Planet of the Orange-red Sun

Series Volume 2

Dark Ages

1

Planet of the Orange-red Sun Series Volume 2 Dark Ages

by Vic Broquard

For Morgan and L. Ron Hubbard

Table of Contents
Part I The Setup

Part II Angel Adaptions

Part III Escalating Chaos

Part IV Rise of the Towers

Part I The Setup

Chapter 1 Theosophy

Lightning flashed relentlessly. The ensuing rumbling sounded more like the Drums of Hell to Bishop-king Gil Granville, quite deafening. Deep inside the castle at Wycombe, he watched the surface of his tea vibrate in unison. *Action and reaction*, he thought. The opened secret letter from his Archbishop Mata Hatta only confirmed what he knew to be true, Hell had come to Tierra, the cold storms of Hell or the *Tormentas Frías del Infierno* as the Archbishop had written, underlining those words with a wavy line. Here in the foothills, it was midsummer, yet nearly every night the relentless rain turned into sleet. Not infrequently, traces of snow could be seen in the dim morning light of the orange-red sun, though the snow quickly melted. The planetary climate had changed for the worse, drastically so.

Bishop-king Gil had finally ceased allowing his holy flock to complain or even ask advice on how they were to grow their crops. *Zounds, I do not know!* he thought for the thousandth time, casting aside into his wastebasket two more requests for his Holy Blessing on nearby farmers' crops. He ruled the Kingdom of Bettingham now, or more to the point, what was left of it, the greater Wycombe area. Last year as he came into power, the original kingdoms of Tierra splintered into many tiny kingdoms. He was not too concerned with this fracturing, since his greater Wycombe area had the largest population density of the old Kingdom of Bettingham and hence the riches.

Upon receiving this latest secret document from the Archbishop Mata Hatta a half hour ago, he'd sent a summons to the Holy Rectory. Impatient, he thought, *They ought to be here by now!*

So much had happened and all for the worst. To begin with, the whole climate of Tierra seemed to have gone loony, completely batty! Last winter, Wycombe had broken all records for snowfall as far back as anyone could remember — well over ten feet. Now it was midsummer and the temperatures ranged from near freezing at night to quite warm in the late afternoons. Yet, three out of four afternoons brought these infernal heavy rains. Even the two moons of Tierra no longer seemed to know where they should revolve, drifting all over the skies as if they were just as lost as the people of the world below them.

Lost, that is most appropriate, he thought. He had had a very workable arrangement with the aliens who called themselves Rigels. Now that too was gone. Cezar no longer answered the mechanical device, which the Psychman had given him last year. *Well, that is not really important now, I have gotten rid of all the evil witches and I have control of the kingdom. I don't need Cezar any longer.* He really didn't believe all those wild tales the ignorant peasants blabbed in the local pubs — something about the alien's base having blown up last fall. True, he had seen the huge dust cloud, but to believe these ultra-powerful aliens blew themselves up was preposterous. No, something else had happened, something wicked, sinister, something evil. After all, shortly after that, the evil spread throughout the known world. *Lucifer has returned to claim dominion over Tierra. I am certain of it!*

Why was he so certain? All over Wycombe and even within his own COG, Church of God, Lucifer had struck, twisting and altering men, women, and children, giving them unnatural powers, known locally as the *mentales*. Oh, it was wild. Some could hear other's thoughts; those were the least affected. Others could start fires just with their minds. He'd seen it done! Others could control or dominate people. Some had devilish control over animals. The list of Lucifer-endowed *mentales* gifts seemed endless to the Bishop-king. Yet, he, one of the true believers in the Lord God, had been able to resist such Unholy Temptations and remain pure of heart and soul.

And now, at long last, Archbishop Mata Hatta had finally issued his formal decree. All those Lucifer-infected were to be slain by any means possible. Hence, he'd summoned his inner circle of priests to share this incredibly good news with them.

Brother Sheridan Abrams pulled his hooded cloak around him even tighter, as if that action would somehow prevent the driving rain from penetrating him. Just twenty-five years old, he had been affected with this *mentales* curse of Lucifer, though he did not attribute it to the devil. Not only could he hear other's thoughts, but he was learning how to become the master of his body. At first, he found it shocking when he was able to lower his body temperature. Then by accident, he'd spilled boiling oil on his legs. His *mentales* gift kicked in at once, and he'd somehow had seen what needed to be done with his legs. A half hour later, all traces of the burns had vanished — a Holy Miracle he began to believe. Now the chilling rain no longer affected him. Mechanically, he adjusted his body and felt perfectly warm as he walked swiftly from the Holy Rectory to the Royal Palace. He was a tall, thin man, blonde, as were most of those in Wycombe. He put up his mental block against others reading his thoughts and fell into step with the priest who moved into position on his right.

Beside him, shivering from the sleeting rain, Father Shane Zadok, also twenty-five, kept pace, their footfalls landing in unison, splashing in the accumulating waters on the grey cobblestone street. Father Shane likewise had the *mentales* gift, though he, like Brother Sheridan, kept this to himself. In fact, neither man had yet come to any firm decision about their altered state of mind. To Father Shane, it was merely amusing to be able to hear the inner thoughts of his parishioners, knowing what they were hesitant about or refusing to tell him during their confessionals. *This infernal cold rain will destroy all our crops. How the devil will people survive this? Maybe the Bishop-king finally has some answers for us.* He was a few inches shorter than Brother Sheridan, but far more muscular. The son of a coppersmith, Father Shane chose to mend souls and not copper pots, much to his father's displeasure.

Six other priests followed behind them, all grumbling about the seemingly perpetual summer rains. Their thoughts fairly screamed into the two men's minds. Father Shane smiled though, recalling their equal complaining about all the snow this past winter. *Some are never satisfied. We should give thanks we are still alive and that some of us have perhaps received the Lord God's Blessings.* Brother Sheridan smiled as he picked up Father Shane's thought.

At last, the eight men entered the Royal Palace on the ground floor of the great castle, depositing their soaking cloaks in the entrance hall on drying pegs. Still shivering, Father Shane formally bowed to Brother Sheridan who respectfully returned it. They led the eight into the Throne Room, where Bishop-king Gil was impatiently awaiting them. Both men sensed the impatience of their leader. He was now very overweight, sporting a thick yellow beard and a countenance that filled others with dismay and perhaps awe and fear. Father Shane was never quite sure what he felt from his leader. *I swear he's put on thirty pounds since last fall,* Father Shane thought. After bowing respectfully, he said softly, "We came as quickly as we could, Your Holiness."

"Ah yes. Good," he grumbled, but his dower look changed almost at once to one of glee, as if a dark curtain rose. "We have it at last! News from our Archbishop!" He waived the document in the air for emphasis. "Please, be seated. Help yourselves to the hot tea. I can see you are shivering from this infernal cold rain." The eight did as he suggested, though Brother Sheridan was neither cold nor shivering as the other seven were, a fact lost on all present, save Father Shane who made a mental note of this.

"*Tormentas Frías del Infierno!* Yes, those are the *official* words of our Archbishop Mata Hatta. The cold storms of Hell have struck all Tierra. It is as many of us anticipated: Lucifer has come, altering our weather so crops will perish and, even worse, altering many of our minds, seducing them with gifts of his devil powers. Our Archbishop has decreed that all those who have accepted Lucifer's *mentales* gifts have thus forsaken our Lord God. They have succumbed to temptation and eaten of the bitter fruit. Their souls are now lost to us utterly, belonging to Lucifer not our Lord God. Woe and alas to them all, for in so many ways, we, my fellow priests, have failed them. Yes, we have failed to lead them to the Holy Path of Righteousness. Having tasted of the bitter fruit, these pitiful folks have now willingly joined the ranks of the devil."

"Your Holiness," Father Shane interrupted him, "I fail to see how it is that we have failed our parishioners. Lady Ellen, for example, has been a loyal and faithful follower of the

COG all her life. She has never failed to cook and serve at all our meetings. She's given of her time, effort, and even funds to the COG. Yet, as we all know, she now has admitted to having *mentales* gifts. I have prayed, as you suggested, to learn how it was that I have failed her so horribly. Yet, I have not received divine guidance on how I failed her. She is one of our most ardent supporters."

With a hint of smugness in his voice, Bishop-king Gil replied, "You must pray harder, my son. Beseech our Lord God and you will be enlightened. If we had not failed her, she would have been able to resist the temptations of Lucifer, even as I have. Temptations come in many guises and forms, my son, far too many, I am afraid to say. Yet there are others — many others — who have remained faithful to our Lord God, resisting all his Unholy Temptations and beguiling. Now we have the answer to these new devil-spawn."

He continued, "Always, there has been a constant battle between our Holy Father and the very devil himself, Lucifer. Both we and the faithful must not be led into temptation. Archbishop Mata Hatta has decreed it is our Holy Duty and Obligation to remove from Tierra all those who have fallen or succumbed to Lucifer and his temptations."

Growing ill at ease, Brother Sheridan asked, "What does our Most Holy Archbishop propose that we do?" This was not what he had been hoping to hear from his Archbishop.

"I quote," Bishop-king Gil replied, "'I hereby authorize you to use any means possible to kill all those who have become possessed of the devil or who have partaken of his temptations, these *mentales* gifts as they are called.' Our leader is quite clear on this point. We are to begin exterminating these Unholy Creatures."

"But are we then saying their souls cannot be redeemed? That our Holy Redemption cannot be given unto them if they accept it?" asked a confused Brother Sheridan. "Can they not be redeemed? Are their souls then lost to us for all time?"

Equally upset, Father Shane asked, "Does this not countermand thou shalt not kill your fellow man? It seems to me we are being asked to break one of the cardinal, fundamental beliefs we hold dear to us."

Father Able added, "Yes, Bishop-king, I am most troubled by this seeming violation of our Holy Commandment. How in good conscience are we to slay these people, knowing we are then in direct violation of Lord God's Holy Commandment and thus become sinners ourselves?"

"Ah, that, my Holy Fathers is quite simple. Our Archbishop is not asking us to break the Holy Commandment: Thou shalt not kill your fellow man. No indeed." He saw complete confusion on all eight faces. *This is why I am the Bishop-king and they are not.* Both Brother Sheridan and Father Shane heard his thought, however.

He continued, "You see, those who have succumbed to the temptations of Lucifer and have accepted him unto their hearts and souls are themselves no longer our *fellow* man. They have become the devil's men, Unholy Servants of Lucifer. Thus, in forsaking our Lord God and accepting Lucifer, they have rejected our Lord God's Holy Protections. Simple. Those Unholy *mentales* are Lucifer's men, filth of the very earth, no more than Unholy Slime. Worse, as you all know, Lucifer continues to enslave more of the Lord God's Faithful. Thus, it falls to us to slay them all, removing Lucifer's men from Tierra, that they may no longer tempt those who have remained Faithful to the Lord God. Cast out the Unholy as one casts out the spoilt grain from the bins that all the grain is not lost. Simple."

Apparently totally satisfied with his own logic, he went on, "It falls to us to work out how we can best implement our Archbishop's order. I know, as you do too, some of these Unholy Servants of Lucifer have been given terrible *mentales* gifts. Some are going to be quite deadly to slay, the fire starters for example. We must strike at those Unholy Servants in force such that they cannot avoid our Holy Justice."

Fighting rising anger and hoping his face didn't show it, Father Shane asked, "Your Holiness, how are we to detect the Unholy Servants of Lucifer from the Holy Followers of our Lord God and even from those who as yet have not joined the COG?" asked. "I mean from all I have seen of these Unholy Servants, they appear to my eyes at least no different from our own bodies. *Mentales* is not visible upon their faces. How are we rightfully to detect the Holy from the Unholy? I fear greatly to make a mistake and thereby break the Holy Commandment, killing my fellow man and thus cast my own precious soul into Lucifer's Hell." *Like Hell, I cannot tell! I can sense a telepath as easily as the perfume of a woman or the odor of pine in the breeze. Gil doesn't have the gift. This is a witch hunt if I ever saw one. Is our beloved Church of God condoning murder now?*

"Hum, yes, I do see your point, Father Shane. It is a valid one. If we slay the innocent, we commit an unforgivable sin. They do look like normal people, don't they?" Bishop-king Gil replied, frowning. He'd not yet thought of this aspect. He only wanted to kill the Unholy Servants. In a flash, he had an answer, "Testimony! Yes, we must gather testimony from our Faithful. They can tell us of those they know who have shown themselves to be the Unholy Servants."

Father Shane grimaced. *I minister to my parishioners nearly every day. Some bear petty grudges against their neighbors, in spite of my teachings and pleadings. What is to keep some of these against giving false testimony?* He shivered and not because he was still warming from the icy rain. "Your Holiness, might I offer a caution? It seems to me some might bear false testimony in order to settle petty squabbles. We have all seen many of these, though we've tried our best to teach our flock otherwise. If indeed false testimony is given, then once again, do not we commit the most sacrilegious sin — killing those of our flock who we are pledged to minister unto our Lord God? I tremble that I, his humble servant, might make such an error."

"Yes, my son, we are all fallible in the eyes of our Lord God. However, let us not condemn as one of the Unholy Servants of Lucifer until we have, say *three*, independent testimonies. Shall not we then be certain our wrath is Most Holy and Justified?" Bishop-king Gil replied. *Now that ought to do it. Three independent witnesses can't all be wrong.*

Father Shane heard his leader's unspoken thought and thought, *Well, perhaps not, if the three are truly independent. Yet, is this not more like a witch hunt, where our faithful bear witness for such minor offenses that might not even be attributable to the mentales gifts? In truth, I have seen this last year when an innocent flower seller was taken as an evil witch. The real witches were easy to spot for they all had herbal remedy shops around the city. She, however, only sold wild flowers. I fear in our enthusiasm, we will do far more harm than good. Besides, does this mean I am now in bed with the devil Lucifer?* This thought greatly disturbed the priest.

They discussed what they were to begin preaching in their respective churches. I say discussed, but it was more the direct orders from Bishop-king Gil. After that, he dismissed them and summoned his Holy Militia captains, veteran COG supporters who served as his local police and guards, if not army. Bishop-king Gil outlined the procedures they would follow to eliminate all these men, women, and children who had tasted of the Unholy Fruits of Lucifer and now possessed his evil *mentales* gifts.

Brother Sheridan had picked up Father Shane's thoughts too and purposely donned his still soaked cloak very slowly, allowing the other six priests to head out into the icy rain. It would soon turn to sleet and perhaps even snow later this evening. "Might I have a private word with you, Father Shane?" he whispered as soon as they were alone and ready to face the strange summer's late afternoon. The thunder rolled over the men as if the very elements were protesting this new onslaught of their flock. *What do I dare tell him? If I am not careful, I can be found out and sentenced to death myself. But I must, if my conscience is to remain clear.*

"Yes, I know a place. My private quarters. Follow me. This devil weather is killing us all," Father Shane replied, taking a deep breath before plunging out into the heavy rain and sleet once more, as if this would somehow protect him and give him warmth. It didn't. A half hour later and once more soaked to the bone, Father Shane beckoned Brother Sheridan into his private room in the Holy Rectory. His manservant had already stoked the fire, anticipating the priest would be drenched upon his return. He also had the copper pot filled with water, steaming on the hearth. Hastily, Father Shane took off his cloak, hung it out to dry, and prepared a pot of hot black tea. *Strong, I need it after that.* He offered some to Brother Sheridan who accepted, sitting on the chair farthest from the warming flames. On the other hand, Father Shane pulled his chair as close to the fire as he dared. He glanced at the heavy oak door. *Good, it is shut.* "We cannot be overheard in here, Brother Sheridan."

How to begin? thought Brother Sheridan. *This will be tricky. Until I know how he feels about the slaying of all of us with the mentales gifts, I best be careful.* "This devil weather appears to be here for a long time."

Father Shane grimaced and looked up at the brother. "Why do you say that?" *I hope not, but maybe it is but punishment from our Lord God, because we have so failed here on Tierra.*

"Observations, my good Father, observations of our world. If you will watch the motions of our moons, the bright white Echador and the pale blue Palidez, and our orange-red sun throughout the day and night, you will see them wobbling. Here, I can show you the motions I have seen clearly with my own eyes, though one must be patient for clear weather these days." He took an apple from the bowl of fruit on the priest's table and three un-cracked nuts. He demonstrated the motion of the sun and moons and what it could only mean. "You see, Tierra has now begun to wobble alarmingly, perhaps over a period of four days — just like a child's toy top. Such a wild motion must be what is behind all this terrible weather."

"Yes, I can see it now. Brilliant, Brother Sheridan. Amazing. I ought to have discovered that myself. It is so simple." *My only justification is I have been too preoccupied.*

"Simple yes, but not until you actually study the motions of the sun and moons and work out what could possibly be the cause. You see, I am convinced our weather will follow the terrible patterns that it has been in since last winter. Something has caused our world to begin to wobble."

"Yes, but won't it eventually die out, like a top?" Father Shane asked, wishing with all his might the man would say so. *I need some good news.*

Brother Sheridan shook his head sadly. "No, I am afraid

it will not. Something enormously powerful has banged our world into this perpetual wobbling. It is not going to stop, not in my lifetime. It will be up to us humans to adapt to the total change in our weather, adapt or succumb."

"Have we so failed our Lord God that he has inflicted such a harsh punishment upon all of us? Have we not been faithful, serving Lord God in every way?" This was the key datum, which so bothered Father Shane since last fall. Had Lord God inflicted this upon mankind? Had mankind so failed their Holy Creator?

"Of that, I cannot say, Father Shane. I am only a lowly brother, who travels the land preaching the Holy Words of our Lord God. But I don't believe our Lord God has done this. I have heard many tell of a massive explosion where the aliens, the Rigels, made their base high in the southern mountains of Goza. Some say the explosion was so massive that all the aliens were slain. Perhaps the aliens were struck down by our Lord God; this I do not know. Yet to my mind that would seem a reasonable explanation. Never have we seen one of those aliens within our Holy Churches. Never has one of them taken Holy Communion or attended Holy Confession of their sins. If Lucifer does have a hold on Tierra, perhaps it is with the aliens who came here unbidden by any of us."

"In that case, perhaps it was ourselves who are to blame for this catastrophe. Did we not make use of the aliens and their machines to rid Wycombe of all its heretical, devil-spawn witches? Have we accidentally become corrupted by Lucifer because of that?" Father Shane began to see an answer to all this madness around him.

"Aye, that may well be, Father Shane, but I cannot say for sure, though it seems plausible. They have never shown the slightest signs of belief in Lord God. In their behalf, they may well be simply ignorant, as so many of our own people here on Tierra are. I have much work to do." He smiled briefly. *So far so good,* he thought, *but how ought I approach my real purpose here, our mentales gifts?*

"Alas, we are doomed to have this hellish weather for all time. How is it that we can possibly adapt? Farmers are complaining their crops will not grow any longer. By winter, we will all be starving."

Ah, the opening I need. "Perhaps our people must move many leagues to the south in search of warmer weather that will support our crops. Perhaps nature will adapt and other types of crops will thrive in this new climate. Already we have seen the various nut trees thriving as never before. There is always sufficient meat in the forest. Hunting will not suffer."

"I see your point. Yes, our own nut trees are bearing three times as many nuts this year as in any previous year, I'm told. Perhaps we will not starve completely."

"Yes, I hope so, and then perhaps our Lord God has taken mercy upon us, his faithful followers," Brother Sheridan hinted, hoping the priest would follow up.

"How so? It seems to me that such is not the case."

Brother Sheridan smiled. *He took the bait.* "Perhaps, Father Shane, our Lord God has seen fit to give unto his faithful the *mentales* gifts such that we can survive this natural disaster which has befallen our world. Perhaps those who have such a precious gift are supposed to use it to help all the others here survive this calamity. Perhaps these people have not touched the temptations of Lucifer after all, but have been touched by our Lord God and challenged by him to use their gifts to help their fellow man. Perhaps."

"But that defies what our Most Holy Archbishop Mata Hatta has declared. Completely the opposite of his Holy Decree!" Father Shane looked positively shocked. His face twisted. Was he hearing heresy coming from the mouth of Brother Sheridan? *No, the man seems most serious.*

"I said only *perhaps*, Father. Just perhaps. I have kept you overly long from your holy duties. I will see myself out. Perhaps we can talk once more later on," Brother Sheridan suggested.

"Yes, I believe we should," Father Shane answered without thinking about it. His mind was reeling. Brother Sheridan rose, went to the door, and left silently, leaving the priest deep in thought and contemplation.

Is this my own doing? Have I really succumbed to the temptations of Lucifer, accepting his mentales gifts? I should report myself to my bishop and beg him to end my Unholy

Life. Perhaps I should be the first of the Unholy to be slain? Yes, set an example. Lucifer can tempt anyone, even those of us in the Holy Church. None of us is immune to the temptations of the devil! I certainly agree with that.

No, wait! I don't! I haven't succumbed to the temptations of the flesh. I am chaste still and will remain so. I eat frugally. I spread the word of our Lord God. I have not spread heresy or taken the Lord's name in anger. I have not killed, or raped, or sought riches. I don't understand! He pulled his long blonde hair, distressed beyond measure.

How is it I have become so Unholy? This mentales gift — how did I become besotted with it? I cannot recall every having met with Lucifer or any of his followers. How was it I was tempted by them, if I have never met the devil? Have I committed terrible sins that I must be punished so now? Well, I did stifle a snicker at Mrs. Smith last Sunday at mass, such a busy body. Oh Shane, get with it! This is not doing you any good! He filled his clay mug with holy wine and downed it rapidly. He felt the rush of the fermented juices of the grapes flooding his senses, dulling them a little. He lay down on his bed and stared at the ceiling, trying to get his mind completely blank.

Look, Shane, if my sudden mentales is due to my failures as a priest of the COG or even as a man, then I should do the honest, honorable thing and turn myself in, and be one of the first to be executed. He had an urge to do just that right now. Surely, the Bishop-king would be more than willing to accept his confession. As he started to rise up, he thought, *But would that somehow save my soul? How could it? All that we are doing with this new program is removing the devil-tainted people from our world. No, I am doomed, doomed utterly.*

Still, he could not figure out what he had done to become a pawn of the devil. This more than anything else bothered him, giving him no rest, no peace of mind. He declared violently to his four walls, "Somehow I absolutely must figure out what I have done to have gotten this accursed *mentales* gift! If it is the last thing I ever do, I have to find out how I have fallen from the Lord God's favor unto the arms of the very devil himself!"

He began with the earliest memories he had, playing ball in the streets with his older brother. "Those were just silly childhood squabbles," he grumbled. He'd kicked his brother in his shins on several occasions, and once he'd slugged him nearly breaking his nose. "Surely that cannot be my downfall! If so, there isn't a man alive who ought not be condemned!"

"I did have lustful thoughts when I was fifteen. Mary was so pretty." He recalled her long, curly blonde tresses as they played gaily in his parent's living room that spring. Again, he rejected this. "Everyman is tempted with young women. Yet I did nothing unseemly; it was merely thoughts, nothing more." Time slipped by and the supper gong sounded, rousing him from his meditations.

"Father Shane! You have known me all my life," Mary pleaded with him, terror in her eyes. She along with five others who had been found guilty of having the *mentales* gift was tied to six poles. COG militia men were now piling up bundles of pine branches around them. The air was heady with the sweet odor of the resin. Three witnesses had come forward swearing they had witnessed these six using *mentales,* and thus per the new law of the Archbishop Mata Hatta, they were about to be burned at the stake as Lucifer-spawn, devil worshipers. Father Shane and many other priests were standing before the six: three women, two men, and one five year old boy, bearing witness to the elimination of these corrupted people.

Father Shane repeated the Holy Psalm of Repentance over and over, fearing to even raise his eyes to the young mother whom he'd known since childhood. He dare not listen to her pleadings, but her words could not be drowned out by his prayers. Her terror flooded his mind, more real than his own heart beating, pulsing dangerously high. These last terror-filled and painful minutes of her life — he was living them in his own mind! He could not dampen out his telepathic *mentales* gift. The only thing keeping him from going utterly mad and jumping into the fire himself was that he also was experiencing the other five's stark terror and burning pain as well, all jumbled up into a massive ball of mind-clobbering

14

emotion and pain. He no longer knew if he was even repeating his Holy Psalm. He did not exist, only the terror and pain of the six were real.

And then, it was gone. His mind: a void, a vacuum of emotion and sensation, as if he had never experienced it. The blaze was roaring now, while around him the crowd was cheering, exalted the Satan-tempted were destroyed, as if somehow these six deaths could so alter the terribleness of the weather and harsh life. The six were dead now. Analytically he knew that. Yet the images of their deaths were now burned indelibly into his mind forever. Father Shane knew he could never get them out of his mind, not ever. Tears wetted his cheeks.

The other priests were backing off, returning to the rectory, but Father Shane could not get his own feet to work properly. How he had remained standing, he knew not. "Come with me," a voice whispered in his ear or was it actually a whisper? He could not tell if it had just appeared in his mind or if his own ears had brought it there. Vacantly, he looked to his side. Brother Sheridan stood beside him now. How long had he been there? The solemn face of the holy man moved slightly to the right followed by the rest of the man's body. *How strange bodies move.*

Having no will of his own, Father Shane merely observed his own body following Brother Sheridan. The orange-red sun was out for a time, drying the rain-soaked ground a little. Blankly, he noted the large crowd was dispersing as well, for there was no more excitement to be had here, though three men stood by with rakes and water barrels in case the fire got out of hand. Fires were always the topmost concern in any town or village of Tierra. Uncontrolled, a fire could wipe out an entire town, caring nothing for nobleman or peasant. Shane followed the tall man in black.

Brother Sheridan wore tall black boots, tied at the knees, his black leather britches tucked in just below his knees. He wore a black cloak over his black cotton over-shirt, as befitting a monk of the COG. *Where is he going?* Shane finally thought. The walk was beginning to clear his mind from the horrors he'd just experienced.

Brother Sheridan had also felt the telepathic contact of the six minds reaching out in desperate attempts to save themselves by any means possible. However, he had already worked out how to block such unwanted mental contact. He called his method the Block Perception. Essentially, it did just that. When it was in force, one no longer received the telepathic thoughts of those around him. He also worked out Hide Thoughts, which did the reverse, blocking his own thoughts from being broadcast to all other telepaths near him. *Everyone who has mentales ought at least to know how to do these two basic, simple actions. Yet they do not.*

However, he knew Father Shane had not been able to block the six victims and was now suffering from telepathic overload and shock. He led the priest into a back entrance of a pub and took a seat in the very back, far from the noisy bar. The priest followed him, almost like a zombie. Brother Sheridan signaled the bar wench, who brought over a large clay pitcher of ale and two somewhat clean clay mugs. He tossed her a couple of coppers and poured the two mugs, sliding one over to the priest.

Mechanically, Father Shane downed the mug and Sheridan refilled it. "There, isn't that better? You should learn to block such things from your mind, Father Shane. A couple of pints and the color will be back in your face."

"I, I don't know how to do that," Father Shane mumbled. "I knew her, Mary. We grew up together. She is no more a devil than I am! She's never harmed a fly in her life! This is madness, utter madness." He downed the second mug in a long series of gulps and the monk refilled it again.

"I will not debate that issue with you, Father Shane. Now we are murdering children. Where will it stop? Able was a blacksmith, good at his craft. Lord knows we need all the able-bodied craftsmen these days. Ben was a skilled miller, one of the best in Wycombe. No bugs or stone in his flower. I ask you, Father Shane, how can these people be so utterly evil that our Church of God must murder them and so painfully? Answer me that one, if you can?"

"That's blasphemy! You know it! Archbishop Mata Hatta has declared it so. He is our most holy leader," Father

Shane declared, flushing a little, wishing he'd not heard such scandalous words.

"Call it what you will, Father Shane, but you and I both know it is the truth. They are no more Lucifer followers, devil-tempted, than yonder barmaid! If you truly believe those of us with *mentales* gifts are of the devil, then you should turn yourself in at once and be burned at the stake tomorrow noon, weather permitting that is," Brother Sheridan growled, almost angry with the pitiful priest. However, he carefully kept his own thoughts blocked so Shane could not pick them up.

Father Shane could take no more. At last, his grief and remorse overflowed and he began bawling like some small child. Brother Sheridan smiled and put a comforting hand on the priest. *Perhaps the dam has broken at last. I hope so. I am not going to wait around much longer.*

He cried out the death of his childhood friend. He cried out the loss of such a young child who never even understood why he was being put to death. He cried for the blacksmith and his family. At last, he stopped, blowing his nose and wiping his eyes. "You are right, all this is not right, just not. We are committing the gravest of sins, I know it, I feel it, but what can we do?"

Brother Sheridan smiled, "My son, there is much we can do. I for one am going to preach for the goodness of the *mentales* gifts in we men and lead those who will follow me into the mountains there to build a monastery in which I and my followers can teach and train others who have this God-given gift to use and control it for the betterment of all men."

"But what about the women and children?" the priest asked, seeing the great wisdom in Brother Sheridan's action.

"I am sorry, truly sorry, but I am sworn to a life of chastity. Having women around is just entirely too much of a temptation now. With our telepathy gifts so strong, I find it almost impossible to resist women. I will not give up my vows of celibacy. It is the underpinning of my existence; you can understand that, father. If I cannot control my body's lustful urges, then I am less of a man, no more worthy to lead than the blacksmith who was burned today. Until last year, no woman could interest me in the slightest. Now I am almost afraid to admit this, but it takes all my will power to resist even yonder barmaid! Women and girls must find their own path. I am not strong enough to lead them, only men," Brother Sheridan admitted.

"I cannot forsake women and children, though I long to follow you and help others to learn to control their gifts," Father Shane stated with a longing sigh. *Oh, how I would like to go away with him right now, seeking guidance and tranquility of a chaste life, but I cannot get Mary out of my mind. I am sworn and pledged to minister to all my people, my flock, be they men, women, or even children. I cannot desert them now, not like this.*

"What will you do then?"

"It seems to me I should journey to the Holy City of Valcia and speak with our Archbishop Mata Hatta personally. Somehow, I must get him to reverse his decision."

"Ah, that is a noble undertaking, worthy of you, Father Shane. Our world has been shattered by the aliens. It is my belief that our Lord God has given some of us this *mentales* gift so we can help our people survive this calamity, and flourish and prosper once more. Perhaps there, Father Shane, you can get our Archbishop Mata to understand this."

"Yes, he has it all backwards. If we could somehow unite all those who can somehow affect the weather, then they could help us get good enough weather to plant our crops. If not, I see only starvation ahead of us all," Father Shane admitted.

"You can foresee this?" Brother Sheridan asked. *Could it be he has the gift of precognition?*

"Not with my gift, Brother Sheridan, with my logical reasoning. If all crops fail, what then do we eat? I need no gift to see such a future."

Brother Sheridan smiled. "Before you embark, perhaps I can teach you how to block others from your mind."

"Is that even possible?" The priest's face looked at the monk in utter wonder. He realized Brother Sheridan knew he had the *mentales* gift and he knew the monk also had it. However, neither man actually admitted such to the other; confirmation was not needed. They were telepaths.

18

A week and another ten deaths later, Father Shane finally passed the ultimate test. Each night he'd spent laboring with Brother Sheridan, learning how to put up a Block Perception and Hide Thoughts. Apparently the monk was now satisfied the priest was sufficiently trained — at least he'd said so last night. Today, the priest would find out. He, along with his fellow priests, was once more called to bear witness to the burning of another batch of Lucifer-tainted. To his horror, this time he saw Brother Sheridan, hands tied behind his back, being led forward through the crowd to be burned at the stake! He'd had no idea his mentor was to be burned at the stake this day!

While the other man and two women were terrified, shrieking and screaming wildly, Brother Sheridan, still wearing his black outfit, walked calmly ahead to the appointed stake. Bishop-king Gil Granville read the charges, but Father Shane didn't listen. His mind was in turmoil. *He can't do this! He is one of us, a Holy Monk! Lord God, help us!*

The priest's eyes met those of the monk. *This is your final test, my son. Put up your Block Perception now. Fear not. I will not be harmed.* Like a clap of thunder, the thoughts of Brother Sheridan echoed in the priest's mind.

"Last words?" the harsh voice of Bishop-king Gil resonated, silencing the crowd momentarily as the onlookers strained to hear what these wicked people had to say.

Brother Sheridan spoke loudly and commanding, "Here yea one and all! Shortly I will be leading my faithful followers out of this Den of Hell ruled by the Insane Bishop-king. We will build a tower to our Lord God in the far reaches of Tierra where we will be safe from the insanity of such men as these. Faithful men, follow after me in a few minutes."

"What?" Bishop-king Gil didn't realize he was screaming in reaction to the monk's words. "Torch these devil worshipers immediately!" He screamed, ignoring his usual protocol. At once, his faithful COG militia men did so, touching a dozen torches to the dried, resin heavy brush. Flames caught quickly. Soon the terror shrieks of the burning man and two women pierced the central square, while many onlookers cheered.

This time, Father Shane's will won, and he was not overwhelmed by the telepathic contact of the three burning people. His mind was quiet though he was anything but calm. He was thankful his *mentales* gift was not the killer type. He'd heard some men could kill another man merely by thinking it so. He knew if he had that type, the Bishop-king would be quite dead. *Thank you Lord God for not tempting me with that mentales gift!*

What happened next became part of the legend of Brother Sheridan Abrams, founder of Skylar Abbey. Soon the other three perished from the roaring flames. However, Brother Sheridan seemed wholly unaffected. His clothing burned, and at last, the ropes binding him to the post burned through releasing him. He stepped naked out of the fire as if the flames were neither present nor hot! The crowd shrieked, dismayed at such a sight. Some yelled, "Lucifer walks among us!"

"Shoot him fools!" screamed the Bishop-king. At once, three of his COG militia men notched arrows. Above the roaring flames, three twangs announced the flight of arrows. Three deadly shafts shot through the flames to where a naked Brother Sheridan stood, having stepped back out of the inferno on the opposite side from the Bishop-king. The monk reacted, his hands flashing this way and that, catching each arrow mid-flight. Solemnly, he tossed the projectiles into the flames, turned on his heels, and walked through the crowd, which rapidly and fearfully gave way to the naked monk. Most held hands over their mouths, afraid to speak fearing the devil before them would hear them and slay them on the spot!

A few blocks away, he stopped before a group of fifty men. Solemnly one held out fresh clothing for their leader, who donned the thin wool shirt, pants, and socks. After slipping on a pair of knee-high boots, he slung a leather cloak over his shoulders and began leading his followers out of Wycombe, heading up the northwest road towards Wyth. Behind him, the fifty men walked, leading horses laded with supplies for their long journey. All of them were now dressed alike; all wore black. Thus began Brother Sheridan's Walk of

Salvation, as the exodus came to be known.

Chapter 2 Suffering

Father Shane headed back to the Holy Rectory. His mind was now clear. Time to act, he told himself. Quickly he packed a change of clothing and his Holy Prayer book into a saddlebag. He quietly walked to the kitchen and added some provisions for his journey, enough for a few days. He looked around at the two women chefs who were preparing supper for the priests. *God, I hope they don't have the mentales gift. They have done nothing but care for us priests for the last few years!* He quietly said a prayer on their behalf, turned and left the kitchen, making for the stables. There, he asked the stable hand to prepare his horse. The lad nodded and did so. *Am I really stealing the horse? No, I fully intend to return here once I put a stop to this insanity.*

The lad held the reins and the priest mounted. "Thank you, Ben."

"Go with God," the lad replied, opening the outer doors. He took a last look around the stables and then rode out into the street. *I am actually doing this!* Never in a thousand years did I think that one day I would be riding down to the Holy City to meet with the Archbishop Mata Hatta! Yet, I am doing just that. His conscience was clear. The murdering of ordinary men and women just had to cease. They were violating the Holy Commandments of Lord God!

Tormentas Frías del Infierno, he thought, tightening his cloak about his body and pulling the hood over his head. Distant Lightning flashed; the freakish late afternoon thunderstorms were moving in from the southwest. "Cold storms from hell, well that's a good name for them," he said to his mare. He was following the southeast road out of Wycombe, which led after some six hundred miles to the Kingdom of Rusden, which until last year had been the southernmost town of the old Kingdom of Bettingham. Now that once great kingdom was history. So were all the other fourteen original mighty kingdoms, broken into many smaller kingdoms. Why?

Father Shane found himself reflecting on the

unbelievable events of the last year or so. First, old King Aaran Wycombe had been assassinated in his own bed. Well, no one shared any real grief over the death of that man. He was a tyrant to the end. Rumors spoke of his ordering his eldest daughter's hands cut off, treating her as a common thief merely because she chose to defy him. "Prince Norwood, he was a good man, that much I do know, horse. Somehow, he won the war with King Chester of Rockton up north and that alone was a miracle. He rebuilt all the hamlets and villages that the cavalrymen from Rockton burned down. Yes, he was a good king, but why did he abdicate his throne?"

That was a complete mystery. It happened suddenly and without the slightest warning. One morning, his Bishop Gil received a dispatch stating Norwood had abdicated and that his very own bishop was now the monarch. "Horse, I still find unbelievable! Why would Norwood abandon his throne?" No one knew or if they did, they were not saying. It was only months later that their second largest city, Wyth, to the far northwest, seceded becoming the Kingdom of the Angels. Indeed, rumors suggested Norwood was there, perhaps running that smaller kingdom. Like dominoes, the other powerful noblemen, the *Jefe*, followed suit, carving up what remained of the kingdom.

Now the northern quarter of old Bettingham was this new Kingdom of the Angels. Immediately to the south of them was the Kingdom of Haverhills and below them, the Kingdom of Oakham. The large southernmost town of Rusden declared independence shortly after that. Worse, many smaller towns in the heartland of the old Kingdom of Bettingham declared their independence as well, but these were all tiny kingdoms, hardly worthy of such a noble title. Perhaps dukedoms would be a more accurate term.

Over time, word came to Wycombe that similar divisions had occurred in all the other fourteen kingdoms. Whatever the cause, it was both widespread and complete. Not a single original kingdom now existed. For a time as he rode along, Father Shane wondered if all this had anything to do with the Church of God. It seemed to his keen mind that all the original kingdom's largest cities now were under the control of the COG. Bishop-king Gil ran the Kingdom of Wycombe as it was now called. He'd changed its name so everyone would forget that many years ago; the Bettingham clan ruled the kingdom, before Aaran took control. The Bettingham clan now resided in the Kingdom of the Angels, which he knew. Shane wondered why his bishop had changed its name, for the proposed reasoning made little sense to him.

Still he could not shake the fact that all the original capital cities of the original kingdoms were now under the control of the new Bishop-kings. A few, he could understand. After all, the COG was everywhere and most of their worshipers were concentrated within these largest cities, but all fifteen? That was too much for chance. Had his own church been behind this breakup? If so, why? Obviously, the situation now was beyond deplorable.

Boom! A loud blast of thunder brought him out of his reverie. Rain began to fall. He pulled his hood tighter around his head and trusted his horse to find its way along the rutted, well-traveled road. "This accursed weather," he muttered to himself. He rode on for another hour before the rains changed to sleet. The winds howled around him; the tiny ice crystals pelted his face relentlessly, sticking to his beard and eyebrows. "We need to find shelter soon, mare." His horse seemed to understand that point, nodding its head a few times. He knew the sleet would soon change to ice and probably to snow after dark.

Shivering in his soaked clothes, he finally spotted a light off to the right. A Lightning flash revealed a farmstead, and he found the lane during the next flash and turned his mare down the farmer's rutted path, heading for the light. Shortly, he spotted a heavily loaded wagon standing before the gaping barndoor. Two men were standing, arguing, it seemed to him. Several more forms were huddled on the wagon, shivering from the cold. He closed the distance, straining to hear the men, unwilling to use his *mentales* gift for such a mundane thing.

"I tell you, this ain't no damn inn! You want shelter for the night, and it'll cost you a silver!"

"But we don't have a silver! I've got my wife and three

children in the wagon. We cannot stay outside, not in this weather. Be reasonable. We only want to stay inside your barn for the night. Surely that can't be a whole silver!"

He rode up and dismounted. His *mentales* gift kicked in anyway, and he realized at once that the farmer was charging an exorbitant rate for simple shelter. "Hello. Might I and my horse spend the night in your barn?" he asked, already knowing what the farmer would say.

"Cost you a silver, mister. This ain't no inn!" the farmer called out.

"Might I ask why an entire silver? For that, you could get a heated room in an inn along with a warm meal and ale," Father Shane asked.

"Look, mister, like I said, this ain't no inn. I am a humble farmer, and with this accursed weather from hell, I can't grow no crops. If I don't have no crops, I don't have anything to feed my own family. The hay fields are not even growing proper and right. What are my cows going to eat this winter? I am only trying to get funds so I can support my own family. A silver or be on your way. Mind you, I got *mentales*, but I don't want to use it on folks."

"I should think not! To me, wasting Lord God's precious gift to harm our own people is doing Lucifer's work."

"You sound like one of them preacher fellows," the farmer declared.

He sensed the man had little respect for the COG. "Well, it so happens I am. Father Shane Zadok," He undid his cloak, revealing his priestly shirt and collar, completely soaked.

"Well, that don't matter to me none. Silver or be on your way."

"You would throw this poor family, wife and kids, out in weather like this?"

"Ain't got no choice. Don't you realize that every damn night wagons pull in here looking for a handout? If I gave shelter to them all, I'd be totally out of food and hay myself."

Disgusted, he growled, "Here, let them stay too." He tossed the man two silvers. "Now let's get inside before we freeze to death!"

The farmer bit down on each coin. Satisfied, he waved his lantern toward the barn. "Help yourselves to the hay fer yer horses. Be gone in the morning though." He turned and headed into his own home.

"Thank you Father! I don't know what we would have done. Thank you kindly."

"Come on, let's get inside. I'm frozen to the bone."

He rode on inside and the wagon followed him. To his amazement, he saw three other wagons and families were already inside. One man was waiting by the doors, closing them after the wagon got inside. "Welcome. I am glad you were able to get inside here. It's not much more than a barn, but we have a fire going over on the blacksmith's hearth. Jane, my wife, has got some hot cider ready. You are welcome to have some and warm up. Fred Beckingham's the name."

"Father Shane Zadok. Thank you, I am soaked clear through."

"I'm Sam Saddle, my wife, Betsy, and the three young'ens. I owe you, Father, for paying that outrageous fee for us," the man whom he'd helped said, climbing down.

"Hey, we are all in this together," Fred suggested warmly. "You are all soaked. We've made a women's shelter over there where your wife and daughters can change. Men's area is over there." Several blankets shielded each group from the other. "Get changed into something dry and bring the wet things by the fire and share our dinner."

"Mighty kind of you, Fred. We will do our part," Sam replied.

Father Shane dismounted and untied his saddlebags. As he stood staring at his horse, Fred jested, "Don't you know how to handle your horse, father?"

Shane flushed. "Honestly, I must admit I don't. I ride, but always the stable hands handled her from here. I feel like an utter fool."

Several men chuckled and Fred said, "Tom, you be taken care of the father's horse for him, son." After thanking him, Shane headed for the men's blankets area, shivering and eager to change into something dry. A while later, he joined the others by the warm fire. Jane handed him a wooden plate and a clay mug of hot cider, bowing slightly to him. She took his bundle of wet clothes and cloak, and hung them to dry.

Not long after that, Sam, Betsy, and their three children joined them, receiving plates as well. All six ate hungrily and said little until they finished and began sipping the cooling cider. "So where you be heading?" asked Fred.

"I'm heading south to the Holy City of Valcia. Church business," Father Shane replied.

"We're heading south in search of warmer weather where crops can grow," Sam added. Fred smiled as did the two other men.

"Same with us. Crops are not growing. We are all farmers here. Had a small spread north of Wycombe. This infernal weather is so bad I can't get a crop in this year. Without it, we'd never make it through the winter. So we packed what we needed and are heading south too. Same with the others. All that we have left is our honor. We're pretty broke," Fred replied.

He went on, "We've been pooling our resources, Sam. You are welcome to join us. You too, Father, if you've a mind to it. We're poor farmers, but we still have our honor. We'd be pleased to have you with us."

"Thank you. I believe I will do just that. I rode all afternoon by myself and found that rather lonely. I have some silver coins I can donate to our cause, but very little food I'm afraid. I had thought I could purchase meals at inns along the way," Father Shane explained.

"We have a goodly supply of food we can donate," Sam put in. "We would be honored to share it with the rest of you." The four men shook hands, sealing their agreement.

Shane wondered why there was so much strife in the world when men could be as helpful and honorable to each other as these men were. He was soon to find out, though. Fred pointed out, "We have to be careful though. There are more bandits and robbers traveling these roads than ever before. Now that the kingdoms are all broken up, there are no guards patrolling them. We're fair game to them all. So there is safety in larger numbers."

"I heard many others from the far northern kingdoms

are coming down south to escape the bitter cold there. They are raiding and pillaging," Sam pointed out. "We were going to try and stay in Wycombe a bit, but then we heard they are burning at the stake poor folks who have the *mentales* gifts!"

"What? How can they?" Fred asked, shocked. "That's murder! Father, what do you know about that? Is this true?"

Father Shane tensed up; his face felt very hot. *Truth, these men want truth.* "Yes, the Bishop-king Gil Granville got word from Archbishop Mata Hatta, declaring all those people who have gotten the *mentales* gift are evil. He seems to have decided they were tempted by Lucifer and have become devil worshipers."

"That's insane! I never trusted that COG and now I know why! No offense, Father Shane," Fred exclaimed and became slightly embarrassed. Shane picked up his thought, *Damn, and I have already accepted this COG priest into our group!*

"I agree, Fred. I think this is an outrage, nothing less than outright murder, a cardinal sin of magnitude." Father Shane decided on dispensing with more religious words. These were not COG followers. "Whether a person has *mentales* or not doesn't make them in league with the devil. It is insane and it's murder. That's why I am going to the Holy City to meet with Archbishop Mata Hatta. Somehow, I intend to convince him to stop this insanity immediately. The measure of a man or woman lies in their conduct, their actions."

Fred visibly relaxed, Shane noted. "Well now then, that's a horse of a different color, father. For a moment, I was really worried. Some of us have got a bit of the *mentales* ourselves."

Sam spoke up, "It is so strange. Until recently, hardly anyone had *mentales*, excepting perhaps the witches, bless their departed souls. Now we keep finding more and more of us have gotten this strange thing. Does anyone know why or how we got it? Will everyone get it sooner or later? Is it a curse or something? They killed all the witches so perhaps they cast a curse on us all."

Father Shane answered, "No one I know of knows why or how, only that it has appeared."

"Surely you must have some ideas about it, seeing as how you are going to your bishop fellow," Fred probed a bit.

"Well, if you want my opinion, and this is only my opinion, I think it is a gift from our Lord God given unto us to help us survive this disastrous change in our weather here on Tierra," Shane explained his own hunch. What else could have caused such a giant miracle to occur? Some people had enormous powers. He could not help but recall the burning images of Brother Sheridan, standing there flames all about him, his clothes burning up and yet his body was wholly unaffected. It had to have come from the Lord God.

"Now that makes sense, *if* there is a Lord God somewhere," Fred had to admit. "Of course, if no one can see or hear a god, then how does one even know he exists?" Shane decided not to answer that tricky one. It had to do with faith, but the man had a point.

Betsy brought Shane a blanket. *Am I ever foolish? Going off on a long trip and I didn't even think about bringing along simple necessities!* "Thank you, ma'am, for your kindness. As you can tell, I am most inexperienced in traveling in such times as these." She smiled and he read her thought, *I knew he wasn't!*

The group rose before dawn, somewhat earlier than Father Shane ever did. At dawn's first light, the small group headed out of the barn and back onto the road. The morning was clear; the two moons were plainly visible in the far southwestern skies. A light blanket of snow covered the ground, melting rapidly as the orange-red sun rose. Soon he removed his cloak. This was more like summer weather, if only it warmed up another twenty degrees or so, he thought. Almost at once, fog developed, turning the world into an eerie scene. However, it soon burnt off, leaving no trace of the uncommon summer snow. Shane could see how crops would fail. *How are we ever going to survive this? Perhaps it is far worse than I ever imagined.*

The lands were hilly and heavily forested here in the old Kingdom of Bettingham, the foothills of the mighty Goza Mountains. The craggy, snow-covered peaks could barely be seen low on the horizon when the travelers topped taller hills.

Large outcrops of rock occasionally broke the rolling hills. Pine trees heavy with resin dominated the various deciduous trees. In the valleys, grasslands and farms predominated closer in to the towns and villages. However, with the strange weather, few crops grew; the fields lay barren and muddy, as was the well-traveled track, which led southeast towards the far distant town of Rusden. As expected, the further one traveled from a town or village, the fewer the farmsteads. These foothills were sparsely populated, compared to the more easterly lands.

Three days out of Wycombe, Father Shane's *mentales* control was tested. The road wandered through a dense patch of pine and maple trees. "Keep close together. I don't like the stillness of the woods," Fred called out. Shane picked up Jane's thought: *Ambush ahead! Do careful, Fred!* She had the *mentales* gift too, he realized. Dutifully, the three wagons moved closer together with Father Shane leading the way on his mare. He kept alert, eyes roving from tree to tree.

Without warning, a dozen men armed with axes, clubs, and a few bows stepped out. Their leader carried the only sword in the lot. He looked ragged — patched leather pants, a worn cotton shirt, and muddy boots. "Halt. What have we here? Search them for anything valuable."

Father Shane focused. He felt the leader's mind. *Dominate! You will order your men to leave us alone and let us go on our way. If not, you will perish.* He could not quite come out and say I will kill you, so he substituted a more benign word. He had total certainty the man would obey his order — that was his gift, to bend anyone to his will.

To the amazement of the others, the leader spoke up, "Leave them be, men. They are poorer than we are. There will be better game for us soon. Back into the trees now." Hastily the rag-tag band obeyed. Almost as suddenly as they appeared, the bandits were gone, and Shane gently urged his mare on, waving for the wagons to follow.

After they had gone another mile, Fred called out, "Did you do that, Father? None of us can figure this out. Why didn't they rob us? Jane thinks you influenced them somehow."

I have to make a choice. Honor. In the end, that is all we can truly say is ours. Such wisdom from mere farmers. He spoke up, "Yes, I suggested he leave us in peace. I am glad it worked."

"Much obliged, Father!" Fred called back. After that, he noticed the small band treated him with far more respect.

As he rode along, he had time to reflect on what he'd learned this past ten-day. Brother Sheridan played a pivotal role. *Without him, I'd still be so ignorant of my own mentales!* He closed his eyes, trusting his mare to trudge on down the road on her own. Almost at once, his own body's energy field came into view. There were the energy lines, running up and down his body and on out to his extremities. The *mentales* gift allowed one to see these lines, the body's communication lines if Brother Sheridan was correct. He spotted a little blockage or buildup of energy in his right foot and realized it was cramped. He sent soothing wave flows down that line and watched the pent up energy go into flow once more and the cramp was gone. *Amazing!*

Further, he now could "see" the energy lines of other people's bodies, thanks to Brother Sheridan. For a moment, he wondered how that man had learned all he did know about this strangest of gifts. Shane shrugged that one off; he had no way to answer that one. Rather, he looked behind him at the other families rolling slowly along behind him. He looked not with his body's eyes, but with his *mentales* gift.

Jane had the gift as well as her son. Sam had it and so did one of his daughters. *It is so easy to tell others like myself. Their energy fields shine like a beacon, if one only looks. Thank you Brother Sheridan!* The bodies of those who did not have the *mentales* gift looked merely dark. True, he knew if he really focused on one of them, then their energy communication lines would appear as well, but they were always dim to him, not the bright and clear lines of those who also had the gift.

During the ensuing two weeks, they added five more wagons to their small caravan. All were farming families heading south to find a warmer climate, which would support their crops. Twice more, Father Shane had to use his gift to drive off would be bandits, much to everyone's gratitude. He was given noticeably larger portions at meal times, much to his embarrassment, but he sensed he dare not refuse their generosity. It was a matter of honor among them that they provide for their protector. More and more, Father Shane came to believe that indeed the *mentales* gifts were given unto man by the Lord God to help them survive this natural disaster.

Mid-July, they were within a hundred miles of Rusden proper. Already the weather was far warmer. While there were frequent rains, neither sleet nor ice came by nightfall and no snow. The farmers' spirits rose, their plan would likely bear fruit. However, that changed quickly. They came upon a large group of soldiers, blocking all passage on the main track to Rusden.

"Halt. You are heading into a battle zone, Father," the captain advised him as he reined in close to the marching men. He no longer needed to wrap himself in his cloak to stay warm. His black collar was now plainly visible to all. The weather was almost summer-like at last. They were about eight hundred miles further south and just east of the foothills of the Goza Mountains. "King Rusden has issued a summons for all able-bodied men in his kingdom to come to him at his fortress in Rusden."

"Why? Who is attacking him?" asked Father Shane.

"The neighboring Kingdom of Hammil, which lies to the east of Rusden. They have invaded and even now, King Hammil is marching his army towards Rusden, burning the villages as he passes through them, confiscating food and conscripting able-bodied men into his own army. It is not safe for you to continue on the road to the city, unless you want to join King Rusden's army."

"No indeed not. I am a COG priest, sworn not to kill others. These others with me are mere farmers. We will seek another route. Thank you sir," he replied. The captain looked over the men, satisfying himself none would make a passable soldier. Then, he signaled his men and the soldiers marched on down the dirt road. As soon as they were out of sight, Father Shane turned to discuss the situation with the farmers.

Quickly, the farmers reached an agreement. None wanted to enter a war zone, for that was far too risky. Fred estimated how far they had come and the amount the weather had improved. His conclusion was to somehow get across the shallow but wide Brockton River, which ran from the southern Goza Mountains in the Kingdom of Oakham eastward across to the ocean. This was the historical barrier marking the southern boundaries of the old kingdoms of Bettingham and Pinewood from the extreme southern old Kingdom of Boshir. Father Shane's goal was the Holy City of Valcia approximately two-thirds of the way down central Boshir.

The farmer's goal was to see if the countryside just across the river was suitable for their new farms and crops. Until now, they merely had to follow the well-marked track leading to Rusden. Fred knew they could not just head cross-country with these heavily laden wagons. Thus, they were forced to retrace their path for several miles until they found a side track that led nearly due west.

For two days, they followed this trail, not much more than wagon ruts. Frequently, they had to stop to clear fallen trees from their way. Only once had they had to do this on the long ride down from Wycombe. Obviously, this was a far less heavily traveled path. About a hundred miles west of Rusden, the track veered southward once again, raising everyone's spirits. Finally, the countryside opened up into gently rolling grasslands. A small town appeared ahead of them.

Hayden's Crossing read the sign at the edge of the town of about five thousand, or so Father Shane estimated. A fair number of people came out onto the street to stare at the arriving wagons. Evidently, he assumed, they didn't get many visitors in Hayden's Crossing. Father Shane was trail dirty. He couldn't recall when he'd last had a bath. His clothes were worn and in sore need of a good cleaning. His companions were in as much need as he, but Shane also realized these people didn't have the funds to spend. Thus, he volunteered to put everyone up at the inn for one day and pay for a public bath. In return, Betsy and Jane washed his clothes and darned some holes in his socks.

While they were at the inn relaxing with a good warm meal that cost him two silvers, a *Jefe* or nobleman entered. He walked up to the group, nodded to Father Shane. "I am *Jefe-*

king Mark Hayden. You are new to Hayden's Crossing. We don't get many travelers here. What news have you brought?" He pulled up a chair and motioned for the barmaid to bring a pitcher of ale. Shane tossed her another silver.

Hayden's Crossing was a rather isolated kingdom, nestled between the larger kingdoms of Oakham to the west and Rusden to the east. *Jefe* Hayden was very willing to have this group of farmers settle in his kingdom. The only problem was how these families could survive until they got their crops harvested more than a year from now. *Jefe* Hayden offered to support them until their first harvest, but for a price. He wanted them to swear fealty to his rule. Father Shane sensed the men were unwilling to make such an obligation, for it meant he could call upon them to take up arms and fight for him, if the kingdom was attacked. They were farmers, not soldiers.

Father Shane interceded. "What if I loan you a hundred silver? Will that be enough to tide you over until your harvest?" It was and the men were extremely thankful for his generosity.

"But how will we repay you, Father?" asked Fred. Shane knew this had become a matter of honor between the farmers and himself. Unless they could find a way to repay him, they could not accept his offer.

"I'll pass this way after your harvest season. You can repay me then when I am on my way back from the Holy City."

Jefe Hayden commented, "You are going to Valcia, Father? Have you not heard?"

"No, heard what?"

"Central Bashir has become a vast desert. All crops there have failed and the people are fleeing to the coasts. It is a vast no-man's land these days or so we've heard from the occasional passerby. If you are determined to go there, I urge you to take your own water with you," the plump, but fit *Jefe* replied. Shane sensed he was very pleased to share news with him. News, it seemed, went both ways.

Sam spoke up, "Father, as part of our repayment, please accept one of our horses to be your packhorse. We can rig a cradle so the horse can carry two large water barrels for you."

They discussed this and agreed they would repay Shane only seventy silver when he returned.

The next day, Father Shane waved goodbye to his new friends and headed on his way, leading a packhorse carrying many gallons of precious water along with food supplies. Hayden's Crossing was so named because just south of town the great Brockton River was shallow enough to ford easily. Reaching the other side of the nearly mile wide river, he turned and waved once more, keenly aware some of the children were still watching him ride off in the distance.

Now he followed the directions *Jefe* Hayden gave him. Simple enough, follow the river eastward until he came to the main southeast track, which led down the center of the old kingdom of Bashir. It too had become splintered into many smaller kingdoms. The largest three cities, Nasik on the northeast coast, Karnatalka on the extreme southern tip, and Madya on the eastern coast where the Brockton River delta emptied into the ocean, formed the heart of the three largest and strongest kingdoms in Bashir. Yet rumors suggested there were also many smaller kingdoms here as well. However, that the central country had become a desert greatly disturbed him. His Holy City was there, the origin point for the entire Church of God worldwide and his ultimate destination.

Two lonely days later, he picked up the trail that led south by southeast towards Valcia, some fifteen hundred miles distant. Already he missed the constant companionship of his group of farmers and their families. He steeled himself as he turned to the south. He had a mission, a vital one. He had to stop the wholesale slaughter of the innocent, those whom the Lord God had blessed with the *mentales* gift; those who could help everyone survive this disastrous change in worldwide weather.

For several days, he rode through rolling grasslands and watched the afternoon thunder heads slowly build up. However, rain seldom came, rather, the rains began somewhere across the Brockton River. Still, for several days, he enjoyed watching the clouds forming, passing the seemingly endless time. He met few travelers for which he was grateful.

By the fourth day, the clouds no longer appeared and the late afternoon temperature soared. Streaks of brown appeared among the rolling grasslands. Ahead, a dark and thick jungle appeared along with a COG dispatch rider way station. He pulled in to the station where a dozen horses were corralled ready for the riders. He knew the Archbishop often sent out dispatch riders from Valcia, carrying his official orders to the fifteen Bishop-kings. These men rode their horses at top speed and thus periodically needed fresh mounts. These periodic way stations provided them. As he rode up, a dispatch rider came galloping up from behind him.

Father Shane reined in and watched the action. The station manager and another rider came out. The fresh rider mounted another horse; he'd failed to see one of the dozen horses was already saddled and ready to go. The incoming rider handed a leather pouch to the new rider and dismounted his lathered horse. The new rider kicked his mount into a canter, heading on down south to Valcia, Shane assumed. The manager took the reins and began walking the exhausted gelding, cooling him down.

"Ah, welcome, Father," the very dusty rider said to the priest. Even though the temperature was stifling, Shane continued to wear his black shirt and collar, identifying his profession. Traveling alone through unfamiliar lands, he trusted his collar to identify himself to would be bandits who might think twice.

"Well met yourself. I have heard of you dispatch riders, but I've never seen or met one. Believe me, we priests do appreciate your efforts," Father Shane replied.

He smiled, pleased to hear the compliment. "Sammy Jones. Thanks. It's actually a lot of fun. Where else can you ride flat out? Where are you headed?"

"Valcia. I have to meet with Archbishop Mata Hatta. I'm from Wycombe." Sammy was barely twenty, armed with a sword. He wore a thin cotton white shirt, very loose fitting and leather britches and tall boots.

"Want some company? I'm off duty now and am supposed to take my time returning there myself. Have you been across our new desert yet?"

"No, I did hear something about that. How can this be? I thought the interior of Bashir was a thick jungle," he answered, hoping for more information.

"Was. That's the operative word now. The weather has altered drastically. It's spooky, riding through the dying jungle. Closer to Valcia, all the vegetation has died. It has become a desert now. I see you were wisely advised to bring along extra water. That's our biggest problem now. We've had to double the number of way stations here in the central highlands so we and our horses don't perish from the heat. You also need to bring along a sack of salt."

"Oops. No salt. Do I really need extra salt?" he asked.

Sammy explained in detail, and then asked, "Say, want to join me? I could use the company on the long ride. The station manager here can give you a salt sack. We'll be staying at the various way stations along the way, Father Shane."

A bit later, as the two rode along heading into the dying jungle, Sammy explained, "We must be extra cautious about fire. The jungle is a tinderbox right now. The manager says to be alert for a wildfire just beyond the next station, that is, about thirty miles from here. He says we ought to smell it before we see it."

"Have there been many such fires? If all this jungle is dying, I would expect some."

"You bet! There's been a rash of them. I almost got caught in one last run out of Valcia. Burned out one station two months ago. Everyone's leaving, you know."

"Leaving?"

"Sure, animals and people. No water. And with the jungle dying, you can't blame them. They are moving to the coasts I've heard. Makes sense, though you can't drink the salt water. What's the weather like up in Wycombe? I heard all sorts of wild tales. Snow in the summer? Is that really true?"

"Quite true. It rains usually every late afternoon, changing to sleet and ice by sunset. Frequently, we wake up to a light snow cover, but it does melt rather quickly and many mornings are foggy for a time," Shane explained.

"Incredible! Are the trees dying like they are here?"

"Yes and no, pines and nut trees are surviving well, but

not the crops. Farmers are in a bad way. Several farming families traveled south with me, stopping around Hayden's Crossing where crops are thriving. They are making new homes there. I've heard horror stories about lands further north though. Some claim there are no seasons there, just always winter. I don't quite believe that story."

"Father, can I ask you a question?" Shane nodded. "Is this weather the devil's doing? Some claim this is Lucifer's revenge on us, but I don't quite know what to believe." Shane's *mentales* senses indicated the young man was deeply concerned, quite troubled. Well, who wasn't? Shane thought.

"My son, I cannot speak for the COG, but it is my opinion that this is some freakish natural disaster; perhaps the aliens were behind it. Who can say? Certainly, the devil had no hand in it. Think about it, Sammy. Are we to claim *we* are the center of the *whole* universe out there, that Lucifer *personally* takes a hand in *our* planet's *weather*? No, we are merely Lord God's humble children. We are not the center of some giant power struggle, that would be wholly egocentric of us. I have not that big an ego." *Sammy has the mentales gift too! My god, he is also hiding it!*

Hastily, he added, "No, my own personal opinion is our Lord God has shown us, his followers on Tierra, his Holy Mercy and has given some of us the *mentales* gift so we can help our people somehow survive this calamity and flourish once more. That is the reason for my visit to our Most Holy Archbishop. I must get him to stop executing those who have this precious gift from our Lord God."

The relief emanating from Sammy was almost overwhelming, and Shane had to dampen quickly his heightened sensitivity down. Sammy was literally mentally screaming in relief. "Thank you, Father Shane! Thank you." He still didn't reveal to Shane that he had the gift. Sammy wisely kept his gift a closely guarded secret. Rightly so, thought Shane, because if I don't get the ruling changed, Sammy could be killed too.

Sammy suddenly halted and sniffed. "Fire?" asked Shane. He thought he could smell a faint odor on the light hot wind. He looked around at the enormous dried vegetation.

Great trees were leafless. Dried brush and smaller plants turned the landscape into a brownish hue. Perhaps even more alarming, Shane realized he'd seen no animals, no birds since they entered the dead jungle! His mare was fidgeting nervously and his lack of horsemanship showed as he futilely struggled to control her.

"Yes, fire ahead of us. Could be bad; we don't want to get too close to it. Perhaps it isn't too close to the path. Come on, but keep alert," Sammy replied. His gay expression changed to lines of worry. His whole countenance altered. "Be prepared to retreat as fast as possible. I heard we lost a rider to a fire last week. They say he couldn't outrun it, but I find that hard to believe. Come on. There is a rider ahead of us by several hours. I hope he is okay." He kicked his gelding and headed on down the well-marked path.

As the miles passed by, the smell of smoke grew steadily until at last they could see the grey fog of smoke drifting across the trail ahead of them. Shane followed Sammy's lead, tying a spare shirt across his face. It helped a little to keep out the pungent smoke. Sammy cursed, "The worst part of this is we cannot see far enough ahead of us to see what the situation actually is." For a moment, Shane considered climbing one of the taller dead trees but decided that might not be a good idea.

They rode on into the growing smoke for another half mile. Suddenly, they heard hoof beats and reined in once more. Shortly, the rider that had taken over for Sammy came galloping madly their way, his horse well lathered. He slowed down and yelled, "Flee, fire's coming! Can't get through." He was covered in soot and his shirt mask over his face was blackened. Quickly, the two wheeled around and followed the rider, going back the way they had come.

Several miles later, the rider's horse collapsed from exhaustion. The man ducked and rolled off the horse, momentarily stunned. Sammy and Shane pulled up and Sammy leaped from his saddle to tend to his comrade. Shane dismounted and took a hold of Sammy's reins. "Tom, are you hurt?" Sammy called out. He reached his friend and helped him stagger to his feet.

A myriad of curses filled the air, but Tom calmed down

quickly. "Yes, poor horse. We have to get out of here fast, though." He mechanically retrieved the dispatch pouch, slinging it over his shoulder, and then began undoing the saddle and bridle.

"We can use my spare horse," Shane offered.

"Thanks, I am afraid I must. Abandon what you don't need. It will be a race for your very lives, gang," Tom explained, coughing up some black phlegm.

"I've got two water barrels there, wash off a bit," Shane suggested.

"Right, thanks. We should water our clothing down too. Come on, Sammy; help me get this one saddled before the flames get us." The two men quickly removed the pack rack and put Tom's saddle on, cinching it tightly. Shane felt a bit out of place. These two young men knew precisely what to do, and he felt more like the packhorse just along for the ride. However, he realized he owed these men his life. Alone, he would not have known about the fire until perhaps it was too late. At last, Tom broke open a water keg. All three men soaked their face masks with water and their shirts as well. Finally, Tom did his best to wash the black filth off himself a little. He rinsed his mouth out and then his nose. Black mucus covered his hands.

Feeling a bit better, Tom explained, "Okay, fire is coming our way. Let's backtrack to the next side path and take it. With luck we can get around the western edge of the fire before it gets to us," Tom explained. The three men headed on down the path to the north. This time, Tom set a pace the horses could handle. All three often looked back over their shoulders. Shane breathed a sigh of relief, for the smoke was definitely thinning. A half hour later, Tom veered to his left and the trio headed westward now. He yelled back to Shane, "Keep your fingers crossed we've put enough distance between the fire and us."

For two more hours, they alternated between a canter and a trot, pushing the horses slightly but still keeping something in reserve. This is surreal, Shane thought. All around him was a brown, dead jungle, save for the well-traveled path they were following. Before long, they entered a village, a ghost village of empty houses, now in disrepair. Tom said most all people had long ago fled these central highlands, no water.

A mile beyond the ghost village, Shane again saw billowing balls of smoke pushing up like soap bubbles out of the dense, dry underbrush, just left of their path. He thought about calling it to Sammy and Tom's attention, but decided the men probably already saw it too. Tom had picked up their speed a little.

Soon, Father Shane heard a loud rumbling, crackling noise coming from the dense smoke. Tom yelled, "Fire is close! Gallop for your lives!" He kicked his horse into an all-out gallop. Shane's horse didn't need any encouragement; it followed the other two without Shane's doing anything excepting holding on. Even his mare knew this was a race for life! Now the roar from the fire became deafening. They felt intense heat on their left side and the smoke was almost too dense to breath, yet they continued their mad dash.

They came out onto a dried up riverbed. Tom veered to follow it a ways. At this point, they could see the flames reaching a hundred feet into the air. The once tall jungle trees burst into flames, like roman candles. Ahead, Tom spotted an abandoned mine and made for it. He did a flying dismount and led his horse inside the dark opening. Sammy followed behind him, but Shane didn't dare such acrobatics. He reined in and hopped off. As he led his mare inside following the other two, he saw the flames leap across the dry riverbed. Any longer and they would be right in the middle of the huge fire!

Tom led them far back into the mine and then said, "We should be safe here, but we have to walk the horses some, until they cool down a bit. We don't want to be stranded out here on foot!" He coughed again and Shane found his dry, parched mouth gagging him. He too began coughing up black phlegm. The poor horses snorted out streams of the foul stuff. While they could hear the roaring inferno outside the mine, inside, they were safe for the moment.

Meanwhile, Sammy found an abandoned rusty sluice pan and carefully used half of their remaining water to give the three horses a critical drink. "Horses come first. Without them we don't stand a chance of getting to safety when the flames die down." Shane nodded, thankful for the wisdom of these dispatch riders.

All three men were caked with soot and Shane began laughing. The two looked at him. "I've never been this filthy in my life!"

Sammy grinned, "Yes, but we are alive." Shane couldn't argue with that point. "Now, we rest. Can't do a thing until the fire's out and cooled down some. Might as well rest up. What grub have we between us?" Father Shane had some dried meat and a couple of apples in his saddlebags, which he shared with the two riders. "We don't carry food with us because we spend nights at the way stations."

"But won't they be burned down too?" Shane asked.

"Some maybe. Let's hope we can hold out until we get to one the fires missed," Tom replied. "Sammy's right. We'd best get some sleep while we can."

Shane couldn't get to sleep. Besides the constant flickering reddish glow coming from the entrance, the stony, hard ground was just too uncomfortable, but he did rest. Finally, he managed to doze off. He slept fitfully, dreaming of their race against the fire. He awoke to pitch blackness, a darkness he'd never experienced. Panic constricted his stomach for a moment until he realized it must be night, that the fires must have died down, and that they were deep inside a mine. The air did feel a bit fresher and cooler. He rose and stumbled his way to the entrance. Outside, he could see the redden embers of the giant jungle trees flickering just across the dry riverbed. He relieved himself and headed back inside, feeling his way with his hands and feet. Once back to his saddle, he lay down once more, relieved the worst was probably over.

When daylight came, Tom and Sammy went to the entrance to relieve themselves and survey the situation. When they returned, Tom suggested, "Lots of hot embers out there. I think we'd best stay here another day. Try hitting the trail tomorrow morning. How's our water situation holding out? Food?"

"Sorry, we ate the last of my food last time," Shane

replied. "We have half a skin of water left. Will that do?" Careful rationing began in earnest but failed. Tom began coughing up black phlegm again.

"We need water bad. Tom's lungs are filled with fire soot. He's had it worse than us two; he ran into the fire first. If we don't get our systems flushed out with clean water, we're going to get sick. The horses have it even worse, look at them," Sammy pointed out. All three were hacking and spewing up more of the blacken mucus. "All our lungs got filled with the smoke. We'd best use the rest of our water, and try to clean out our lungs and throats. Mine feels like I swallowed sand or something." They split the remaining water three ways, but Shane gave a goodly portion of his to Tom who was more desperate for it. At last, Tom got his spell under control, but the horses were still not doing well at all.

"Where is the nearest water?" Shane asked, growing more worried by the moment. His mare looked none too good, but then he knew little about horses and their care and afflictions. He trusted these two men in that regard.

Tom shook his head, "Way station, unless they used all theirs to keep from getting burned up in the fire. I was about thirty miles from it when I ran into the fire. I couldn't tell how much had burned. If we," he paused for another great cough, his body heaving wildly. Not a good sign, Shane thought. Tom finished his thought, "If we are lucky, the next way station has water. If not, we are doomed. I don't think the horses can make thirty miles without water, let alone seventy miles to the next station after that."

Shane didn't like the way this whole situation was developing. Apparently, Sammy didn't either. "I suppose we could wait along the path until the next rider came through and ask him for help."

"Yes, we all carry a water skin, but lord knows when the next dispatch rider will come. Messages are growing more and more infrequent these days," Tom lamented, fighting against another round of coughing.

Shane's mind was rather open at this point and he suddenly picked up Sammy's unspoken thoughts. *Damn, I could find us water, but then the mouse will be out of the bag.*

They'll know I have the mentales gift, and I'll be executed! Hell, what do I do now? Shane looked at Sammy from the corner of his eye. He saw a tall, thin youngster, covered in a sooty black mess, filthy beyond all measure. His hair was thick with soot and disheveled. *I probably look like him too,* Shane thought.

I have to make it all right for Sammy to use his gift to save us and yet maintain his secrecy. How? He thought faster than he ever knew possible. An avenue of workability opened before him. He focused as Brother Sheridan had taught him. Into Sammy's mind, he sent, *Say you knew a friend who knew where water might be found. Lead us to the water, Sammy.*

Sammy's head jerked slightly, his eyes falling onto Tom first, but the man was holding his head in his hands, staring at the uneven ground and fighting from coughing once more. Slowly he turned his head to Father Shane. The priest nodded his head ever so slightly, hoping this would be enough to satisfy Sammy. It was. Sammy volunteered, "Hey, I might be able to find us some water. I knew a guy once who told me where there was a spring. Don't know if I can find it now, but it isn't too far from here, I think."

"Hey, that's better than trying to ride thirty miles. I don't think the horses could make it. Tom needs water badly too. Let's give that a try first. If you can't find it, then we can head for the next way station and gamble it is still there," Father Shane spoke up. Tom was too ill to object. They saddled up their horses and led them out of the mine.

Around them, the brown world of dead leaves, brush, and trees had been replaced with blackened earth and burned shells of what had once been mighty, tall trees. All around them, the land took on an eerie form, a ghost world, a dead world. The three and their horses were the only living things in sight, which only added to their uneasy feelings. Several larger trees still smoldered, sending acrid fumes into the clear blue sky. "What I wouldn't give for some of the perpetual rain we keep on having up north in Wycombe," Shane said wishfully. Tom cracked a slight smile.

"Walk the horses. We need them alive, if possible," Sammy ordered and led the way. "It's hard to imagine we once had hundreds of men clearing the constantly growing jungle from our paths." Father Shane tried to imagine how this jungle once looked, but could not. Stark, barren land was all he could see.

Sammy expanded his senses, using his new *mentales* gift, searching for the nearest water. *I wish I knew how I can do this. Strange. I am definitely being pulled that way.* He led them across country, Shane assumed, since the path was nearly invisible. The fire had turned the world black and confusing. Dutifully, the other two followed him. Shane dare not say a word for fear of interrupting Sammy's concentration and Tom was rapidly growing too ill even to care. However, Father Shane kept glancing back at Tom making sure he was still with them. He could sense the man was failing; the coughing fits grew more and more frequent.

Around noon, Sammy halted at the base of a small hill or rather what used to be a jungle hill. Here a bubbling spring issued from an underground aquifer, forming a small pool of water, barely five feet across. The horses made for the water of their own accord, and wisely, Sammy suggested they allow the horses to drink their fill first. There was even a small ring of grasses still living around the outer edge, preserved from the fires, most likely by the pool itself, Father Shane guessed, though he was not an expert in such matters.

They dismounted, unsaddled the horses, and hobbled them. Soon, the horses had their fill and quickly devoured the remaining grass, clipping the greens close to the ground. The men allowed the waters to settle a little and then each knelt down and drank deeply. The water greatly revived Tom. Once their thirst was quenched, they filled all their water skins and then proceeded to wash off their faces and hair as best as they could manage.

"Sammy, you have saved our lives! Good thing you remembered where your friend said this spring was at!" Father Shane spoke up, validating Sammy's efforts. "What do we do now?"

"Well, we have water enough now. While our bellies will protest, we can go for several days without food. If we cut across country, we ought to be able to find the main track again and head on to the next way station," Sammy suggested. "Of course, in this mess, finding the path and following it will be tricky." Father Shane also picked up Sammy's unspoken thoughts, *That is, if the way station wasn't burned too. If it has, am I just postponing our deaths?*

Sammy took his bearings from the sun and the smoldering hills. He seemed satisfied enough, Father Shane thought. The three headed off over the charred landscape. *Could this be what the surface of our moons look like? Barren, desolate, no living thing as far as eyes can see? Barren, death. Shane! Stop such silly thoughts! Trust in Sammy or your bones will lie out here among the burned-out trees.*

The devastation was beyond anything Father Shane had ever seen. True, back in Wycombe, the summer snows were wreaking havoc, but the trees still had leaves in spite of the cold nights. People were going hungry, but there was still game to be had in the forests outside the city. Here there were no people, no game, no plants, nothing at all but smoldering, blacken spires of what had been the great trees of the central jungles of Bashir. Where did the people all go, he wondered not for the first time. Then, he remembered something Sammy had said. Many villagers had migrated to the coastal areas. Well that certainly made sense.

It struck Father Shane: why had Archbishop Mata Hatta not moved the Holy City and the central administration of the worldwide Church of God from Valcia to the coast as well? Why had the Archbishop remained here among such desolation? Perhaps things were better in the Holy City. Perhaps it had been spared after all. He was about to ask Sammy about it when they crested a rise and saw birds circling overhead, great giant scavenger birds, the rocs. With wingspans of some fifteen feet, these monster birds could carry off a small antelope in its claws. Four of these monster birds were slowly circling something in the valley ahead. But what? More unfortunate travelers caught in the fire like themselves?

Sammy headed towards the birds and Father Shane's apprehension grew. The rocs would fight fiercely to protect their carrion feed and he had only a small knife to fight them off, hopeless at best. As they approached the valley, two more rocs were on the ground, savagely ripping flesh from several horses. Sammy veered to the right of them, giving the beasts a wide berth. He said soberly with a hint of sorrow in his voice, "That was our way station and our fresh mounts." He added somberly, "And our food."

Father Shane could not force his eyes off the rocs and the dozen carcasses. Although a sickening sight, this was Nature providing for her birds, the clean-up crew, who were always the last to leave an area. As they passed by what had been the corral, the smoldering ruins of the way station proper came into his view, forcing his attention off the rocs at last. "Shouldn't we stop and see if there are any bodies to be buried?" he asked. After all, he was still a ranking priest of the COG.

Sammy shook his head, "Father, we have not the strength or water to spare on such. If we get to safety, we can send others back to tend to that. The dead really do not need us to join them. Here is the track to the next way station, I think. It is so obscured that it's hard to tell."

The trio rode on slowly over the blackened landscape, something out of a nightmare, Shane thought. No, a nightmare could not be so hot and so real. Smoke still clung to the very air they breathed. Heat waves rose from the land, distorting vision. Sweat rolled down their foreheads, collecting for a time in their days-old stubble, adding to the misery of their trek across the central highlands of Bashir.

Time slipped by Father Shane as the land slipped by his mare, who plodded along, step after step. Drenched in sweat from head to toe, he felt weary, tired beyond belief. Perhaps it would just be best to fall onto the hard ground and give up this impossible quest. His horse ran into Sammy's gelding before he was even aware Sammy had stopped. "Take some salt," Sammy muttered, struggling to get his bag out of his saddlebags. "Salt first then a little water, before we all collapse. Heat exhaustion," Sammy muttered. Father Shane tried to obey, but felt so dizzy. The whole world was spinning. No, he was lying on the ground. He vaguely realized he must have fallen off his mare.

Sammy poured a little salt into his mouth. Never before had felt the body's cravings like this. He sucked on it and he was sure if his body could yell, it would have sung praises to Sammy, who was helping Tom with some salt as well. Then, they passed around a water skin, emptying it. "Thanks Sammy, I don't know what came over me. I feel lots better," Shane said, his voice sounding still a bit distant.

"Heat exhaustion, maybe heat stroke. Happens sometimes. I should have seen it coming sooner, but I was affected too," Sammy admitted. "Come on; let's get some salt and water into our horses." They used the last of their water to revive their horses. After the rest stop, they mounted and continued following the barely visible track.

At the top of the next rise, Sammy pointed out, "We are in luck! Look, there is the brown jungle once more. The fire didn't get beyond this hill! The next way station ought not be too far now."

As they reached the bottom of the valley, Father Shane's eyes caught sight of a bunch of sun-bleached bones off to their right. "What's there?" he called out to Sammy.

"A bunch of bones from a lot of jungle animals that died there when the water hole dried up. Hundreds of them. I stopped to look last trip north, but we don't have time to stop now, father," Sammy replied. "How's Tom doing?" Shane took another backwards look. Tom was definitely feverish and swaying in his saddle.

"He's still with us," he answered. *Not for long. I suppose we can tie him to his horse. I hope he makes it.* "Just a little further, Tom, hang in there." He did his best to encourage the dispatch rider.

Near sunset, they spotted the way station. Never had a crude adobe building with attached corral and lean-to looked so heavenly to Father Shane. A dozen horses were milling around, munching on dried vegetation of which there was no lack. A tall man came out, followed by another rider. "Praise the Lord! Tom, we thought you were a goner, what with the fire and all," the station master called out.

Chapter 3 Changes

Mid-September, Sammy and Father Shane crested the last hill and halted, overlooking the Holy City of Valcia, the centerpiece of the Church of God on Tierra. The once marvel of the world was now a ghost town. True, the marble columns and grey-white stonework remained along with the grey slate roofs, untouched by the drought and fires and still dominating the whole valley, an architectural marvel, a feast for the eyes. Yet this city of some twenty thousand seemed eerily deserted. From their hilltop, Father Shane did not see what he had anticipated: throngs of people going about their Holy Duties, overseeing the great COG.

The Great Stable was quite visible, hundreds of horses milling around inside the stone fenced-in pasture and shelter. The Holiest of Holies, the Mother Church of God rose like a beacon, calling to Father Shane. *Here is where our mighty church first began,* he thought humbly. He said a brief reverent prayer and followed Sammy as he headed down the hillside to the stables. The city covered many square miles, the entire valley in fact. Yet even as they entered the city, Shane could see very few people. "Where is everyone?" he found himself asking the stable master, who came out of his building to assist his arriving dispatch rider, Sammy.

"Who are you? Man, you two look like you have been through Lucifer's Hell and back," the man replied.

"Father Shane Zadok from Wycombe. I've come to seek an audience with Archbishop Mata Hatta. Long story, ran into fires. Sammy saved our lives."

"A priest? Man, you sure don't look like one. You'd best get to the Rectory and clean up, father." Plainly obvious, the man didn't think he was a priest, but he would let those in the Rectory make that determination.

"This is my first visit to our Holy City. Please, sir, where might I find our Rectory? There seems to be so few people around. Where is everyone?" he repeated his unanswered earlier question.

Begrudgingly, the man gave him the needed directions.

He added, "Many have lost their faith and fled the city."
Clearly, the man did not have a high opinion of those who had
left the city. Shane thanked him, shook Sammy's hand, and
started off on foot to the Rectory, his nearly empty saddlebags
slung over his shoulder.

As he walked through the empty streets, he had an eerie
feeling. *So desolate. Not what I expected.* Houses stood empty,
shops deserted. The light breeze clapped a pair of shutters idly
back and forth, announcing yet another empty shop. *Has our
Holy City become a dead city? Has everyone left? I don't
understand this.*

"Welcome Father Shane Zadok of Wycombe. I am
Hannan, the Rectory Caretaker. Come in, come in." Shane
took an immediate liking to this man, whose brown skin was
ideally suited to the warmer climate here in Bashir. He was tall
and thin, with bowl-cut short black hair and a moustache,
carefully trimmed. What struck him most was the man's face,
one of those that exude kindness, a gentleness seldom found
these days. "If you will follow me, I will show you to your room
and to the bath. I will bring you a fresh set of clothes while you
bathe. Yes, we do have enough water for bathing," he grinned,
adding, "there are so few of us left now, so water is not a huge
problem, though it will be before long. We've gone four
hundred days now without a single drop of rain. Incredible.
How is the weather in Wycombe? Is it truly snowing at night
in the summer? We've heard rumors." Hannan stoked the hot
water heater and listened to Shane's description of the
incessant rains, sleet, and snow up north.

An hour later, bathed, shaved, and sporting a new
hastily done bowl haircut, Shane felt like a new man. At long
last, he had the acrid smoke smell out of his hair and nose. He
felt human once more and proud to be a priest of the COG, as
he put on the new black shirt and fastened its black collar.
Hannan led him to their dining room and kitchen. "We still
have a bit of food left, but I am afraid we are running out.
There are just a dozen of us left here in Valcia."

"What? A dozen?" Shane replied, his face displaying the
utter dismay he felt. "But this is the center of our religion, its
birthplace."

"Aye, that it is, but with no food, the animals gone, and very little water, one by one, families moved out. Only a few priests and advisors are left, along with some dispatch riders and their managers. Grim. The Archbishop Mata finally did listen to reason and moved the Doctor College down to Karnatalka on the southern coast. Quite a few families joined them. At least with the exodus of so many, our food supplies have held out far longer than I estimated." Hannan chatted with Shane for over an hour.

At last, his hunger satiated, Father Shane could not put off the purpose of his visit any longer. He got directions to the Archbishop Mata Hatta's office and headed there, unsure of exactly how he would present his case. Months ago when he left Wycombe, he assumed he would have three months to work out the best way to convince his Archbishop, but that had gone by the boards. As he approached the Holy Office, another priest stepped out from a side room. Shane glimpsed a small placard that read Advisors Only.

"You must be Father Shane Zadok from Wycombe. Hannan sent word you came to see our Holy Father, Archbishop Mata Hatta. I am Father Ramal, his Holy Advisor. May I have a word with you first?" The man had sharp eyes — the kind that searched your soul, divining your worth and mettle. Shane bowed as appropriate and followed him into his plush office, taking a seat. He could not help noticing the elegant mahogany table and matching chairs. Expensive tastes, but fitting for the Holy Advisor, he thought. More importantly, Shane did not detect any hint of the *mentales* gift in Father Ramal. This he accepted as fortunate.

After the perfunctory hand shake, Father Ramal motioned for him to have a seat. "Before you enter the presence of His Holiness, I must alert you and swear you to utter secrecy." The man was dead serious and many ideas flooded into Shane's mind. He so swore, refusing to probe the man's mind for more data. "You see, all this drastic weather has driven our Archbishop — well, there is no easy way to say this. It has driven him slightly mad. Please do not say anything that will upset him any further."

"I shall say my prayers for his swift recovery," Shane

promised, thinking this would be the most appropriate reply. He asked, "Are others taking over the responsibilities of leading our Church of God?" Perhaps there was someone else he really needed to talk to, if the Archbishop was indeed mad. In that case, there would be no need even to speak with the man.

Father Ramal sighed and slumped heavily into his chair. "If this had happened a year ago, five priests would have battled to become our next Archbishop. Alas, now it seems, due to the wild weather, all seem to believe the end of the world has come. No one wants to have anything to do with it. In fact, all five have long ago fled from Valcia and I can't say I blame them."

"I see. How come you are still here, if you don't mind my frank question?"

"Mata and I have been friends since we were children. I owe him my position here. Even though his mind is nearly gone, I am sworn to look after him until the end."

"Bless you. So few display such loyalties these days," Father Shane sought for the right words to both comfort and praise the man. What was really going on here? Had all the other priests decided there was no hope mankind would survive? Was his beloved church doomed? "Hasn't anyone stepped in to help Archbishop Mata with running our COG?"

"It is down to me and Father Banalthan, I am afraid to say. All the others have deserted the COG here in its Holy Time of Trial. That's what Father Banalthan and I are calling these impossible days. Come, I can see I have truly upset you, Father Shane. I felt I owed you an explanation. If you will follow me, I will take you to our Archbishop now."

Crestfallen, Shane rose and humbly followed Father Ramal. Was this trip all for nothing? Could nothing at all be done to stop the wholesale slaughter of the innocent whose only crime was somehow they had received the Lord God's Holy *Mentales* Gift? Was Ramal right? Were they facing the total extinction of mankind? Father Shane was troubled as he walked along the red carpet into the Archbishop's Office, located behind the High Altar of the Great Founding Church of God.

"Father Shane Zadok of Wycombe to see you, Your Holiness," Father Ramal spoke up as they entered. Shane saw an overly plump man slumped over in his plush purple chair. His purple robes trimmed with real gold embroidery hung like an albatross around his neck, as if he bore the entire weight of the total failure of all mankind upon his shoulders. The forty-five year old man looked as if he were seventy-five! Mechanically Shane sat down in a chair opposite the Archbishop. Father Ramal quietly left them alone. Whatever business Father Shane had with his master was private and not meant for his ears.

Shane spoke quietly, "I have come from Wycombe, Your Holiness."

"Wycombe? Wycombe. Why do you comb a bee? To get more honey, I say," Mata mumbled.

"The Kingdom of Wycombe, Bettingham, Your Holiness. The northern kingdom," Shane attempted to orient the man.

"Why do you bet on a ham? Because only a fool will survive the End of Days I say. World's End? I was so close and now all I have done is a fool's errand. Today is Wednesday, I do believe. Perhaps it is time for High Mass, but only rats come, you know. We have lots of rats these days. Some suggest rats will become our staple meat in the coming days. I for one do not like staples. I say, a good old nail is far stronger and more reliable than a staple. No, I don't need my nails trimmed, good man," he said while examining his fingers closely. "I used to be stronger, but then so is everyman in their youth, stronger that is. I, however, prefer strong tea, black, no sugar. How about you?"

Shane stretched his mind to its limits trying to make sense of His Holiness' words, as the man continued his babbling. "I'm afraid there isn't any more sugar to be had unless you go to Karnatalka for some. Send a dispatch rider, why don't you? Do I need to write another dispatch? Where was I? Oh, I remember, it is these infernal headaches that have afflicted me, striking me down in my youth. Do you have headaches? Mine are pounding ones. I haven't slept for days. Can you please ask the builders to cease their pounding and hammering, at least for today? Perhaps that will give me some peace."

Father Shane finally realized Archbishop Mata Hatta was not making any real sense, that he was mad. The mention of headaches triggered something. What was it? Ah, something the Brother Sheridan had told him. Some of those who received the *mentales* gift could not handle it and went mad. The usual symptoms were intense, debilitating headaches. Usually, the person so afflicted died. He focused his mind and reached out to the Archbishop Mata, touching the man's mind with the gentlest, feather-like touch. The instant he contacted the man's mind, he knew Archbishop Mata had the *mentales* gift and that he was suffering mightily from it. In a flash of understanding, he knew why. Self-denial.

The Archbishop considered all those who had the gift to have been tempted by Lucifer and thus corrupted. Yet, he was the supreme leader of the COG, the world's most Holy Man. Force-counter-force battled for control of the man's mind, neither side budging or yielding to the other. If he acknowledged he had the *mentales* gift, then by his own decree, he had to be burned at the stake. To survive, he had to attempt to deny and force out of existence his *mentales* gift. Since neither avenue was acceptable to him, his mind had almost ceased to function.

Zounds! There is no way I can talk to him and get him to see reason and rescind his orders to execute all those who have the mentales gift! This whole trip has been wasted. We are all doomed! For a minute, all hope left Father Shane.

Get a grip. He obviously needs to step down as our COG leader. Yet, Father Ramal has said all those who coveted his position have also fled, abandoning our beloved COG. Oh, yea of little faith! You do not deserve to lead our COG! I will. I will lead, since no one else will. Something must be done, and I darn well better do it!

Carefully, Father Shane planted a carefully worded thought into Archbishop Mata's mind. *Appoint Father Shane here to be the next Archbishop. Then I can retire in peace and find relief from my headaches.* This was Father Shane's primary *mentales* gift, Dominate.

"Yes, I shall do just that! Father Shane, you are hereby appointed to fill my shoes and become the next Archbishop of the Church of God! Father Ramal, Father Ramal, come, come," Mata called out loudly. The door opened and a fearful Ramal looked in. Shane sensed the man's worry over his lifelong friend. His thoughts screamed into Shane's mind: *Has Shane upset him?*

"Ah, Father Ramal. Take this down. I am hereby appointing Father Shane What's His Name here to take over the COG for me. I can retire in peace and find relief from these hideous headaches of mine. Take care of the paperwork will you? I believe I feel better already, Ramal. I should have done this long ago."

"Yes, Your Holiness. I'll draw up the proclamation immediately. Please rest while I am writing it. Father Shane, if you will follow me? He needs to relax a little." Shane followed Father Ramal back to his office. "Oh dear me, Father Shane. Sometimes the Archbishop doesn't know what he is doing. I am sure you don't want his position. If so, perhaps the wisest thing would be simply to leave. By tomorrow he will have forgotten all about it."

"No, that is okay with me, Father Ramal. Someone has to lead our beloved COG out of these Dark Times. I will be honored to do it. Besides, I think giving up his post and retiring may greatly aid his mental state, don't you think?" Shane replied diplomatically.

"Are you sure? None of the others want such terrible responsibilities — what with the world coming to an end and all that." Father Ramal looked both terribly shocked and surprised.

"Yes, I am sure. I am a priest and it is my responsibility to help lead us forward. The world is not coming to an end just yet. Rather, it is changing and our Holy COG must change with it and lead the way to salvation."

Father Ramal let out a huge sigh of relief. "Bless you, my son! God bless you! I will draw up the proclamation at once."

An hour later, Fathers Shane, Ramal, and Banalthan stood beside Archbishop Mata Hatta as he signed the formal proclamation. "There it is done!" Mata stated with relief, his handwriting barely legible. He took off his heavy purple robes and handed them ceremoniously to Shane. "It is my Highest Honor to be the first to place this Holy Robe of office upon you, our new Archbishop Shane What's His Name."

"Zadok," whispered Father Ramal.

"Yes, Archbishop Shane What's His Name Zadok. There, it is done. Ramal, I am retiring to my room to sleep now. My head is still aching, but not so bad. If he takes sugar in his tea, send a dispatch rider to Karnatalka for some. We are long out of sugar." Mata shuffled on out of the office for the last time.

"Thank you Archbishop Shane! Truly, this is the Lord God's Holy Blessing for us all," Father Banalthan said enthusiastically. "Now our beloved leader can finally find the peace he needs. Thank you. Ramal and I are your only remaining advisors. Your first action must be to send out a copy of this proclamation to all our bishops."

"Yes, that is wise. I would also like to send along my first official proclamation as well. Then, I will need to be fully briefed. I admit I know nothing about our situation and my new duties to our Church of God, but I am a quick learner."

"Excellent. I will prepare the copies now. You can get started on your first proclamation. I will inform the dispatch master that riders will be needed soon," Father Banalthan replied. He was fifty years old and a faithful administrator, but he had no aspirations for the topmost position. Shane sensed he enjoyed being an administrator, a follower and not a leader. Shane sat down and picked up quill and paper. Now to undo the disaster.

16 September 1001

My Holy Bishops,

Contrary to many rumors, our world is not coming to an end, mankind is not on the verge of becoming extinct. Rather, Nature had undergone a fundamental change, a change that will forever alter the weather of our world. But that is Nature, she does as she will, as our Lord God has designed.

That said, yes, the hardships forced upon us all are monumental in scope. Our Lord God is testing us, we, his faithful followers. Do not give up hope or abandon the Holy Commandments, for we, the people of Tierra, have not been forsaken by our Holy Creator, the Lord God. Nay, Lord God has seen what Nature has done to us and has given us another of his Holy Miracles — a Holy Miracle that will help us all survive the effects Nature is bestowing upon us all.

Until now, the gravest of mistakes has been made concerning our Lord God's Holy Gift. The gift I refer to is widely being called the *mentales* gift. In the past, some have mis-interpreted this as having come from Lucifer himself. This is utter folly. Lucifer would never give unto us mortal men such powers as many who have this *mentales* gift now have. No, Lord God has given his Holy Gift to some of us so they may be better able to help all mankind through the awful changes Nature has given us. The *mentales* gift is God's Grace upon his children that we may be able to survive what Nature is doing to our world.

On my way to the Holy City of Valcia, I found the great jungles of the central highlands of Bashir had died. I am told it has not rained here for four hundred days. Nothing but dead brown leaves lay everywhere and great fires come in their wake. I very nearly died in one of these fires. If not for a humble man who had the *mentales* gift from our Lord God, I would have perished. His *mentales* found us safety from the raging inferno and more importantly, found us life-giving water afterwards.

Lord God has distributed his *mentales* gifts among some of us, his faithful followers, but not all of us have received this precious gift. Why? It has nothing to do with God's favoring one of us over another of us. Rather our Lord God wishes us to learn to be thankful for what he gives us and to be tolerant and respectful both of those who have and those who have not this precious gift. Do not pick sides. Do not pit one against the other. This is Lord God's Great Holy

Test for we, his faithful flock, to see if we can use his Holy Gift for the betterment of all mankind.

And yet he has also given his Most Precious gift to non-believers as well. Why? For the non-believers, Lord God is also testing them to see if they will use their precious gift for the betterment of everyone or if they will succumb and use it for their own personal gain.

In short, all mankind is now undergoing our Lord God's Holy Test. I am certain we will pass his test as will many of the non-believers.

Effective upon receipt of this proclamation, the COG will cease all harassment and executions of anyone who has the *mentales* gift. Yes, in the past, we made a terrible mistake, and have slain many who had our Lord God's Greatest Gift. Alas, we do not have the power to bring back the dead. That is in our Lord God's province.

If asked by others, you must state clearly and with no hesitation that the COG has made a mistake and that we are now correcting it. Be humble. We are only mortal men and prone to making errors of judgment. Let us instead move forward.

I urge you to call upon those who have received Lord God's Holy *Mentales* Gift to come forward and lend their precious gift to helping all others survive this natural disaster Nature has given unto us. Those with the gift and who are members of your congregation are to be seated in the front pews, given the COG's highest honor at our holy services.

Catalog the forms the *mentales* gifts take and put them to work in the areas for which they are best suited.

Protect those who have these precious gifts, even if they are non-believers, for they all have been touched by our Lord God. Guard them well and let them help us survive.

We now know this is the reason Lord God gave them this Holy Gift, they have a heavy responsibility to use their gift to help others.

All of Tierra is undergoing massive change. Nothing remains as it was before. This is the Lord's Holy Will. We too must adapt and use new ways.

Worse, so many men, women, and children have already perished and more will undoubtedly perish as well before we all have adapted to Nature's climate changes. Thus, it is vitally important women bear our children, for in our children comes our future. Without children, we are doomed to extinction.

Guard and protect our women that they may bear the children who make our future possible. Families must be bound together by love. Men, bind your wives to you for all time. Together, begat as many children as you are able to support.

I know from personal experience some newborn children have also been given Lord God's *mentales* gift. He wants us to survive and to prosper once more. I do too.

Expect more changes to come. You may have heard rumors our Holy City of Valcia is nearly uninhabitable. That is true. Nature is forcing me to move our Holy City elsewhere. Expect to hear more from your new Archbishop in the weeks and months ahead. Likewise, I expect to hear from you, my Holy Bishops. What can I do to help you and your brethren?

Humbly Yours in God,
Archbishop Shane Zadok

"There, I hope that is as clear as possible," Shane said to the empty room. "If I accomplish nothing else, I will be content if they stop those hideous, senseless, and cruel executions!" For a time, his mind revisited the slayings he'd witnessed. Those horrors Shane could not forget. He knew they would remain with him until his dying day.

"They are not Lucifer-spawn?" asked a shocked Father Ramal. He and Father Banalthan had just finished reading the proclamation. Both men were quite surprised by what they read.

"I admit to you, at first I too thought these people were somehow cursed by Lucifer. Yet, after much prayer and readings of our Holy Scriptures, I have come to see the Holy Hand of our Lord God in this matter. This is his way of giving us the *means* by which all his children can survive this natural disaster. Now it is up to us, his faithful, to implement His Holy Gift to mankind," Archbishop Shane answered him. He looked at the brown skinned man with a crooked nose and bird-like eyes. A slight resistance formed in Father Ramal's mind but then it evaporated. Shane sensed the priest's acceptance of his will.

He held out his hand in friendship. The gesture was accepted, and Shane shook the old priest's hand and turned to face Father Banalthan. He too was brown skinned, as were most all the inhabitants of Bashir, where the orange-red sun had always burned hottest on Tierra only now more so than ever. The priest was homely and overly tall, thin and sinewy. Sweat poured off his forehead. He said, "Your Holiness, we accept your word, but will others, the many bishops?"

Shane sighed and sought for the right response. "Faith, Father Banalthan. In the final analysis, all that we have is faith. The bishops have faith that the many priests they oversee will preach Lord God's Holy Words. In turn, the priests have faith in the guidance they are given by their bishops. Likewise, the bishops have faith in their Archbishop, as I have faith in them. Without faith, we have nothing; we are nothing. So I have faith in my many bishops. They will follow my guidance, though at first, they may resent and disagree with my position. They have faith and we must not betray their faith in us. Faith makes us human."

Part II Angel Adaptions

Chapter 4 Organizing Chaos

Mid-March 1001, Palmer Wycombe, Norwood's younger brother now twenty-three and still unmarried, arrived at the Bedworth *Círculo de la Torres* to escort Marisol Bolivar back to the tower and mansion just northwest of Wyth. He had his older sister's good facial bones and smile. Like Ally, he was very comely. Unlike Norwood, he had always fancied himself as a ladies man and had dated more women than either Ally or Norwood could count. His naturally wavy, shoulder length blonde hair and deep blue eyes added to his personal charms, or so he always claimed. If his track record was any indication, he was not mistaken. However, the love-bug had finally struck the young man. Marisol Bolivar.

Last fall, Isabel Bolivar and her daughter Marisol immigrated from Benito, Trujillo, Westerlings to Wyth, Midlands to avoid the COG witch persecution. Isabel and her life-mate, Luisa Camila, along her daughter Ria were witches but now all four had the *mentales* gift as well. Isabel, forty-one, and Luisa, a year younger, were masters of illusions, able to create very believable illusions. In past, they used their psi-crystals to power their illusions, but now with the gift, they no longer needed their psi-crystals. Both had trained their daughters to follow in their footsteps as great healers. All that ended with the systematic extermination of all witches worldwide by the COG and the alien Psychman Cezar. The four had fled for their lives along with others of their coven.

Like her mother, Marisol, twenty-two, had lustrous black hair, long and full. Her face was round and her bushy eyebrows accented her eyes, making her irresistible and a highly attractive young woman. Marisol's *mentales* gift was so far unique, the ability to tell what another's *mentales* gift was, whether or not they were hiding it. She had spent the winter helping her mother, Luisa, and Inez get the Bedworth *Círculo de la Torres* up and running, taking some of the pressure off everyone up at Wyth, a hundred-fifty miles due north. The third tower was at Brom, nearly the same distance north of Wyth, while the fourth tower was at Bettingham, five hundred miles nearly due east of Wyth.

The spring thaw had come early, but that was not saying much. Winter snowfall here in the rugged foothills of the mighty Goza Mountains had broken all records, accumulating upwards of ten feet before the thaw came. However, three out of four days, the warm morning sun gave way to huge thunderheads by noon. Rain changed to sleet by evening and a dusting of snow greeted the early risers the next morning only to melt forming a dense, low fog by midmorning. Strange weather indeed. A dozen soldiers accompanied Palmer and they provided protection and handled the camp duties for the three nights on the muddy road. The journey took four days and three nights at this time of the year, a third longer than summertime.

"Glad you can ride, Marisol. We'd never get a wagon through all this mud," Palmer said as he helped her mount and then adjusted her heavy cloak.

"Of course I can ride. I'm not like my moms. When is it supposed to warm up around here?" she asked.

"Dunno with this weird weather. Dita doesn't think it is going to ever warm up like it used to do in the hot summer — something about Tierra wobbling, but I didn't follow her. So how's it been down here? Miss me? I sure have missed you, Marisol."

She picked up his unspoken thoughts. *Missed you is an understatement! I have been going nuts since you left! I have to convince her to marry me.* Marisol chuckled, "No way, Palmer. I know all about you from mom via Dita and Norwood. So how many women have you dated eh?" she teased him.

"Hey, no fair reading my mind, since I can't read yours!" he protested slightly; his flushed face told her she'd scored. "I am madly in love with you, Marisol. I am going to marry you if it is the last thing I ever do! You are just going to have to say yes one of these days. I know you are."

"Why? Because I am the first woman who has not fallen over her own feet to drool over you?" Marisol replied, her mouth forming an enticing grin, totally disarming Palmer. "Or is it my charming Westerlings accent that has so enthralled you?"

"You are one gorgeous woman, Marisol. Okay, that too, charming. Bright, intelligent, beautiful — oh, did I mention gorgeous?"

She chuckled, "Yes, you did. Glad you appreciate me, Palmer. Now why would a bright, intelligent, beautiful, gorgeous woman be interested in you?"

Palmer's face crimsoned. Marisol turned to face him, startled by his unspoken, sudden thought. She flushed, "No, I am not like my mothers. I like men, Palmer, not women, though I do appreciate what my moms share between themselves. True love knows no gender mom says. I believe her." Somehow, her taunt of Palmer had backfired and she attempted to change the topic, glad he was head blind, that is, he had not gotten the *mentales* gift of telepathy. "So how is Drina faring?"

Drina Esteban had also been part of her mother's coven of advanced witches and she and her family had immigrated to Wyth along with the others last fall. Marisol always had a special place in her heart and mind for Drina, who was born with a genetic defect. She had no arms and worse, her three children also were born armless as well, much to Drina and Ernesto's dismay. He was a stonemason and was helping build the four *Círculo de la Torres* here in the Kingdom of the Angels. There wasn't anything Marisol would not do for Drina; she'd proven that many times over, ever since she was five years old. Drina's gift was to sense what another wanted to know, a most useful gift indeed. Actually, Marisol thought she knew why Drina had this particular gift: because of her deformity, everyone Drina met wondered about her.

Change the topic eh? Well, okay, but I am still going to get you to marry me, Marisol! "She's doing well as always — a powerhouse in a small package. So are her children. She and they constantly amaze me. There is nothing they cannot find a way to do. Of course, Ernesto is always there to make suggestions or inventions. Clever man, clever woman, clever children. She's been a huge help now that all the babies are coming. Drina always seems to know what to do, what needs to be done. Amazing," Palmer replied. *But not as amazing as you, my lovely Marisol.*

"Good. You know how much I admire her. You'd better take good care of her for me," Marisol added.

Palmer laughed, "Ernesto does a fine job of that. He hovers over her constantly when he's not off working."

"Of course, they are still madly in love with each other, silly boy. Mom introduced him to Drina thirteen years ago now. He fell for her big time, as we witches are wont to say. No love potion needed." She chuckled, but Palmer didn't know what was funny. Perhaps it was an inside witches' joke, and he wished he had paid more attention to the witches when he was growing up in the castle at Wycombe.

"Wooly bear. That's the kids' nickname for him. He's spouting a stubby beard these days. He claims it helps keep his face warm in our freezing climate," Palmer explained. *I bet she doesn't know that detail. I have to impress her somehow!*

Marisol gave Palmer another glance. *He is observant after all. I'll give him this one, though Drina already told me about that when we chatted telepathically.* "Makes sense. We are used to a much warmer climate down in Benito. It is so cold up here."

"Not anymore. Everything's changed for the worst. We've heard news from other of Holly's Advanced Witches who managed to elude the COG witch hunts. I'm keeping an accurate accounting, you see. I have this big map of Tierra in my room. I plot everything I can find about the world's weather." *She seems interested.* Palmer continued, "Everything is going on a forty-five degree angle, from the southwest to the northeast, in straight lines. There is this band that begins just south of your Brozas River — some five hundred miles north of Benito that is, down to just above Nasik. Between those two southern edges and stretching clear across Tierra going nearly due northeast is the eternal precipitation band, as I am calling it — constant rain in the lower elevations to snow here in the higher ones. Benito's temperatures are at least twenty degrees cooler than normal, Marisol. This past winter was especially hard on them, since hardly anyone was prepared for such a cold winter and spring."

He glanced at Marisol, saw she was paying close attention, and he continued. "Haruk up north in the Midlands is now eternally icebound. Likewise, your Westerlings' Zamora is so stricken, as is the Easterlings' old kingdom of Domei over on the extreme northeastern edge of Tierra. We've heard people are fleeing those lands because it has become just too cold to survive. Worse, your Westerlings' Abvera and the Easterlings' Domei, Arad, and eastern Alba have not had any precipitation for months. They are becoming deserts, we think. Likewise, all but the coastal regions of old Bashir have become a vast desert where there once were dense jungles. These areas are not getting any precipitation at all, not a drop. I don't see how all those people can possibly survive either. I am keeping very accurate records."

"Impressive, Palmer. I give you this one. Did Dita put you up to it?" She could not help but see the hand of the Rigel's alien Dita Ewa in this analysis. Dita had gone native and married his brother, Norwood. Her friend, Doctor Zosia, had also gone native with her, marrying Captain Able Smith, Norwood's lifelong friend and protector. Since then a new batch of alien Rigels had returned late last fall and had promised to cease interfering with humanity on Tierra. Still, she knew Dita and Doctor Zosia were reporting back to the Rigels at least once a month. Drina had told her so.

"Yes, I am tracking the weather patterns and Norwood is tracking plant and animal changes for her. Dita is the smartest person I have ever met, but then she is an alien," Palmer admitted.

"Well, true, she *was* an alien. Now, she has become one of us. Doctor Zosia too. I don't think the color of one's skin or where one was born has much to do with being human. Do you?" Marisol mused.

"Nope. The babies are doing fine, though I think both the new arrivals will have a skin color closer to the grey of the Rigels. I'm an uncle now. Pretty cool, don't you think? Twice an uncle, counting Ally's."

"You are proud of the babies, aren't you?" Marisol asked, sensing a deep seated pride coming from Palmer, something she had not sensed before in him.

"You bet I am! Ally and Alford's little Adrian is a fine little boy and Dita and Norwood's Stefan is cute too, but he's only a few days old." Palmer had a wild thought. *Zounds! Perhaps Marisol doesn't want to have children! I never thought about that.*

"Of course I want to have children of my own, Palmer," Marisol answered his unspoken question. He was fairly screaming it in his mind, and she spoke up without thinking about having overheard his unspoken thoughts. "Look, even my two moms wanted children, though I wish they had had more than one each, but I understand why. It is no fun giving birth, to say nothing of enduring the nine months."

"Whew! You had me going there for a bit. That's about the only thing that would turn me off to you, Marisol. If I knew you didn't want to have any children, to raise a family, why, I could never marry you." At last, Palmer realized he had not actually spoken that original thought aloud. She'd read his mind and he flushed again. *Oh god! That's why she doesn't want anything to do with me! I don't have any mentales! Damn! Damn! Damn!*

Again, Marisol could not help but pick up his realization, for he was fairly screaming it to the world around them. She flushed, but he was absolutely right. She did find Palmer very attractive, a sexy man, but she was now a telepath. If she were merely an Advanced Witch, why, she'd have said yes to his proposals long ago. Not now, though. He was head blind and she was not. That alone was a huge barrier between them and would always remain so.

How can Ally, Aurora, Dita, and Doctor Zosia manage to mate with head blind men? Are they that desperate? Well maybe so. After all, Ally and Aurora lost their hands, and are pretty darn helpless without the fancy mechanical hands Doctor Zosia gave them. She and Dita are aliens after all, quite unlike the rest of us, so maybe those four were desperate. Mom and Luisa are not head blind and they are madly in love with each other, have been as long as I can remember. I don't know how I could possibly marry a head blind man! Why, you'd have to outright vocalize absolutely everything, completely destroying such intimacy. I don't think I could ever be happy doing that, not ever, not since I have seen my moms. What do I say to poor Palmer? This is something he has no control over at all!

If I lie to him and say it isn't so, that true love can surmount this barrier, he will still hold out hope I will one day succumb to his charms. Yet, that is not really fair to him. He needs to find someone else. I could never marry a head blind man, not ever. Oh god, what do I say to him?

Palmer recognized her long silence and sighed. "You don't have to say anything, Marisol. I understand. You could never be happy with someone like me who can't read thoughts and all. I've been deluding myself otherwise, thinking I could somehow get by like my brother and brother-in-laws have been." He took a deep breath and asked, "So how has it been going there at Bedworth? Having lots of folks coming to learn how to control their *mentales*? How's your massive research project coming along? Added any new *mentales* gifts to the log?" Palmer desperately wanted to change the topic before he broke down and cried. He fought hard to keep his eyes from watering.

Damn! This is destroying him! It's eating him alive, but he knows the truth of the matter. He's about to lose control. Thank god, he had the wherewithal to change the topic. He is more observant than I ever imagined. If only he had even a little telepathic skill. Marisol replied, "Busy, busy, busy. Once we got the first floor of the tower opened — work is going on on the other floors, we have had a steady stream of folks braving the snows, seeking our help." For quite some time, she discussed these mundane activities of her *Círculo*, grateful for the change of topic. Sometime later she sensed Palmer had regained control over his emotions and she relaxed again.

"So tell me about this emergency that requires my presence at the *Círculo* in Wyth?" she asked him. She need not have since she'd been fully briefed by Ally and Aurora already, telepathically that is. However, she wanted to get a head blind person's point of view, though she dare not say so.

"It's quite a mess, actually. Something happened with Aiden and Alford, right after their wives gave birth. I'm not sure what it was. Then, Dita and Doctor Zosia had their babies

— a day apart, if you can believe that timing. Anyway, Able and Norwood have somehow gotten really, really sick and now Aiden and Alford are bedridden too. It's a mess, what with the four newborns needing so much attention. Holly, Wendy, and Sissy are doing their best to deal with all those who have come seeking to learn how to control their gifts, leaving only Drina to care for the four men. Honestly, Marisol, we truly need another set of hands right now. I've never seen my brother so deathly ill. Aurora is really worried, so much so that she used her gift to look into the future. Apparently, she saw you somehow helping and sent me to fetch you. I hope you can help my brother and the others somehow."

"I'll do what I can, I promise you, Palmer," Marisol replied. From her tone, he knew she truly meant it.

Late afternoon, the cold rains came again. They made camp while some light remained and as the sleet began. Palmer and Marisol had to share one tent, though he made sure they had many blankets for warmth. She had no choice but to lie beside him for warmth. He could smell her scent, which nearly drove him wild with passion, but he forced himself to suppress it, treating her with the utmost respect as she snuggled close for warmth.

My god, this is driving me almost mad too. Poor Palmer is doing his best, treating me with honesty and dignity, but being this close is driving him out of his mind. Me too. I'd give anything to embrace him now, but I dare not. He's head blind. It would never, ever work out. We would both deeply regret it. Oh god, why did I ever have to fall for him? Why did he have to fall for me — the one woman he dare not have? Just be careful not to encourage him, that's the best I can do. Sleep came mercifully and swiftly to both.

Late afternoon on the fourth day, they rode into the gated estate of the Bettinghams. The rustic manor house chimneys tossed smoke upwards into the gentle rains. The tower here was really taking shape. Scaffolding rose to the third floor already. Ernesto was doing a fine job of its construction. More importantly, Marisol saw all the early spring plants either sprouting or in bloom. She'd spent many long hours getting the unattended gardens out front tended last fall and now the fruits of her labors were clearly visible. Crocuses, daffodils, and several others were in full bloom, as if the cold temperatures meant little to them. Tulips were growing as well, but it would be another month before they came into their own, along with the rows and rows of irises.

"You did a super job on the gardens," Palmer praised her. He noticed her attention was on the plants and made the connection.

She smiled, "Such a pretty garden. These flowers are truly a touch of beauty in the early spring, a harbinger of things to come, I always say. I do love plants, you know, but then I am a witch, even if we are outlawed nowadays." He chuckled and held her horse so she could dismount. While Drina waited for her near the front door of the large manor house, he led her mare into the stables following his men.

"Marisol! I am so glad you could come on such short notice. Thank you, thank you. Come in, I have got a hot bath waiting for you and then a warm meal," Drina gushed out as Marisol walked up the stone walkway to the ornate main doors. The thirty-two year old woman wore her usual sack-like dress, white with the finely stitched embroidery, which Marisol had done for her two years ago. The dress was warm and easy for the woman to slip on by herself.

"Hi Aunt Drina. You are looking well. I like your shorter hair, easier to take care of?" Marisol replied just as enthusiastically. She always considered Drina to be her aunt, though of course there was no familial relation between them.

"Yes, what with all the confusion around here and sickness, I had to cut it shorter. Much easier for me to handle this way. Ernesto grumbled about it though. Men, but then he doesn't have to wash and brush it. So was the trip okay?" *Did Palmer behave himself? I bet he made constant passes at you.* Drina gave Marisol a mischievous grin.

Marisol's lips returned her grin. *He sure did. He's nuts about me, but I am not encouraging him.* "Yes, it was fine, a bit cold and muddy. I sure could use the bath. I smell like horses."

Drina led her to the waiting bath, though Marisol knew where it was. She wanted to talk privately a bit with her

Planet of the Orange-red Sun Series Volume 2 Dark Ages

"niece." *You could do far worse. Palmer is a fine young man. Are you still holding out for someone who has mentales? Ernesto and I don't really have any problems with him being head blind. But then, it's none of my business. Anyway, I am really glad you could come.* "Let's get you cleaned up and fed before we tackle the seriously ill men."

"Yes, let's." *I just cannot see myself marrying a non-telepath, Aunt Drina. Too many problems to overcome. Maybe we can talk about it later tonight.* "Ah, a hot bath. Lavender?"

"Yes, I knew you prefer it, so I added some for you. I'll leave you to it. I best check on the feverish men again. Holler when you are ready for some supper. The rest of us have already eaten. Thanks again for coming on such short notice, Marisol. I really need your help with this mess." She turned and left Marisol to bathe.

She ran into Palmer as he entered the main hall. "Hi Palmer. No change to report. Your brother is at least holding his own. Go get bathed. I've kept some supper waiting for the both of you."

"Thanks Drina. Damn, still no better. How's Dita and Stefan doing? Are they still recovering?" he asked.

She sensed his deep fears over his brother's illness, but she purposely did not probe into his personal thoughts. "Dita and the baby are doing fine, though she's really worried about Norwood. I'm insisting she stay in bed a few more days, just to be safe. Same with Doctor Zosia. You can't imagine how difficult it is to play nurse to a doctor," she teased.

Her grin was infectious and Palmer chuckled, breaking out of his worry for a moment. "Thanks Drina. You are a doll. I'll get cleaned up and dine with Marisol. Can I check on Dita and my nephew after that?"

"Sure, I'm sure she will be relieved to have you back safe and sound. Holler when you are ready. I'm off to check on the sickbeds now."

An hour later, Palmer and Marisol walked into the spacious dual kitchen. Along one side was a standard kitchen with stove, oven, counter tops, and sink. Along the opposite wall, Ernesto installed a second complete kitchen. Each item was low to the ground so Drina could cook using her feet while sitting on her chair with rollers. In the center of the kitchen was a small table that doubled as a dining table for times such as these. "Have a seat, stew is coming up," Drina announced. Both watched the shapely woman as she scooted about, using her feet to ladle out the steaming meal onto two wooden plates. Marisol never tired of watching just how Drina managed to do nearly everything by herself. Both she and Palmer, as well as everyone else, knew better than to butt in and try to do things for Drina.

For a moment, Marisol drifted into the past, when she was barely ten years old. She'd done just that, butted in with good intentions only to have Drina scold her for it. "Look, I can do most anything, but I just have different ways to do them. You must let me do things for myself. I refuse to be a helpless cripple, Marisol." Her face had turned beet red and even now thinking about that time, her face flushed, but she hoped Drina wasn't noticing it.

Palmer, too, had learned well. Only when Drina had their plates ready did he volunteer. "Okay, Drina. Thanks for the stew. I can carry the plates to the table. I'm not completely helpless in a kitchen, just mostly." He was jesting and it brought a chuckle to the young woman, who allowed him to carry the two plates over to the table. All three knew this was a most difficult task for Drina to handle, and by reversing the roles, Palmer had made it seem acceptable to Drina for his help. She busied herself with the teapot before joining them, sitting at the low table, where she could use her feet to sip the tea laced with honey.

"Drina, you are by far the best cook around here," Palmer praised her, his mouth full of the tasty stew. She smiled appreciatively.

"Well, I suppose we should get down to business," Drina began. "After you eat, let's visit the four mothers and their babies. Then, let's check on the sick men. After that, Palmer, I really do need you to watch over my kids until Ernesto gets done with his work. Tomorrow, I leave the three in your care for the day. We are so shorthanded around here as you know and I don't dare leave them totally on their own. You know kids and the mischief they can get into, especially since they can play outside some in the mornings before the rains come."

"You got it, Drina. I love to play with them. I'll see they don't get underfoot or into any real serious mischief," he replied.

Drina teased him, "Why is it I don't like the sound of that: any *real* mischief? Please, *no* mischief at all would be quite nice. While you were gone, they claim they fell down in the mud, but I doubt that." All three laughed. She added, "I had a devil of a time cleaning them up!"

After the two finished their stew, they followed Drina to check on the four new mothers. Because all four of their husbands were quite ill, the four had moved into Ally's master bedroom. This was a pragmatic solution, as Ally quite often had to use her special *mentales* gift to force raiding bands from the kingdom. She'd leave her body lying in her bed and patrol the borders of the Kingdom of the Angels, looking for signs of invading groups. Hence, most of the time Ally needed someone to look after her six week old Adrian. Doctor Zosia and Dita's week old babies required constant monitoring and Aurora acted as head nurse and go-for the four of them, though the two Rigel women insisted they should not remain bed bound much longer.

"Palmer! You're back. Marisol, so good of you to come. What a mess we have," Dita exclaimed as the three entered the master bedroom in the Bettingham manor house. The twenty-four year old Rigel woman was sitting up in bed, nursing her newborn. Her skin was grey but her hair and eyes were coal black and shiny. "Come see your nephew. I swear he's already grown several inches."

"Will he be as tall as you, Dita?" he asked. They chatted a bit and Marisol noticed both Ally and Aurora had removed their prosthetic hands.

Ally picked up her thoughts. "Aurora and I are not totally certain we might not injure our babies with them. You know, squeeze too hard. Zosia claims we should not be able to do that, but we are too worried we might injure them, so we are playing it safe. Glad you are here. Something is really wrong with our four husbands. It's totally weird. You'd think we mothers would be the ones having problems with giving birth, not our four husbands. Honestly, we think they might have somehow gotten poisoned or something."

"Look, I am perfectly recovered," Doctor Zosia protested. "Tomorrow, Drina, I am going to give the men a thorough examination with my diagnostic machine. We've got to get them over this illness and soon!"

A few minutes later, Drina led the pair into the makeshift infirmary, Aurora and Aiden's master bedroom. Wendy Lane looked up; she had bags under her eyes, and evidently, she'd not been sleeping well. "Oh hi all. No change in the four of them. I've been wiping their feverish brows constantly and doing what I can to help the men. They are so ill." She had been the victim of the Rigel-3 Psychman Cezar and had been Behavior Modified. Though she was much improved, she still hovered around men, trying to do whatever was needed to help and please them. In this case, she was a perfect choice to stay with them while the others handled the flood of other activities. At least she no longer ran about chanting the mantra with which she was brainwashed.

Alford, Aiden, Norwood, and Able lay on four beds, delirious and fever-wracked. Palmer held his brother's hand, "Come on, Norwood. You have to fight this and get better." He fought hard from breaking down. Fighting back tears, he rose and left the room, muttering to Drina that he'd go check on her three children.

Just then, Holly Sprigs quietly entered. *Thanks for coming, Marisol. I don't want to bias you, but could you take a look at these men?* She looked exhausted too. From morning to night, she and Sissy were handling the training sessions for over fifty men, women, and children who had the *mentales* gift, teaching them how to control and use their gifts.

Marisol looked up at Holly and nodded. She sat on the bedside of Alford and placed her hand on his forehead. "He's burning up," she whispered. One by one, she sat beside the others. At last, she rose and beckoned Holly and Drina to come with her.

"I could use a cup of tea," Holly finally spoke. "Laced

with honey. I am so exhausted." The three headed to the kitchen once more and Sissy joined them. Outside in the hallway, Marisol heard the laughter of Elena, Filipa, and Emilano. Palmer was chasing them up and down the hallway playing tag with them. She smiled; laughter was good to her ears.

"Well, your diagnosis?" Holly said, pouring out four cups and adding a mountain of honey to hers and Sissy's before handing them out.

Marisol paused a moment, taking a sip. "Well, they are certainly ill. It does rather look like they are undergoing Verge Sickness, but they are grown men!"

"Well, we do know children are the most vulnerable of all to the Verge Sickness," Holly stated dryly.

Sissy added hastily, "That's because the body's nerve channels that carry our psi-energies are also the same ones that carry sexual energies. So we know now the most critical period is when the child becomes sexually mature. The nerve channels get all confused with which signals are being sent and the energies simply pile up, blocked from going into flow. High fevers and death are often the result unless the blockages can be removed and the person trained."

"Still, none of us have experienced Verge Sickness," Marisol stated factually.

"I suspect that is because all of us were Advanced Witches, attuned to using our psi-crystals before we received the *mentales* gifts," Holly theorized. "Normally, the adults we've been seeing are not suffering from Verge Sickness, but rather a Psi-insanity, which apparently comes about from their not understanding their gifts and how to deal with them properly. True, they often die from Psi-insanity as well, but it isn't Verge Sickness. Different symptoms entirely. We've got four really sick men on our hands."

"Perhaps we are seeing a third kind of psi-illness," Sissy speculated. "There is a two to one chance of that, I believe."

"Well, I am inclined to allow Zosia to do a complete diagnosis on the four men tomorrow and then see what she comes up with. I'd have let her do it sooner, but she had a rough birth, and I want to make darn sure our only doctor is healed before she goes back to work. If they do have some awful illness, we cannot afford to have her get sick too," Holly advised.

Just then, the booming bass voice broke in on the foursome. "Well, hello Marisol. Good to see you again." Ernesto stepped into the kitchen and planted a kiss on her forehead. He was filthy, having worked all day on the construction of the third floor of the tower. He was twice the mass of Drina, a huge, well-muscled man, a skilled stone mason and inventor.

"Glad to be back, Uncle Ernesto. I've missed you all more than I care to admit," Marisol replied, pleasing the thirty-four year old man who smiled and excused himself to go bathe.

The next morning after breakfast, Doctor Zosia with Marisol's assistance brought her portable diagnosis machine into the bedroom. One by one, she ran every test in her extensive medical training on the four men. By noon, she was quite fatigued and Marisol had to help her back into her bedroom. "I guess I am not as fit as I thought I was," she admitted.

"Well, you did just have a fine baby a week ago," Marisol replied.

I know, but I never thought of myself as an invalid, Marisol. I don't think I can take being one, not with my services so urgently needed. "I'm okay. Just need to rest. Go tell Holly about our findings, please."

"What did you find out? Are they going to be okay?" Dita pleaded with Zosia. Ally and Aurora listened anxiously to hear her reply.

Zosia fought back tears. "I don't know. I ran every test, honestly I did. Tested all four of them, but there is nothing in the database. It is as if their illness does not exist! Yet, they are seriously ill. They are running a high fever, but I can find no source. No poison. Their white count is perfectly normal as if they had no infections at all. I just don't understand it." As brave as she was, she lost control and began sobbing. "I can't cure them because I don't even know what ails them! I am a total failure as a doctor!"

Ally put her arms around her and sat beside her. "There, there, no you are not. It is as you said: something that is not known to you. Honestly, you cannot expect to know all the illnesses in the vast universe out there, now can you?"

Marisol quietly left the nursery and headed off to find Holly. As she passed by a window, she saw Palmer and Drina's three children running around out on the grounds of the manor. They were playing kick ball and she smiled. Holly dismissed her dozen students, sending them home for the day and looked eagerly at Marisol. Quickly, Marisol relayed Doctor Zosia's findings, adding, "She's overdone it and very nearly collapsed herself. I have her back in her bed for now."

"Okay, let's get some lunch and think this one through," Holly suggested, her face stern and grim. Marisol knew of all the women here she was the wisest and most knowledgeable. If there were a cure, Holly would come up with it.

Drina had lunch waiting for them and she listened in on their conversation. "Well, they are displaying all the symptoms of Verge Sickness. Zosia has in effect confirmed it," Holly declared, sliding her empty plate away from her and pulling her tea closer.

"But how? They are all adults. They are long past puberty; they are fathers now," Marisol protested.

Holly stared at her cup before replying. "I think we can let slide the how for now and focus on curing them first. We need to deaden their *mentales* for a time and then get their fevers knocked out."

"*Bacal* tea?" Marisol asked. Last year they had discovered this bitter tea temporarily neutralized a person's psi potential, making them temporarily head blind. For those suffering from Psi-insanity, this was a major blessing, allowing them to begin to recover.

"Yes, and then we are going to need to rapidly Regulate their bodies, unblocking their overloaded nerve channels, especially their channels which control their sex organs," Holly added. Marisol blushed. The older woman picked up her thoughts. "Surely you have seen a man's — oh dear! You haven't, have you?"

Marisol crimsoned. "Well, no I haven't." Her voice

sounded thin and stretched which only added to her discomfort. *Damn, we don't have any male healers here do we?*

"No we don't, so it falls upon us to do it," Holly answered her unspoken question. "I think it will be of great benefit if Doctor Zosia aids us in the Regulation process. It will give her back confidence if she can help heal these men. Will she be strong enough this afternoon?"

"I hope so. I'll go check on her and take her some lunch." Marisol was very glad to have an excuse to leave the room. *Am I really such a prude? Male sex organs? Why am I so embarrassed about them?*

"Hi Doctor Zosia. I brought you some lunch. You were right in your diagnosis. The four men have the Verge Sickness. We need your help curing them later this afternoon," Marisol relayed the news to all four women.

"How? Verge Sickness?" Ally asked very much surprised. "Marisol, can you help me get my hands on? I'm going to go down to get lunch. Dita is going to watch the babies for us first."

"Me too," Aurora put in, holding her arms up.

After the two women left, Dita asked, "But how did they get Verge Sickness? Isn't that confined to children who reach puberty?"

"Honestly, Dita, there is so much we simply do not know about this *mentales* gift. Apparently, adults can get it too," Zosia answered, feeling a bit more relaxed. *Perhaps I am not a total failure as a doctor after all. Verge Sickness. Incredible. It sure isn't in my medical database!*

"Well finally something is making some sense! They can be cured, can't they?" Dita asked, suddenly images of the many that had died from the Verge Sickness came flooding into her mind unasked for.

"Very likely, Dita. I don't think you need to worry about becoming a widow just yet. Marisol, is someone brewing some *Bacal* tea?" All her fears of unworthiness evaporated. She had a proper diagnosis and some knowledge of the needed cure. She was not hopeless any longer, and she slipped back into her formal doctor image, much to Dita's relief.

"I think Drina is."

"Good old Drina! God, how we have really needed her these past weeks! She's a life saver, you know."

"Yes, that's my Aunt Drina," Marisol grinned.

Zosia glanced around the room and then whispered, "I don't want her to hear this, but when I first met her, I thought she would be so completely helpless that she would be better off dead. Yet, I've come to realized that was just my own stupidity. I don't think there is anything she cannot do. She is an inspiration to us all!"

Marisol smiled, but added, "She can't sew worth a darn."

Dita laughed, "Marisol, that is not saying much! I can't sew a stitch! And I have two good hands."

"But not the patience for it," Zosia reminded her, and both women laughed. "Okay, I'm finished and feel much recovered. Let's get this healing going."

"I have the tea ready, but I am afraid I am totally useless on this kind of Regulating," Drina admitted with a sigh. "It takes hands to follow the nerve channels and those I don't have. I can monitor just fine, though."

"Thanks for preparing the tea. Drina, you don't have to be able to do everything in the whole wide world. You don't see me doing Dita's anthropology stuff. What a bore. I don't sew either, except stitches that is. I have a black thumb, not a green thumb."

"No, it is grey," Drina teased her, but both Marisol and Zosia felt the relief and appreciation flowing from the young woman. All three laughed at her jest.

"It will be up to you and I to clean the psi-energy blockages, Marisol. Ally and Aurora have no hands and Sissy and Dita do not know how to do it. Holly does, but she is handling twenty others at the moment. So it is you and I." Marisol flushed. "Oh good grief! I didn't know, Marisol." Doctor Zosia picked up on her embarrassment. Quietly, Drina stepped out of the kitchen, leaving the two women alone.

"Look, I've examined many men. It really is not any big deal, ordinarily. The thing you must remember is always to maintain a professional, doctor-like demeanor. However, in this case, we will be clearing out psi-energy blockages more than likely locked up along their male genital nerve channels."

"Yes, I've done Regulating of a dozen women and cleared almost that many blocked channels, but never a man before," Marisol admitted sheepishly.

"Well, there is a first time for everything, I always say. I should warn you, sexual responses in males are quite — well they are very easily aroused. Light flirting often arouses them sexually. Undoubtedly, clearing out these blockages will result in an arousal, possibly even an ejaculation. Just remember to do or say nothing that might possibly be misconstrued as a sexual flirt or advance. In their state, it could well push them over the edge. If they do have one, they will likely be highly embarrassed about it, so try to act as if this was simply a medical procedure we are doing, which is what it really is."

"I'll try, but I am so embarrassed about it."

"You'll do fine. Men arouse at the drop of a pin, if I do say so myself — from much experience with Able. We women take quite a lot more to get our motors a going, which is a good thing." Marisol gave her a strange look and she added, "Otherwise, we'd be pregnant all the time." Both women chuckled at her jest.

"Excuse me," Drina poked her head into the room. "I hate to do this to you, but there is a man in the hallway who needs to see you Doctor Zosia. His wife has the *mentales* gift and she has gone into labor."

"Hells Bells! When it rains, it pours! Okay, come on, Marisol. I am still weak. You are going to have to help me a bit with this too."

The man was wringing his hands and constantly shifting his weight from one leg to the other. Marisol didn't need telepathy to know he was extremely worried. Rightly so, she thought. So many women with the gift died in childbirth, especially so when their unborn baby also had the *mentales* gift!

"Hello, I am Doctor Zosia. How is your wife doing? Is this her first child?" she asked quite professionally.

"Ben Smith. Lena. It is her second. She's feverish and not doing at all well. The midwife pleaded with me to come for your aid. Please, can you help us?"

"Yes, of course we can, Ben. First, we have to see to four very sick men here. If you can wait a bit, we will come as soon as we can."

"Thank you, thank you doctors. Lena is everything to me. I don't want to lose her."

"That's the proper attitude. Drina here will see you get something to eat. We'll join you as soon as we can." The two left him in Drina's care. After fetching the *bacal* tea from the kitchen, the two headed to the four sick men.

"Okay, you get a half cup of the brew into each man. As soon as it takes effect on one, I'll start in on the Regulating process and see about unblocking the nerve channels. When the second one is under the tea's influence, you take care of him. Ready?"

"No, but I will do my best." *God, I hope I don't embarrass myself or the men too badly!*

A few minutes later, Able showed signs of relaxation, and Doctor Zosia pulled down his covers and then his pants. Carefully, she began running her finger tips lightly along his nerve channels, beginning at the top of his head and moving down his spine. As she anticipated, the blockage was in his groin and she rolled him over onto his back. Marisol glanced over at him and watched as Zosia's fingers followed the nerve channels. Her face reddened and she felt quite hot, as Able became aroused. She took note of how Zosia reacted. She didn't. She was deep into concentration and focused solely on the energy channels as if nothing else was happening.

Then Norwood sighed and relaxed, the *bacal* leaf had done its job, disconnecting his budding *mentales* gift from his body and mind, at least temporarily. Marisol took a deep breath and tackled him. She focused her attention onto his body and then slowly his nerve channels appeared, like illuminated flow lines. At first, she was a little surprised; they appeared as they did in someone who already had the psi gift, not in those who were head blind. *Worry about his mentales gift later,* she thought, forcing herself back to the task at hand, blockage detection and removal.

Heartbeat, strong. Blood flowing properly. Body

cooling down. Breathing a bit shallow, but acceptable. Okay, follow the nerve channels, beginning at the top of his head. Slowly, she touched his head with the lightest possible touch and felt his nerves. Pain. Lots of pain. He had a wall of pain sitting around his head with no place to flow. Down his spine, she moved until she reached his lower back. There she sensed a huge black mass, but it was on his front side, not his back. She rolled him over and had to slip his underpants down. Again, she fought to keep her focus and concentration. Then, her fingers continued down the nerve channels.

There was the blockage and it was huge. As she worked to get it to begin to flow, Norwood became aroused. It took all her concentration to keep her focus and continue. At last, she got the block freed and the mountain of pent up energy began flowing, rapidly dissipating. As it did so, he ejaculated and woke up from his trance-like state.

"Oh!" His face flushed a brilliant shade of red, and he quickly pulled his pants back up and the sheets too.

Maintaining as professional an attitude as she could manage, Marisol said, "There, you are going to be all right. You had a severe psi blockage that very nearly killed you. Rest and relax. I have to attend to the others, Norwood." She rose and headed for Aiden as rapidly as she could, averting her eyes from Norwood's body, hoping he could not see her face.

Already, Zosia was working on Alford and Marisol hastily began on Aiden. Twenty minutes later, a terribly embarrassed Aiden pulled his covers up and Marisol hastily told him what had happened. Doctor Zosia then took charge. "You four men have had a very nasty bout of Verge Sickness. We very nearly lost you. Yes, we sent for Marisol seven days ago."

"But how? I don't understand," Norwood blurted out.

"We don't either. We'll worry about that tomorrow. Right now, you need to rest and drink all the liquids you can. We have another emergency to handle in Wyth, so we are leaving you in Drina's capable feet." All four men broke into a smile at her choice of words.

Drina, assisted by Aurora, brought in cups and water pitchers, and the two left. They grabbed their heavy cloaks and headed down to deal with Ben and his wife. Ben had brought his wagon, and the two women were thankful they did not have to walk the two miles into Wyth. It was already starting to rain and heavy thunderheads were massing over Wyth as they entered the large town of some ten thousand. Ben was a miller by trade and his home was a cozy stone structure.

He took them inside and to the main bedroom, where Sally was tending to Lena. The woman was sending out enormous streams of uncontrolled *mentales* energies. She was spooked. "She's overdue; the baby is having a hard time of it. I think it needs to be repositioned, but I can't get the job done. Every time I try, I get repulsed by Lena and the baby too. Can you help?"

"Yes, of course we can. Marisol, get them both calmed down. Regulate them both if you can. I will see to the bodies," Doctor Zosia took charge once more. Adrenaline flowed in both women. If they could not get the two calmed down and the baby repositioned, both would die. That was a certainty. Both women had seen it happen many times before. Marisol focused again and lightly touched Lena's head. Pain. Overwhelming pain. Down Lena's nerve channels went Marisol's gentle touch. Pain began to flow once more, bringing relief to Lena, who began to calm down. Her utter panic subsided, though both women kept their mental blocks fully in place, dampening out Lena's wild thoughts.

For Marisol, handling women was an easy task and soon she got into rapport with the baby girl as well. That was enough to enable Doctor Zosia gently to reposition the baby. Then she too added her fingers to the rapport and Lena relaxed completely. That was all that was needed; her body took over and slowly the baby girl emerged unharmed.

"Okay Sally, you can take over now," Doctor Zosia said, as she laid the newborn girl on Lena's chest. "Lena, you have a fine looking baby girl. Well done." Lena managed a smile.

The two then left the room, relaying the good news to the very worried father. An hour later, Ben dropped the two off at the Bettingham mansion and both headed to the bathroom to bathe. Around four, they checked on the four men.

Aurora and Dita were also there with Drina, caring for

their husbands too. "Hi, how did it go?" asked Drina.

"Mother and baby girl are both doing fine. Without our help, neither would have survived. The baby has a strong *mentales* gift, which very nearly killed them both at birth," Doctor Zosia answered. "So how are our four patients here doing?"

"I've been giving them lower doses of *bacal* tea and a lot of liquids. They claim they are starving to death, but I thought it wise to let you tell me if they are able to have solid food. If so, I'll rustle up something or perhaps we can all eat at suppertime in about an hour or so. I am going to need some time to prepare it though," Drina replied.

"I'll lend you a hand, Auntie," Marisol suggested, glad to have a reason not to be in the room with these men. She still felt ill at ease over what had happened.

"Okay, keep it on the light side, Drina. I am so tired I'm going to nurse Irena and rest up myself. I've rather overdone it today," Zosia explained.

"I'll help you," Dita volunteered. She kissed Norwood on his forehead and Zosia did the same to Able. Both left, leaving Aurora watching over the four men.

"I hear all sorts of voices in my head, faint though," Aiden whispered to his wife, Aurora.

"Yes, the *bacal* is wearing off. Those are the stray thoughts of the twenty-some folks who are in the tower learning to control their *mentales* gifts. Holly and Sissy are working with them," Aurora explained. "Looks like you guys are going to have to learn the same things too." She grinned.

"But how? How did we all get it all at nearly the same time? We were unaffected for so darn long. How come now?" Aiden asked for the tenth time.

"We don't know, my love, but we will figure it out. Besides, we have Marisol with us now, so there is nothing to be alarmed or worried about. You rest and get your strength back. Honestly, it is supposed to be we women who are recovering from our pregnancies." She chuckled a little and Aiden smiled, pulled her close and gave her a loving kiss.

Palmer, accompanied by the three children, poked his head into the room. "Hi big brother! Glad to see you are recovering. All of you fellows. It's been murder these past couple of weeks. I'm stuck babysitting," Palmer laughed as Elena playfully bumped into him with her hips. From the size of his grin, Norwood could tell Palmer was having just as much fun as the kids.

"Well, we babysat a while back, so it's only fitting you take your turn," Alford managed to tease the younger man.

"Good to see you awake and recovering, catch you at supper. Gotta run, Elena says I am it again. Man, can she run." Palmer dashed off after the three children, leaving the four men with a smile on their faces.

Chapter 5 The *Mentales* Rule Book

Several days later, the four men had fully recovered their strength. Holly and Sissy took time off their hectic training schedules personally to work with the four men, helping them master the basics of their newly acquired telepathic *mentales* gifts. Specifically, they learned how to Hide Thoughts and Block Perception of Others. Without the latter skill, the four were wide open to any stray thought anyone had anywhere around them, highly disturbing, particularly when they were in a crowd. Imagine hearing dozens of dis-related conversations in your mind simultaneously. Without the former skill, they were literally broadcasting their own thoughts in all directions.

While Holly and Sissy wanted to teach them a whole lot more, at this point, they were at least stable and everyone finally relaxed at long last. Now it was Marisol's turn to apply her own special skill to the mix. Her special ability was to be able to ascertain the nature of someone's *mentales* gift, whether the person knew it himself or not. In this case, none of the four knew precisely what they could do, save telepathy.

She started with Alford. "What do I have to do?" he asked a bit nervously. All this mental stuff was totally new and foreign to him. He accepted it in his wife, Ally; she'd nearly always had such skills. "How do I use whatever I have?"

Marisol grinned, "Now that I am going to have to leave up to you and others, unless you have some of the skills that I have. All you need to do is to quiet your mind. Think nothing. I am going to step into your mind and have a look."

He flushed, thinking of how he and Ally now joined when they were together at night. He had no words to describe it, the merging of two minds into one, beyond intimate. "Don't worry, Alford, I am not going to, well, you know what I mean, I hope." She too was a bit embarrassed. *This is so easy to do with women and total strangers!*

She focused and lightly touched Alford's forehead, making physical contact with his body. His energy field came into view. This she passed over and concentrated on the control portion of his mind. As she did so, she was again reminded of the immense power she now wielded over Alford. With a single thought, she could kill his body or heavily damage his mind. Hastily, she let that thought pass by. *Focus. Focus. What have we here?* Marisol was inherently a highly curious person. Even as a child learning witchcraft from her mother, she always wanted to know why a certain plant had the effect her mother said it had.

Images formed and she studied them before breaking her connection with Alford. "You have a touch that is utterly remarkable, like a lavender feather. I could almost smell your presence in my mind. Is that what's supposed to happen?" he asked.

"That's what several have said. Okay, Alford. Yours appear to be aligned with your personality and ordinary goals. You can sense when danger is near. When you are going to fight someone with your sword, you will have some kind of special combat sense of how your opponent will fight you, which you can use to your advantage. You ought to be able to give someone or some object a hard push or punch. I can't tell which. Like your wife, you ought to be able to dominate others and make them go along with your will. Careful with that one. Finally, you have something I have not seen before, potentially a very dangerous thing. I can sense you can somehow explode inanimate things and plants. Please be extremely careful with that one, Alford. You could cause a whole lot of harm with it. I think Ally can help you develop some of these and gain mastery over them."

Alford was impressed and they chatted a while longer. Ally dutifully wrote down what Marisol's suggestions were. Next, she tackled his twin, Aiden. As she expected, his *mentales* gifts were quite similar, except instead of somehow causing objects to explode, he could manipulate the internal state of objects. She said, "I can see that you can change a section of a stone wall into something so soft you can cut through it with a knife, like it was butter. Do be extra careful with this one!"

Marisol then tackled Able and was very surprised with what she discovered. "Wow, I would never have guessed your gifts, Able." Zosia was rather pleased that her Able was somehow not what Marisol had expected. "I think your wife has somehow rubbed off on you," she teased him a little. "You have the unique ability to fully heal your body, no matter how badly it is injured or how ill it is. I see you somehow using that to absorb others' illnesses, curing them and then curing yourself. You ought to be able to detect poisons too and easily Regulate others, perhaps even so far as helping your wife with surgery. Incredible Able, I would never have guessed them."

Zosia looked extremely pleased and Able smiled, saying, "I would. That's what I have been doing all my life, looking out for Norwood here. Keeping him safe. No wonder I am so attracted to my incredible wife!" Zosia's grin was infectious; she was intensely proud of Able.

Finally, Marisol tackled Norwood, while Dita looked on eagerly. She was barely able to Hide her thoughts from everyone as Marisol began. "Well, you can sense danger too. Oh wow. This is interesting, Norwood. I'd never have guessed this either. You can look at an object and know its history. You can look at a place and know what has happened there. Oh, that is a good fit with your wife, since she is an anthropologist. I guess she is rubbing off on you too." Everyone chuckled. "But there is more. Yes, you can dominate others too. I guess that goes along with your penchant for being a king. And one more thing, you ought to be able to move objects, telekinesis it's called. What an interesting package, Norwood. Dita can help you with some of them."

"Thanks Marisol. What I'd like to know is how do you do this? How can you tell these things?" Norwood asked.

"Dunno, I just can. Unfortunately, as yet, we have not encountered another person who can do what I do. I hope there are others around. It would be really strange if I was the only person on Tierra who could do these things," Marisol answered humbly.

"Well, there is still one burning question I need answered," Alford broke into the conversation. All heads turned to face him. "How come we got it now and the Verge Sickness? Why didn't we get it when everyone did last year? Does this mean others who have not yet gotten any *mentales* gifts will wake up one morning with it too?"

"He has a very valid point," Holly spoke up. Until now, she sat back with Drina, quietly observing the group. "Will Ernesto one day suddenly wake up with *mentales*? That can have enormous ramifications to everyone who does not yet have *mentales* gifts. Then again, just how did you four suddenly have it? Personally, I am very bothered by the whole episode."

"How so?" asked Sissy, suddenly curious. "I can see this is very important. Fifty to one it is vital for us to know how it happened. No, make that five hundred to one!" Everyone roared with laughter at her sudden increase of odds.

"Okay, okay, let's try to sort that out," Holly said, stifling her chuckle at last. "Let's begin at the beginning. Before your wives gave birth, did any of you feel different in any way? Any hints something had changed in your minds?" she asked.

"No, not really. I was extremely happy for Ally and I was excited about becoming a father," Alford replied. The other three agreed with him. Until the birth of their children, all four men were normal.

"Okay, then for Marisol's benefit, I'll go over what happened then. As we all know now, when a woman who has *mentales* gives birth, the trauma of the birthing process makes it very difficult for her to control her *mentales*. If the husband also has *mentales*, we like to have him join with his wife and share the whole process with her, providing a sense of stability and lending her his strength. With head blind husbands, this is far more difficult to achieve and we don't normally do that. Except in these four cases, we did. We knew all four babies had strong *mentales* gifts. They too experience the pain, trauma, and fears accompanying the birth of their tiny bodies. However, their minds are wholly untrained and their *mentales* gifts wildly affects their mothers and the attending midwives. In these extreme cases, we try to have the head blind fathers joined with their wives via a Regulator. One of us brings them into close contact with their wives and urge them to flow power and strength and calmness to her. This we did with all four men."

"Holly, that was the most fantastic thing I have ever

experienced, the birth of my little daughter, Alanna," Aiden spoke up. "I will treasure those memories forever, but I was okay with it. I wasn't different after that."

"Hum, how about you three?" Holly asked. All shook their heads.

"No, I was just fine afterwards. Then, Alford and I took turns playing with Drina's children, freeing her up so she could help our wives with their newborns. She's been invaluable in that department. After all, she's had three, more than anyone else here, excepting the del Fuegos over in Bettingham's tower who have had four children."

"He's right. We spent most of the days playing with her three little angels. Okay, we allowed them to get into some mischief, but hey, they are just children," Alford added wryly, remembering the mud fights he helped instigate with them. Oh how they loved playing in the mud. Drina would never have let them do that and they loved it.

"Yeh, it was a week or so later that I began to feel feverish," Aiden spoke up. Alford agreed.

"Right, that's when Dita went into labor and I took over for you fellows," Norwood added. "I spent several days looking after Drina's kids. The next day, Able joined me because it was Zosia's time. I think we got sick a couple days later, but my mind is really fuzzy on that point."

"No dear, you got sick the day after Zosia gave birth," Dita corrected Norwood. "And the day after that, Able came down with a fever too, but he looked after the three children for another day before we got wise and put all four of you to bed."

"This is utterly silly!" Alford declared, exasperated. "The only thing we four had in common other than the birth rapport was playing with Drina's children. There has to be something else going on."

Marisol bit her lip and twisted some strands of her long, thick black hair, lost in thought. While the others continued to chat, her curiosity was roused. She broke into the chatter, "Drina, has anyone checked your children for *mentales* yet?"

Drina flushed. "No, there has been no need. My oldest, Elena, is only eleven, and has not yet reached puberty and become a maiden. That's when we have been checking children, not before. Why?"

"Would you mind if I checked them, Aunt Drina? The children seem to be the only common factor here. It could be important and then again it may be totally nothing," Marisol answered.

"Sure, I'll go call them in. Palmer is watching them, though I know for a fact he is as bad as you men were with them — allowing them to get into *all* sorts of mischief," she declared.

A few minutes later, four red faces joined the large group who were sitting around the large dining room table. All were out of breath, having been running madly around the huge manor house. "Hey, we kept clear of the nursery," Palmer protested, figuring he had somehow gotten them all into trouble with the adults. "Just having a little fun," he added.

Holly noticed he was rubbing his head. While Marisol dealt with the three children, she took Palmer aside. "Don't fret so, Palmer. You are not in trouble. I think it is good for the children to run and play. I've never seen the three of them as happy as they have been these past weeks when you five men have taken care of them for Drina. Now tell me, are you experiencing a headache? You keep rubbing your temples."

"Well, as a matter of fact I am. Got a splitting headache that just won't go away. Got it yesterday. Thought it would be gone by now, but I'll be damned if I'm going to shirk my duties with the children. Drina needs the help and she deserves it," he declared.

"Palmer, humor me. Go with Doctor Zosia and let her give you a complete checkup. It won't take long. The children will be tied up here for at least that long. Doctor Zosia?" She sent, *Check him out fully. I suspect you will find he has a mild case of Verge Sickness too.*

Doctor Zosia rose, giving Holly a strange look. "If you will come with me, Palmer. This won't take too long. Marisol is going to examine the children."

"Oh, you think they might be ill too? Hardly, they are running me into the ground," he teased her and followed her to her medical room.

Meanwhile, Marisol had Elena sit down and catch her breath. She pulled up a chair and sat before the eleven year old girl. "I am going to gently look into your mind, Elena. This won't hurt and I won't pick up any of your thoughts."

"Oh cool! Filipa, she's going to look into our minds too, just like she did with the fellows!" Elena became rather excited about it and sat very straight in her chair.

"Relax. Take a deep breath and try to not think of a thing," Marisol whispered to her. She watched as Elena slowly relaxed and then she focused and began concentrating. Soon the bright energy flow lines around Elena's body came into view. She had a powerful *mentales* field about her, so much so, that Marisol was slightly taken aback by the surprising discovery. She forced such thoughts out of her mind and moved to the control center of the gift. *What do we have here?* Her curiosity was definitely pricked!

I don't know. What is there? Elena's thoughts filled Marisol's mind, rather startling her.

It has to do with other people, I can tell that much already. Marisol decided to chat with Elena, since the girl had no formal training on how to block her thoughts.

I know. I sort of push it into others. Alford couldn't read my thoughts. We three had constantly to speak them aloud to him, so I just pushed it into that black mass in his mind. Now he can hear us. Isn't that just great?

Did you do that to Aiden and Norwood and Able too? Suddenly, Marisol began to realize what Elena's gift actually was!

Oh sure. It is so tiresome when we have constantly to say our ideas aloud. I did it to Palmer too. Maybe he can soon hear us as well.

Okay. Can Filipa or Emilano also do this like you?

Oh no, but they can do other things. Emilano is getting pretty good at lifting things and moving them about. Soon, I think he will be able to lift himself up in the air. Pretty cool. I can't do that. Filipa and I keep telling him if he does that, it is cheating at kick ball. Is that cheating? I mean if he can lift his body up out of the way of the ball, isn't that not playing fair?

It certainly is if you two do not have a way to counter

that move.

We don't. But Filipa can make animals do what she wants. Sometimes when we are bored, she makes mice do tricks for us. She's real good at it. That's not wrong is it? We are not being bad if we do these things are we?

No, of course not, Elena. However, I want you to promise me before you push someone else's black mass that you check with your mother first.

Okay. This is fun. Can you play with us some, Aunt Marisol? We all miss you terribly.

I miss you three too, but the adults at the other tower need me too. I will try to come and spend more time here with you three. How's that?

Cool, Aunt Marisol!

Marisol ended her contact. Although she had all she needed to know, Filipa and Emilano would be heartbroken if she did not examine them too. Hence, she gave each one a similar examination. Both also chatted freely with her as well. When she finished up with Emilano, she suggested they run off and play a while longer but promised them she would join them in a little while.

The gathered adults knew something was up because Marisol had not spoken a word since she began with Elena. Although quite curious, none more so than Drina, they respected Marisol and did not attempt to eavesdrop on her. Once the three scampered out of the dining room, Marisol sighed.

"Well, this is a first! Drina, all three have some of the most powerful *mentales* energies I've ever seen! However, there is a whole lot more. It's Elena. She has a natural ability to remove *mentales* blocks. It was she who has unlocked the *mentales* in all five men! Furthermore, it took almost no effort on her part! She and the others wanted you men to be able to hear their thoughts so they don't always have to speak the words aloud, which is a vastly slower form of communication, especially to active children."

"Oh my goodness!" Drina exclaimed, sitting down before she fell down. "Do they all have this ability?"

"No, each has a different gift. Filipa has a fantastic

rapport with animals while Ernesto is able to move things and perhaps levitate his own body. When they mature, they will gain a much better mastery of their gifts, Drina. They need to be taught how to Hide Thoughts and Block Perception, though. I suspect they already have worked out mechanisms to do that in some manner, but we ought to teach them properly. All three are strong telepaths, no question of that!"

"Wow, I never suspected," Drina replied flabbergasted. "No," she corrected herself, "I had some indications, now that I am aware of it. I ought to have been more alert for it. Darn, I am proving not to be such a good mother."

"Oh no, you are a great mother, Drina. They love you and think highly of you. This whole business of *mentales* has thrown us all *vast* curves. Who would think of young children as having such powerful and untrained *mentales*? No one, so don't go blaming yourself, Drina," Marisol countered her aunt.

"She's right, Drina," Holly spoke up. "Do you realize with all the people we've encountered, Elena is the only one who has a *katalyein* ability. She is a *mentales* catalyst. From what I've seen, she is extremely valuable and you are too, Drina. She is able to undo the mental blocks a person has that prevent them from using their *mentales* gifts. Incredibly valuable, incredibly rare."

Drina beamed as any proud mother would. "My little Elena! Ernesto? Has she tried it on him? Does he have a block too or is he head blind? Oh god! Please don't tell him I said that of him. He hates that term and so do I."

"No, she didn't mention Ernesto. I promised to go play with them soon. I'll discretely ask her about it and let you know. Honestly, Drina, I think she would have long ago undone any block he might have had," Marisol replied, just as Doctor Zosia entered the dining room.

"Well, that is interesting, gang. Palmer has a mild case of Verge Sickness too! I sent him to bed and he was elated for some reason," she reported. "Why aren't you all astonished?"

Holly laughed. "Sit down; we already knew that would be your diagnosis. Marisol, tell her what you discovered."

A bit later, the doctor exclaimed, "Well, I'll be — so there is a form of *mentales* that can undo mental blocks in others. Incredible. Well, I should have thought one would sooner or later appear. It makes sense that there would be. Still, Drina, that makes Elena incredibly valuable to others. She can unlock the potential in other people!"

Drina beamed. Doctor Zosia added, "Okay, I am going to nurse Irena. Meanwhile, Drina, please make up some *bacal* tea for me. I'll start treatment of Palmer as soon as I finish nursing her. I sure don't want Palmer getting it as badly as you four got it! We almost lost all four of you men!" She pivoted and left, heading for the nursery.

Marisol rose to go fulfill her pledge to play with Elena and the others. As she left, her face felt rather warm. Drina sent her, *So now what Marisol? Looks like Palmer is not going to remain head blind any longer.* Marisol flushed bright red, but was thankful her face was hidden from the others. She focused on regaining her composure before she found the three children.

"See, I told you Aunt Marisol would come play with us. We want to play dolls, but Emilano doesn't," Elena replied tartly.

"Dolls are sissy things. I am a man," little Emilano protested.

"I have it. We will pretend we are playing kings and queens. You two get your dolls. You will be the queens. Emilano, you will play the role of the king, kind of like Norwood. Your sisters will have to follow your orders, you see." A big, broad grin appeared on the eight year olds face. Marisol had found a good solution to the problem. The girls could play dolls, but Emilano had a way to play too. Later she sent Drina a private message. *Ernesto doesn't have any mental blocks. Elena keeps checking on him now and then, but has never seen any. I told her if she ever sees some, then she should ask you about it before she does anything.*

Whew. What a relief. Thanks Marisol! Thanks for everything!

Marisol wondered about that for some time. Drina was perfectly happy that Ernesto was head blind while she and now her children were not. This puzzled her for a long while.

Meanwhile, as Holly and Sissy headed back to their

work, Holly said, "You know, we are going to have to make up a *Mentales* Rule Book and share it with the other *Círculo de la Torres*."

That evening after supper, Drina produced quill and ink. "Okay, let's get this *Mentales* Rule Book going. I can see now it is going to be invaluable to everyone. Just look at my own family to see why."

"Aunt Drina, will you allow me to do the writing? I want you brainstorming with the others," Marisol deftly suggested. She knew Drina could write using her feet, but she was very slow at it and she suspected the ideas would fly thick and fast.

"Thanks dear. If you would be so kind, I hate to hold things up because I write so slowly. Now then, where do we start?" Drina asked.

"The problem is that ninety-nine percent of Tierra is illiterate," Sissy pointed out. "So how is this going to work if they can't read it?"

Holly took charge before things took a wrong turn. "True, Sissy, but most of us in the towers can and the average person ought to come to a tower to get help. Now then, I think the first and most important rule is that anyone with *mentales* must be trained to Hide Thoughts and Block Perception. Lacking that, an untrained *mentales* is a danger to themselves and to others."

"Perhaps we should write why the rule is needed," Drina suggested. "Some people want to know why something is before they will follow it. My kids, for example." That brought a few chuckles. After a time, Marisol read back what they had agreed upon for the first one.

Rule 1. Anyone who has the *mentales* gift and who is past puberty must receive basic training from one of the *Círculo de la Torres*. This basic training consists of learning how to block out unwanted thoughts of others who are around the person and not to broadcast one's own thoughts indiscriminately to everyone else around said person.

Why? Sensory overload can occur if one is wide open

to everyone's thoughts. In a crowd, the person can receive hundreds of dis-related thoughts simultaneously which has been known to drive the person mad, psi-insanity. If one cannot hide his or her own thoughts, then they are often screaming their personal, private thoughts to everyone around them, which can be both embarrassing and reveal things that should not be revealed to others, state secrets, for example.

Next, they tackled Verge Sickness, since that caused an alarming number of deaths. Several days passed before they finally reached agreement on this one. Some thought it was necessary to explain how the psi energies worked by following the body's nerve channels. However, that was only a theory. No one truly knew how or why *mentales* actually worked. Of course, Doctor Zosia wanted the diagnosis of Verge Sickness fully described along with the various remedies they had discovered thus far. Complicating matters was the fact that the adult men had just gotten it as well, not just those undergoing puberty with all its hormonal changes.

Rule 2. Children who are known to have *mentales* must be carefully monitored for Verge Sickness when they reach puberty. Similarly, adults who suddenly come into possession of *mentales* must also be carefully monitored for this illness.

Symptoms: a high fever, headaches, inability to eat or drink anything, non-responsive to external stimuli, often there is uncontrollable vomiting at the onset of the illness.

Possible Cures: Get a half cup of *bacal* tea into their systems. When they begin to relax, a full Regulation of their body's nerve channels must be done. Expect to find a severe blockage along the nerve channels, which also handle reproductive processes. If the blockage is not removed, death usually occurs. Once

the blockage is undone, gradually bring the patient
off *bacal* tea and train them as per Rule 1.

They tackled the childbirth issue next, made overly
complicated by the possible variations of which parent or both
had *mentales* and whether or not the child did as well. The
situation was also impacted by whether it was an easy birth or
filled with physical complications. Holly pointed out that this
rule would be vitally important because so many women were
now dying during childbirth, particularly so outside of the
Kingdom of the Angels. She added, "If we do a good job with
this one, we ought to see that all midwives receive this
training. After all, they deliver the vast majority of all babies
on Tierra." Doctor Zosia fully agreed with her on this point.

Rule 3. Childbirth is a critical time for both mother
and baby. Some births are easy, while some are filled
with all manner of complications. When *mentales* is
thrown into the mix, even more complications arise.
We have identified seven known situations.

Case A. Father, mother, and baby are known to have
mentales. If it is an easy birth, the father should act
as the Regulator for mother and baby, lending his
strength and calm to the mother and baby. If there
are physical complications, father and midwife must
Regulate and handle the situation. If needed, *bacal*
tea can be administered to reduce the psychic
overload in mother and baby.

Case B. Mother and baby are known to have
mentales, but the father does not. Treat as Case A
when possible, with midwife bringing the father into
rapport with mother and baby.

Case C. Mother and father have *mentales*, but baby
does not or baby's state is not known. Treat as Case
A to be safe.

Case D. Mother has *mentales*, father does not and
baby does not or baby's state is not known. Treat as
Case B to be safe.

Case E. Father and baby have *mentales*, but mother
does not. If it is an easy birth, the father should act
as the Regulator for mother and baby, lending his
strength and calm to the mother and baby. If there
are physical complications, father and midwife must
Regulate and handle the situation. If needed, *bacal*
tea can be administered to reduce the psychic
overload in baby.

Case F. Father only has *mentales*. Treat as Case E to
be safe.

Case G. Baby only has *mentales*. If midwife can act as
Regulator, then she should. *Bacal* tea ought to be
administered at the onset of labor and given as
needed to keep baby calm during birthing.

Doctor Zosia then appended a lengthy writeup on
proper delivery methods and the need for sterile water for
cleaning the newborn. She added a lengthy outline of
treatments for problems that could be encountered in both the
mother and child. Her addendum was five times as long as the
rest of the final document.

Holly then insisted on adding a behavioral rule. In time,
this one took on enormous significance. The anthropologist in
Dita kicked in and she absolutely demanded Holly's rule be
added. "Look, we are rapidly becoming a telepathic society.
We have to have this rule!" She even wanted it to become Rule
2 and not Rule 4, but she lost that argument.

Rule 4. No one will enter or pervade or invade
another's mind without first obtaining their freely
given consent.

Why? To do so uninvited is psychic rape!

During the ensuing weekdays, the five men worked on developing their newly acquired *mentales* gifts. Meanwhile, Marisol dutifully made a number of copies of the new rule book and then sent them off to the other *Círculo de la Torres*. She also spent time with Drina's children, carefully avoiding Palmer. As the days passed, she became more and more overt in avoiding being alone with Palmer. Finally, in early May, Drina took her aside when she came to take care of the children.

"Look Marisol, I don't know what is going on with you and Palmer, but whatever it is, it is creating quite a psychic disturbance. So much so, that those coming to the tower for training are being bothered by it. Holly told me to tell you to handle it pronto."

Oh god! Now everyone knows! Marisol's face reddened noticeably. *Whatever am I going to do now?* She was so shook up by Drina's announcement that she failed to put up her barriers and Drina heard her thoughts as if she had been shouting them.

Drina flushed. "I'm sorry, Marisol. I really don't like picking up another's thoughts like this, but you are broadcasting them wildly. Calm down. Why don't you tell me what is going on? Maybe I can help somehow." She leaned her body comfortingly into Marisol's. Her leg wrapped around the young woman's body, her unique hug.

Marisol sighed, "Forgive me, Aunt Drina. I was taken by surprise. It's so embarrassing."

"What is so troubling you? Has Palmer made unseemly advances to you?"

"Oh no, no, he's been the perfect gentleman. It's me. Drina, I'm, I'm scared, that's all." *There, I've actually said it aloud.* "No, I'm terrified," she corrected herself. *If I'm going to talk to her, I best be honest with myself.*

"Come sit down. Whatever are you terrified of? I don't understand you, my dear."

She did and found sitting was more conducive to talking about it. "It's Palmer. He's a man. I know he is madly in love with me. He's asked me to marry him many times now."

"Are you scared of him?"

"Not of him, per se, rather of any man, I think. You see, when he was head blind, I thought I had a good excuse to refuse his offer of marriage."

"I don't see why that is an excuse, not unless you really don't love him in turn," Drina replied, wishing she had a hand to rub her forehead. She just was not following her niece at all.

"But I do love him; at least I think I do. Oh, Aunt Drina, it is me that is the problem! Now that he is also a telepath, the problem is a hundred times worse!"

"There, there, Marisol," Drina said in a comfortingly way, but her mind was far from offering comfort. *What **is** she talking about? I don't understand her at all! Terrified? Of what? How can it be worse? Can it be she is like her mothers — a lover of women? Well, that would explain it.* "Dear, are you afraid of saying you are like your mothers — that you are attracted to other women and not to men?"

"No! Well, maybe I should be. I don't know. I am so scared, Aunt Drina." She began crying softly to herself, while holding onto Drina.

What the devil is this all about? Oh hell, I'll just use my gift. Let's see. Ah, Palmer needs to know what is troubling her. He has sensed her plight for days. That is the source of his upset that is affecting everyone to some degree. Now what does my little Marisol really need? Ah, she needs him here with us. Well then, so be it. I'm never wrong about these things, though she may curse me for it at first. Palmer? Ah good. Come to my bedroom. Marisol needs you here to work this mess out.

Wow! Sure thing! Is she in trouble? Like Verge or whatever?

No, but there is something that has her absolutely terrified and it concerns you somehow. You both need to be in each other's presence, something that she has been avoiding for days now, I think. Come please.

Marisol's arms hung around Drina's body as if she were a little baby being comforted by her mother. She didn't speak, just cried, and shook nervously. Shortly Palmer knocked and Drina said, "Come on in Palmer. Marisol dear, Palmer is here with us. It is what you both need to get this all sorted out."

"Palmer! I can't face him. Not like this. Make him go away," she wailed.

"Marisol! What is it? What have I done to you? My god, whatever it is, I ought to be drawn and quartered!" Palmer exclaimed, emotion swelling in his chest. He came over to the two who were sitting on the edge of her bed. Kneeling on one knee, he put his arm over her shoulders, gently touching her as he had been advised to do by Norwood. Instantly, he was flooded with her fear and terror. His first reaction was to reject it wholly, but analytically realized that was the wrong approach. He opened his mind and accepted it for what it was and the rapport was established. He felt her draw upon his own strength and allowed her to do so.

"Oh Palmer. I do so love you, but I am so terrified of it and marrying you," Marisol finally had the courage to admit it to him, drawing upon his own strength to help her master her weakness.

Drina said softly, "Marisol, can you tell us why you are so afraid? Are you afraid of dying in childbirth?" *I am grasping at straws. What the devil is she so afraid of anyway?*

"Huh? Oh, no, not that, Aunt Drina, but I suppose I ought to be afraid of that. So many women do, you know."

Somewhat exasperated now, Drina said, "Then please, Marisol, tell us what this is all about. We are wholly in the dark. I am running out of things to guess." Suddenly, she had another insight and added, "So you have had so darn many love affairs that you don't want Palmer to know about? Is that it?"

That broke the dam. Marisol giggled. "No! That's silly. No, how do I explain this and not sound like an idiot? Look," she pulled away from Drina and wiped her eyes. She couldn't quite face looking into Palmer's eyes, but kept the rapport going between them. "Since I can remember, I have been my own master. I do what I want to do. Well, I was a witch and planning to be an Advanced Witch, like my moms. What I mean is I have always been the cause of things, not the effect of things. I hate being the effect of things. You know that well enough, Aunt Drina."

"Yes, that I do, but I am still not certain what this is all about, dear." Palmer looked as frustrated as she did.

"If I marry Palmer, then I am always going to be the effect and never the cause anymore," she finally said it. Relief flooded over her, that much was obvious to both Palmer and Drina.

"Dear Marisol, I am an ignorant man. I don't understand how come you are always going to be the effect if we marry," Palmer said softly, looking with confusion at Drina who returned his expression. He felt a bit better that she was just as perplexed as he was.

Marisol flushed beet red. "You, your, well, your thing comes into me always. You are the cause and I am the effect. I can't be cause, only effect. I've been in close rapport with my mothers. They share a deep intimacy and take turns being cause. But they are both women you see. With us, you being male, you will always be cause and I will always be effect, receiving you, and that terrifies me somehow. I think I'd die if I had to always be the effect."

Drina listened to this and broke into a hearty, roaring laugh, embarrassing both Palmer and Marisol. "Drina, what is so funny? Marisol is deadly serious about this." Palmer felt stretched to the limit.

Finally controlling her mirth, Drina replied, "I thought there was some hideous blockage here, Marisol. This is so simple. I am flabbergasted your mother didn't teach this to you. Okay, I will teach you both. Let's start simple. Palmer, fetch those lovely irises over there that Ernesto picked for me this morning. Good. Now, hand them to Marisol. Marisol, you love flowers and as you accept them, feel which direction the flow of the flowers are coming, either into you or out from you."

"Into me, I love them. He was incredibly thoughtful of you," Marisol replied.

"Right, when you agree with something, you naturally pull it in towards you. Agreement in an inflow into you. Now then, imagine he is handing you a pair of rotting dead rats."

Marisol cringed and pushed the flowers away from her. "Which way did that go?" Drina asked.

"Outward, obviously," Marisol replied without any hesitation. Palmer nodded his agreement.

"Right, when you disagree with something, you push it away from you and that is an outflow. Now then, here comes the kicker. Suppose Palmer here wants you and pulls you in towards himself. He is agreeing with his desires for you and that makes an inflow to him, but which way is it then going from your point of view, Marisol?"

"Er, it is going from me to him. Oh, I see, an outflow from. Oh! Oh! That would be disagreement. I don't want it. He wants me but in doing so, it makes me not want him!"

"Precisely. Now suppose you want him and that desire is coming in towards you. What will it be from him? Outflow and he will feel that he doesn't want you, disagree again," Drina explained.

"Zounds! I have seen that at least a hundred times in dad's court when I was growing up. Ladies try to pull in guys, but they resist. Guys try to pull in ladies, but they resist. I thought the women were just being fickle!" Palmer gushed out his revelation. Marisol giggled, as she too understood what he was saying.

"So there is no hope, is there? I want him, but then he won't want me. He wants me so I won't want him," Marisol suggested.

Again, Drina laughed heartily. "Dear child. No. Look, you are not your body. A body is part of the universe, but we are not our bodies. Certainly, every witch knows that!" Marisol flushed to the roots of her hair. She had entirely forgotten that. "We do not have to follow the laws of the physical universe because we are not of the universe."

"I see what you mean. My terror is really just my body experiencing an outflow every time I see Palmer wanting me."

Drina replied, "I won't pretend to tell you what your terror is, dear child. Know this; you are right about male-female sex. It is always a one-way flow from the man to the woman. Nothing can change that, not unless men start having the babies. Now personally, I think that would be a very good thing, to have the men carry the babies for nine months and then deliver them." Both women chuckled and Palmer flushed a little.

She continued, "Marisol, a marriage is far, far more than just sex. It is an intimate sharing of each other, especially among telepaths. In such a rapport with each other, nothing can be hidden — each is fully revealed to the other, the best sharing in the universe, if I do say so myself. Of course, with Ernesto, I have to bring us into rapport since he is not a telepath.

She continued doling out her advice, "In your case, Marisol, it will be very important for you to be cause and initiate things between you two, but please don't hog cause. Allow Palmer to also initiate too. Mutual and equal sharing is what a marriage is all about, though non-witches usually believe and act otherwise. In your case, if you two decide to get married, you owe it to each other to make such a pledge to always share the driver's seat, as you put it Marisol."

"I feel like such a fool, Aunt Drina. All this time, I've been fearing nothing at all."

"My dear Marisol, that's not true," Palmer caught her self-invalidation and decided that was not a good thing for her to do. "You were right to be frightened. I've seen many ill-fated marriages while I was growing up in my dad's court. You are a powerful person; I can't imagine you being any less strong. I think a marriage is supposed to help both of us achieve our goals, not just one of us. But I have seen it go that route all too often in court-dictated marriages where women marry into money or position only to find the price too steep, but by then it was too late for them. I remember the awful case of Lena. When I was a boy, she was a stained glass artist, who made the most fabulous windows, albeit for the Church of God buildings. Still, I greatly admired them, but to gain position and social standing, she married John Weathers who was an advisor to my despicable father, King Aaran. He would not let her make any more of her windows, insisting her proper place was by his side in dad's court. Grim. She died two years later. Rumor had it she killed herself, but I was only a lad at the time and could not find out the truth. So you are right to be scared of this."

Marisol sighed, "You are right, Palmer, but I refuse to

end up like that Lena. I can't and I won't."

"I promise you never to do that to you. If I even try, kick me in my butt," he teased her slightly, bringing a grin to both women's faces.

"Deal, but you do the same if I stop or hinder you, promise me Palmer," Marisol insisted.

He did so, but they were interrupted by a telepathic message from Holly. *All hands to the Great Hall. We've another major situation developing with our farmers.* The three headed down stairs, but Marisol flashed Drina a huge thank you and took Palmer's arm, surprising him but also pleasing him.

Chapter 6 Environmental Changes

The group of farmers had left, presenting the group a most severe problem. It was mid-May and the crops ought to have been all sewn and up. Yet, the constant rain, sleet, and late night snow was causing a huge problem for everyone in the kingdom. Only the winter wheat crop was doing well. The usual crops of corn and many vegetables were not even planted. They could not survive the cold weather, let alone the amount of rain that had already fallen. However, they reported a bumper crop of mushrooms and by fall, a wide variety of nuts. The nut trees seemed to know there was a severe disruption in the weather patterns as well.

"I saw this coming, but I am afraid the solution is beyond my knowledge," Aurora began after the farmers left. "We have to do something or by fall we will all be starving."

"Our problem is none of us are botanists," Doctor Zosia replied. From the many strange looks shot her way, she added, "A person who studies plants and knows all there is to know about them."

Dita inserted quickly, "There are other cold and wet worlds out there. If I had access to a computer, I could research the problem. I am sure there are crops, which would thrive in these strange conditions. Ordinarily, I could send off for some seeds which looked promising, but. . ."

"But what?" Aurora asked.

"They have applied the hands-off rule which they ought to have done in the first place. Even if I could find plants which would thrive here, they'd not let me import them," Dita explained.

Ally laughed, "The sword cuts both ways." Others echoed her.

"Well, we're still witches," Sissy declared. "Come on; let's put our collective knowledge to work."

"Hay, grasses, alfalfa, and winter wheat are going strong. I bet spring peas would thrive," Holly suggested. "And at least the hardy apple trees seem unaffected and have a bumper crop coming."

"With all the nuts, we could have the millers grind them into nut flower," Sissy suggested. "Plus there are numerous tubers that would probably grow well."

"With all the flowering, the honey bees are going strong. Perhaps we could increase honey production," Aurora added.

"You know, I was thinking," Dita mused, "with the severe climate change, many plants are likely to adapt in various ways. Already we've seen many northern animals migrating down to our foothills. The reindeer and those snow bunnies, Norwood, remember? I think in time we'll have a different economy going strong here. If we put more into grasslands, sheep and cows could thrive."

"Hum, good idea. Horses might as well," Norwood added. "We just don't have good horse breeding stock around here. Maybe we could get some from the Westerlings, but that's several thousand miles just to get them here."

"Hey, that is something that I can focus upon," Aurora broke in. "Let me see if I can get a glimpse of the agricultural future around here. I've not tried to look for that before." Everyone encouraged her to do so and Aurora closed her eyes and worked her special *mentales* skill for quite some time.

She finally opened her eyes and smiled at everyone, "Well, you guys are geniuses. You are right. Down the line, our kingdoms will be producing lots of honey, dairy products, apples, dried meat, wool, sheep, peas, mushrooms, and a host of tubers. Looks like our grains will be a combination of wheat and nut flower. But I also saw something really strange. Some of our trees are going to mutate, just as Dita suggested. To protect their fruit from the evening cold and snow, they develop these folding pods, which open during the day and close during the night. What is fascinating, I saw you, Marisol, using your fingers to pull out these thin white strands of fiber from the pods, twisting it into thread. So we will have a home grown substitute for cotton, and we won't have to always be wearing woolen clothes which itch me something terribly."

She shared her images of this with the others. "Hey, Marisol, you are pregnant there!" Sissy exclaimed.

Marisol flushed beet red. She mumbled, "Palmer and I are going to get married soon." That changed the topic for a while.

"Way to go, little brother!" Norwood patted Palmer on his back. After the many congratulations ended, they got back to the task at hand.

"I also saw that falconry would also become a big industry here in the foothills, not so much over by Bettingham," Aurora continued. "I think the big hawks will be moving closer to us from up north, where it is becoming too cold for much of anything to survive. Another curious thing, our pine trees are also going to change somehow, but I am not sure what that implies, save we will have more forests and that they somehow grow more rapidly. The question is: how are we going to get enough seed to get this implemented?"

"Right. A typical farmer hasn't a clue about raising and sheering sheep," Norwood added. "Growing corn is very different from some of these other things. We will need an education program. Let's have those who know how to say handle sheep train those who want to take up sheep herding. We'll need a plan or else we'll have all the farmers growing peas on us." Everyone laughed but knew he was right. Orchards would have to be planted and maintained. Hives would have to be expanded and more trained in the care and handling of the bees. The list was lengthy.

This was the arena of Norwood and Palmer, the large scale organization of the workforce. They'd had a lot of practice with it when Norwood was king. Aiden and Alford were widely traveled, and knew the lay of the land within the Kingdom of the Angels very well. Between them, they drew up likely areas where each type would do the best. Here in the rugged foothills, orchards and pastureland would predominate, along with nut trees and the occasional winter wheat field. Over by Bettingham at the easternmost part of the kingdom, the terrain was rolling grasslands, though hills were still heavily forested there as well. Crops could be grown more readily there. Once they had their best guesses laid out, they then had to sell all the local farmers on the ideas and get the projects implemented. It was late in the season for many, but they did their best.

All that summer, they traveled throughout the

kingdom, meeting with every farmer they could find. Gratitude abounded, for many had nearly given up all hope, and considered picking up and moving southward to find better growing conditions. In the short view, even more beneficial was their advance planning for the coming long, cold winter. They arranged for numerous hunting parties to scour the forest for deer and established meat drying locations and tanners to make use of the leather. Knowing what was where and in what quantity, the men managed to get food supplies distributed uniformly around the kingdom, though barter was the frequent mode of exchange. Further, they encouraged every household to lay in a huge supply of firewood. Norwood's idea was somehow to get all his people through this coming winter and hope for a new, productive growing season next year, as the farmers adapted.

Unfortunately, the myriad of other kingdoms did not fare so well.

Part III Escalating Chaos

Chapter 7 Wycombe Mutiny

Just after noon, on the first of December 1001, the Gang of Six was once more meeting secretly near the edge of the once thriving city of Wycombe, amid the creaking of the mill by the stream at the west edge of town. Phil Street was one of the better millers and during the daytime, many folks came here either to have grains ground while they waited or to purchase flower, which was in extremely short supply. Crops had mostly failed this year, naturally.

The gang chose Phil's place because their coming here would not draw any attention to themselves. He was forty and the oldest of the group. Phil was also a talker, ordinarily quite jovial, which suited his profession admirably. All six had powerful *mentales* gifts. To counter the Church of God's arresting and burning at the stake all those who had the *mentales* gift, these six quietly joined forces and formed a resistance movement back in September. Phil's gift was the ability to Push and Move rather heavy weights, which also aided him in his work.

"Do you really believe what Bishop-king Gil was saying? That the COG has made a mistake and that those of us who have *mentales* are now to be highly honored in services?" asked Anna Wycombe. She was thirty-five and a housewife, an older cousin of Norwood, Ally, and Palmer. Her gift was that of Domination. All had just heard the latest service, attendance was mandatory ever since the Bishop-king took control over Wycombe.

"I wouldn't trust him any further than I can throw one of my chickens!" Becktold Hams exclaimed bitterly. His brother had already faced the burning stakes and his other brother had run off with Brother Sheridan Abrams, hoping to create a safe place called Skylar Abbey somewhere in the far northern mountains. He was thirty and raised chickens at the edge of the city. His primary gift lay in Controlling Animals. He was very bitter and quite outspoken against the COG.

Janice Wells, a twenty-three year old who worked as a maid at an inn, commented, "I don't trust him. It seems to me to be a sneaky way to get us all to come forward and identify ourselves, only to have him burn us at the stake next!" She too was quite bitter; her husband had been a bit too overt with his gift and had been murdered three weeks ago. Like Anna, her gift was that of Domination.

The coppersmith, Jasper Hodkins, thirty-three, was normally the quiet type, rarely saying much of anything. His gift was the ability to Create Fires, which he quietly used in his trade. "There has to be more. He is two-faced. One month we are the devils and the next month we are the angels. You can't have it both ways. I don't trust him either."

"What do you think, Kyle?" Phil asked. Kyle Bettingham was twenty-eight and an ex-soldier who fought in King Norwood's army in the great battles against King Chester's cavalrymen. Now he stayed in the background, doing odd jobs, refusing to join the Bishop-king's fanatical militia soldiers. For good reason. They were ill-trained and often cowardly, as witnessed by their latest action. Last week, soldiers from the neighboring Kingdom of Leedward, some fifty miles southeast of Wycombe, launched an invasion. When the militia encountered the invading and trained soldiers, their morale broke and they routed all the way back to Wycombe.

Kyle cleared his throat. He said softly, "Well, if you ask me, the Bishop-king is getting desperate now, what with the kingdom being invaded by the upstart *Jefe* Leedward. Shoot, Leedward used to be part of our own kingdom, but now all the kingdoms have broken down into dozens of smaller ones. He's seen his fabled COG militia is a dismal failure. With the invading army a few days from Wycombe, he's getting plenty worried about an attack on Wycombe. I know I would be. He's got no real, trained soldiers. Old King Norwood was sure clever when he disbanded his army before he fled the bishop. I'd say he is probably speaking the truth when he wants us brought into his fold. That way, he can beg us to come to the defense of Wycombe."

"Ah, now that makes real sense! Thanks Kyle," Phil replied, shaking his head in total agreement. "Maybe it wouldn't be such a bad thing to have them invade Wycombe and remove the Bishop-king from power."

"In principle, I would agree," Kyle cautioned him, "but the reality of an invading army is they will kill all who stand in their way, loot everything of value, and rape or steal our younger women. Janice and Anna would be in serious jeopardy if an invading army hit the streets of Wycombe. Whether we like the bishop as our ruler or not, it behooves us to see to it that the invaders are repelled."

Janice shuddered and then said, "So you think we should report to the Bishop-king for active duty? What's to prevent him from murdering us once we have done our part in repelling the invading army?"

"We are vastly stronger than that man and his fanatical followers," Anna pointed out. "I know men. As soon as we are no longer needed, our lives won't be worth chicken feathers. No offense Becktold."

"None taken, Anna. I agree with the women. Once we've done our part, why should we, the ones with the gift — presumably from God if Gil is to now be believed — why should we become puppets at his whim? We are the strong ones; any one of us could take him out with our hands tied behind our backs," Becktold replied.

"Now there's a point on which we all agree!" Phil exclaimed highly animated. "Hell, Anna ought to have the throne! She's a Wycombe after all or even you, Kyle, you are a Bettingham, and we all know King Aaran Wycombe somehow stole the throne from the Bettingham clan."

Anna laughed, "They'd never accept me. I am a housewife with three children and my husband, bless his soul, is something of a moron. Don't know why I ever married my second cousin, but I did. No, for my money, Kyle ought to take the throne."

"Well, if we do stand up and fight off the invaders, Bishop-king Gil ought to have an accident. We can then put Kyle on the throne, one of us," Becktold declared. "That would go a very long way to putting all the rest of us who have gifts at ease and it would be justice for all our friends who have been burned at the stake."

"I can arrange an accident," Jasper whispered. "Just say when and the man will become toast."

114

Kyle laughed, "No kidding. I've seen you in action. Good man!"

"Okay, then are we all agreed that we will come forward and help defend Wycombe against these invaders and then once that is settled, have Gil replaced with Kyle?" Phil asked for a consensus. It was unanimous.

"What about this other idea that he was preaching? That it is vitally important that women bear our children. He speaks the truth well enough, in our children comes our future. We've already lost a good quarter of our population. I'm not too happy with his ideas that we must guard and protect our women that they may bear children. I'm perfectly able to take care of myself. I was and still am very perturbed about his idea to bind your wives to you for all time and to begat as many children as you are able. You men don't have to endure nine months of agony and the pain and risk of childbirth. If you haven't noticed, most of the women who have died have died in childbirth of late," Anna asked and pointed out the part of the bishop's speech that most bothered her.

"Part of that is simple math," the miller Phil pointed out. "If there are more women dying than are being born and growing into adulthood, the city is slowly succumbing and one day will be no more. We need more female children being born and surviving to bear children than we are losing in childbirth or we are doomed. Simple math."

"True, but you don't have to risk death each time," Anna declared with a slightly hostile tone. Then, her lips curled in a coy smile, "On the other hand, I would not mind carrying one of your children."

"Huh? What *are* you saying?" Phil asked, taken aback by her sudden shift and flirting eyes and grin.

"Simple, fellows. We all know those of us who have *mentales* are giving birth to children who also have *mentales*. That is well known among us who have the gift. We six are among the strongest endowed here in Wycombe, right?" They nodded. "So think what our child, Jasper, might possess, given my endowment of Domination plus your endowment of Create Fire? Or my Dominate plus your telekinesis, Phil. Or my

Dominate plus your Detonate, Kyle. Our offspring would likely be doubly more powerful than either one of us! Now for that I would risk childbirth!"

"Hey, so would I!" Janice added her opinion to the mix. "If we mated, think of how powerful our lines would become! Then we mate the Dominate-Create Fire child with Kyle's Detonate and we have a child who would be three times more powerful than any one of us. For that, I would risk all. Think of it, guys, immense *mentales* power, so much so that none could ever again subject us to burning at the stake! Not ever! Think of all the *mentales* children the Bishop-king has already murdered! Never again I say. We have the power to make it so!"

"I like your thinking," Kyle grinned. "It helps that neither of you is bad-looking either." The men chuckled and the two women grinned. "But what about your husbands and our wives? Such children would be bastards, illegitimate children, ostracized kids."

"You have a point there. Well, when you are king, Kyle, you can issue new proclamations making it honorable to have such children. We can call them fosterlings and make them as valuable and honorable as normal children," Anna declared.

"But what about birthrights, Anna?" asked Phil. "Would the fosterlings have the same rights as normal sons? I think we'd get into a lot of trouble with folks if a fosterling son inherited his normal family's estate as they do now."

"Men! What about us women? We inherit nothing at all," Anna cried out exasperated with Phil's attitude.

"He's got a point, Anna," Janice spoke up. "I would want my son born in wedlock to inherit before any fosterling son I might have. Besides, if we do it right, the fosterlings will be immensely powerful and will not need the extra benefits of inheritance."

"We could allow fosterlings to inherit if there is no regular son to inherit," Becktold suggested. "That would likely fly, as I certainly would not want others dividing up my chicken farm if I had no legitimate son heir. If I had a fosterling, I'd rather it go to him."

"Okay, okay. I will go along with this. It makes sense,"

Anna admitted. "But what about that binding of women business? Bind your wives to you for all time."

"She has a point there," Janice spoke up. "I have been married four years now, but you would not believe the number of men who try to pick me up! I wish I had a way that would show anyone who looked that I was married so they would not bother me so."

"It is because you are too good looking," Phil jested but he was also speaking truthfully and could not hide his feelings. Not from these other telepaths. All six were blonde with blue eyes, typical for this part of the Midlands.

"Whatever we do about it, it cannot involve too great an expense, not if we declare all married women have them," Becktold suggested, waxing pragmatic. "It cannot be some fancy jewels, for example. Three quarters of Wycombe men couldn't afford them."

"Are we to take the word bind literally, though? Bind your wives to you for all time," asked Kyle.

"Oh you are being kinky, Kyle. Are you going to tie me up? I might like that," Janice flashed him a coy smile and flicked her long eyelashes several times. Everyone chuckled.

"Well, if we were somehow bound physically, we'd not be able to do our work properly, guys. Besides, you'd get a whole lot of women protesting, I think," Anna declared.

"I wonder if the COG women would protest? After all it was their revered bishop who announced it," Janice countered.

"How about being more symbolic? A ring would not do. They are very hard to see and can easily come off. A wristband would be more prominent, but that might interfere with work. How about a neck ring? That would be unmistakable. We could use copper, good for my business and very affordable, don't you think," Jasper suggested quietly.

"I like that idea," Janice mulled it over. "It would not interfere but they would have to be attractive, ornamental. You know how we women like our jewelry, when we can afford it."

Anna supported her, "Yes, she's got a good point, Jasper. Good idea. We can have simple, plain rings, easily affordable and readily noticed by men. Those who have more funds can have fancier ones, perhaps with a jewel or two in them, but still basically a neck ring."

"Okay then, I have only one question," Kyle changed the topic to one that concerned himself. "Look, I am okay with your putting me on the throne of Wycombe, but, and this is a big but — not yours, Anna," he couldn't resist teasing her a little, "I insist all of you become my top advisors in this business. I am not willing to try to run the whole kingdom by myself. You five have to share in the responsibilities. I won't do it alone. I am not that power-hungry."

The others agreed to share the duties of governing Wycombe. As they had already spent considerable time in this meeting, they hastily adjourned. All promised to think this over and meet again in two days ready to share ideas on how to best proceed.

December 8th came along with a howling snowstorm. *Jefe* Abrams Leedward surveyed his small army of rag tag soldiers and six *mentales*. As planned, they would attack at noon. Once again, the Bishop-king had marched his army out to meet his and *Jefe* Abrams intended to strike first under the cover of the snowstorm, greatly aiding his chances for victory.

His was a desperate one. Last year, it seemed wise to secede from the Kingdom of Wycombe. He had everything to gain and nothing to lose. Now all that had changed with the fickle weather! Most all crops on his holdings had failed. His people were starving and all requests to purchase food supplies from neighboring kingdoms had failed. He was left with only one real choice: invade and capture Wycombe and take the food supplies his people needed. That there was barely enough food in the city was not known to him. Wycombe had always been the capital city, the largest and most prosperous city in the old Kingdom of Bettingham. Surely, there was plenty of food to be had there, plump for the taking, especially since they were now ruled by the puny COG folks. No standing army, only the religious fanatical COG militia, who had already been routed once.

He had two hundred men, well-armed, good soldiers, though they complained bitterly about having to fight in a snowstorm. He had chosen six of his best *mentales* gifted people — three men, two women, and a boy. He expected to be fighting the COG militia and not any *mentales* gifted, because everyone knew the COG was burning all those with the *mentales* gift at the stake.

Two of his *mentales* were prepared to breech the castle walls. He fully anticipated eventually he would have to take the castle in Wycombe, figuring the Bishop-king would hold up there to the bitter end. One woman could manipulate the weather and had nursed this snowstorm along as a cover for their attack. The other woman was a healer. The boy could Dominate others, while the remaining man had several combat related skills and he was given charge of the fighting forces as his general. He was totally confident of a swift and complete victory.

Some distance away, Bishop-king Gil rode his horse up and down his battle line. He had well over two hundred of his prized fanatical COG militia men at the ready, all armed and swearing to defeat the invaders. Today, he was confident of victory. Why? At long last, the *mentales* gifted men and women accepted his formal apology and stepped forward to help defend Wycombe, even though it was winter and blizzard conditions. For days, he fretted these men and women would not accept the COG's abrupt reversal. After all, had it been his people being murdered, he knew he would not have accepted it. It still baffled him that these men and women did come forward and offer to help unconditionally to boot. *All praise to our new Archbishop Shane Zadok! He is wiser than I ever anticipated. Timely too! Without their support, I don't know if we could stop Jefe Leedword!*

Somehow, two dozen *mentales* men and women volunteered. He'd never seen so many of them in one place before. Besides, he thought that they had already murdered nearly all the *mentales* gifted people. Obviously, he hadn't and wondered how they could have all escaped his dragnet.

They seemed to have some leaders, he had noted. They took their orders from a former soldier, a Kyle Bettingham, but there were five others, who carried nearly equal weight. He was a keen observer, if nothing else. He could not have become Bishop-king without that skill. Still, a skilled soldier would be very useful on the battlefield. He already knew his COG militia was not battle-hardened soldiers. Only days ago, they had routed from their first encounter with *Jefe* Leedword's army.

Now bolstered by many *mentales* gifted and some ex-soldiers Kyle had brought along, some fifty men, his COG militia seemed to have a higher morale. Gil certainly hoped this would prove to be the case. However, he had to make one concession to the *mentales* gifted. In hindsight, Kyle had been right, Gil thought. He had to ride out with his army and face the attackers. "Any leader of any kingdom would do no less. To hide in your castle while your men are out fighting your battles is a certain way to lose the battle. A leader must be present to inspire his men," Kyle had patiently explained to him three days ago when they came to him with their proposal of unconditional aid. Well, it was darn cold and miserable even on his horse, but surely the battle would be over swiftly now, if only it would start. He wondered now how it would start.

Kyle had said to allow the enemy to make the first move. He'd gone along with his suggestion, trusting to the man's soldiering skills. His horse snorted, frosty spray mixing with the soft white flakes flying across the field of view. Gil was behind the line of men, just where Kyle had suggested he position himself. He had three COG guards beside him, armed with crossbows. He felt totally safe and knew he would not actually be in any real danger, not unless his entire army was defeated, but then he could easily ride back into Wycombe and prepare to defend the castle proper.

Suddenly a trumpet sounded from perhaps two hundred yards distant. *Jefe* Abrams Leedward finally began his main assault on Wycombe's forces. His men charged forward through the near blinding snow towards the line of defenders. In this part of the world, combat between armies took on an entirely new style of fighting, never seen before in this area. Normally, the two opposing sides would join in fierce hand to hand combat, sword against sword, or in better weather, archery volleys would soften up the opposition first. Still, until this day it had always ended up sword against sword in the end.

Becktold and three others made their move, sending

four large bears charging into the right flank of the attackers. Phil and six others began sending out massive Push waves against the advancing enemy lines, knocking them off their feet. Snow footing was treacherous at best. Jasper and five others began igniting those who drew closer, the ones who had somehow avoided the telekinesis pushing. Kyle watched carefully to detect who was the enemy leader and pointed him out to Anna and Janice. Dominate versus Dominate, but with two to one odds, the women won.

With his leader out of commission, his ranks on the ground or being torn apart by the berserk bears or going up in flames, *Jefe* Abrams Leedward had no choice but to surrender. "We give up! We surrender! We surrender! Call off your bears, for heaven's sake!" he screamed as loudly as he could. Hearing his cries, his men dropped their swords, save those trying to stay alive as the bears rushed them.

Becktold heard Kyle's order in his mind. *Okay, release the bears, Becktold.* He also heard, *Jasper, do your thing now.*

Bishop-king Gil shouted for joy! Victory in less than five minutes! This was unheard of! His men had hardly anything to do but confiscate the enemy's weapons. His newly acquired *mentales* men and women had carried the field. He cheered his army loudly and thought, *All praise to Archbishop Shane Zadok!* His three guards shouted with joy as well. In the next instant, his clothes burst into flames!

Dressed heavily against the cold winter's day, he was burned alive. Even though he fell off his horse and the three guards tried to put the fire out, he perished. The three intervening guards also burst into flames when they tried to roll him over in the snow to put out the flames.

"I am the new King of Wycombe, Kyle Bettingham. I accept your surrender, *Jefe* Abrams Leedword. Come to me and let's discuss the terms. I have a warm tent waiting. Bring your *mentales* with you," Kyle's voice thundered, aided by a simple Magnify Voice.

All two dozen of his friends and the fifty ex-soldiers watched the COG militia men carefully. While Kyle suspected they might offer resistance to his proclaiming himself the new king, they were too thunderstruck by the sudden demise of their leader to offer any effective resistance. Besides, they too had been completely awed by this entirely new form of combat, far, far beyond anything they had ever seen before.

Ten minutes later, a humbled and defeated *Jefe* Abrams Leedward and his six mentales entered the warm tent, which had been the field tent of Bishop-king Gil only an hour before. "Have a seat, there is warm tea. Help yourselves. These are my associates," Kyle motioned to the steel-faced five men and women standing behind him along with a small boy. All watched the six enemy *mentales* closely. The seven looked half-starved and greedily accepted the warm tea.

"What are your terms? My people are starving. We tried to buy food, but Bishop-king Gil would not sell us any. What else could we do?" *Jefe* Abrams finally asked.

"Times are hard. We are short of food as well, *Jefe* Abrams, but we are not so desperate that we would attack our neighbors," Kyle pointed out. *Jefe* Abrams lowered his head in defeat.

"Terms. Well, first, what are your *mentales* gifts? State them truthfully, we will know if you are lying. Billy here may be a boy, but he can spot a lie easily," Kyle stated flatly.

She can control weather? Kyle, we need her and her gift. The healer woman too, Anna sent to him.

We can't throw them to the wolves or kill them. That would not be honorable, Phil sent him.

"Okay, the terms of your surrender are simple. We will keep the two women *mentales* with us here. You and the rest of your men are free to return to your homes. You may take your weapons with you. I give you permission to hunt for deer and rabbits on your way back. We will provide you with some flower for bread and some tea." The fact that they would be allowed to keep their weapons was very significant. On this metal-poor planet, iron was precious. One of their swords was worth ten horses.

That they would not be sent home without any food also made an impression on *Jefe* Abrams. However, the old man protested, "But Jana is my daughter!"

"All the more reason she should stay here with us. She will ensure you do not attack us in the future. If you do, she will be the first to die. I give you my word she will not be harmed but will be accorded a status appropriate to that of a daughter of a *Jefe*. Will you accept these most generous terms?" Kyle asked flatly.

"I have no choice." He looked at his daughter and tears streamed down his eyes.

I will be all right, father. You must accept these terms or surely, all will be lost. Please promise me to raise Tom. Tell him I love him. Ask the king if you can somehow buy enough food to get by until spring.

I will, my daughter, as my own, Jefe Abrams swore to Jana. Bent and defeated, he looked way older than his age.

Although wondering what had passed between the two, Kyle ignored it and looked at the two women. "Will you abide by this agreement and come willingly with us? I give you my word you will be well treated and not harmed."

Kyle was impressed with Jana's reply. He expected hostility and defiance. Instead, she faced him squarely and said, "I will do so as long as Betsy and I are well treated, not harmed, and if you help my father and our people avoid starvation. We can pay for food."

She has spunk, Kyle. I like her attitude, Janice sent him. *It will play out well for us if you are seen to make this small concession to her. Trust me; it will go a long way with her.*

Kyle grinned. "Jana, you drive a hard bargain. I will accept your addendum as far as we can. Food is scarce here too, but I will send back what we can spare."

"Thank you, King Kyle. You have our pledge," she replied. Kyle nodded and shook *Jefe* Abrams hand, sealing their terms.

While they left the defeated leader to assemble his troops and tend their wounds with the help of Betsy, Kyle and his group headed into Wycombe to take possession of the castle and the palace. They met little resistance and the chaos of the switch of rulers began in earnest.

During the next week, the Gang of Six took over control of Wycombe. King Kyle's first action was to remove all non-*mentales* people from the castle, offering these many positions to those who had the gift. Confusion reigned for quite some time as the new rulers tackled the immense challenge of determining what was where. Because it was wintertime, few problems were pressing, other than the ongoing shortage of food. Kyle did have the good sense to send a dispatch to the Kingdom of the Angels, outlining their takeover of Wycombe, asking for food aid, for assistance in training those who had the precious gift, and for a peaceful alliance between their adjoining kingdoms.

By the end of the week, he kept his word, sending two wagons of supplies to *Jefe* Abrams. He wisely decided to pay for the food by giving King Kyle two dozen swords before he and his defeated soldiers began their long march home.

Each of the Gang of Six moved their entire families into the castle, though Jasper, Phil, and Becktold continued to operate their businesses. By spring, they appointed some of their relatives to handle the daily operations. Jana Leedward and Betsy Trout were given a pair of rooms in the castle. Each was given a lady in waiting and told no one would violate their private space, as long as they behaved themselves.

Jana was twenty-four with long, curly brown hair. Her face was quite prominent, with angular cheekbones and bushy eyebrows. While she was not a beauty, she had an attractiveness about her. Her husband had died last year, leaving her to raise their two year old son, Tom. Betsy also had brown hair, shoulder length. She had just turned eighteen and had secretly been training as a witch before the COG began their systematic elimination of all witches. Betsy now depended on Jana; she was frightened of being held a virtual prisoner here in Wycombe. "We watch and listen and learn, Betsy. We stick together and see what fortune has in store for us." Both women did just that, shocked to learn King Kyle and his group had just taken over the throne right after the ill-fated battle.

On New Year's Day, 1002, King Kyle assembled a group of a hundred key people to hear the many new proclamations, which would define the rule of the *mentales* in Wycombe. Among the throng was the newly appointed Bishop Lloyd Raine, a forty year old priest pressed into service with the sudden demise of the Bishop-king. He came very hesitantly, fully expecting either to be murdered himself or to be somehow punished for the COG's earlier murders of many *mentales*. His wild thoughts were plainly obvious to all the assembled telepaths of the new court. Many smiled, enjoying his discomfort and fears. King Kyle also had Jana and Betsy in attendance, as befitting Jana's status as a princess.

"Welcome everyone to our first of many Formal Exchanges. During these meetings, we will be explaining our rulings and asking you to inform us of situations you feel we need to address. As you probably already know, we who possess the *mentales* gift have defeated the invading army of *Jefe* Abrams Leedword. In truth, we have now entered into a new era in which those of us who possess these incredible gifts are taking over the reins of government and protection of our kingdom. I call your attention to the simple fact that not a single soldier of ours was injured in the recent battle. It is only fair that, if we who have this precious gift put our lives on the line protecting our kingdom, then we should have a major say in the running of our kingdom. Thus, I have accepted the position as your king. My five top advisors and I will do our best to run a fair and just kingdom, but we will not tolerate any more attacks or harassment of our people who have been given the *mentales* gift."

"Next, I want everyone to know we hold no animosity to the COG for their murdering spree of our people. We have accepted their humble apology, feel confident they are both sincere, and will cause us no further harm. Yet that does not mean we totally reject their teachings. It is not our intention to go around and murder all those who support the COG. Rather, we want to work together with the ideas that are vital for us all."

"Specifically, we wholly agree with them that it is vitally important women bear our children. Your Bishop Lloyd speaks the truth well enough: with our children comes our future. We've already lost a good quarter of our population. We must guard and protect our women so they may bear children. Our miller pointed out to us it is simple math. If there are more women dying than are being born and growing into adulthood, the city is slowly succumbing and one day will be no more. We need more female children being born and surviving to bear children than we are losing in childbirth or we are doomed. Simple math."

"There is another aspect to all this. We who have *mentales* have managed to thwart this recent attack. The enemy only had six *mentales* gifted with them, while we fielded two dozen. Thus, by mere numbers we were able to win the day. Can you imagine what would have happened if we faced a large army which had fifty *mentales*? We would be easily conquered, just as *Jefe* Abrams was. Thus, in addition to needing more women bearing our children, we need more who also have the *mentales* gift. That should be obvious to you all."

"Jana here can Control Weather to some degree. Come spring, I will be asking her to help us obtain better weather so our crops will grow. Yet we need far more people with these powerful gifts. Some of you already know that frequently the children of women who possess the *mentales* gift also inherit this precious gift. Thus, we who have the *mentales* gift need to, pardon my crudity, mate with each other to ensure far more children in the future will have this precious God-given gift. If we fail to do so, then in time other kingdoms will be able to conquer Wycombe. That, I and my friends will do our very best to avoid."

Jana also picked up on what he wasn't saying. He hoped to mate specific men and women who had specific gifts in hopes their children would inherit both of their parent's special gifts. If so, their children would become far more powerful than either parent. She didn't quite know whether or not she approved of this idea, save the idea of her children would likely be far more powerful than she and thus with the right coaching could achieve what she could not, revenge for their lost battle.

King Kyle continued. "Of course, such children would normally be considered bastards, illegitimate children, and thus likely become ostracized children. This must be avoided at all costs, since our future survival depends upon these powerful, young well-gifted children. Hence, today I hereby proclaim that from this day forward, it is highly honorable to have such children. We will call them fosterlings and make them as valuable and honorable as normal children."

A lot of hushed gasps and whispers echoed through the Great Hall. "I know, I know, this raises a serious problem with birthrights. That has been considered carefully. Sons born in wedlock will always inherit before any fosterling son might. If a family has no wedlock son, then their fosterling inherits." Kyle felt a growing sense of acceptance from the crowd. He moved on to his next point.

"Next, according to your own Archbishop's proclamation, we must bind our wives to us for all time. I know I am perhaps not saying this as eloquently as your Archbishop, but that is the basic intent, as I understand it. With our women now so utterly valuable, we cannot have them subjected to harassments once they are married. We need a foolproof way for anyone to tell a woman is legally married and thus to be honored and protected, for she is bearing our future, our children. Bishop Lloyd, I hope I am not misinterpreting this. Surely you do not mean to literally bind, to tie up our women in some manner."

Bishop Lloyd had not given this serious thought. He'd had far more serious matters, such as the possibility of Kyle taking revenge on the COG. Hastily he shook his head no. Kyle smiled and continued. "I am glad I have not misinterpreted it. We've decided to use nicely made, easily affordable, copper neck rings. Advisors Janice and Anna are wearing two of the proposed styles. Please inspect them and give us your feedback. By spring, it is my wish that all married women in Wycombe be given a neck ring so these precious women can always be easily identified and protected by us all. Oh yes, I'm told those who have the funds can have fancier ones made, perhaps with a jewel or two in them, but still basically a neck ring."

"Finally, I want everyone to know I have just received a reply from King Norwood of the Kingdom of the Angels. He is backing us here, promising to send along food supplies if we run short this winter. Come spring, his towers will train our people, and he has sent along a large number of suggestions for our future crops. We are not alone; we now have a powerful ally. Okay, that's all I have for this first meeting. Please check out the neck rings and if you have other matters we should know about, contact one of my five advisors or myself. Refreshments will now be served. Happy new year to us all."

That evening, Kyle and his gang met to discuss how the big first meeting had gone. In fact, they had done remarkably well, just as Anna had predicted. They had made just enough concessions to the COG that the new bishop fully supported them. As the COG went, so went Wycombe as a whole, for the COG wielded a great deal of influence in the city. However, no one knew this also marked the decline and fall of the COG worldwide. They were never again to have the influence they once had had.

Kyle said, "There is one thing we overlooked. There needs to be a queen on the throne. I picked up numerous thoughts of who's to be our queen among some of the women in attendance."

"He's right. While there could not be a queen during the COG's rule, they being celibate and all, the people expect there to be a queen," Anna backed him up.

"Well, I have never married and to be honest, I don't have any girl friends," Kyle admitted. "Been a soldier most of my life, but I have two suggestions."

"Do go on, old fellow," Phil teased him, curious about what Kyle would do about this oversight.

"Janice, we are good friends. I'd be honored to marry you and have you become our queen."

Janice smiled, "Well, we are good friends, Kyle. I think love is overrated anyway. As long as you still accept my advice, then I agree to your proposal. We do need a queen. I too picked up at least a dozen people wondering about that detail. I'm curious though, who is your second suggestion?"

"Jana. She is going to be a constant threat to us and her position here at our court is very tenuous. It cannot be pleasant for her to be effectively an enemy prisoner of war and hostage. We need her blood and *mentales* gift in our kingdom. I thought perhaps by marrying her, she'd become one of us, in time."

"He has a point. Her position here is not a pleasant one

at best. However, I would advise against marrying her. You might find a dagger protruding from your chest one fine morning," Becktold suggested.

"I thought as much. Still, if I could make her my Royal Consort, give her an actual position and say in our group, then she might be persuaded to assist us and not work against us."

"I can live with that," Janice replied. "We definitely need her to give us a number of children and hopefully they will have her weather control *mentales* gift. Betsy can either become her handmaiden or we can find her a suitable husband so we can add her *mentales* gifted children to our fold. I like this. Now I don't have to have Jasper remove the fine neck ring. He's got them made such that we cannot take them off, not even by accident. Good work, Jasper."

"Okay then I will speak with Jana tonight. If she is willing, we will give her the position of Royal Consort and an appropriate suite of rooms in the palace. Jasper, should she not also have some kind of binding ring?"

"True. True. I am making a pair of very fancy ones with gemstones in them. Anna deserves to have a very nice neck ring and now Janice should have an impressive one, as befitting our queen. The Royal Consort ought to have one perhaps as fancy as Anna's. What do you all think about that?" They agreed.

A short while later Kyle knocked on the door to Jana's private room. "Come in. I don't really have a choice do I?" she called out. There was a note of bitterness in her voice.

"Good evening, Princess Jana. I wanted you to know Janice and I will be married soon. We did indeed overlook the fact that we need a queen on the throne as well."

"Did you come here to ask me for congratulations?" Jana answered testily.

Kyle chuckled. "No Jana. Not at all. Your position here in Wycombe has got to be extremely rough and unpleasant for you. I am not a cruel man, just a pragmatic soldier. I really don't want to see you as a kept hostage."

"No, you want to farm me out to as many of your men as you can, right? Bear a bunch of *mentales* children for you," she replied, antagonistically.

"I came to make you the best offer I possibly can. I want you to become my Royal Consort. As such, you will have both a position in my court and a say in the governing of Wycombe, much as my close advisors do. You will be a highly respected woman in your own right and your own palace suite. As you have heard today, our children will become fosterlings. Should Janice and I not have a male child, if you and I had one, he would legally become my heir. Jana, times are changing. We must accept new ways or face extinction, just as your father was. As the Royal Consort, you will also be giving your father a great honor and strengthen the ties between our two kingdoms. Naturally, I would need to send as much aid and assistance to the Royal Consort's kingdom as possible."

Betsy and I fully expected to be raped anytime now. He's not doing that. Royal Consort? Is he really serious about this fosterling situation? If we had a son and he and Janice did not, my son would inherit the throne of Wycombe! How ironic! It would help dad and my people tremendously, if he kept his word. As Royal Consort, I suppose I could work to see he did keep his word. What about Betsy, I wonder. After a moment of reflection, she replied, though he had already heard all her private thoughts. Neither had been trained in one of the towers as yet. "You would really send help to my father? What about Betsy? Are you going to throw her to the wolves then?"

"I give you my word on the assistance to your father. Betsy can either become your handmaiden or we can both work together to find her a suitable husband, one who has the precious gift, of course."

He seems sincere. I know I'll never have a better offer. There is always the chance some good can come from this. "Okay, then I agree to become your Royal Consort. For now, Betsy can be my handmaiden, but if something better can be found for her, I want her to have it. Agreeable?"

"Yes, of course. I will have a special neck ring with a gemstone in it made up for you, second only to that of the queen's neck ring. You will see, you will soon become a much honored person in my court," Kyle promised.

Historical note: Originally, there were fifteen kingdoms of Tierra. With the breakdown of the large political units, the COG and their new Bishop-kings took control of the fifteen capital cities, because these were the largest cities in each kingdom. Beginning with Wycombe, one by one, the *mentales* gifted people slowly, one way or another, took over control of these cities. The normal human Bishop-kings were no match for the *mentales* gifted. Many quietly abdicated their thrones, though some were slain as Bishop-king Gil had.

This also marked the appearance and acceptance of the post of Royal Consort and fosterlings. Inherent in this was the beginnings of intentional breeding for enhanced *mentales*.

Chapter 8 The Fall of Hilliard Heights

At the westernmost edge of the old Kingdom of Rockton, Hilliard Heights cradled snugly against the eastern edge of the mighty Goza Mountains, some two hundred miles north of the *Círculo de la Torres* at Brom, Kingdom of the Angels. Hilliard Heights was the ancestral home of the Hilliard clan, breeders of horses for King Chester. The fortress complex of grey stonework clung to the very base of the mountain locally called Devils Peak, a rugged peak that protruded skyward like some giant finger.

The Hilliard Heights fortress was large, containing a huge stable where their prized horses were wintered. The vast estate stretched off to the east into the rugged, rolling foothills of the mountains. While heavily timbered, there were numerous valleys rich in grass where their herds grazed from spring through autumn. The fortress was also quite isolated and with the breakup of the Kingdom of Rockton, Orson Hilliard, the forty year old patriarch, saw no reason to not declare his own independence, calling his vast lands the Kingdom of Hilliard Heights.

Life was always harsh this close to the Goza. Brutally cold winters were marked by snow depths that often exceeded ten feet before the spring melt in early May. As a rule, the first heavy snowfall was expected by early September. During the warmer months, the extensive staff at Hilliard Heights worked vigilantly at laying in sufficient firewood for the coming long winter, collecting honey, hunting and preserving meat for the inhospitable months, as well as stockpiling hay for the horses. Additionally, three purchasing trips to distant towns were made, laying in many wagonloads of staples, including flower, dried fruit, and vegetables. Usually late fall, the workers made large vats of ale enough to tide them over the long winter months.

The *mentales* gifts were bestowed on Orson himself and his primary gift was that of Domination, as one might anticipate of such a ruler as he. His wife, Vana, did not receive the gift, but she made up for that with her charm and beauty.

Her long, flaming red hair was widely known throughout the land. She also had a sharp tongue and knew every inch of their extensive pantry. Vana was a superior steward and Orson had no idea how he could possibly manage Hilliard Heights without her.

They had three children, all of whom possessed the *mentales* gift. Their eldest, Peter, twenty-one, had his father's black hair and an uncanny fighting ability, aided by his special gift. The twins, Melissa and Belinda, were eighteen, as lovely as their mother was and with her flaming red hair. The twins had never cut theirs and their hair was both rich, thick, and quite long now, falling just to their thighs. Their special gift was the ability to control animals, especially horses, as you might be guessing by now. Orson always allowed his twins to break the new two year old horses that they would eventually sell to the highest bidder. Though it was unseemly for young maidens to wear pants, Orson had compromised. He allowed them to wear pants and tall men's boots, as long as they also wore the customary long plaid dresses over them, effectively hiding their pants. This worked well, for the climate at Hilliard Heights was always cold, bitterly so in the winter season. Both young women were gifted singers and played the vielle and lyre well. They provided hours of entertainment for everyone during the long winters when everyone was cooped up for months on end within the stone walls of the fortress.

Then came the huge climate shift. However, while the lands beyond the actual mountains suffered enormous changes, here this high and close to the Goza, the altered weather patterns were not so pronounced. True, the winters were somewhat longer and far colder and snow depths nearly doubled, no one cared much about the frequent rains, which often changed to sleet in the late afternoons. These were rugged people, they had to be in order to survive here all these years. The only difficulty Orson had was laying in enough food supplies that could not be obtained via trading. However, mushrooms now multiplied tenfold and became a new staple food.

By early spring of 1002 and the twins' eighteenth birthday, other physical changes occurred, though for months, none here knew that these changes were widespread across all Tierra. One morning, Melissa came wailing and running into her mother's room. "Mom! What's happened to my eyes?" Belinda was right behind her, sobbing as well.

"Oh dear god! What's happened to your eyes?" exclaimed a usually unruffled Vana. Both twins' eyes had turned yellow with a few brown speckles. Hastily, Vana looked in her mirror. Hers were their usual hazel color. "Come on, let's check the others. What the devil is happening around here? Eyes don't change colors this drastically."

"Mom! We look like freaks now. No one has yellow eyes, no one," Belinda wailed, but followed her mother and sister.

They found Orson going over his books. He looked up at the three women, but before he could react, Vana screeched, "Orson! Not you too!"

"What?"

"Your eyes — they've turned yellow! Look at our twins. Oh Orson, have you gotten some kind of plague? Are you all feeling ill? I must send for Doctor Runthal at once." Vana dashed out of the study, calling out his name as she rushed down the hallway.

"Oh dear, your eyes really are quite yellow, aren't they? Bit of brown speckles here and there," Orson said, growing slightly alarmed.

"Dad, we're freaks now! What's happening to us?" Melissa demanded to know.

"I don't know. Let me look at them. Are mine as yellow as yours?"

"Yes, dad, just as Belinda's. Are you sick? I kind of feel sick at my stomach," Melissa asked.

"No, I feel perfectly fine. I suspect it is just nerves, dear child. I seem to be seeing everything just fine. How about you two?"

"We are seeing okay. I can't tell any difference," Belinda answered.

"There, see, there is nothing to be really alarmed about."

"But dad! No one has yellow eyes. We are freaks now. We'll never find boyfriends, not looking like this," Melissa complained bitterly.

"Oh I highly doubt that. Come on, let's see what the COG doctor has to say. Melissa, go fetch Peter. He's out checking on the stables." Glad to have something to do, she dashed off, her boots slapping on the stone floor. Meanwhile, Orson put his arm around Belinda and ushered her down the hallway, following Vana's distant voice.

A half hour later, Doctor Runthal finished examining the household. Peter also now had the same yellow eyes as did three other hired men who also had the *mentales* gift. Easton and Samuel were masters at creating very believable illusions, while Bert could start fires. All three were on Orson's staff, valued men pledged to help defend Hilliard Heights and well paid for their services.

"Well, if I were to venture an opinion," the COG doctor finally gave his diagnosis, "I would say only those who have the *mentales* gift have yellow eyes. Perhaps it is nature's way of allowing us to identify easily who has been given this precious gift. I can find nothing wrong with anyone's vision. Ho wever, I suggest we all keep a close eye on things. There may be more changes in store for you."

"But I want my hazel eyes back! Change them back this instant!" Melissa demanded. "I don't want to look like some freak."

Doctor Runthal chuckled. "My dear Melissa, if I could do that, why I would be a god or something. No, I am afraid there is nothing at all that I can do about the color of your eyes. Look, you cannot see your own eyes, so what's all the fuss about?" *Women! I'll never understand them!*

Melissa and Belinda picked up his unspoken thought and stormed out of the room in a huff. "Women, I will never understand them," Orson complained, echoing Doctor Runthal's unspoken comment as well. Vana smiled, she sympathized with her daughters, but was powerless to do anything about it.

The surprise eye color changes caused everyone to pay far more attention to their bodies during the ensuing days. The women began to feel discomfort in their breasts. This time, all the women around Hilliard Heights were affected. Poor Doctor

Runthal was run ragged, as day after day he was forced to examine twenty women's breasts, sometimes twice a day.

"I am not imagining it, Doctor Runthal. Something is happening to them. I can feel it. They seem to be swelling, as if I was pregnant, but obviously I am not," Vana complained. "Look, can't you see that they are enlarging? So are my twins and every other woman in the fortress. What is the matter with us? Have we all contracted some strange disease? You are supposed to know these things. Why else are we paying your keep and salary if you are not able to handle our illnesses?"

He flushed red. "My Lady. I can see they are becoming larger, yes, but as to why, I am not a mind reader. They seem perfectly healthy. You have not those bumps or growths that I have seen on women who have contracted the rotting disease. Perhaps it is something in what we are eating."

"If that were so, why are only we women being affected and not a single man? Tell me that?" Vana asked rather annoyed with the brown skinned man.

"Okay. Let's see if we can find this out, shall we? We will study what everyone has been eating and drinking and see if there has been something unique to the women around Hilliard Heights." That appeased Vana for a time. For days, they made lists and cross checked. However, it soon became clear there was nothing exclusive to the women. So worried were the women, that the men also began checking themselves, just to be sure they were not being impacted as well. None were, only the women.

As May 1002 rolled around, bringing the great spring thaw with it, the women's breasts were very noticeably larger, so much so, that they began altering their dresses and blouses to accommodate their larger bosoms. Accompanied by the sounds of rushing, gushing water sluicing down the side of the mountain and off the outer stonework the women patiently did their needlework on dress after dress and blouse after blouse.

The twins were now solemn-faced about it. Days ago, they ceased complaining and demanding cures. Nothing worked and at last, they took some comfort in the simple fact that all the women in Hilliard Heights were having the same problem. In fact, Vana had only today insisted all the women temporarily move into the manor house with her. Company in misery, she'd explained to Orson, who had agreed. Daily, the twenty women sat in the large Great Hall, stoically altering their clothing. Fear predominated and the twins were bombarded with the terrified thoughts of the other eighteen women, ranging in ages from fourteen through forty. Two much older midwives, far beyond childbearing ages, were the only women unaffected.

I can't take this any longer. We have to do something. If I hear about another horror story, I simply am going to go mad! Melissa sent to her sister.

Me too. They are not saying anything aloud, but their thoughts are horrid. Come on; let's play some music. Perhaps one will be kind enough to alter ours for us if we can distract them, Belinda replied mentally. She added, *I wish there was some way to block all their thoughts. I am so tired of hearing them.*

Well, another few weeks and we can go riding again and then have peace and quiet, sis. The two picked up their vielle and lyre and began playing and singing ancient mountain songs. As anticipated, this brought the women some relief and the twins some mental quiet. A couple of the women graciously worked on their current dresses for them.

As the days in May passed, the women's breasts continued to swell and enlarge. All noticed they were now drinking a far more liquids than normal and their appetites were almost voracious. Well, such was the attitude of the younger women who were still fretting over their thin waists. The older women no longer worried about such trivial matters. Linda thought to herself, *Just wait until they have had a couple of babies, and then they won't be worried about it any longer.* She had no idea Melissa and Belinda heard her thought, however.

As June came bringing better, warmer weather, at least for Hilliard Heights, the women's breasts finally ceased growing. Uniformly, their breasts were now at least as large as their heads, positively huge. The women were at least thankful they no longer had to work daily on altering their clothing, which now looked like a patchwork quilt. All promised to begin making whole new dresses and blouses made to fit their current sizes. Vana was the first to recognize what was happening, though she did not know the effect was universal in scope. "My goodness, I think I know why they have become so large. Food is getting scarce. If I have another baby, with these knockers, why, I am sure to have an awful lot of milk for the child. Maybe this is Nature's answer to the food shortage, thereby ensuring our babies survive these times."

"Well, my baby will be drowning in milk if it keeps up this way," Louise giggled. She was due in near the end of the summer. The twins didn't find this at all funny. Besides, this was keeping them from their usual duties this time of year. They ought to be helping the men get the corral cleared of horses and herded out into the grasses of the foothills. Usually, they would head out for a couple of days, spending nights at one of the dozen line shacks, temporary emergency shelters scattered around the foothills. Because of the situation, Orson forbad them to leave. The twins grew more and more agitated with each passing day. Knowing this same phenomenon was occurring to every woman on Tierra at roughly the same time would not have lessened their agitation.

One afternoon in mid-June, Captain William came galloping into the fortress. "Invading army! Invading army!" he yelled. After a flying dismount, he raced for the large gong and began pounding it madly. This was the universal sound signaling a dire emergency was at hand, usually a forest fire that had to be fought. Over fifty people came dashing out of the various doors.

Orson came out on the high veranda overlooking the cobblestone entrance way. He yelled down, "What's this? An invading army? Who? What? Where? How many? Captain, here at once!" His bass voice was almost that of Dominate or Command. His captain raced inside and up the steps, quite out of breath. Peter and the twins beat him to their father though.

"My Lord. A hundred men, some on horseback, but most are riding reindeer with a few a pulling wagons. They are heading this way from the north path. All are fighters, armed with bows and swords. From their leather armor, I suspect they are from somewhere in Haruk, possibly Bafra. Henry was in their path, leading a string of horses out to the foothills. I saw them cut him down without any warning. They left him where he fell, but took his horse. The string galloped off, so we've not lost those horses yet. I thought they might head off after the string, but they didn't. They are on a direct line to us."

Orson yelled down to one of his men, "Sound the attack signal. Get everyone inside and bar the gates with everything we have. Captain, breakout all the weapons from the armory. Position the men as you see fit. Summon all the *mentales* to me. We'll make a stand from up here where we can see down over the outer ramparts. Hilliard Heights can withstand any siege, but we must be prepared. Women, get water boiling and bandages ready, and then get water pails ready to douse fires. Hustle, hustle everyone!"

Everyone scampered, especially after the gong sounded the attack signal. From their high veranda, the twins saw the men dashing about below, scurrying to grab weapons. Captain William dashed about like a mother hen, positioning the men in proper defensive positions. Shortly, Easton, Samuel, and Bert came onto the veranda, joining Orson, Peter, and the twins. "Good, everyone is here. Bert, you shoot fire where it will do the most good. I leave that up to you. Easton, Samuel, make illusions as you have never made them before. Make it seem we have hundreds of men defending the walls. Add in anything else you can think of. Twins, your task is to help identify any *mentales* folk the enemy may be using against us. As you locate them, point them out to me and I will smash them utterly."

"Dad, my skills are best suited down there manning the walls with the captain. I can do little from up here," Peter insisted.

I know that well enough, damn it, Peter, but I want to keep you safe. You are my heir.

Yes, but if we don't repel these invaders from the north, there will be nothing for me to inherit.

Damn it son, I know that! All right. Join William, but be damn careful!

The twins overheard the two and both gave their brother a brief hug as he smiled and turned to leave. He'd won this round.

Vana appeared, "Dear, we have the healing supplies ready. Doctor Runthal has got the Great Hall ready to tend the wounded. I've got the women ready to help with the fires and the wounded. Where do you want me to stand?"

"You best take charge of the women, but be careful, Vana. I will have my hands full up here. I will leave firefighting in your capable hands." She gave him a hug and kiss, and then gave her daughters one as well, before leaving and heading down the stairs, where her group of women were gathered. The twins sensed the overall nervousness of the group. A bit of fear was hard to ignore. At least once a year, Orson had drilled everyone for this very day. However, since the breakup of the kingdoms, he'd done it twice a year. Nevertheless, for everyone here, this would be their first real combat situation and none knew what to expect, least of all the twins.

As they waited, Orson turned to his twins. "Daughters, if the gates below should fall, I want you to promise me that you both will dash to our secret escape tunnel and flee for safety. I trust you can summon up some horses and get away. Head south, ahead of these men and alert others. Perhaps you will be able to bring aid to relieve us."

"But dad that will mean Hilliard Heights will fall. You and Peter and mom will be killed," Melissa exclaimed, suddenly reading her father's unspoken thoughts.

"Dears, if they breech our walls and take Hilliard Heights, they will rape you and hold you as slaves. I love you both too much ever to allow that to happen. I will fight to my last breath to give you both time to escape these renegades. Promise me you will do as I say. Promise me. I will hold you to that."

He used his Command *mentales* on them and they agreed to do as he asked, though both were protesting. They had no choice but to agree, but it didn't mean when the time came, they would obey. Now they waited. That was the hard part, waiting for the unknown. Thunderheads coalesced overhead and the afternoon rains came. The twins went inside, got on their heavy cloaks, and brought their father's to him. Below, they saw their mother and the other women doing the same thing for the other men. They waved at Peter, as Vana handed him his warm oilskin cloak. At least they would stay somewhat dry and warm while they waited.

As bits of ice pelted their faces, late afternoon, they spotted the large army coming their way. Battle would be joined within the hour. Nerves began to fray.

The Karli Clan dwelt at the southern edge of Bafra, the western coastal town of the old Kingdom of Haruk. They made their living as fishermen during the short summer. During the long ice-filled winter, they trained reindeer either to a saddle or to pull sleighs, making a tidy profit. When the witch hunts began, they ignored the whole affair. Later, when the old kingdom broke up and the COG gained control over the other port city and capital, Kozan, on the far eastern edge of Haruk, again they ignored the events. It had nothing to do with them or their business.

However, the arrival of the *mentales* gifts did affect the clan. Four of them received the gift. All claimed God had blessed them. For a month, a clan power struggle ensued, before Uncle Kertme Karli effectively used his Dominate skills to assume the clan leadership over the hundred plus Karli's. He kept his cousins, Tepe and Azay as his right-hand men. Tepe's gift was a telekinetic Push, while Azay's gift was the ability to Crush other *mentales* minds. When used against non-*mentales* minds, the victims either went into a temporary coma or simply died outright. Finally, he kept his widowed sister, Tepecika, at his side, for she had the gift of Healing. Besides, she was an excellent cook.

When the weather turned bad, things changed drastically. The summer melt never occurred, eliminating all the huge fishing industry, though some attempted ice fishing. Soon, the ice became so thick they were unable to punch a hole through it. Still, the clan had their reindeer business, more profitable anyway. However, as the bitter cold persisted, even the reindeer began to migrate southward. At last, Kertme gave the order to abandon their homes and head south as well. He had no choice. To stay here meant certain death by starvation or by freezing from the bitter cold.

141

Worse, as they headed south, food became a constant problem. There simply was not enough game in the ice lands Haruk had become. Twice, they had been attacked by other bands from Haruk and had managed to repel them primarily by use of their *mentales* gifts.

Tepecika advised, "Kertme, we need to be on the lookout for more *mentales* people. We should capture them and force them to help us or die. Think how powerful we can be if we could get ourselves a dozen more like Tepe and Azay. None could stand in our path. We could have all the food we desire. Perhaps we can even capture one of those fortresses we've heard about down in Rockton. We could hold up there and have a good life, don't you think?"

"Aye, Tepecika, you have a point. We need more *mentales* people. Somehow, we will get them, but there is a fatal flaw in your plan, sister. How can we prevent them from using their *mentales* on us once we have captured them? Eh? Answer me that one?"

Tepecika glowered and replied, "That one requires an ale. Give me one and I will give you an answer." Ale was being hoarded now, for supplies were low.

She's got the right idea. We need to capture mentales people, but how to prevent them from attacking us after we capture them — that's the real problem. Okay, I'll give her the ale. "Woman, you darn well better come up with an answer or you'll not get any ale rations until we find more ale somewhere." He knew she had a passion for ale and could drink almost any man under the table. He'd seen her do just that. Kertme measured out the cup and handed it to her.

"Thank you brother. I will give you your answer soon." She sipped her ale, nurturing the brew for as long as she could. Tepecika was addicted to the stuff, and their low supply of ale was annoying her no end. She felt its warmth entering her body and relished it.

At last, Kertme's patience wore thin. "Okay woman, out with it. How do we keep the captured *mentales* from attacking us until they submit to our will and rule?"

She belched a good one. "Okay, okay, don't get testy with me. We've got a lot of copper with us. We make a copper helmet in two halves that goes over the person's head, leaving an opening for their nose and mouth only. We braze the halves together around their necks so the helmet cannot be removed easily, not without undoing the brazing. Likewise, we make hand cups. Stick their hands balled up into a fist into the cup and braze the halves together around their wrists. They cannot then be undone. They will be helpless and yet mobile and can be fed, but they cannot harm us. When their wills are broken, we can then remove the copper and use their skills for our clan. Clever eh?" She belched once more and added, "I think that idea deserves another ale."

"Hum, I like it, Tepecika, I really do. No more ale. If this plan of yours works, then I will give you all the ale you can drink."

"I'll hold you to it, Kertme, I surely will. Want me to get with our coppersmith and see about making some?"

"Yes, do it. Make say six sets. That ought to be enough for a good test. I wonder how long it will take to break their spirits so they will join us willingly?"

"Not too long, I reckon. Blinded and crippled, they will be and feel completely helpless and at our complete mercy for everything, even peeing, Kertme." She roared with laughter. "Hey, do you know your eyes are now yellow?"

"What? Say, yours are yellow too." Quickly the four discovered their eyes had turned yellow with brown spots, while the eyes of those in their clan who did not have the gift remained unchanged.

Shortly after that, Tepecika and the forty other women in the clan band began experiencing the same breast development all the other women on Tierra were undergoing. By June, their breasts were uniformly as large as their heads or slightly bigger. Often they jested they would have enough milk to feed the entire clan. Still in spite of putting up a good front, the women worried about their overdeveloped bosoms. Compounding the problem was the simple fact they were out of doors and on the move, continually setting up a crude camp each late afternoon, chopping pine for firewood. They were all bundled up heavily to protect themselves from the cold. Few had time to alter and sew their clothing.

Later that evening, Kertme lay down beside his sister beneath their wagon. They had covered the ground with several reindeer hides and lowered the reindeer hides affixed to the sides of the wagon to protect them from the rain, cold, and sometimes snow that came in the night. Tepecika finally whispered to him, safe from his eyes in the darkness, "I think our breasts have finally stopped growing, but they are so huge now."

"God, that is good news. Honestly, I think our midwives speak truth. With food so scarce, when babies come, you should have plenty of milk, and we will lose no more children. Perhaps it is Nature caring yet for us." She accepted his wisdom.

"Well, there's the fortress our scouts spotted yesterday afternoon. What do you think? Good place for us to settle down?" Kertme asked his two cousins.

"Yah, we've seen plenty of game, and horses too. Fine place, not too hot either. I like that. I was half afraid you'd be leading us into a desert or something," Tepe replied. Azay chuckled. He'd had no such thoughts, but this fortress built at the base of the towering mountain looked like heaven to him. Snows still covered its tall peak and some of the higher valleys behind it.

"I sense the presence of seven *mentales*," Tepecika announced. "Use caution."

"Okay, arrange the wagons here, far from the battle. We'll form up in two parallel lines and advance to the walls. I see several standing watch from that high position, a balcony or something like that. Good vantage point, that's where I'd place my strongest defenders. Sister, keep an eye on them; see if they are the *mentales*. Our biggest barrier will be getting through those heavy gates," Kertme took charge.

"God, maybe we are out matched, Kertme. Look at the number of men manning the battlements and gates! We're outnumbered three to one," Azay pointed out.

"If they have that many men inside, think of the food and ale that must also be inside, just waiting for us!" Kertme shouted encouragement to his men as they began scrambling to form up lines as ordered.

We won't be effective until we get to around fifty yards from the walls. I can get off two of my devastating Push attacks, Tepe sent his clan leader.

"Right, fifty yards. Use arrows to pick off the men on the walls near the gates while we get in range. Give us cover men. Azay will get the gates open for us," Kertme yelled. *Tepecika, stay alert for their mentales.*

Oh, I thought I would just take a nap, she sent testily. *Men, they are all fools.*

I heard that, sister. Now is not the time. This is serious business!

Tepecika scowled. She continued to issue her own orders to the many women, who were arranging the wagons and reindeer some four hundred yards from the walls. The stone path that led up to the fortress was steep, winding along the grey base of the tall peak. A great pine covered ravine fell off sharply to the south or left of the path. She maneuvered their wagons down into the protection of the timber. Here their precious reindeer would be safe from errant arrows and the battle. Although some distance from the walls far above her, she had a good view. Now she began to probe for *mentales* minds, hoping to gain some idea of where the persons were physically located.

She watched the men of her clan moving into positions, two lines, two waves, approaching within bow shot range of the walls. They were focusing on the section with the main gates. *Funny, I don't see the hundreds of men I saw before. Hey, Kertme, where did the hundreds lining the walls go? I can't see them from way down here. I have the reindeer and wagons secured. The women are ready for healing work. Don't go getting yourself killed now; you've promised me a barrel of ale.* She exaggerated the bargain slightly, but right now, she'd give anything for a good mug of stout.

Are you blind sister? They are all right there along the top of the walls. Must be hundreds of archers! We are about to be bombarded.

I don't see but a handful of men. Some crossbows and some with short bows. Most are closer to the barbicans over the main gates.

What is going on? He strained his eyes. He felt a little energy tingle in his mind. He rubbed his eyes with his hands and looked again. Some of the supposed archers looked awfully thin. "Men! It's an illusion! There are only a handful of archers and most are over the gates. Ignore the illusions!"

Lightning streaked across the skies, with some striking the distant top of the peak. Thunder rolled and echoed down the valley; the skies darkened and the rains came. Even the wagons vibrated. Small stones shook loose and rattled on down the ravine in which the women were huddled. They wrapped their oil-skinned cloaks about them and watched their brave men launch their assault. Most were thinking ahead to the warm fires and feasting that lay just ahead of them, just beyond those impressive grey stone walls.

"Aim for those in the front lines. Steady men. Now!" Captain Williams barked his orders. Twenty arrows rained down upon the front line of the northern invaders approaching the main gates of Hilliard Heights.

Peter had his sword drawn and was watching the approaching men closely, identifying their leaders. Those would be the key men he needed somehow to take out. He focused his *mentales* gifts. Slowly through the thunder and lightning, the enemy's plan of attack came to him. They would be breeching the main gates with *mentales* power.

"Captain, give me half the men to go below. They will be breeching the gates with their powers. I'll hold them off, while you keep their ranks from joining them," Peter yelled, dashing down the stone steps to take up his position before the heavily barred main gates. At first glance, it seemed impossible mere men could somehow bust through those heavy timbered doors; the two cross bars were a foot thick, heavy and solid. Still, he trusted his *mentales* sense.

"Damn, my men are still wasting arrows on the illusionary archers," Kertme bellowed. *No use yelling at them; they can't see they aren't real. Okay, I've got to take the illusion creators out myself.* He focused and his mind contacted the two minds who were holding the impressive illusions in place. He sensed male minds and acted accordingly.

Easton and Samuel were totally focused; their illusions were working. Sweat poured down their faces, mixed liberally with the rain pelting them, though neither even was aware of the heavy, cold rain. All their attention was focused far below them, maintaining believable images of archers upon the walls. At first, their illusions were working well, drawing off many arrows from the invaders, arrows falling harmlessly inside the fortress, clanking and sliding across the cobblestones. Now, fewer arrows were being wasted on their illusionary men, though still they were drawing fire away from their own men.

Suddenly, both men heard a loud, sneering, condemning voice appearing in their minds. *Your pathetic attempts to confuse us are failing miserably. You are not worthy of your gifts. Never have I ever seen such pathetic and simpleton attempts at illusions. You must be about the dumbest excuses for mentales men anywhere on Tierra. Even your Lord is a hundred times more powerful than you are with your ridiculous attempts to confuse us. You must be a complete moron, an idiot; what a pathetic excuse for a man you are. You would do better to go down and shoot an arrow with the real men — the brave, heroic men than stand there and toss off your laughable excuses for illusions.*

Unexpected and unprotected as their minds were, the loud words blasted into their minds. The grain of truth, that their illusions were no longer as effective as they had been, allowed the first part of agreement with the voice to happen. Once they agreed they were not being effective, the rest of the attack slammed home. Both men stood there reeling, dazed, and unable to do anything. Their illusions faded instantly.

Kertme took advantage of his small telepathic victory. To his second line of archers, he called out, "There, those two men there on the balcony. Send a hail at them." Some twenty arrows went flying upwards through the downpour, while Kertme wiped the rain and sweat from his own face. This was exhausting work. Destroying the two men's egos, at least temporarily, had cost him over half of his available energies. He was breathing hard, and took a moment to flood calm back through his body. Thud! Pain! That momentarily lack of concentration on the overall battle had cost him. An arrow sunk into his left thigh. "Damn!" He took a firm hold of the arrow with his right hand, grit his teeth, and slowly pulled it out. Blood flowed freely down his rain soaked pants. *Good, bleeding freely. Best thing for it right now.* He put his full attention back into the battle at hand. *Good, Azay is at the gates now. It won't be long now.*

"Dad, look out, arrows!" Melissa barked out her warning. She, Belinda, and Orson ducked for cover, but five arrows found their marks on the two stunned and reeling young men. Easton and Samuel went down.

"Move them back inside!" Orson barked, as he stuck his head up to see what was happening now. The first line was now at the gates. Melissa and Belinda rushed to the two wounded men and dragged them by their feet across the balcony and into the study. Vana and several women came rushing in, answering Orson's telepathic summons. Vana motioned for her twins to get back to their father, while she and her companions took over.

Shock and terror crept into Melissa and Belinda's minds. They'd never seen men being wounded before. The arrows protruding from Easton and Samuel looked horrible and quite frightening. Neither man was conscious, and they didn't know if they were dead or not. Shaking visibly, they rejoined Orson, who now had worked out who the enemy *mentales* were. He sensed too his daughter's fear, for they were broadcasting it wildly. "Take deep breaths. Calm down. The gates will hold; they cannot scale the walls. We can hold out here indefinitely. Bert, flame that man standing before the gates there. He looks like he is about to do something to the gates."

Somehow, his words comforted the twins, and they relaxed and stopped thinking wildly disastrous thoughts. Meanwhile Orson acted. He focused and reached the mind of Kertme, who had somehow attacked his two men, and he sensed the man's painful throbbing leg. *You cannot win. Hilliard Heights has never been taken in its long history. The gates cannot be breached. The walls are unscalable. We can hold out for years. We have food and water aplenty. Face the stark reality, the truth; you have already lost the battle! Surrender and I will spare your life.* Orson tried to Dominate the opposing leader by invading his mind.

We are losing. My men are down already. We cannot scale those walls; we have not rope and grappling hooks. They are too tall. Self-defeating thoughts echoed in Kertme's mind, finding points of agreement with Orson's dominating words. Kertme felt his own will to continue the battle rapidly flowing away, like the rain waters sluicing down the steep stone path from the gates. All was lost. Pain! Another arrow thudded into his chest. *Pain, all is lost!*

At this same moment, Azay, shielded from arrows by his fellow men, focused his mind onto the thick wooden gates proper. In his mind, he saw the small vibrating particles that composed the heavy pine, though he had no name for them, only that they were vibrating and formed the essence of the wood. Using his gift, he began exciting the particles further. Faster and faster. Farther and farther apart the tiny particles flew. This he enjoyed doing. He had no idea why he so liked to see these tiny particles vibrating so wildly, it just appealed to him. More. More, he poured his own mental energies into the particles. Suddenly a four foot section of the thick, heavy gates exploded inward, as if some giant blast had disintegrated the very wood itself.

Inside, ten defending men were hit by the exploding bits of timber; all were wounded or killed outright. Peter, standing back from the gates, recovered his stunned senses first. "We're breeched! To the gates!" He screamed his orders and launched himself into the battle. At that same instant, Azay's heavy clothing burst into flames, sending the man screaming and running wildly back down the roadway. Eventually, he slipped on the treacherously slippery stone and fell into the ravine.

Although taken aback, the men followed Tepe's last order and charged in through the breech. Peter's blade came down hard on the exposed neck of the first of the many coming through. His body dropped like a rock. Still standing back a bit, Tepe acted rapidly. He focused and his blast of mental energies acted as if they were some kind of giant wind or hand, pushing Peter and five others running to help man the breeched gates, slamming them back some ten feet, landing all in a heap on the ground.

"Charge them!" Tepe yelled, though he need not have. A dozen men from the second line raced up and squeezed through the four foot hole in the gates. Peter leapt to his feet and took on four of them at one time. His combat *mentales* kicked into high gear. He sensed where each would strike and thus parried and dodged effectively, but took the opportunity to strike with deadly accuracy. Quickly, two went down with nasty gashes across their sword arms, their weapons clanking onto the rain slick cobblestones. More and more men poured through the breech. Now the remaining defenders, who were above the gates, arrived to help repel the attackers, giving Peter some much needed support.

"Damn! Damn! How is this possible?" screamed Orson. "I've got to get down there now!" He drew his sword and turned to his twins. "Melissa, Belinda, we are breeched and overwhelmed. I order you to flee now. Use the secret escape tunnel. Go get help before it is too late. That is an order! Move!" He used his Dominate voice on the two stunned, shocked teens. He saw their bodies turn and start to run into the study, and he followed them, but not before ordering Bert to flame some of the others rushing to get through the breeched gates.

All dashed down the hallway and down the steps. After making sure that the twins continued down into the cellars where the secret door was located, he raced on past the women who were tending to many wounded men and on out to the fierce battle at the main gates, a battle that Peter, despite his superior combat skills and senses, was losing. There were just too many invaders left. He threw himself into the thick of the battle, felling the first man he met.

Peter finally fought his way through the men to Tepe, the most dangerous foe currently in the battle. The two exchanged blows, their swords clashing, their bodies spraying drenching water in all directions. The cobblestones were slippery with blood and rain. Ice pellets struck all the men now, as the cold rain drew even more threatening. Tepe and Peter both slipped and their sword thrusts went awry, but managed to cut deeply into each other. Nearby, Orson slipped as well, and one of the four opponents he was battling found his mark, slicing a terrible gash across the man's chest. Blood poured down his tunic, mingled with the rainwaters, and ran diluted across the hard, unforgiving stone. At once, three men jumped on the fallen man, who still managed to stab one in his heart as he tried to hack at Orson. A great peal of thunder echoed in Orson's ears, then cold blackness. His body moved no more. All his hopes and dreams faded into nothingness.

Reeling, shocked, terrified, the two twins raced into the cellar and to the secret door behind a moth-eaten tapestry near the ale barrels. Only then did their father's Command over them wear off. Shaking, Melissa whispered, "What about mom? Peter? Dad? We can't we just leave them! Where will we go?"

"Dunno, but dad ordered us to flee. He will be plenty mad at us if we don't! He's almost never used his Command Voice on us, Melissa. We best hurry us. Light a lantern and I'll open it." Melissa reluctantly obeyed and regretted having not cleaned the accumulated lamp black off the glass. Such a silly thing to be so worried about just now, she thought to herself.

The dim lantern provided only poor lighting inside the cool, dark tunnel. They heard scampering sounds in the darkness ahead of them. Neither dared comment upon it. A few cobwebs latched onto the hoods of their heavy cloaks, but Orson had always been conscientious about keeping the secret escape tunnel in good order. Melissa said a private thank you to her father for that as she walked slowly along, her left hand holding the lantern and her right feeling along the stone wall for security.

As children, they had been down this tunnel several times, but then it had always been fun and exciting. Now they were fleeing for their lives. Belinda whispered, "Good thing we are wearing our pants and tall boots under our dresses. We won't freeze with them and our cloaks on, but we've no food. Melissa, maybe we should go back and get some to take with us."

"I, I don't think we should. I have a horrible feeling that — that dad is dead. I don't know how I know it, but I feel it."

"Me too. Maybe we should have brought mom with us," Belinda whispered forlornly, barely able to hold back her grief. She too had the same sense of foreboding. She could no longer sense her dad's mind and morbid ideas flooded her mind, releasing her tears. Melissa sobbed too, breaking down just when her sister had. Together, they walked on down the dark tunnel, which seemed to echo their mood, utter despair.

The exit point was deep in the steep and pine covered ravine, some four hundred yards from the walls. Unknown to the twins, their exit was not too far from where Tepecika had strategically placed their many wagons and reindeer for safety, far from arrow shots. Already, some of the women were bringing their wounded men down from the battle close to the walls for treatment. However, she heard a strange scuffing noise and wisely paid attention to it. It was coming from about a hundred feet further into the ravine. She focused her mind and sensed the presence of two *mentales* gifted women moving somewhat towards her.

She sent, *You three. Come with me. Be silent and grab something for a club. Someone is trying to sneak out of the fortress. Follow me, but be quiet!* Three startled women looked up and over at Tepecika, rather spooked. They knew it had to be her, but even now, they disliked having their leader's sister's thoughts somehow appearing in their heads. It wasn't natural they often claimed. Fortunately, Tepecika didn't do it to them frequently, just enough to garner their respect.

Holding stout fire logs, the four crept on into the ravine, trying hard to avoid slipping on the treacherous, rain-soaked, stony ground, holding onto bits of pine trees to keep from sliding down. They spotted a grated gate. Using hand signals, Tepecika positioned her three companions and they waited silently.

The two grief stricken teens finally stumbled to the exit grate. Outside, they could see bits of sleet in the heavy downpour. "Come on, we'll just slide our way on down the ravine, Melissa," Belinda whispered. "Careful, we don't want to fall and break a leg. We best be quiet too." Cautiously, she opened the gate and stepped out of the tunnel. Melissa was right behind her. Just then, Tepecika swung her log. Belinda saw the woman's arm and log, but was too late to avoid being struck. Pain rushed into her head and mind, and then all went dark. Her body slipped to the ground. Behind her, Melissa tried to avoid the four women, but was dropped with a solid blow to her head.

Tepecika bent over the two and raised a closed eyelid. "Yellow. Good. We've captured two *mentales*. Let's get them to the wagons, but easy does it. It is damnably slippery here." After a good deal of struggling, the four got the two teens to Tepecika's wagon. "Go find Copperman. We need his services here pronto before these two wake up. Go on, woman! You there, get a fire going. We will need lots of hot water and heat for Copperman too."

"Tepecika, come, it's Kertme! They've brought him from the battlefield," a woman called out, sending a pang of fear into her bosom. Slipping and sliding on the rough rocky ground, she headed to her brother. She saw two wounds. Automatically, she dismissed the leg wound, focusing her attention on the broken shaft of an arrow protruding from his chest. *Damn. Fool.* She sighed and began to focus, wishing all the while she had some ale to calm her nerves. He was still alive, that was a good sign. Blood oozed from his lips, not a good sign. For a moment, she studied the situation. Should she or should she not pull the arrow out? *Well he can't live with it stuck in him like that.* She pulled it out as gently as she could, though it took all her strength to manage it so tightly was it wedged between rib bones. Blood oozed out in pulsing puddles. *Damn.*

As she looked him over, it quickly became apparent to her that she would have to use her ultimate gift just to save his life, though it would cost her. Just then, Copperman walked up. "You sent for me?"

"Oh, yes. We captured two *mentales* gifted women. Go to work and do your thing. Do their hands first, in case they wake up before you get fully done. We don't want them attacking us with *mentales* now do we? I've got to work on Kertme; he's in a bad way."

The tall, thin man, scarred from many burns from his coppersmithing, grinned, baring two missing front teeth. "You got it." He headed on down to her wagon where a woman had a small campfire going with a pot of water over it.

"God I need an ale! Oh well. To the business," she complained. Closing her eyes, she focused her mental energies and then opened her eyes. Before her, she could now see Kertme clearly. Using her gift, she began to peer into his body, below the outer skin, concentrating on the area of the wound. The tip had nicked his heart, the source of the pulsing flow. One cell at a time, she commanded the healing to begin. She moved a particle from one location to the breech and while holding it in place, she moved another. Sweat poured from her head as she worked, oblivious to the pounding rain and sleet. After what seemed an eternity to her, the small hole was plugged and healing.

Now she eased back outwards slightly to his left lung into which blood was steadily seeping. Again, she began to move a particle here and there, using them to plug the much larger gap. How long it took, she could not have said. After an eternity, she had the lung puncture wound healing. Blood no longer entered it.

Tepecika sat back utterly exhausted, drained of all her energies and then some. As expected, her body had burned up an enormous amount of energy, funneling it through her nerve channels to her mind, which had converted it in this case into healing actions. That was the liability of using nearly all her *mentales* energies: she was ravishingly hungry and totally exhausted.

As she pulled back from Kertme, her voice sounded distant, somehow disconnected from herself. *Is this really my own voice speaking?* "Someone bind his leg wound." She slumped into a deep sleep. The women folk were used to their *mentales* gifted personnel passing out like this, especially so after they'd worked some incredible miracles. Indeed, the women who brought Kertme to her had written him off as dead. In fact, some had even begun to spread word of his demise. Kind hands lifted her up, put her into a wagon, and covered her with several reindeer blankets. Others tended to their leader's leg wound, commenting upon the miracle they'd just witnessed. Tepecika had somehow saved him from certain death.

Melissa came too at last, her head aching from the woman's log strike. She was sitting with her back against a wagon. The smell of burning pine filled the air. She raised her hands mechanically to rub her sore head and got the shock of her life. Her hands, balled into fists, were entirely encased in round copper bowl-like cups that were fastened around her wrists. She could wiggle her fingers slightly, but no more. Her wrists felt slightly burned and she noticed the copper had been fused or forged forming a seam that could not be undone. She let out a startled shriek, which roused her sister, who was also sitting beside her.

"Keep quiet and you will not be hurt. Try anything and we'll knock you out again," a tall thin man said. He was ugly. Melissa could not keep from being revolted by his appearance. He only grinned, adding to her discomfort, showing his missing teeth. He came towards her holding another large copper device. "I am going to put this over your head. Don't move or resist or I will just knock you out again."

The twins had their really long hair tied up in a bun around their heads, which was fortunate. He slipped the copper helmet over her head. When he shut the two halves, she was totally in the dark. She could breathe through a nose hole and there was an opening for her mouth, but the rest of her head was entirely inside the copper helmet. She felt heat rising at the back of her neck. "It's burning me!" she wailed. She could barely hear her own voice.

"Nah, just a little heat, only copper. See, I got plenty little burns. Nothing major from copper. Now steel, that's a whole 'nother story!" Copperman said. She heard him only faintly. "There, you are finished up." A bit later, she heard Belinda's wail and knew her sister's neck was being burned as hers was. She could only guess he was forging the joints together so the helmets could not be removed either. Encased in total darkness, Melissa finally broke down entirely. All the pain, suffering, loss, death, and destruction overwhelmed her and she cried and cried, banging her copper-encased hands against her copper-encased head. Nearby, she faintly heard Belinda also crying, though the sounds were quite muted. At least, she had on her clothes and warm cloak, which kept her warm as the icy rain continued to fall on them.

Chapter 9 The Plight of the Hilliard Twins

Tepecika roused, her stomach ached, ravishingly hungry, as if she had not eaten for days. It was dark and snowing lightly now. Torches illuminated the wagons and many bonfires were blazing. With an effort she rose and stretched, weakly. *I used more mentales energy than I ought to have used this time. Damn. Food. I need food now!*

"Over here, Tepecika. Food's waiting for you," a woman called out.

Slipping and sliding on the snow-covered, icy rocks, she made her way to the food wagon. Without a word she accepted the wooden bowl of hearty stew and began gulping it down. After a time she managed to ask, "What news?"

"Figured you'd want to know. We won the battle. The men claim they've slain all the defenders and captured a few older women. However, it's pitch black in there so they are tending the wounded out here tonight and at first light they will go inside and make sure there are no traps waiting for us or other hidden defenders. We lost half of our men and another quarter are wounded but will survive, we think. Kertme is still alive, thanks to you, Tepecika, though many say he should be dead already. His pulse is weak but he breathes yet. We lost Azay; he was slain long before anyone could reach him. Tepe has taken a couple of bad wounds and has asked for your healing when you are able again. He's in charge now until Kertme recovers." *If he ever does,* she thought, but did not say so. Tepecika heard it anyway. Her senses were wide open at the moment. She felt the pain and suffering of nearly fifty men but was too weak to do anything about it, if she could. In the past, her only remedy was to drink enough ale to deaden her to the world around her. *Why is the world always in so much agony?*

"How about our two *mentales* prisoners?" she thought to ask.

"Bawled their heads off for a time. We think they are

unconscious now or else asleep. Want us to wake them and feed them some stew?" the woman asked.

"In a bit. Let me recover my wits please. How bad is Tepe, really?"

"Not good, not good."

"I best check him, though I can't do much until I have recovered a whole lot more." Finally quite full, she rose though her legs were still a bit wobbly. She followed the woman's directions and found Tepe lying beneath a wagon, heavily covered up. "How's it going, old man?" she tried to make light of his pain which she could feel — his and fifty others. *God do I need ale! And sleep!*

"Not so good. Chest gash is pretty bad. Can't move my left arm at all. How's Kertme, really, Tepecika, how is he really?" *Is he going to make it? Be honest with me woman, no lies, not when I am like this. We lost Azay.*

"I got to him in time, but barely. He's breathing and the heart and lung wounds were healing when I finished up on him. I will know better in the morning, Tepe. It took all I had and then some to save him. I don't have much left in me tonight, but I will at least examine you and do a little. In the morning, I'll tend to you first thing." She tried to focus, but simply could not, the pain of so many wounded in so close a proximity overwhelmed her exposed, raw senses.

I can sense you are beyond exhausted, Tepecika. Go get some sleep. I will live til morning.

I am sorry, Tepe. I promise to come to you in the morning. She gave him a loving kiss on his forehead. She slowly returned to the food wagon. There she picked up two bowls and headed back to her wagon where the two captive women were being held. As she approached, she saw the two women still sitting where Copperman had left them. A light covering of snow hid their cloaks from view. She smiled; her idea was working only too well.

She kicked the feet of the two women slightly to get their attention. Both twins jerked alert from their emotional daze. "I have some food for you. Open your mouths and I will feed you some stew. We don't want you to starve." She began spoon feeding the two women. While neither wanted food, the moment the stew hit their tongues, their stomachs became ravenous. They had not eaten since breakfast. They ate greedily.

As she fed them, she outlined her plans for them. "We know you both have the *mentales* gift. We've encased you in these copper devices. We will keep you encased in them until we break your spirits, and you willingly join us and use your powers to help us. Oh you can protest now," she said, sensing both teens rising anger, "but you will be kept helpless like you are now, until such time as we are sure you will join us and help us. You might like to know we won the battle. I'm told everyone in your fortress is dead, except for a few servant women and a young girl. The men are having some fun with them even as we speak, spoils of war and all that, though I don't see why men have to rape women after a battle. Yet they always do. Men. Anyway, as long as you cooperate and eat for us, you two will not be harmed or raped. We need your *mentales* gifts. Your people killed one of ours, you see. In time, you will join us and make up for that loss. Hell at that time you probably can have your pick of the men to mate with, if I know my brother, Kertme. God, I need ale!"

"I'm full," Melissa said, though her voice sounded tinny and distant.

"Good. It was a good stew. I needed it. Used up too much energy today healing Kertme. God, I wish to hell I had a keg of ale! Damn."

Melissa's mind absorbed all that Tepecika had said. She'd cried her grief out and had somehow dozed a little. While still emotionally raw, especially with the woman confirming what she already had sensed, that her parents and brother were dead, Melissa became coldly calculating. She was helpless and knew it, but she wanted revenge or at least some justice. Her father's last orders were to get help. Well it was too late for that but not for justice. Although totally in the dark, her mind was not. *Ale, a keg of it? Why?* "What do you want with a keg of ale?" she asked.

"To drink, silly. I need it and we are out of it days ago. It's the only good thing in the world, ale. I can and have drunk any man under the table. What I wouldn't give for a good keg now. I need it more than I ever have before."

"We have kegs of ale," Melissa volunteered.

Why are you being helpful? Belinda sent.

"You do? Lots of it?" Melissa nodded her copper head. "Where is it at? They have not yet searched the fortress. Men are spooked of the dark. They think you have laid traps for them or there are more of you lying in wait for them."

"No traps. We only got word of your coming this morning; at least I think it was this morning. I can't see anything at all. Is it night or day?" Melissa asked.

"Early evening I think. It's starting to snow as always. Kegs? Where? Oh hell, the men will not let me go through the smashed gates by myself. Damn, ale. *So* close and yet *so* out of my reach! God, what I would do for a keg right now!"

"We can show you where. It is not too far from where the secret tunnel starts. You could get in that way, 'cause the men probably have not even seen the tunnel where you surprised us," Melissa said softly, though she had no idea if it was loud enough to be overheard or not. She hoped not.

"Can't you just tell me where it's at? I've been kind to you, fed you. I'm keeping you both safe from the men," she begged.

"No. That's just it. If you sneak off and go for the ale, then the men will think we did something awful to you and will beat and rape us. We only feel safe around you. We can't do anything to you now; we're helpless and cannot even defend ourselves from the men. We can't even see," Melissa played her unseen captor.

Belinda caught on partially and added, "It is really very good ale and stout. There are several huge barrels of it, tapped and ready to go. We know where it is, but dad hardly ever lets us drink much. Can we have some too? Our heads really hurt where you all hit us."

Tepecika was quiet for a moment and the twins waited anxiously not knowing what was going on. *God, ale this close! I can taste it. I can't get all the wounded men's pain and agony out of my mind! It's driving me nuts! I can't possibly sleep, not around here. Ale, god I need it!* Aloud she whispered, "Okay then, I see your point. You lead me to the ale and I will make sure you are not harmed. We are at the very southern edge of the camp. Mine is the last wagon, which is uphill from your tunnel's exit about a hundred feet or so. You can't see, so slide down on your butts, but be damn quiet about it. I'll guide you by touch. Don't say a word; you can't hear how loud your voices actually are."

Carefully, the two began scooting down the ravine. From the cold on their rears, they knew there must be some snow over the ice. That was the usual situation in the early evening this time of year. They slid awkwardly, getting jarred left and right, with more than one bruised butt. They stayed alert for the gentle touch of the unseen woman. After an eternity, she said, "Okay, you can stand up now. We are in the tunnel. I've found your lantern and I am going to light it. We can't be seen from here. Go on, get to your feet, you can't be that helpless." The two obeyed.

"Come on, here we go."

"But we can't see," Melissa complained, waving her copper covered hands about, trying to orient herself. Tepecika looked back and saw the twin's plight. They could not see and were walking into the sides, struggling to figure out the proper direction to go.

"Okay, okay. I will put my arm around you and you put yours around your sister. I'll lead us. Come on. I want that ale. If this is a trick, you will both pay dearly for it!"

With her guiding, the twins managed to walk the slightly uphill tunnel with little difficulty. After quite a walk, they reached the end of the tunnel. "Now what? How do we get out and where's the ale?"

"There should be a lever on the right side. Pull it down," Melissa said. She heard the familiar grating sound and knew the door had opened. She felt the gentle push and stepped hesitantly forward, pulling Belinda along with her. She heard the door shut behind them.

"Now what?"

"We are in the wine cellar. The ale kegs are about ten feet that way, if I am facing the steps coming down."

"Well, you are not. Ok, there I see them. You to stay put while I check on these kegs."

"There are some lanterns on the walls you can light to see better," Melissa volunteered. "The one marked 95 is the best ale."

"Found it. Let see." Melissa thought she heard a slurping sound. "Ah. Now that is some mighty fine ale! Mind if I drink the barrel? You two want some?"

"No, we want to sleep. Is it okay if we lie down for a while? You can drink all you want," Melissa asked.

"Sure, you two are probably just as exhausted as I am. Go to sleep. You are safe here. So am I. The voices, pain, and agony are rather faint in here. I'm going to get good and drunk. Damn good ale! Damn good!"

Carefully, the twins lowered themselves to the floor and sat down. *Are we going to sleep?* Belinda asked.

No, we are going to let her get good and drunk and fall into a stupor like some of the men do. Then we will escape somehow. For now, rest up.

The two sat quietly straining their senses to hear what the unseen woman was doing. A couple of loud belches echoed inside their copper helmets, bringing a smile to their faces. Sometime later, they both heard the copper mug clunk onto the floor followed by what was probably her body slumping onto the floor, her dagger clanking on the cold stone floor. They waited a while longer before rising.

Pretend we are playing blind man's bluff. Find the secret door's level, Melissa sent. Occasionally, their coppered hands tapped into the stone wall, but the tinny sound was muffled by the moth-eaten tapestry. Before long, Belinda found the lever and managed to get it pulled down. Feeling their way along, they both entered the tunnel again and listened for the door to close. Hearing the familiar grating sound followed by a distinct click, they relaxed. So far so good. They'd left the drunken woman behind; she'd probably sleep until the morning.

They hooked an arm around each other and extended their other arms out, feeling for the side walls. "I have it here. Okay, let's walk down the tunnel slowly. I'll keep feeling the wall and guide us," Melissa whispered, hoping she was not shouting. Step by step, the two headed down the slightly sloping tunnel until at last they reached the exit point once more. "We'd better listen first and see if the coast is clear."

"But what are we going to do next?"

"Slide down the ravine on our butts. I can't think of anything else to do. I hope we don't tear up our clothes or get hooked on something. I can't see to get it undone nor can I do anything with my hands like this," Melissa replied.

"You hear anything?" Belinda eventually whispered.

"I heard something. It sounded like a Montaña Beast." Faintly, the two, straining their ears, heard the unmistakable meowing sound of the great cat. These carnivores grew ten feet tall or more with huge canines and claws that could rip a man to shreds in mere seconds, a horse in three times that. Swift and sure hunters, they often tracked their prey for miles before striking at the most opportune time. Montaña beasts were greatly feared throughout all Tierra. They were found primarily in the Goza Mountains and its foothills. That was one factor, which had gone into the design of the Hilliard Heights fortress. Its huge walls prevented these giant cats from leaping over the walls to get to the horses and people inside. With its back against the mountain, there was no way inside for these top predators.

"I think I hear two of them," Belinda whispered. "Are you thinking what I'm thinking?"

"You bet. Justice. Of course, we have a choice. If we stay with these invaders, at least they will feed us and keep us alive. But I will never be their slave so we will be imprisoned like this forever. If we call the cats, then we will be on our own, helpless in the wilderness, but we can then try to go for help. Dad said for us to head for a tower. There is one to the south of us and up in the mountains. Remember seeing it last fall when we were out riding?"

"Yes, but it is way up in the mountains. How will we ever get that far? We can't see where we are going?" Belinda countered.

"I don't know, but I don't want to remain their prisoner like we are, and I'll never work for them. I'd rather die first. Does rape hurt?"

"I don't know, but I think it's very awful to endure.

Okay, I'm with you. Let's do it."

The two sat down and relaxed, focusing their minds. They reached out with their special gift. Before long, they felt the touch of the animal mind. Each made sure they were not touching the same big cat, however. They could sense intense hunger in the huge, powerful bodies. They planted the thoughts: *Lots of food here. Men and reindeer, all for the taking. They are asleep.* They felt the great cat's body growl, an incredible sensation, and then felt their powerful muscles spring into action. The twins broke their rapport with the Montaña beasts and began sliding on their butts out into the ravine.

They were aided by the totally dark night. The two moons were hidden behind the huge clouds. Neither could tell whether or not it was snowing, only that the ground was hard and cold. Sliding and feeling their blind way, the two scooted slowly and carefully on down the ravine until at last they stopped scooting downwards. "I think we are down to the valley floor now. What do we do now?" Belinda asked, hoping her voice was not too loud and draw the attention of the invader's guards, if there were any. Behind them, they heard a huge commotion and knew the Montaña beasts had come upon the recovering invaders. Both knew they would not want to be in their shoes at the moment.

They got to their feet and locked arms together, while feeling ahead with their free arm. They took hesitant, feeling steps and found they could at least walk, albeit extremely slowly. They knew the tower was to the south and that meant turning right once they were down to the grasslands. "There is that creek that runs mostly southwards. If we can find it, we can maybe follow it for a while," Belinda suggested. "Ouch, I think I bumped into a tree." They did a bit of a side step and hesitantly moved forward again. "My hands are getting really cold."

"Mine too. We have to keep on going for a while so they can't find us come morning." The two stumbled along not knowing if they were even traveling in a straight line or even roughly southward. At last, both were too exhausted to continue. They lay down beside each other, struggled to get their cloak hoods up, and then snuggled together, falling at last into a dismal sleep.

At last, Tepecika woke. Her head felt like mush and she had to urinate badly. Once done, she took another cup of the ale and only then noticed her two captives were missing. "Well, I would have done the same thing, tried to escape. They cannot have gone far. I wonder if the men have begun their search of this impressive fortress yet? Hum, if the captives headed up into the fortress proper, then the men will come across them. If they went on down the tunnel again, then I had better go that way. Besides, I promised Tepe to heal his wounds today. But before I go, I am going to take a bunch of this fine ale with me. I sure as heck am not going to leave it for the men to guzzle!" She scrounged around and found a water skin and filled it up. Then she lit the soot- coated lantern and headed back down the escape tunnel. At the exit point, she saw sliding marks beneath a light coating of snow heading on down the ravine. "Well, I know which way they went. They can't get far. I'll have to go round them up after I take care of Tepe."

She slipped and struggled up the slippery slope to her wagon and stood gaping with her mouth open, speechless. Everywhere lay destruction and parts of bodies. Arms, legs, and reindeer parts lay interspersed in one bloody mess. Wagons were upturned and some were shattered. She saw giant claw marks here and there and suddenly she realized what had happened in the night — Montaña beasts! She shuttered. "My god! If it were not for those girls, I'd be dead too! They saved my life!" Stunned into silence by this revelation, she continued to stare at the horror-filled scene. Then she saw sweeping shadows passing over the ground. Looking up, she saw the giant scavenger birds, the rocs, coming to claim what the giant cats had left behind. She shuttered and quickly began searching for survivors. She found none. Then she walked up the slippery road that led to the fortress, hoping against all hope that some of her people made it into the fortress. She found dead bodies lying where they fell during yesterday's battle, flies buzzing around as thick as fleas on a reindeer.

For a time, she yelled and called out, but heard nothing but a ghastly silence. At last, she sat down to think. Mechanically, she pulled the water skin around to her front and began sipping some ale to clear her head. *Well, I definitely am alive only because those girls took me to the safety of their wine cellar. I owe them my life. Hell, I've got them encased and helpless and Copperman is gone. Even if I can find them, I haven't the faintest notion of how to get them out of my damnable invention! But I owe them a life. There is now a life between us, mine! Hell, what else have I even got left but my own sense of honor! Crap. I had best see about finding them and then see what, if anything, can be salvaged here. Who would have thought I owe my captives a life now? Ah well, there is plenty of ale to be had. Come on old bones. Let's get to finding them.*

She began walking back down the long path that led up to the fortress. A half hour later she reached the grasslands and headed south until she found the ravine down which the captives had slid the night before. She picked up their trail; it was easy to follow, wandering about in many directions. Tepecika began to admire the spirit of these two teens. Despite being as helpless as they were, they were endeavoring to flee on foot, albeit blindly. Well, they seemed to be trying to head southwards, she noted. After a half mile of meandering tracks, she came upon the two women, lying snuggled together in the tall grass. She smiled.

"Wake up sleepy heads. The sun's up. It's a bright morning and the snow's melted."

Melissa woke from a hideous dream only to discover the dream was reality. She shrieked, frightening Belinda who also woke, terrified of the darkness and her helplessness. She too cried out. "Calm down. You are safe and sound," the voice of their captor reached their ears and their hearts sank. Captured once again.

"I got to pee," Melissa said miserably.

Quickly, Tepecika helped both teens with that. "Come on. Let's head back to what's left of the camp. I owe you my life. My honor says I must repay that debt. So I am your slave until I can find a way to repay you. There are only us left alive now. Montaña beasts came during the night and slaughtered all my people and all the animals, if they didn't run away. They are food for the rocs now. I'd be dead too if it were not for you two having led me to safety inside your cellar. So like it or not, I owe you two. Unfortunately, I have no idea how to get those copper things off you. So for the moment, I will have to nursemaid you both. We don't have much choice. Come on. I've got my arm around each of you. I'll lead you. Do you realize you were very nearly walking in circles in this grasslands? Mostly you were going southwards. My name's Tepecika Karli, by the way."

"I am Melissa Hilliard. My sister, Belinda. How are you feeling today? You were pretty bad off last night." She tried to comprehend what the woman was saying. A life owed? What did that mean exactly?

"Yes, I've never quite been that bad off before. I over did it with my gift. As it turns out, it was all for nothing anyway. No, not for nothing. It saved my life. If I had not been so bad off, I would not have allowed you two to take me to the ale, and I'd be roc food this fine morning. Oh, I didn't answer your question, did I? I am doing pretty good now, what with a bit of ale to remove the fuzziness in me head. How about you two?"

An hour later, they arrived back at the carnage scene. Miraculously, her wagon survived unharmed, being at the end of the line and with neither reindeer nor people there when the cats attacked. She sat down leaning against a wheel and helped the two teens sit down. "Well, it is a good thing you cannot see what is here."

"But we can smell it," Melissa replied. *What are we going to do now? She cannot get us out of these copper things.*

Belinda sent back, *I don't know. We can't stay here, not like this. Maybe we should still do as dad asked and head south to that tower and ask them for help.*

"Well, my young charges, I am going to have a drink and think. What are we to do now?" They heard her taking a long drink and then a belch. "First thing, I have to find a way to get you out of those darn copper restraints without hurting you. Okay, you two stay here. I'm going to rummage through this mess and see if I can find anything useful to free you. Yell if you need something."

"What if she can't get us out of these things?" Melissa whispered.

"Hey, there are still a couple of riders out, leading the horses out to the pastures, where we ought to have been. When they come back, maybe they can help get us free," Belinda suggested. The two took heart with that hope and knowing at least two of their father's hands were still alive.

"Hey, girls, I found some tin snips. I'm going to see if I can cut these things off you," Tepecika's voice sounded close to them again.

Melissa felt her head being moved around and relaxed. "Please try. You can do it," she said encouragingly. *I'd keep my fingers crossed, but they are balled up. Please work, please work.*

I am working, really I am. I think it is working a little. Hang in there. Don't move your head. Melissa realized Tepecika could easily read her thoughts too and kept her mind still as well as her head. After what seemed to her an eternity, she heard a snapping sound and the head shell broke free. A moment later, she was free of it.

"It worked! My head's out of it, Belinda! Way to go Tepecika! Thank you!"

"I need another drink before I tackle your sister. Ah," she belched again and set to work on Belinda. This time it went faster and soon her sister was free too. "Thank goodness the copper is thin and easily cut. Now to free your hands."

While she worked on them, the twins looked about. They were in the ravine below their fortress. Stretching for several hundred feet on up out of the ravine to the main winding road that led to the entrance gates, they saw the remains of many wagons. Several large, black rocs were pecking away at remains on the ground. Fortunately from where they were sitting, they could not see exactly what the scavengers were ripping into pieces and they didn't want to for that matter.

"Oh my god! What if the rocs are eating mom and dad

and Peter and the others?" Belinda suddenly gagged at what the rocs here implied.

Grimacing, Melissa said, "Well, as soon as we're free, we can see if we can drag them inside and somehow get their bodies buried. We can maybe do the same for your brother, Tepecika."

"He's roc food already. Nothing left to bury, I'm afraid." She paused a moment, wiped tears from her eyes, and added, "He was only trying to find a way for our clan to survive." She continued her painstaking work. "You see, we lived in Bafra, way up on the north coast. Had a pretty good living until the damnable weather changed. It's all frozen over now, all the time. Even the reindeer began to migrate south. We train reindeer you see. Kertme, that's my brother and clan leader, he said we had to go south too, but there was almost no food to be had and pitifully little ale. Honestly, we were running out of everything and had no place else to go."

"You could have asked dad for help," Melissa countered. "He'd probably have helped you out."

"Men. You know men. Well, maybe you don't. They are overly proud and greedy too. He'd never have resorted to asking for help. He was too proud, besides he'd have lost face in the clan leadership. Men. For my money, which I haven't got any, we women ought to be the clan leaders. There, your hands are free, Melissa. One more set to go. Where was I?"

"Thanks," she replied, rubbing her sore wrists and extremely grateful to be free at last. "What about your husband and children?"

Tepecika tossed her head back and laughed. "Lost him two years ago. Then my boy died of the fever that no one could cure. Lost a lot of children to the *mentales* fever, we called it. My brother took me in, since his wife died of it too. Hard life up in Bafra."

"Thanks, what do we do now?" Belinda asked. "Too bad about your family, Tepecika."

"I'm hungry, why don't we head home and see what we can fix up in the kitchen and see if mom, dad, and Peter's bodies can be rescued from the rocs?" Melissa suggested.

All three headed through the remains of the camp,

dodging the rocs's loud calls and wing flaps, as the great birds refused to budge from their feast. Both teens gagged several times before they finally reached the stone roadway. "Told you it was no sight for such young faces," Tepecika whispered and finished off her water skin of ale, drowning her own emotional upheaval. The twins guessed that was why she was drinking so much, but didn't say so.

As they approached the carnage at the gates where five more rocs were busily feasting, they heard horse hooves coming up behind them. The three turned to face the unknown. "Maybe it is dad's hired hands returning," Melissa said hopefully. Dread seeped into her mind though. She knew she couldn't face more trouble.

All three held their breaths. As soon as Melissa saw the two men rounding the bend and coming into view, she called out, "Ben! Frank! Thank god you are alive! We need help! Invaders from the north wiped us all out."

Already white-faced from having just passed the carnage and having seen the rocs up by the fortress, both men feared the worst. They dismounted and came to the twins, looking them over. "Are you two all right? What about my wife?" Ben asked, pleadingly.

Tepecika sighed. "I think they are all dead, save these two. They saved my life and now there is a life between us, though I don't know why they did save me, but they did. We were just heading there to find something to eat and rescue their family's bodies from the rocs."

"You three stay back until we get those birds away. Frank, look at that hole in the gates! How in the world did they do that?" Ben asked shocked at the four foot, splintered hole.

"Probably *mentales* force. One of our clan can do that sort of thing, well used to. He's dead now," Tepecika answered him. Ben nodded grimly, handing his reins to Melissa and drawing his sword. He walked on up to the gates, yelling and waving his sword. Frank emulated him and soon the rocs begrudgingly rose into the air, forgoing their dining for a while. All took up positions on the roofs of the various buildings within the fortress, waiting for the chance to resume. The two crawled through the gaping hole and shortly swung one gate open, waving to the three to come.

Bodies lay everywhere, but they found their three family members and the two young men dragged them into the stables, where the rocs could not get at them. After unsaddling the two horses, the twins finally broke down and cried once more. Their grief was interrupted by Tepecika, who said, "Damn, I need more ale!" That brought the two out of their emotional upheaval. They realized she too was full of grief and was picking up on all of theirs, as well as her own. She, like they, had no way to block out all the surrounding agony and suffering.

"Has anyone searched the complex for survivors?" asked Ben. Melissa picked up his thoughts. *I haven't seen Louise's body yet. Maybe she and our baby somehow survived this.*

"I'll take Tepecika to the cellar and check the basement," Melissa suggested. They divided up and began going room to room, calling out names, looking for possible survivors. "I know you need more ale, Tepecika. Now I know why. Come on. There's lots of it for you." She resumed her searching.

A bit later, they heard Ben's voice yelling as loudly as he could, "Survivors! Survivors in the top tower!" When she finally got there, she was amazed to see that ten women had somehow survived the disaster. Two of whom were their midwives, Becka and Linda.

"Lord be praised! You twins survived!" Becka exclaimed, jubilantly, hugging both teens. "You look awful. Your clothes are a fright. But you seem fit, both of you."

"We are, we saved Tepecika here, and she saved us. How did all of you survive?" Melissa asked, noticing Ben was holding his pregnant wife tightly, as was Frank with his Linda.

"My doing," Becka explained. Ever practical, Becka, thought Melissa. "When I saw your father and brother fall, I knew it was all over. I ushered these women back into the main house and led them up here, where your father has a secure room. We bolted the door and waited. I had one sword and we swore we'd not be taken without a fight. Didn't we ladies?" Many nodded. She went on, "They didn't come, and later last night, we heard Montaña beasts growling and raising quite a ruckus outside the walls. We didn't know what to think, only hoped, you see. Nothing can stand against them Montaña beasts, you know." Tepecika grimaced as the ghastly images of her campsite came back into her mind. Quietly, she took another long drink from her refilled waterskin. "So we waited. Then, we heard Ben calling frantically and well, here we all are. I am so sorry about your family, misses. They died protecting all of us. Heroes, I say."

"Well, there's plenty to do now, but we are starving. How about we get something cooking?" suggested their cook, Irena. As they all headed out of the secure room, Melissa caught Ben and Louise embracing as well as Frank and Linda. She smiled; at least they still had their families. That thought brought another twinge of loss back to her and to Belinda. Tepecika took another long drink, and Melissa also knew Tepecika had similar raw emotions too.

The two men set about the cleanup operations, while the twins and Tepecika headed for the bath. Later over lunch, Ben pointed out that Amos was still out and was due back in the morning. That was something anyway, Melissa thought. Clean and with her hair washed and brushed, she felt human again.

"So what do we do now?" Ben asked what was on everyone's mind. "You ladies are now the owners of Hilliard Heights, so it is your call. Do we abandon it and try to find safety somewhere? Do we stay? If so, how are we going to manage with just three men around?"

"Well, we still have the herd, so we have resources. Does anyone know anywhere we could move to?" Melissa asked. None had. Hilliard Heights was a very isolated kingdom. She added, "Dad's last order to us was to go to the southern tower and ask for help. Maybe that's what we should do. I don't want to leave Hilliard Heights. I love it here, so do you. Somehow we need to get by."

"Well, in that case, we need to repair the gates and clean up the mess," Ben suggested. "Louise and I are behind you. We'd like to stay too. After all, where else have we to go?"

Frank added, "We should gather up all the metal

weapons. Those ought to fetch a fair price. Metal is rare around here."

"Okay, we'll lend you a hand with it. After all, we women are going to have to pull a man's load around here now. I wish I had paid more attention to what all mom used to do. She always ran the estate and knew what needed to be done and when," Belinda added.

"Well, trust some of us, dear. We know what has to be done too. You two know the horses so you take care of them. Leave the estate stuff to us," Becka suggested. "Of course, only Orson knew where to get supplies, though they have been pitiful this last year."

Thus, the cleanup and organization began. The twins and Tepecika helped Ben and Frank on the outside cleanup work, while the women scampered about the complex taking stock of what supplies were present. Becka began an exhaustive list of them and what was needed and a rough guess by when.

Near dusk, it began raining once more, but the five had filled an entire wagon with weapons. "These will fetch a huge price, Melissa," Ben proclaimed. "If only we knew where we could sell them for the things we need." All five sighed; none had that answer.

That evening after supper, they held a funeral for the fallen. Here against the Goza Mountains, graves simply could not be dug in the rocky ground. Hence, cremation was the rule. A giant bonfire blazed through this night as the remains of so many fallen were given back to Nature. Tepecika sat beside the twins, drinking heavily, drowning her senses once again. The painful emotions flooding into her mind from everyone present was too much for her to bear. She had her own losses as well, but she was grateful for her new surroundings. The twins had given her new clothes, a room of her own, and all the ale she desired. She knew she was bound to them even more now, though she had no idea why they would be so kind to her. After all, it was her idea to cripple them with the copper bonds and her people who had attacked them, killed her family, and caused so much pain and suffering here. The latter was once more overwhelming her, and she drunk deeply, relishing the numbing sensation that finally deadened the agony in her mind.

The next day, the twins busied themselves sorting through their parents' things and their brother's as well. What to do with all their possessions was solved by dividing everything up among the survivors. What would not fit anyone was put into the sewing room to be later recycled into new clothes. No one knew when, if ever, they could get their hands on more cotton bolts or even wool for that matter.

Meanwhile, the two men began to see what they could do to repair the damaged gates. Neither was a woodworker and they laughed as they bungled their way through the repairs. Around noon though, they sounded the alarm gong as a precautionary measure. A number of horse hooves against the stone path echoed up the ravine before the fortress. Only Amos was unaccounted for and the two men were rightly concerned with the number of horses making their slow way up the long path to the fortress. The fifteen survivors congregated at the gates, though only Ben and Frank carried a weapon.

We are simply going to have to learn how to fight and defend ourselves, sis, Melissa sent worriedly to Belinda.

Count me in on that too, Tepecika sent back, having overheard her.

"Oh thank god it is Amos!" Belinda called out. "But who are those men with him?"

As Amos pulled up near the partially destroyed gates, he called out, "What happened here? We saw all that mess down in the ravine."

Hastily, Melissa took charge and gave him and these strangers a brief synopsis, leaving out some of the worst details. "This is all that are left? Betsy is dead too?" Grief finally hit him as he realized his wife had perished too.

Belinda also realized her father customarily had greeted all the strangers to Hilliard Heights. With all that had happened, they had not given any consideration to hosting guests. She spoke up, "I see you have brought some visitors. I am Belinda Hilliard, my sister Melissa. We are all that is left of our family. Dad would usually offer you sanctuary and well I don't know what all is customary. You will have to forgive us. Everything in the universe is all topsy turvy right now. Please, we do welcome you to Hilliard Heights. I am sure we can find rooms for everyone; it is just all so confusing at the moment. Mom always handled that." Her eyes went from man to man obviously uncertain whom she ought to be addressing.

Two men looked nearly identical, though, with long blonde hair falling loosely to their shoulders. They too had yellow eyes, hard to miss. None of the other men did, at least she couldn't see any other yellow eyes. "Forgive us, My Ladies Hilliard. We had no idea of your plight. I am Alford Bettingham, my twin brother, Aiden. We are from the Kingdom of the Angels some two hundred miles due south of here. We heard your horses are some of the finest in the land, and have come on a rather large buying spree for our king and towers. Please allow our men here to assist yours in any needed repairs."

"Thanks, we only have three men now that Amos has returned," Melissa admitted. "For your help, we are most grateful. We do have a lot of horses we can sell. We've just taken them down to their summer pastures, but it is a small matter for Belinda and me to round them up. How many do you want? We need food supplies, but mom always took care of that. Right now, Becka is trying to work out what we are going to need. Please come on in. We will find places for everyone to stay."

Ben whispered to Melissa, "Their men should stay in the stable bunk house. The two lords should be in the manor house with you. Use the guest rooms." Melissa flashed him a thank you sign.

A couple of their men took their horses for them, and Alford and Aiden followed the others into the manor house within the fortress. "Incredible place. The walls are so high, and the mountain is at your back. No attack from that direction," Alford commented.

"Yes, the only direction is up the stone trail. The walls are as tall as they are to keep the Montaña beasts from getting in. We have a lot of those big cats in these parts. We share the land with them, you see," Melissa chatted, glad to have something that she could relate. *If I'd only paid more attention to what mom and dad did with guests!*

Becka brought them all some hot wild berry juice and Melissa decided they ought to discuss business first, since their guests came to buy. "We could use fifty good mounts," Aiden explained. "By the way, we saw a lot of reindeer out there too, and some still had the remnants of hobbles or halters on them. How strange."

"Those are probably ours; some must have been lucky enough to escape the Montaña beasts a couple nights ago," Tepecika broke in.

"Well, are they for sale too? With these impossibly cold and snow filled winters we are having, reindeer do better in the winter than our horses do," Alford asked.

Tepecika opened her eyes, quite surprise. "Of course, buy all you want. My clan and I used to train them you see. I'm all that's left of the Karli clan, but I know how to train them. Been doing it since I was ten."

"Excellent! Say, will they spook if we take them back with the horses or do we need to keep them far apart?" Alford asked.

"Mine are all trained to tolerate horses side by side. A lot are used to pulling wagons, though, not riding."

"We could use both. Aiden, we sure have come to the right place. Perhaps, we could arrange a standing purchase arrangement with Hilliard Heights. We'd take all your available horses and reindeer each season in return for whatever you need and want, that is, if the horses are up to our standards."

"Well, that would certainly simplify things enormously for us. We don't know where or how dad always sold them in the autumn. Our horses are really the best," Melissa explained. "Belinda and I are the only ones dad ever trusted to break them and train them for riding. We've been doing it since we were nine. You can check out our mares in the stables if you like. They are representative of our stock. They are sturdy trail horses, well rounded girths, and smarter than normal horses the cavalrymen ride."

Belinda added, "We always train them to come when we

whistle too. Makes it a whole lot easier to manage hundreds of them, you see. Come on. We'll show you."

Off to the south of the manor house lay the wintering corral, large enough to hold several hundred head at one time. A dozen horses were currently grazing on a patch of hay tossed out by Ben in the early morning. Already though, the rain clouds had gathered and they felt the first sprinkles of the afternoon rains. As they approached, the twins whistled, and Aiden and Alford watched rather amazed all dozen came trotting over to the two teens, nuzzling each of them as they patted the horses lovingly on their noses. Each had a halter on and Melissa snapped a lead line on one mare and tied the end to the halter as well.

"Don't need a bridle, really. Watch." She hopped onto the horse and arranged her flaming red hair across its back and then her dress. The men saw she wore men's pants beneath the dress and smiled. Melissa put her mare through some paces, and then came up beside him, and slipped off, handing her to Aiden. Meanwhile, Belinda readied another mare for Alford.

The two men climbed up, but not as gracefully as the teens. They were used to saddles. However, both we amazed at how well the horses responded to the slightest nudge or command, even backing up. When they finished, Alford commented, "These are the best trained horses I have ever seen. Wide backed. Easy gait. We certainly came to the right place! Name your price!" The two teens smiled. They already knew their horses were tops.

"Well, we have ten four year olds and thirty-one three year olds we could sell you right now. We've twenty-four two year olds we need to finish their training this summer before we would consider selling them. Is that too many?" Melissa asked.

"Not at all. Perfect. If they are out in the grasslands, how will you round them up?" asked Alford.

"Oh, it will take us a couple of days. They can't have gone too far yet. The grasses are tall and there is no need for them to head too far to the east yet. I don't know about Tepecika's reindeer though. We can start in today or wait until tomorrow, since the rains have already started. It will ice up by supper and snow after that. Morning will be better all round. We have line shacks out there in the foothills we can use while we round up the ones to sell," Melissa replied.

Later at dinner, they chatted and at last, Tepecika asked, "You both have *mentales*, right? Yellow eyes?" They nodded and she continued, "I thought so, but how is it that I cannot read your minds? I am always hearing the twins and they always hear me, but I've listened all day and not heard either of you."

Alford asked instead, "Have you three gotten your tower training yet?" From the blank looks on the three faces, he knew they hadn't. Well, that was to be expected, Hilliard Heights was incredibly remote. "The towers are our short way of saying *Círculo de la Torres*. We have four such towers in our kingdom. Their purpose is to train we *mentales* gifted. Our wise women have written a book of rules for us *mentales* gifted. Our first rule is that anyone who has the *mentales* gift and who is past puberty must receive basic training from one of the *Círculo de la Torres*. This basic training consists of learning how to block out unwanted thoughts of others who are around the person and not to broadcast their own thoughts indiscriminately to everyone else around them. Why? Sensory overload can occur if one is wide open to everyone's thoughts. In a crowd, the person can receive hundreds of dis-related thoughts simultaneously, which has been known to drive the person mad, psi-insanity. If one cannot hide his or her own thoughts, then they are often screaming their personal, private thoughts to everyone around them, which can be both embarrassing and reveal things that should not be revealed to others.

"Oh my god! You mean you can get so you don't have to hear all the voices around you?" asked Tepecika, totally shocked such was even possible. "I don't have to get totally drunk to drown them out! What I wouldn't give for that! Does it cost anything? For this special training?"

"Not at all. It just takes a few days or a week or so. You know, the tower women have also gotten a good handle on curing the Verge Sickness," Aiden added.

None knew what this was and after he explained it, Tepecika nearly broke down into tears. Her son had died of it and she'd seen so many others get it as well. No one up north knew what it was, let alone how to cure it. "My gift is healing. I simply have to learn how to cure this sickness. My son died of it and I felt so helpless, so useless."

"We are training all midwives in it as well. Perhaps your midwives here could come and learn how to deal with the birthing process. There are a whole lot of things that can help prevent needless deaths of mother and newborns. There is also one other rule, Tepecika. No one will enter or pervade or invade another's mind without first obtaining their freely given consent. Why? To do so uninvited is psychic rape!" Alford added.

"We must get this training," Melissa stated. "All three of us, and also for Becka and Louise who are our remaining midwives. How can we do it?"

"Oh simple. Come back with us and the herd. Get trained and then return with all your needed supplies. Hey, if you do come, we can help you find others who might like to return and live here with you, working your horse farm. Many people are struggling just now because of the terrible weather changes. Some would love a good job as you can offer them," Aiden suggested. He knew the two twins needed a whole lot of new workers and Wyth was a likely place to find them.

"Can we learn to fight and defend ourselves?" Melissa spoke up. *We need to be able to defend Hilliard Heights somehow. It's up to Belinda and me now. We have to learn how.*

"Yes, that can be arranged too, but you will need to spend months at it. Perhaps we can send back one or two to train you and your people who want to know how to defend and protect themselves and others," Aiden suggested.

"Now you are talking! That would be ideal because the summer is when we do most of our training of the next year's horses. If we are gone all summer, we won't have many ready for you next spring, and you will have to wait until autumn to get them," Melissa explained.

"Hey, that was Abbey. She's already volunteered,

Aiden," Alford broke in on the conversation. "She's our younger sister; she and Adam are also twins. Abbey is a superior archer and a darn good fighter and tracker. She and Adam just never get lost and can follow a trail that neither Aiden nor I can even see. She just contacted me wanting to know how it was going, and I told her all about the situation up here. Abbey wants to come back with you and teach everyone how to fight, particularly your women. You couldn't get a better person than Abbey for my money."

"How? Oh, *mentales*. I didn't know you could use telepathy that far. Sure, tell her that would be great. I think we need archers most of all," Melissa replied. So much good was now happening, and it was all tied to these new and strange towers. She wanted to leave at once, but knew she had to round up the horses and help Tepecika gather her reindeer too.

Alford suddenly started laughing. "Great! Oh, Melissa, Belinda, Abbey is at our Bettingham tower and one of the women there is Sammi, who is married to her twin brother. Sammi's gift is to be able to appear anywhere and view what's there. She prefers flying as an eagle. Well, Abbey is so excited about all this that she has Sammi hovering over Hilliard Heights right now and has Mink Linked her sight to Abbey and Adam who are looking your fortress over. Abbey says this is a fabulously looking place. Oh heck. Why don't I just Mink Link you three into those three?"

Suddenly, Melissa, Belinda, and Tepecika were joined with Sammi, Adam, and Abbey, viewing Hilliard Heights from the viewpoint of an eagle circling high overhead. The twins got a view of their home they never had before and were elated with the experience as was Tepecika.

Abbey sent, *You have a perfect place for a refuge for women in need. I am going to see how many able bodied women I can round up for you. I'm calling it the Sisters Place for now. When you all get here, I will have a bunch of women and a few men for you to select. What a cool place you have, Melissa, Belinda. I can't wait to get there!*

The next day, Melissa and Belinda loaded a large bag of carrots onto the backs of their saddles. Ben led another horse carrying food supplies for a few days. Tepecika, Alford, and Aiden followed them, along with six of their men. Out into the waving grasslands of the high foothills the small group rode. Constantly the twins were amazed at how easy the roundup of the horses was. Melissa or Belinda would pause at a likely meadow and give a sharp whistle or two. Their horses would come trotting up to them to get their carrot treat. The young newborns were more hesitant, but followed their mothers and also got a carrot. The older horses to be sold were weeded out and tied into an ever-growing string.

Before long, isolated reindeer that had been part of the Karli clan's herd were spotted and gathered up as well. After three days, they headed back to the fortress with forty horses and fifty-one reindeer. Tepecika was shocked to learn her reindeer were going to be worth half as much as one of the twin's horses. She was soon to be independently wealthy, much to her surprise. She vowed to have more reindeer trained by next year. Her fortunes had definitely changed for the better.

Early July, the large group arrived at the Bettingham estate just outside Wyth. Abbey was also there, along with forty women she'd rounded up. Most of the women had lost their husbands, and some even had small children to care for as well. All manner of occupations were represented, something that would be of great benefit for the twins. She also had a blacksmith who wanted a fresh start and four other men who were good around farms and horses. She also had one stone mason. Melissa and Belinda interviewed all of them and took them all on and thus was born what in later years would be called the Sisterhood. Furthermore, seven had *mentales* gifts.

A final agreement was also reached. Since the twins accepted so many women and promised to take more as time went on, particularly those women in dire need, the Kingdom of the Angles promised to provide protection for Hilliard Heights. King Norwood explained it this way, "Twice each day, Sammi flies over our borders and is on the lookout for invaders. When she spots some, our *mentales* protector takes over and she gets rid of them. Thus far, we've repelled all invading bandits and armies. We aim to keep this kingdom safe from the battles that are so commonplace in these unsettling times. Sammi will now fly over Hilliard Heights twice a day as well. If she spots invaders, we will handle them for you as we do here. We need a really safe haven for battered women and those women who are in true need. Hilliard Heights is a perfect place for them. Besides, we need your horses and reindeers."

Chapter 10 Exchange City

November of 1001, the aliens from Rigel-3 held the first of their bargaining sessions with representatives of the three kingdoms, which bordered the desired location for their space transfer station on Plateau Grado. The entire western side was claimed by the new Kingdom of Valen, Westerlings, while two Midlands kingdoms claimed the eastern side, Angels and Haverhills, though Haverhills owned the vast majority of the eastern side. Norwood asked Inez Anacleto, who now ran their Bedworth tower some twenty miles north of the plateau to handle the negotiations for the Angels. Why? Her gift was the ability to tell when a person was not telling the whole truth.

She was forty and had long brown hair with a stern countenance. Dita figured she would blend well with her boss, Ania Anka, the Sector ID Minister, that is, the Intelligence Division. Ania was also quite stern and extremely powerful, controlling most all aspects of this whole sector of space. Besides, with her gift, they would have confidence in any deals made. The other representatives were *Jefe* Ben Haverhills and *Jefe* Basilio Ventura of Valen, both powerful men in their own right. Both also had *mentales* gifts, though at this time, precisely what their gifts were was unknown.

The meeting was held on Plateau Grado in the same meeting room of the giant spaceship in which Dita and Doctor Zosia had met with Ania. Of course, the three representatives were awed and impressed with the huge battleship and were given a brief tour before sitting down for the negotiations with Ania. Only the four were in the large meeting room, again designed to impress the three representatives. Ania knew precisely what she was doing, making it appear as the four were on wholly equal terms and of equal importance. Certainly, they were not. Appearances meant a lot in bargaining and Ania was an expert at it. Armed with vast knowledge supplied by her Intelligence Division, she almost never was taken by surprise data.

She began, "Let me begin by telling you what it is we wish from this meeting. We are going to build an interstellar space station here, where many transfers can be made. Since the development of this base will require an enormous expenditure of men, equipment, and expense, we want to sign a five hundred year lease on the entire Plateau Grado. Our people will set up a defensive perimeter around the plateau. None of our people or those arriving will be allowed beyond that perimeter and likewise none from Tierra will be allowed onto the base."

"The Imperial Directive #5 will be strictly enforced, unlike our predecessors. This means there will be no contact between our people and yours. No trading. We will not be selling or marketing our devices, machinery, and weapons to anyone on Tierra, for example. We will not interfere in anything that goes on on this world, outside of Plateau Grado. Your planet and your cultures and your governments will be your own affairs. Under no circumstances will we get involved, save to guard and protect our space station here. I might add that if our predecessors had followed that, none of the mess that occurred here would have happened. There are valid reasons why that directive should be enforced. So while we are here, there will be minimal interaction between us. However, we don't just take what we want. Instead, we are prepared to make a fair trade for our use of this land and our total sovereignty over it and what goes on here."

"Of course, with the Imperial Directive #5 in play, there are limits to what we are allowed to trade for this five hundred year lease. For example, we cannot trade technology that you do not possess here on Tierra. That would wholly upset the balance of power and culture on this world. Sorry, no blaster guns, no flying shuttles, though I know that they would be of immense value here. We do know that this world has a severe shortage of all heavier elements, such as iron and gold. I have given this considerable thought, and I believe that payment in high quality iron ore and gold would be appropriate, unless you rulers have some other ideas to present."

Jefe Ben said, "Iron that can be turned into strong steel blades is incredibly valuable here. Gold is so rare that little use is made of it, save for some ornamentation for our women. As I see it, if you pay us in iron ore, does that not also upset the balance of power for we three kingdoms would suddenly have it in quantity?"

"Your point is well taken. Yes, in a way it does. However, the population of each of your kingdoms is sufficiently small that I don't believe it will become a culture-destroying trade. You've not enough men to set out to conquer the rest of the world. On the other hand, you could become the makers of the finest blades on your world and trade them for other things that you need. Obviously, no matter what we trade for the use of Plateau Grado, your three kingdoms will be the primary beneficiaries. No question of that," Ania pointed out.

"Now to keep this from making huge changes all at once, we will be paying you equal yearly payments, say on the first day of each new year. While the overall grand total is quite large, as you would expect, divided into five hundred payments, no one payment will be enormous and thus upset the balance of power, as near as I can estimate," Ania said sternly.

Inez decided to try a different approach. "While iron ore is valuable, what about lending us a hand coping with the horrific changes in our weather caused, as I understand it, by the explosion of your previous station here on Plateau Grado? The weather is really causing tremendous problems and upheavals all over Tierra. Can't something be done to help this situation improve somehow? To me, that would benefit everyone on Tierra, something that we in the Kingdom of the Angels would prefer from this land lease."

"She brings up a very valid point. Ordinarily, my first action upon coming here would be to attempt to undo the awful damage done by my predecessors. Indeed, I have had our best men working on that since we learned of the exact nature of the problem. However, to date, they cannot guarantee me that any action they could attempt to remedy or at least improve the drastic climate changes will not in fact make things even worse. Until they can give me a hundred percent assurance that a corrective action will not make it worse than it now is I will not authorize such."

She went on, "But she does have a valid point. How

about a stipulation in the lease agreement to the effect that if we can devise some way to improve or rectify the weather changes that will definitely not make it worse, then we will do so, but only with the agreement of the leaders of the lands that abut Plateau Grado?"

Inez sensed that she hedged her wording and realized why. Who could say what political kingdoms would be adjoining the plateau five hundred years from now. Certainly changes would occur, much as they had recently with the breakup of the original fifteen large kingdoms. "I can agree to that stipulation, Minister. Please continue to try. Aurora has seen just how awful it will be in the near future, a total upheaval of nearly every kingdom. Any improvement will be most welcome by all on Tierra." The two *Jefes* agreed with her.

Jefe Ben brought up another detail, almost as if reading Ania's mind. "Your predecessors made contractual agreements with several thousand miners to mine for psi-crystals in return for gold. Since the explosion, they have been left in a sort of limbo. Some have not been paid for their more recent work."

"Yes, we have about a thousand men and some of their families in a sort of temporary camp just to the east of the plateau," Ania replied. "We need to settle that situation. I have a suggestion. What about hiring them to construct a small Exchange City there on the eastern slopes? We will need a convenient location to transfer the iron and gold to you, though we can make provisions for Valen on the western side as well."

"I like that idea," *Jefe* Ben replied. "Surely there can be other things that could be safely traded between our world and the universe out there." He had thought long and hard about this detail. An Exchange City would be a toehold that no other kingdom would have. He was after a closer alliance with the aliens, if possible. "We have leather and furs, for example. I've heard that furs are in vogue elsewhere besides Tierra." Inez wondered where he'd picked up that tidbit, but didn't dare interrupt. His was a very key point. Perhaps other things could be traded.

"Well, yes," Ania replied. Inez also picked up Ania's surprise that he knew this datum, but the woman quickly suppressed it. "Furs and leather could well be traded, but again, it would have to be for such things that are indigenous to Tierra. No technology that you don't already have, no flying shuttles. If we could agree on that, it would make the Exchange City much more valuable to us both. However, I would insist that any person on Tierra, independent of their home kingdom, would be allowed to bring their goods to the city for trade unfettered by any taxes or fees on your part, *Jefe* Ben. The Exchange City would have to be an open city, open to anyone on Tierra who would like to come and trade. We four would, of course, have to agree on what items would be accepted in trade."

Jefe Basilio spoke up. "In order to make this Exchange City fair for we Westerlings, we would need a new road built from our western side over the plateau or nearby to the city. You cannot expect all of us in the Westerlings to have to travel thousands of miles to the south just to get across the Goza Mountains to the proposed city."

"Point taken," Ania replied. "If we did build such a road for the Westerlings, we would have to have a signed contract between you three that anyone wishing to travel to the Exchange City and thus have to pass through your kingdoms would be allowed to do so untaxed and unchallenged. There has to be a bargain of free travel and access to the city. No fees, no taxes on said travelers."

"I think that we can all accept that," *Jefe* Ben replied, seeing many advantages. Travelers would need to stop at many inns along the way and spend money for lodging and food. Inez picked up this thought from him and smiled. He was always looking to maximize Haverhills' profits.

Inez pointed out the obvious next detail. "If we do this, then within the boundaries of the Exchange City, both of our people will come in direct contact with each other. That's obvious, but what is not clear is jurisdiction. Surely, there will be conflicts, perhaps even outright fights, to say nothing of minor disagreements. Who will arbitrate and police the open city?"

Ania smiled for the first time. *These people are extremely wise and intelligent! Do not underestimate them.*

"She has a critical point. How shall this be done? Our people or those who might come to trade do not know your laws and customs. Our laws and customs are not known to your people."

"The proposed Exchange City is on our land and ought to be subject to our laws," *Jefe* Ben pointed out. "I would think it would be the responsibility of your people to ensure that your traders know our laws and follow them."

"Point taken. May I suggest we each have a regent who will meet and handle the disagreements? Our regent will be responsible for punishing our guilty parties and your regent will be responsible for doing the same with your guilty parties. How does that sound?"

"Acceptable," *Jefe* Ben answered politely, knowing that he'd scored another victory.

Men! Inez thought. She'd picked up his thought.

Ania added, "Our regent will be in charge of inspecting all goods coming to the Exchange City for trade to ensure that no contraband items are transferred, such as blaster guns. I would expect the same from your regent."

"That would make sense," *Jefe* Ben agreed with her.

"What about the iron ore? Could we not have high grade steel instead? That would save us time and effort making swords," *Jefe* Basilio asked.

"The direct answer to that is no, although I did consider it at first. I am informed by my engineers that there are many possible additives to iron to produce various qualities of steel that could be used in swords. While I can understand your desires, *Jefe*, I cannot allow that because we cannot guarantee that any batch of steel being imported here does not contain a heavy metal or compound that is not already on Tierra. In short, we could inadvertently be bringing in a form of steel that could not possibly be manufactured here. Again, that would violate our overriding directive. I am sorry about that detail. I can guarantee you that the iron ore will be of top quality, equaling the very best that is infrequently found on Tierra. That way, you can have a consistent, high quality ore to count upon each delivery. No surprises, so to speak." He accepted this explanation, though he did not like it.

"Now then about the actual trading details. Since we want such a long lease and none of us can predict the future, I propose the following payment system. The total annual price will be fifty tons of high grade iron ore and five hundred pounds of gold. The area that we wish to lease will be square in shape, twenty-five miles on a side. Using only the north-south boundaries, that is a total of fifty miles. Now divide that by fifty to get the rate per mile of adjoining kingdoms and we have one ton of iron and ten pounds of gold per mile. That means, *Jefe* Basilio, since your kingdom now owns the whole western side, you would get twenty-five tons of iron and two hundred fifty pounds of gold each new year. *Jefe* Ben, your border is twenty miles long, so you would get twenty tons of iron ore and two hundred pounds of gold each year. Inez, your boundary is only five miles so thus your share would be five tons of iron ore and fifty pounds of gold per year, all payable on the first of each year. Now I realize that is the dead of winter. We could prorate it and make the actual transfer say on July 1st of each year, when the weather, I'm told, will be the most favorable for such travel."

Jefe Basilio and *Jefe* Ben's eyes nearly popped out of their heads. Fifty tons of iron ore was a huge amount! If their miners were extraordinarily lucky during a year, they might discover and mine five hundred pounds. Other kingdoms far from the foothills had vastly lower amounts. Ania did not realize the sheer magnitude of this from the viewpoint of the *Jefes*. Now she saw she should have made this announcement at the very start. If so, she might have had more control over the other concessions.

She then cautioned them, "Realize that if say a hundred years from now, Valen divides into two smaller kingdoms, then the amount given to each of the new kingdoms will be proportional to the number of miles that border with the plateau spaceport. That will have to be spelled out in our contract, of course. None of us can foresee what the conditions will be that far into the future."

Inez also sensed that from Ania's viewpoint, the total price being paid was virtually nothing at all, that she was getting a huge bargain here. However, she did not say anything about this detail. What else could she ask for? Technology to help out was outlawed, even bringing in crops that might grow in the altered climate was out. The very things, which could ultimately aid everyone on Tierra, were out, thanks to that directive. She could not even ask for cloth bolts since they could not guarantee the materials used in them were native to Tierra. However, she also realized that the contract would have to be renegotiated in five hundred years. By then, perhaps Tierra would be vastly more technologically oriented and many more things could be accepted as payment. For now, this would have to suffice. Besides, she liked the concessions involved with the Exchange City. This offered a real benefit to many other people on Tierra, not just these three rulers.

The group discussed a few more minor details and then spent several days drawing up the precise documents. Wording was crucial and far more time was wasted getting just the precise wording used. In short, what was ultimately signed by all four parties would be legally binding for five hundred years, independent of who controlled the fifty miles bordering the plateau. On this point, Ania was absolutely insistent. She'd be fired if she did not make it one hundred percent binding for that period.

At least Inez received the wording that she desired. When the contract was up, a new lease had to be worked out. If terms could not be worked out within a year, the spaceport land would have to be given back to the kingdoms bordering it. Hence, in five hundred years, the people of Tierra had a way to get rid of the Rigel-3 people, if things did not work out and went south. This she insisted upon and Ania finally had to agree to it. Again, Ania was very much impressed with the intelligence and wisdom of Inez.

In fact, Ania asked Inez to come for visits when she could manage it. She liked this native woman and wanted to learn more about her. Inez agreed, for she wanted to find out more about these aliens and their culture.

The first transfer would be on July 1st 1002 at the new Exchange City. Ania promised that the city and the road to the west would be ready by then. She agreed to help *Jefe* Ben get the beginnings of the city constructed in order to meet that deadline. She had little choice. During the winter, the locals would not be able to do much work; the snow depths were prohibitive for native technology, but not the monstrous machines of the Imperium. The day after the meeting broke up, Ania ordered the beginning of the many construction jobs. She easily met the July deadline.

Chapter 11 The Easterlings Response

To understand the situation in the Easterlings, one must first grasp their environment and culture prior to the upheaval. Originally, there were four kingdoms, three vastly different from the others because of the great Buku Hills that ran north-south, ending some five hundred miles from the southern coast. These hills divided the old Kingdom of Matruk from the far eastern kingdoms of Domei in the north, Arad in the central zone, and Alba at the extreme southern tip. Matruk lay west of Alba and east of the great Wyndl River. The climate of Matruk was originally quite similar to that of the Midlands, since it was adjacent to the middle kingdoms.

The Buku Hills consisted of a vast sea of mesas. From the west, the land rose smoothly to the peaks. The eastern sides of the mesas were often nearly sheer thousand foot drop-offs, wholly unclimbable due to the soft sedimentary rock. The width of the hills averaged some five hundred miles and tended to block rainfall further eastward. What rains did come flowed back westward, eventually joining with the Wyndl River. Hence, the three easterly kingdoms were primarily arid in nature, though there was a wide range of dryness patterns.

Domei in the far north was both dry and cold, though not as frigid as Haruk, save in the northernmost portion. Rolling arid hills dominated the landscape, though sheep thrived here. A mostly dry riverbed from ancient days divided Domei from the Arad south of that kingdom. The Arad was a vast, sandy desert with tall, windswept sand dunes dotted with life-giving oases. Another wide, dry riverbed separated the land of the sand dunes from the small Kingdom of Alba along the southern coast. Here, the rolling hills supported scrubby grasses, and water was more readily available for commercial purposes, primarily because the Buku Hills only blocked the northern five hundred miles, leaving the southern five hundred miles of its border free for rains to enter, though not frequently.

Because of the harsh conditions inland, most of the population lived within twenty miles of the seacoast. Some fifteen thousand lived in Teraspoli, Domei and a like number in Tecuci, Arad. Turda, Alba boasted closer to thirty thousand inhabitants. Of course, there were numerous smaller towns dotting the long coastline of these three kingdoms. Yet, there were many inland villages as well. The Easterlings were a hardy folk though their language was not too dissimilar from that of the other two large divisions. Their culture, on the other hand, was different, derived in part from the products that they produced.

The three eastern kingdoms exported vast amounts of colorfully dyed silk bolts, the finest on Tierra. Rainbow dyes were plentiful throughout these lands, and some were also exported to the western lands. Fine blown glass was masterfully crafted and was their second largest export. Closer to the Buku Hills, a few iron mines were found, but there were much larger deposits of copper which was their third largest export. Vast deposits of silicates were located here too, but they did not play any role for centuries. They also exported smaller amounts of the other lighter metals, such as tin, zinc, and a good deal of silver, though silver was rare. Hence, fine silks, copper objects, and fine glass were found in abundance in the three eastern kingdoms.

Because of the high heat, both men and women wore thin, silk clothing. The men always wore white silk, loose-fitting shirts and pants, though the pants were somewhat thicker and were tied just above the ankles. The men's sandals had long pointed toes that curved upwards. Gaily colored waistbands identified the tribe or clan to which the male belonged. Each one had their own unique color scheme, but all were gaily done. When out in the hot sun, the men also wore silk wrappings over their heads, much like a turban. All men of age, that is fifteen and older, carried their unique, curved scimitars around their waists and a wicked curved dagger strapped to their left shins. Men fought with one in each hand, a deadly combination.

The three kingdoms abided by a strict three caste system called the Castas. The Lords Castas consisted of the rulers and those who controlled the power-base. The Craftsman Castas consisted of those who did the fine work, the coppersmiths, the millers, the rug makers, the cloth makers, the smelters, the blacksmiths, the soldiers, the guards, and the weapons makers. These were the gentry. The Labor Casta consisted of the lowest servants, the menial laborer, and the wholly unskilled workers. To help denote one's Castas, fingernail length was used. The Lords Castas kept their nails at least four inches long, though none was allowed to exceed the length of their actual Lord or King, whose nails were often six inches long. The Lords Castas seldom fought, their weapons were primarily ceremonial. Rather, their fighting was done by proxy, utilizing their soldiers or personal guards instead.

The Craftsman Castas men were allowed to have their nails as long as two inches, but often their occupation prohibited such and that was acceptable. The Labor Castas could grow theirs to a half inch beyond their fingertips, but no more. Few could afford such luxury however.

Their women were also bound by the same Castas, and their nails uniformly spoke of the Castas to which they belonged. With both sexes, it was possible to marry into a higher Castas. That is, a Lords Castas could marry a Labor Castas, which would then elevate the Labor Castas man or woman into the Lords Castas. One never moved into a lower Castas; that was not allowed. Ordinarily, one was fixed permanently within the Castas, in which he or she was born, excepting by marriage elevation.

The women's clothing was influenced by their Castas, unlike the men. Dita, the Social-Anthropologist, had a theory about the Easterlings women's clothing, though unproven. Her notion was that in ancient times, the Easterlings men must have feared that their women and wives would run away and desert them. Ignoring the real why that is lost in antiquity, all women of the three eastern kingdoms wore variations of the fetter skirt. Made of heavy silk, these gaily colored skirts fit extremely tightly all down their legs to their ankles with no walking slit. This forced the women to take a shuffling-like two inch steps at most. Women's movement was thus extremely slow and shuffling. None could climb stairs, but that was not a problem since all buildings had only one floor.

The women also wore sandals, but theirs had a rounded

toe, unlike the long pointed toes of the men's. Loose fitting tops varied widely among the Castas and whether the woman was out in the sun or inside. When inside, the women wore the thinnest silk blouses, or none at all, in the case of the Lords Castas. Yes, one could see everything and the women were proud to display their bosoms, using them to help charm the men in their lives. When outside in the hot sun, a somewhat heavier silk blouse was worn, but removed or replaced when coming indoors. Like the men, the length of their nails also indicated their Castas and thus social standing.

With both sexes, one's hair was never cut. To cut one's hair would lower his or her vitality and life energy or so it was commonly believed. The height of disgrace was to have one's hair cut short, which was done to those convicted of crimes. Seeing a man or woman with short hair told all to everyone who saw that person. Men wore theirs in a long single braid, while the women wore theirs in two braids. However, at night, both sexes undid their braids.

Now the women were superior dancers. The undulating and twisting of their upper bodies enthralled the men. Indeed, it has been said that more than one Labor Castas woman enticed a Lord Castas to marry her because of her sexy gyrations on the dance floor. Further, marriage was not monogamous, for the men at least. A man had as many wives as he could support. There were rigid and fast rules though. A man had to prove and continue to prove once each year that he was capable of supporting the wives he had. If it was shown that in a given year he had failed to properly provide for them, one or more wives were dismissed, beginning with the most recently added wife and any children she may have. Hence, the newer wives did all that they could to see that these extended marriages thrived or else they would be dumped. Those in the Lords Castas often had many wives, though those in the Labor Castas were lucky to have but one.

For centuries, when a woman reached her teens, she was considered of age and had her arms bound. To a copper band around her waist, her arms were attached just above her elbows where a pair of leather bands was tied. A copper chain a few inches long fastened her elbow bands to the waistband, allowing her to use her hands and lower arms, albeit awkwardly.

Further, at nighttime, the woman's arms were positioned behind her waist, inserted into a leather tube, and secured. Hence, she could not move her arms and thus not resist the marital advances of her husband. In the morning, the husband or father was required to remove them as his first action upon waking. A good deal of religious notions quickly built up around this binding practice, which also brought the two closer together by forcing the husband or father to attend to the needs of his wife or unmarried daughters.

These were the customs prior to the upheaval. Of note, the few witches in the Easterlings had to import a great many of their herbs and remedies from the Midlands, prior to the COG's destruction of the witches around the year 1000.

When the bishops with the help of the Psychman Cezar attempted to take over the rulership of the four Easterlings kingdoms, again the minor Lords seceded forming smaller kingdoms, often based upon strong clan or tribal ties, leaving the bishops in control of the four largest cities only. Later on, when the bishops began implementing the decrees of their new Archbishop, major changes occurred, primarily because far too many women were being kidnaped by or married into other clans. Bind your women to you took on a whole new meaning here in the far east, just as it had for centuries.

Because women were supposed to be seen and not heard and some were a bit too vocal in their protest of the new COG ruling to bind women, all women were also given eight lip rings, four in each one, usually small copper rings. If a woman was too vocal, her husband or father simply tied the rings together, sealing her lips. As time went on, the practice became commonplace whenever a woman went out of her home. Thus, there could be no chance of her flirting with other men and being taken away from her lawful husband.

These seemingly barbaric practices became necessary because of the horrific weather pattern changes that occurred on Tierra. The northern Domei, always cold, became absolutely frigid. Many perished before they could move southward to warmer lands or died in transit, especially women. Even those living on or near the seacoast became threatened and took to wearing heavier clothing as time went on. The Arad became even dryer, again forcing many to migrate for lack of food and water, many perishing in the attempt or were unable to find new homes. Alba experienced a doubling of its population during several years following the weather change. Men became highly worried about losing their many wives and thus began taking all manner of precautions against that, all shrouded in religious notions, which made it palatable to all concerned. Most women accepted the new restraints out of fear of being abandoned by her husband or father. Alone, she stood little chance of surviving, though many were overly vocal about it at first.

Enter the *mentales* gift or more truthfully, the lack of it. The dust from the refining process on Plateau Grado fell most heavily on the eastern portion of the Westerlings and most of the Midlands. Hardly any got as far as the Easterlings. Thus, as the *mentales* gifts became more widely known in the Easterlings, a huge have-not problem developed. All throughout the three eastern old kingdoms, those few who got the gift became highly prized, highly honored, highly paid, and highly sought after. Being closer to the Midlands, Matruk did not have this problem for they had a reasonable number of men and women with the gift. In time, the Lords began to realize that they were now at a horrible disadvantage because they had so few with the precious gifts! *Mentales* became synonymous with power.

During the first few years, many small battles were fought between clans, small villages, and the tiny kingdoms. The prize was the addition of one or more new *mentales* gifted to the victor. Of course, this further reduced the population, including women who often became collateral damage in the raids.

Later on, it was discovered that mothers and fathers often passed on their gifts to their children. Over time, via the COG churches and bishops, the Lords Castas learned of the breeding programs that were commencing in other kingdoms, especially in the Midlands. This was the last straw for these *mentales* have-not lands. Something had to be done about it.

Early January 1006, Serafino (Fino) Lucca, the thirty-five year old clan leader, held a Lords conference. Their clan owned the oasis called Lucca near the Buku Hills in the Arad, some five hundred miles from the southern border with Alba. They had a lucrative copper mine and also made fine silk bolts. Yet, Lucca was quite isolated. Still, twice a year they made the long journey down into Alba to sell their goods and returning with supplies to enable them to survive another year. The clan was rather large, some thousand members. Fino had only recently come to power or rather usurped it. He had the *mentales* gift of Domination and had used it in a massive power play, yielding him the rulership of the clan.

All had dark brown hair and eyes, though now the *mentales* had changed to yellow with brown spots, and all women had greatly enlarged breasts nearly the size of their heads. By now, the women appreciated their large endowment, as their newborn babies seemed to thrive far better than before. Sitting with him at the meeting were his two brothers, Fredo, thirty-three, and Gavino, twenty-nine. Their wives, Gina and Savina, were also present because Fino insisted that his two wives be present, Adriana, twenty-five, and Donata, thirty. Why? Adriana also had the *mentales* gift; hers was that of healing. Though she was the younger bride, because of her gift, she was elevated to the position of the second most important person in the clan, second only to her husband, Serafino.

"We simply have to do something to get more *mentales* gifted people into our clan. You've heard how the Ciano clan has just capture the whole Vento oasis. How long do you think we will be left alone? What's to keep the Midlands kings from crossing the Buku Hills to take our precious copper mine and silk factory? They have so many *mentales* that we don't stand a chance with them," Fino pointed out.

"We know, we know. But what do we do about it? *Mentales* gifted don't grow on trees. We can't wait for your children to grow up, Fino," Fredo complained.

"The only way I can see is for us to go into the Midlands and steal some *mentales* gifted people from them," Fino declared, drawing instant protests.

"You can't be serious, Fino!" exclaimed Gavino. "My god, we'd all get killed trying to capture a single powerful *mentales* man."

"You speak madness. I agree with Gavino," Fredo growled.

"Men, very likely, but not women. They are easy to spot, yellow eyes. We go among them and look for likely candidates, say younger women. After all, we want to breed many children from them. In time, we can have an entire army of *mentales* gifted in our clan. We can't kidnap men. I wholly agree. Besides, even if we captured them, we'd never be able to bend them to our will. However, as Adriana pointed out to me, young women are susceptible. According to her, the women in the Midlands are not bound as our women are. Such travesty of the teachings of the Lord God. I don't know how they get way with such idiotic notions, but they do. We can kidnap a likely candidate, bind her in our Holy Ways, paying particular attention to sealing her lips that she cannot speak and invoke her *mentales* against us. Once she is here in Lucca, in time, she will break and willingly join us. What other choice would she have? A man would have many choices, fighting not the least. But when was the last time an Easterlings woman fought as a man? Never."

Not bound as we are, my love, Adriana sent him in a coy, teasing manner, causing him to grin, but the others frowned. They hated this special rapport that Fino and Adriana had, none more so than the usurped wife, Donata. Though she often spoke against Adriana, she had learned better, having had her lips sealed for nearly a week as a result.

"I am presuming that these Midlands folks also keep close guard over their young *mentales* women. So I have worked out a fool proof plan that will work."

"But when they find out that we have kidnaped their young women, what is to keep them from attacking us and wiping us out? You know darn well that scimitars and daggers are no match for *mentales* spells," Gavino pointed out acidly.

"That is the beauty of my plan. They will not find out. Further, if they should stop and accost us, why they will not find their lost women with us," Fino replied, withholding vital information. He enjoyed seeing the looks of utter frustration on the faces of his brothers and then their utter awe when he sprang the clinching details on them.

At last sensing both men were at their limit of tolerance, he added, "We will be in two groups, one led by me and the other led by Adriana and you, Fredo. Here's the plan, listen carefully and see if you can find any holes in it that I have overlooked." He talked for an hour, drawing a sketch of the Midlands and the Easterlings in the sand. "On the way up, we can resupply in Matera, where Adriana has close friends. No one will be the wiser. Fool proof." As expected the two men were indeed not only impressed with the plan, but were convinced it would work and their lives would not be in jeopardy because of it.

Fredo made one comment, "The part that I like is that the women will be coming from lands that are a long distance from here. Even if their men should come after them, the sheer distance will make it almost impossible for them to reach us. Brilliant brother, brilliant."

"Okay. Let's get Jovanni and Lauro practicing their juggling acts. Fredo, you see to the wagon constructions and Gavino, you see to the secondary wagons and the boats. Donata, it is supposed to be very cold there, so you and the other wives see what accommodations can be made without violating our honor."

"Is it true that Midlands women are not only not bound but also hide their bodies beneath mountains of thick cloth?" Donata asked curiously.

"That's what I've heard from some of the men in Alba," Fino replied.

"It's a wonder that any Midlands woman could ever attract a husband! They must also be fools." Donata just could not imagine hiding her entire body beneath mountains of cloth, let alone not wear the fetter skirts, unthinkable. Still, she knew that Fino was expecting her to make allowances and to do her part. *Well damn it, they don't leave me any real choice, now do they. If I make any fuss, Fino will back his younger wife, not me. She's got mentales. Curse the day that he found her. I'm lucky that he still keeps me around, he could have dumped me or given me over to one of his brothers, but I'd still be seconds there too. Curse the damnable mentales. It has fouled up our whole lives!*

Little did she know that Fino and Adriana could hear her thoughts, as if she had been yelling them aloud. Fino accepted them for what they were, a first wife being replaced more or less legally by a second wife. If the old rules were to be followed, it would be Adriana who was number two, not a demoted Donata. For that reason, he said nothing. Adriana said nothing for entirely different reasons. Her *mentales* gift made her number one, demoting Donata. Of that, there was no question, for Adriana was a powerful woman in her own right. No, she needed Donata for entirely different reasons of which she neither spoke of nor thought of, keeping them always from Fino's mind. She even went out of her way to insist that Fino prepare Donata for bed each evening before doing herself, allowing the older woman some first-wife dignity. For that kindness, Donata kept her notions to herself.

That evening, the two wives shuffled into the master bedroom. Donata took her seat before the dresser waiting for Adriana to undo and brush out her hair. With their upper arms locked to their waists, it was customary for each woman to do each other's hair, among other things. Again, Adriana made this peacekeeping concession to the older, first wife, although she had every right to insist that she be done first. She had the gift, not Donata. However, it again helped keep Donata on her side, in as much as that was possible. She shuffled to the dresser, bent and retrieved the hairbrush and shuffled into position to do the older woman's hair. This nightly ritual allowed them time to chat and Donata always did so, though about the most mundane things, as far as Adriana was concerned.

After undoing the two braids, Adriana began brushing out Donata's long brown hair. Of course, she often had to stand and reposition her body, due to the extremely short reach of her lower arms, constrained as they were. Small price to pay for having the utter respect and devotion of the men, she thought. Donata's thoughts were still on the grand plan, the details of which she'd just found out minutes ago.

"You know, I do think that this will work. Everything depends upon you and I, doesn't it? We are in the power position with the captured women. Say, how will we communicate with them? I don't speak their language and I would be surprised if they spoke the Easterlings dialect."

"I think that we will have to take time on the way there to learn some of their language. It cannot be helped, I don't think," Adriana replied. "I am not very good at languages, are you?" She didn't say that she could simply read their thoughts, which were independent of language or words. A person had an idea, a concept in his or her mind. That concept or idea was what Adriana easily picked up, language independent. However, she continued to humor the woman, besides, she needed her in more ways than one. Not the least was the simple fact that no Easterlings woman was truly self-sufficient, not constrained as they were. No, these women learned to rely upon one another for many basic needs, such as doing their hair and bathing. She had another need for her, but this she kept locked in the furthest recess of her mind so that Fino would not detect it. So much depended upon it.

"I suppose that I might be. I guess we will see. Thank you for doing my hair." The two women switched places and Adriana's hair was undone and brushed out.

Shortly Fino came into the room and undid his hair, shaking it out too. He seldom brushed it fully. He looked at his two wives and commented, "It is a shame that I will have to cut my nails drastically shorter. None of the Midlands men are cultured enough to allow theirs to grow. However, my beauties, you will not have to cut yours in order to do your part. That's something at least." All three of them had about six inch long nails. "Are we ready for bed now?"

They were. Gently, he helped each one out of their thin blouse and unfastened their fetter skirts for them. Then he fetched the leather tubes and gently slipped Donata's arms into the tube, securely locking them behind her back. He did Adriana's last, only because she insisted that she not make Donata feel like she was being demoted. With their arms secured, he pulled down the silken sheets and helped each woman into bed, crawling in between the two. With their hair intertwined, the three allowed their passions to run freely.

Adriana waited until she heard the even breathing of Fino as he finally fell asleep. Already Donta was sound asleep, quite contented. Adriana was too, for that matter. Rather she wanted to make very sure that she could not be overheard. She focused and expanded her awareness southwards. She felt the familiar mind. *Vanna, Adriana here. All is set. Your plan is going to be executed. I've got Fino to agree to our route. Don't lose hope. I'll let you know when we get closer to arriving. My guess now is that it will be late fall.*

Thank you my love, thank you. I have total faith in you. The two broke the telepathic contact. Adriana smiled and relaxed. All was going to work out after all.

At dawn, Fino rose and helped the two rise. Gently he removed the arm tubes, helped each into their fetter skirt, and then put on their desired light silk blouse. After giving each a kiss on their foreheads, he left them to braid their hair, while he did his. He stepped outside and did his few morning chores while waiting patiently for the women to prepare breakfast. Today, they would begin work on their grand plan to obtain a number of *mentales* gifted women for the clan, hopefully ensuring their long term survival in these unsettling times.

In the Wyth tower, Elena, Drina's eldest daughter, had become a woman. She was fifteen now, and like all other women her breasts had grown positively huge. Even Filipa, her fourteen year old sister, had hers filled out to nearly the size of her head as well. Both teens were elated over this because they looked like their mother and the other women around the mansion and tower. However, Elena was extremely worried and troubled. She had been so for over a year, though she had been too embarrassed to say anything about it. Again, it was her time of the month and her long term worry surfaced yet again, making her irritable.

This day, Drina was not overly busy and picked up on Elena's mental anguish. "Dear, what's wrong? No use in hiding it from me. I can see it as plainly as your face."

Elena blushed, realizing that she'd failed to put up her mental block. *It's private mom.*

"Well, let's go into my room. No one will bother us

there." Almost unwillingly, Elena followed her mother. Sitting beside each other on the large bed, Drina said, "Now then, tell me all about it. Boy troubles perhaps?" She was guessing, knowing better than to simply enter her daughter's mind without her permission. Such was mental rape and she'd never do such a thing. No, she'd wait until Elena told her.

Elena giggled, "No. Well, sort of." She sighed and decided finally to voice it. "Mom, I'm not normal."

"Huh? Of course you are normal, dear."

"Not really. I don't have any arms just like you."

"True, but when has that stopped us?"

"That's not the point, mom. I mean, well look. You and dad had three kids and we all are armless, just like you are."

"Well, that's true, dear."

"That's why you and dad haven't had any more children. I know I heard you two talking about it several times. You both don't want to risk having another armless child. I can't blame you for that. We are weird, not like everyone else."

Drina flushed. "I'm sorry. You were not meant to overhear that. We love all three of you with all our hearts just as you are."

"I know mom. That's not it either."

"Well what is the matter then?"

"It's me. I don't know if I want to have any babies and that means I don't dare ever have a boyfriend and get married, doesn't it?" She nearly broke down into tears, but managed to keep them at bay, barely.

"Why on earth don't you want your own children to love?"

"Cause I am scared that my babies will not have any arms either! I don't want my babies to be a freak like me. Mine won't have arms either, will they?" Elena did break down now, leaning her head into her mother's chest and sobbing her heart out.

Drina knew the smart thing to do was to allow her daughter to get it off her chest. Making sure that her own Hide Thoughts was in place, she began to think herself. *How can I respond to this one? I could tell her that her babies will be perfectly normal, but I can't. I don't know that and I have a notion that they won't, just as she does. Damn. Triple damn! I bet Filipa is thinking similar thoughts. She's been a bit mopey of late. I wonder if Emilano is worried about this too? Ernesto and I ought to have seen this one coming years ago and figured something out. Now it has falling squarely into my lap.*

"We are not freaks, Elena, but our bodies are different than most. Your father and I don't want to have more children not because we are different, but because it is very difficult for us to manage with four of us like we are. I just couldn't put more of a burden on your father. But dear, you are putting the cart before the horse. First, you need to find just the right man for you, one who loves you unconditionally, and one who you also love. Then, the two of you must discuss this fully. There is no reason under the sun, moons, and stars not to have children of your own, whether or not they are different than other children, as long as you and your husband first want to have children and when you have them, love them wholly. If your husband does not want to risk having children by you out of fear they will inherit from you, then for my money, he is not worth marrying. It took me a very long time to meet just the right man for me, your father. So don't fret about not having a boyfriend right now. Trust me; one will come along one day. All I ask is that if your children take after you, don't have so many that you cannot care for them. I can handle all three of you, but no more. I refuse to put more burdens on your father. Remember always, we are not our bodies."

"I know I am not my body. It's just we are so different and I don't want my children to be so different."

"I understand. I did not want any of you three to be like me. Yet, when each of you came, I found that I loved you just as much, maybe more because you three are extremely good children. I would not want to lose any one of you three. But as your mom, I would really like to one day be a grandmother."

Elena giggled a little. "Okay mom. I am still worried about it, but I think I understand. Say, are we going to get to go to see the Easterlings carnival people this afternoon?"

"I've got to fix everyone's supper. Why don't you take your brother and sister to see them? Make sure that they know that they are supposed to be back by suppertime."

It was mid-June of 1006 and three gaily colored carnival wagons from the Easterlings rolled into Wyth, the last stop on their grand tour. Several men with long, braided hair hung out some posters showing jugglers and acrobats and indicating a show in the afternoon. Around one in the afternoon as the rain clouds slowly thickened, a crowd gathered just outside Wyth not far from a small river that drained into the Wyndl River some fifty miles to the northeast. Most were children and young adults, though a few older folks came to watch the festivities.

"Elena, why are the women wearing such tight skirts? They can hardly walk. And why are they chained up?" asked Filipa.

"Yes, why?" Emilano added. "Seems kind of funny to me."

"I don't know. We did hear that the Easterlings bind their women. This must be what they mean. Come on, I want to watch the jugglers."

"I want to watch the women dance. I'll catch up to you later," Filipa insisted.

"I'm going to watch the knife throwers. Now that *is* interesting," Emilano said. "Ben's there. I'm going to watch with him."

"Okay, remember to be back by suppertime." Elena headed to the back wagon where the man wearing gaily colored silk shirt and pants had a small crowd watching him juggle a number of battens. She watched, fascinated by his skill. Then, another of the Easterlings women in her fetter skirt shuffled very slowly up to him and took the battens from him, making her slow way back to a stand, all the while smiling gaily at the audience. Next, he began juggling flaming sticks, at least that's what they seemed to be to Elena, who'd never seen such juggling. The more she watched the more she was fascinated by the man's skill.

After several more changes of objects, many in the crowd moved on to see the other attractions, but Elena stood waiting to see if he would juggle some more. "Hello there young lady. You like my juggling?" the man said with a big grin in broken Midlands dialect.

"Yes, it is fascinating. It's something that I can't possibly do, but I would sure like to know how you can do it."

"Well, I am finished for a while. Have to let the crowd see my fellow acts so I have a few minutes to spare. If you want to come to the back of our wagon where my wife is at now, I can show you how it is done. Only you have to promise me not to tell my secrets to others — spoils my act, you see."

"Sure, thanks. It is amazing how there are so many more objects in the air than you have hands. How do you do it?" Elena asked, joining the pretty, brown haired woman, who was carefully lining up the different sets of objects on the back of the wagon.

"Hello. I am Gina. So you like my Fredo's act, eh?"

"Yes, he's amazing, Gina. He's going to show me how it is done. I can't do it, but I'd like to know. How can you walk in that tight of a dress? Why are you all tied up? Is that part of the act too?"

Gina laughed. "No silly. Every woman in the Easterlings wears these skirts. No one would dare wear a loose fitting dress such as you are wearing. It would be beyond scandalous! All we women have our arms bound to our sides to please our Lord God and our husbands. We are bound to our husbands this way. It is just, how you say here, symbolic."

"I think I understand. It is a symbol that you are married to Fredo?"

"Yes, exactly. I honor him by having my arms at my sides always. It is a great honor, you see. But you Midlands have such strange customs here. I feel very out of place among your women. Don't any of your women here honor your men? And to wear such loose fitting and such thick dresses! Why you would think that all women here are sluts. Pardon me, my dear. You are young and should not hear such words."

Elena grinned and did not see another man slip up behind her, but she did feel the solid thump on the top of her head and the world vanished. He held onto her body and another man quickly wrapped a rug around her body, lifted her across his shoulders, and slipped into the woods, unseen by all the others in the crowd. He laid the package into the small boat and shoved off, paddling swiftly downstream. Later that night, he met the large barge where the small river joined the Wyndl River. There he handed the package to a man on the barge and tied the small boat to the barge. He then headed off on foot in the icy rain.

Gavino carried the unconscious woman below deck, where Adriana and Savina were waiting, ready to help handle their latest captive. "Last one. This makes the eighth. Nice haul. Time to head home. Make sure she gets *bacal* right away. I will get the barge going," he said, laying the still wrapped teen onto a bunk bed.

Adriana shuffled over to her and began clumsily unwrapping Elena. "Oh my. Look at this one, Savina! She has no arms!" She lifted an eye lid. "*Mentales* all right. How strange."

Savina shuffled carefully over to examine the young woman, carrying a small vial of *bacal*. She poured the liquid into Elena's mouth and made sure it slipped down her throat. "Well, it makes our job a little easier. Come on, let's get her undressed and into proper clothing. They wear such obscene clothing here in the Midlands! Honestly, don't any of their women have any modesty or honor?" Adriana shrugged. *Apparently not*, she thought.

Once that was done, they then sat on either side of her head and began making eight punctures in her lips, four on top, four on the bottom lip. Next, they inserted the finely made copper loops, making sure that they were fastened properly. Then they slipped a leather thong through them and tied her lips together. Next, they worked together to get a proper fetter skirt onto Elena and slipped a pair of sandals on her feet. At last, they fastened a finely made, thin silk blouse on her and braided her lovely hair into two long braids. Satisfied, Adriana shuffled over to retrieve her salts and back again. Waving them under Elena's nose, she roused the woman.

Elena wiggled to sit up and tried to speak. She could only mumble and her lips would not move, though she tried to open her mouth. A strange taste was in her mouth, though she didn't pay attention to that at first. She tried to get her leg up to rub her aching head but it didn't move. She looked down and saw that she was now wearing one of those strange skirts that she'd seen the Easterlings women wearing at the carnival. Shocked and suddenly very frightened she made a lot of mumbling noises.

In broken Midlands dialect, Adriana said quietly, "Calm down. Your lips are tied shut until you learn to behave and be quiet unless you are given permission to speak. We got rid of that outrageous clothing of yours. They are not suitable for even a prostitute! We have you properly dressed as a fine Easterlings woman now, for that is what you are now. One of us. We are taking you back to our village, Lucca, to be one of us and help us with your *mentales* gifts. Be quiet; there is nothing you can do. For now, don't try to use your gifts. I've given you a strong dose of *bacal*. I will give you a few minutes to absorb all this before we go into the main cabin and join the others that we are taking back with us. I am called Adriana, she is Savina. We will be taking care of you during the long journey." She rose and Elena watched totally shocked as she carefully shuffled over to a chair and sat down. Now she realized what that awful taste in her mouth was: *bacal*. Her hopes sank, her mind was temporarily dead, her *mentales* gift totally absent.

She wiggled and managed to sit up better, her feet on the floor. It was moving now. Just how the floor could be moving eluded her. Elena's fears only worsened by the unknown. She listened in to what the two older women were saying. Adriana said, "She will have a harder time walking without arms to help keep her balance or to catch herself if she should start to fall. I think it best if one of us accompanies her when she needs to walk."

"Yes, and one of us will have to feed her and help her with everything. Honestly, couldn't they have found a better *mentales* woman? Are they scraping the bottom of the barrel? She will be a liability for us, even if she joins us. Someone will always have to be helping her with everything. I hope her gifts are worth it," Savina replied.

"You are right. She is so helpless that I am surprised with Fino. Yet, I will not second guess my husband. He must know what he is doing. We'll have our hands full taking care of her, no doubt of that, especially on this barge. Well, come on, let's get her to the others, and introduce them." The two women rose and shuffled over to Elena. "Okay, up you go. We will make sure that you don't fall. Our girls wear these skirts as soon as they can walk, so our people are used to them and find them quite comfortable. However, we have arms. Nevertheless, you will get used to learning how to walk properly like a good Easterlings woman.

Elena panicked. She tried to walk but could only manage to move her right foot forward a couple of inches. She wobbled wildly, but the two women helped her regain her balance, though both found it rather awkward to do with their bound arms. "Slowly, slowly," Adriana explained using a tone of voice suitable for a five year old girl. Elena could only make muffled noises indicating her panic and utter dismay.

After an eternity of shuffling, they reached a door and passed into the main cabin area. Elena's eyes rapidly took in the scene before her. Along the sides were narrow bunks on which seven other young women sat rigidly in their overly tight skirts and silk blouses. Each had their arms bound to their waists just above their elbows and each had eight small copper rings through their lips, which were tied shut just like hers. The main area held a table and ten chairs with a large space on either side. "You will be practicing walking in the morning. Now it's time to meet your fellow captives. Ladies, this is Elena or so I've been told. Shake your head if I have your name correct, Elena," Adriana asked. She did.

"Now these are Martha, Sally, Ann, Jill, Molly, Nadine, and Shannen. Now then, since poor Elena here has no arms, each of you can take turns with helping her with her needs. It is past our bedtime. So undo each other's hair and brush it. Tonight, I will do Elena's lovely hair. When we are finished, I will ask Savina's husband to perform his duty for us all." Elena wondered what that meant. Was she about to be raped? Would it hurt? Her terror only grew as the older woman awkwardly undid her braids and brushed her hair. She watched as the other captives struggled mightily to accomplish this task for each other. It was obvious all were in fear; she didn't need *mentales* to tell that much.

She did notice that Adriana and Savina also did each other's hair as well. Finally, Savina slowly shuffled to the door and called out, "Dear, we are ready to honor you." Shortly, the tall man entered and kissed his wife on her forehead and bowed to Adriana. Elena noticed that he had extremely long fingernails and so did Adriana and Savina; she'd missed this detail before. As she watched, he began taking down hollow leather tubes and Elena could not imagine what they were. He went to Adriana first and as she sat with her back to him, he gently slipped her arms behind her back and into the tube and tied them securely there. Adriana then shuffled to one of the bunks and sat down. He helped tuck her into bed, returning to do the same to his wife, who gave him a passionate good night kiss. One by one, he did the same to the other women. At last he came up to Elena. "Well, come on then. It is my honor to tuck you into bed. It is our way." Elena rose and slowly shuffled to the remaining bed and allowed him to tuck her in, pulling up the covers for her. He blew out the light leaving them in utter darkness and left.

Elena, still terrified, listened to the others as they drifted into sleep. When she thought that they were all asleep, she finally began crying as silently as she could. For the first time in her life, she was helpless and she hated it. It was bad enough being so different, but this was a horror. She drifted into an ill sleep.

In the morning, the man returned and helped each woman out of her tube sleeve. After he left, the women helped each other lower their fetter skirt and use the chamber pot. Then they braided each other's hair. At last, the man returned with breakfast and Elena watched helplessly as the other women shuffled about the room setting the table. Then she too rose and shuffled to a chair. Only then, Adriana spoke, "For Elena's benefit, I will now untie your lips so that you may eat. One of us will feed Elena. Remember, do not speak a word unless Savina or I give you permission to speak. If you do not follow this, we will tie your lips again and you will get no breakfast. After breakfast, it is walking practice time. Twenty laps around the long table then you can relax and enjoy the morning."

Elena notice that their tea was laced with *bacal* leaves and realized that they would be kept doped up for some time, perhaps until they reached their destination. *Well they have to do that or we would use our telepathy to get help. At least I haven't been raped and am being fed. Why are they doing this to us?*

Day after day the routine continued. At first, she tried to keep track of the days as they passed, but soon lost count. Daily her walking improved until at last she was able to keep her balance for the most part while making the twenty laps around the table area, which was done three times each day. Always her lips were kept tied except for meals and always she was given *bacal*, though she once refused the tea and had Adriana pour the liquid into her mouth forcefully. After that, she merely drank it as the other women did.

Then one day, the barge's movements became more irregular and violent, so much so that Adriana dispensed with the walking as even she had a good deal of trouble navigating the room. For days after that, Gavino always appeared to help the ten women as needed. She strained her ears and thought that she heard the sounds of the ocean. It was similar to the Westerlings city in which she had been born and raised. Where were they going? At last she decided that they must be going to somewhere in the Easterlings. That would make sense.

Finally, one day the barge stopped rocking. Adriana announced, "We've reached our port city. Time to disembark. From now on, we will be traveling in two carriages. This is a big and dangerous city. You all appear to be normal Easterlings women, and I expect you to behave and act like one of us. You five will walk in a line behind me, and you five will walk behind Savina. We have a fair distance to walk to get to our waiting carriages. It is hot down here; so starting today, we will be wearing a more appropriate blouse as befitting Lords Castas women, which you all are now, even though your nails have not grown enough yet." Elena looked at the other women and notice that theirs were now an inch or two beyond the tips of their fingers. How much time had passed she wondered. She could not know that it was now mid-September and certainly not from the heat that she felt as Gavino lifted her up and carried her to the wooden docks, sitting her down beside Adriana.

She looked around and saw that she was in a large seaport, quite unlike those in the Westerlings. The buildings were different. All the men wore white, save for the multicolored waistbands. Dangerous looking weapons hung from their waists. Several men, including Gavino, took the lead and a couple followed along behind the two lines. Carefully, Elena began her shuffling walk, taking one two-inch step at a time. After an eternity, they reached the stone pavement and the walking was slightly easier.

When they reached the main streets, she saw other women, lots of them. All wore the same ultra-thin silk blouses, which left nothing to one's imagination. All wore similar fetter skirts and all had their arms bound at their waists as well. Uniformly, the men's hair was done in a single long braid while the women wore theirs in two braids. Nearly all lengths fell to at least their thighs or lower. At least one woman's hair, she noted, almost touched the ground.

Seeing all the other women shuffling along as she was gave Elena some comfort. At least here, she did not feel out of place. For the most part, she, like the other ten, seemed to fit in perfectly, except Elena knew that like this, she was utterly helpless. She did not have the use of her legs for hands. Still everyone had been kind to her, assisting her with all her needs. She also realized that if she wore her own dress here so that she would not be helpless, she would look totally foreign and out of place, more so than merely being armless. She sighed as she realized this.

How long they shuffled slowly along, she could not guess. It was pure torture moving like this, but she bore it. All the women were just like her and she felt a bit of kinship with them. *I do fit in with them, sort of.* At last, they reached a number of carriages. Once more, Gavino lifted each woman up and into the carriage. None of the women could climb in by themselves; the skirts prevented it wholly. "Sit back and enjoy the countryside. It will be a long ride, quite a few days, I'm afraid, but we will be staying at some inns along the way. Again, I caution you. Do not speak unless Savina or I tell you to while we are eating."

As they rode along, Elena watched out the windows, and saw more and more of the people of the city and even spotted a sign that read Turda. At last, she realized that she must be in Alba now, thousands of miles from home. Her heart sank. No one could possible find her here and rescue her from this awful nightmare. Still, the women that she saw looked just like she and her captured companions, and she took some comfort in that. Elena thought that she rather blended in with these women. For once, her deformity took a backseat.

During the next twenty days, the temperature grew hotter and hotter. At last, Adriana removed even their thin blouses. "Yes, here in the desert, we women wear no blouses at all, only our fetter skirts. We always wear those. Be proud, our men love to admire our beauty, but please do not flirt with the men with your eyes; it is unseemly for women of the Lords Castas." At first, Elena and the others were horribly embarrassed to wear the thin gauze blouses, but soon they saw that all the women here also wore nothing but the tight skirts and again, they blended in and slowly overcame their embarrassment at being half naked in public.

On the eighteenth day, Elena noticed that their tea had no *bacal* taste in it and wondered if Adriana had made a mistake. Slowly she felt her *mentales* gifts returning, gradually, day by day. She noticed the other captives were also recovering. On the twentieth day, Adriana spoke to all ten women via telepathy. *Ladies. I have stopped giving you the bacal leaves. By now your mentales gifts are returning. If you value your very lives, do not use them and say nothing about this to the other women and especially to the men with us! I am trying to save you. Trust me. More in a while.*

One by one, all ten looked at each other and nodded to each other, indicating that they understood and that they were indeed regaining their precious *mentales* gifts. Now her gift returned and Elena intuitively knew what Adriana needed. She needed these women to do as she asked. There was something vitally important behind it, something beyond what they had been told before. But what? Whatever it was, Adriana was somehow defying her husband and the other Easterlings, of that she was totally certain. Was there a plot within a plot? For the first time, Elena forgot her misery and became wholly curious. This was becoming interesting. A mystery to solve. She vowed to herself that she would solve it.

For the last many days, they had been traveling across what seemed to be open desert lands. Great sand dunes rose way off to the east, while to their west, she could see the huge, sheer cliffs of the Buku Hills, the giant sea of mesas. The temperature was almost unbearably hot, particularly so inside the carriages. For once, she was very happy to be wearing no top at all and to have her hair braided. So were the other women, including Adriana and Savina, who was extremely happy to be so close to her home oasis.

Late that afternoon, they pulled into a small oasis out in the middle of what seemed a vast empty land. There were only a few adobe buildings here. Again Gavino lifted each woman down, and they fell into their usual marching lines.

Adriana again made telepathic contact with the ten. *This is my home village. We are almost to our destination. Remain quiet a little longer please.*

"You take them inside, Adriana, and get them settled. I will handle the carriages and see to the men's needs," Gavino ordered. She bowed and led the way inside one of the adobe buildings. She fought hard to keep her excitement from showing to Savina.

Chapter 12 Ancient Gods Arise

"Where is my baby?" Drina screamed, wholly unable to contain her fear and anxiety. Filipa and Emilano came home on time, but not Elena. Now it was nearly midnight and still no word on her missing girl. "Why oh why didn't I go with them? It's all my fault. I should never have left them go on their own!"

Though awfully worried over the missing teen just as everyone in the tower was, Aurora, became slightly annoyed that Drina would start blaming herself. She countered, "Now you are being irrational, Drina. Look, she is of age and must be treated as a responsible adult. Perhaps she found a boyfriend and has lost track of time."

"It's midnight, for god's sake, Aurora! She's never been up this late. I just know something terrible has happened to her. Why haven't the men found her? Where can she be? Is she lying somewhere badly hurt, bleeding to death? She is so helpless, my precious Elena!" She broke into another round of uncontrolled sobbing. Aurora put her arms around her, comforting her as much as she could.

"I think that we would all know it if she were hurt and in pain. She would call out to us."

"But she hasn't! She must be unconscious. Why can't I reach her Aurora? Why?"

"I don't know. Surely, the men will be returning soon with news. We must be patient." The other two children were now asleep. They had been grilled by the adults when Elena failed to show up for dinner. They both told the same stories. They had been watching the juggler man for a while. Emilano had gotten bored, and went to see the knife throwing man, while Filipa went to see other things. The last that they saw of Elena was her standing near the juggler watching his every move.

Later, Filipa tried and tried to make mental contact with her sister. Nothing. The more that she tried, the more frightened she became. At last, the adults had to put her to bed giving her a slight sleeping drought. The men of the tower, including a very alarmed and worried Ernesto had gone off in search of the missing girl around six. It was raining hard, but they took lanterns and headed off in a pack to search. Ally went with them too.

Periodically, Ally reported back to Aurora, who relayed the information to the others waiting anxiously for news. As the night wore on, all grew more and more worried that something terrible had happened to the young teen. But what?

The men reported that they could find no trace of her anywhere around the Easterlings wagons. Alford had grilled the juggler man. Yes, the girl was watching his act intently. Yes, they had chatted and he had promised to show her how it was done. Yes, she had wandered to the rear of his wagon and listened to his explanations. However, he turned his back. Later when he turned in her direction, she was not there. He assumed that she went back to the other attractions. Alford had even insisted on searching the Easterlings' wagons. While they protested some, they permitted the men to search and they didn't find Elena or even any of her few possessions. There was nothing there to suggest that was not what had happened. Holly even sent a *mentales* gifted woman who could detect lies. She reported that the juggler was telling the truth. He had turned his attention off her and she was not there when he looked back to where she was standing. However, she felt that he knew more than he was saying, but without probing the man's mind, they could not get at what it might be.

At this point, the men were out searching the underbrush and the timber surrounding the outskirts of Wyth where the Easterlings had their camp. Still nothing. Finally, Ernesto gave up the search for the night, swearing to resume at first light. "Surely you folks have ways of finding my baby," he pleaded with Alford and then Ally as they walked back through the sleeting rain, heads hung low, but not to avoid the precipitation.

"Tomorrow, I will have Abbey come and see if she can pick up any tracks. If she rides hard, she can be here in a few days," Alford suggested. *Why can't we make telepathic contact with her? It doesn't make sense. Elena is not the type to just up and run off.*

No she isn't, Ally sent back. I know that she was frightened about the possibility of her children inheriting from her as she did from Drina. She hinted that Elena was really upset about that. Surely, she didn't throw herself in the river. I think that we all would know if she did that. I am certain that she is not dead. We would have surely sensed her dying, that I know, well, pretty sure anyway. What could have happened to her? They entered the manor and had to face Drina without having found the slightest trace of her missing Elena. Ally hated this moment.

The next day, Ally had all the telepaths in their tower and their other three towers attempting to make contact with Elena. Nothing at all. Drina was a nervous wreck and Ernesto stepped in to fulfill her breakfast duties. Then, he and the men set out once more to scour the countryside. When still no word at all came by noon, Aurora decided it was high time that she used her special gift. She went to her room and quietly focused her mind. Slowly she searched the future, looking for signs of Elena in specific. Although she really had little control over what she saw and when she saw it, still she used all her skills to attempt to make such a divination.

Aurora lost all track of time, but when she finished close to suppertime, she had what she wanted. As a very somber group gathered for supper along with a red-eyed Drina, she began, "Well, I spent the afternoon looking for Elena in the future. We can rest a little easier. I did get a vision of her being here in our tower in the future. So there is hope."

"What did you see? Was she hurt? Bleeding?" Drina feared the worst.

"No, it was a very strange vision. It is as if she somehow just appeared among us, startling us all. I got the feeling that there is something really big going on that she is somehow involved in, something that we know nothing about at this time. She looked a little haggard and was wearing very strange clothing and no top, but she looked uninjured and somehow older and wiser, though I don't know what that means."

"When will it be? I want her back now," Drina wailed.

"I think it might have been fall," Aurora answered

thoughtfully, looking over her images of her vision.

"That's almost half a year from now! Surely we can do something long before then," Drina protested.

"I give you my word that I will try to reach her every single day until she returns, Drina. We all will try daily. The only thing I can think of that would be preventing telepathic contact for this long a time is someone has given her *bacal* leaves," Aurora replied.

Sissy spoke up, "Yes, that's it. I am sure. Odds are one hundred to one someone is giving her *bacal* to drink!"

"But why? Why would anyone want my Elena? She is so helpless," Drina protested.

Ernesto grinned for the first time since his daughter's disappearance. "Dear, you and our children are about the *least* helpless people I have ever met! Your ways are unusual but you are certainly not helpless. Neither is our Elena. Thank you, Aurora for letting us know we will have her back. I just want it to be soon."

"We all do, Ernesto, we all do." Aurora sighed.

As the days progressed without any word whatsoever, as their only hope, they clung tightly to the future vision Aurora had. At first, Drina would not let her other two teens out of her sight, which only drove them half-mad. Finally, as the summer wore on, she did relinquish her tight hold on them, much to their relief. "A parent should not outlive their children," Drina kept saying, but Aurora kept on reminding her of her vision and Elena was going to return and would be fine. Still without being able to make telepathic contact, Drina simply could not be consoled.

Adriana hoped Vanna Tiofela had everything arranged. She'd given her as much advanced warning as she dared. If only Gavino did not have *mentales*, it would have been far easier for her to pull this off. As it was, she carefully had to keep her thoughts from straying to her real purpose. She'd spent close to three years to make this happen! The two lines of women slowly shuffled up to the adobe building. Elena began to suspect something was amiss or not quite right here. Where were all the inhabitants? No one was outside, quite unlike the other oases that she had seen. Perhaps that was because of the heat. Never before had she experienced such dry, hot days. Sweat rolled down her bare chest tickling her, but she could do nothing about it. She dare not ask one of the other women to help her with something so trivial. After all, they had all been extraordinarily kind to her, taking turns with her needs.

As they entered the adobe building, Adriana explained briefly, "This is our host for tonight, Vanna Tiofela. As you can see, she is blind. We should be polite and courteous to her. Please walk up to her and give her a little hug. I will introduce you to her as you greet her." Elena was at the rear, her usual position. She noticed several other young women came shuffling into the room from another door. These women and Vanna were Easterlings, she concluded, and were naked from their waists up, wore the same fetter skirt as she, had their arms similarly bound to their waists at their elbows, and wore their hair in two long braids. Again, Elena did not feel out of place, relaxed a little, and observed the proceedings.

"Vanna, this is Martha," Adriana said quietly as the tall woman approached the sitting Vanna, who rose and extended her arms as open as they would go, though from her glazed yellow eyes, Elena saw that she could not see from them. She had no pupils in her eyes. Martha and Vanna fumbled a little getting into a hug position with each other. For a hug, Elena thought that they took a long time at it. Perhaps a minute. Strange. Maybe it was because Vanna was blind, she concluded.

After the hug, Vanna said softly and with a slightly askew motion of her left lower arm, "Please have a seat at our table." One by one the other eight women were introduced, each introduction taking perhaps a minute each. Finally, it was her turn. She wanted to explain that she couldn't give her usual hug because of the overly tight skirt, but with her lips tied; it was only a vague mumble sound.

"Vanna, this is Elena. She has no arms at all, so you will have to find her yourself and give her the hug. Elena moved as close to her as possible and watched helplessly as Vanna moved her lower arms trying to find her. Soon she did and she pulled Elena close to her, their large breasts touching. How strange, Elena thought.

Then, she felt Vanna entering her mind. *At last! Elena, please help me. I am so desperate. Undo my mental blocks. Do whatever you have to do to get rid of them, no matter what it costs, no matter how badly it hurts or pains me. Please, please, I beg you to undo my mentales blocks! Please.*

But it might hurt you. What about the others?

Adriana will watch over them. Please, I would rather die than stay as I am, blocked. Please, if you have any heart at all, I am begging you to do whatever you need to do to remove them, please Elena, please.

Okay. I will. Let me know if it hurts too badly. Elena focused her gift, thankful that Adriana had finally stopped blocking it with *bacal* tea. She saw an enormous black mass pinned into or onto Vanna's mind. She found a small corner of it and gave it a solid push.

She dislodged a part of the blockage. A series of images began to play out, in full color, three dimensions, with sound, smell — vividly real. Both she and Vanna watched it, though Elena began to realize these things had happened to Vanna at one time or other.

She saw a little girl also wearing a fetter skirt trying to keep up with what probably was her father. He kept saying "Hurry up, damn it!" He grew more impatient, took her arm, and began pulling her along. She couldn't move that quickly, and he began simply to drag her along by her arm. Pain, shooting pain, wrenching pain. She felt a bone snap with excruciating pain, yet still the man continued to drag the girl along behind him. After an eternity, he dropped her, but by then, the child had passed out. Some men stood over the girl now; she was lying on some table. "Hast to come off. Never heal right," one man said. More pain, hideous pain, and the arm was gone. Several days seemed to pass swiftly and the pain lessened. At last, this small piece of black mass vanished from Vanna's mind.

Vanna was holding onto Elena tightly, and Vanna's tears and sweat dripped onto Elena's chest. Still there was a whole lot more to go. Elena took a breath, calmed her own body, found another bit of black mass, and energized it. Once more, she and Vanna witnessed the contents of the movie-like strip unfold. Elena now realized that Vanna was actually re-experiencing it, while she was only observing it because she was in such close rapport with Vanna.

This incident contained stark terror. A young girl, Vanna she presumed, not much older than Elena, was cornered by a group of men. Over her protests, she was lifted up and laid across a table. Her hands were tied to opposite table legs and her fetter skirt was cut off with a knife. Her legs were then also stretched out and tied to the other two legs. Elena cringed, for she now knew what her worst fear was. She watched as the young woman screamed and screamed, and man after man had his way with her, leaving her finally in great pain and still tied to the table. After a time, another man appeared, looked at her angrily, cut her loose, and threw her out of her home totally naked. Elena was drenched in Vanna's tears now, but she continued with the next bit of black mass that was obstructing Vanna's *mentales* gift.

This next one held a very severe beating at the hands of what was likely her husband. It must have been earlier in time, for the woman did not have her arms bound at her elbows, but did wear the fetter skirt, making her unable to get out of his way or flee from him, though she did try. Her face was a bloody mess when the man finished pounding her with his fists. He left her alone lying on the floor.

Elena allowed Vanna to recover a little, and she calmed them both before activating the next bit of blockage mass. This one revealed a huge loss. A woman watched helplessly as several men killed her children, the oldest of which looked to be maybe four years old at most. Vanna cried her heart out as this one rolled past them. Even Elena was dismayed at what evil men could do. Both women needed more time to recover from this one, and Elena focused on maintaining the rapport and soothing raw nerve endings.

When she dislodged the next chunk, the images hit almost too close to home for Elena. A young woman, again wearing the traditional fetter skirt and bare chested as usual was being tortured. At least that was what Elena thought it was, for she had no other name for such brutality. A man was trying to get the woman to do something, just what was not evident from the images and really not significant. She'd refused and the man grabbed her arms and tied her wrists together behind her back. Then, he cruelly took another rope and pulled her elbows together tying them tightly together, giving her the appearance of having no arms when viewed from her front side. If that wasn't enough, he then gagged her and blindfolded her. She was then ordered to do her usual work. Again just what that was remained unclear from the images, only the awful fear and helplessness the woman felt. Elena herself had to work hard to keep her own fears from interfering with the process. For a moment, she confused her own helplessness she'd experienced these past months with those in Vanna's images. For a short while, both women were intertwined in confusion over whose helplessness was whose. It took all that Elena had to finally get her focus back and end her own restimulation. This one was just too close to home for the young teen.

Thankfully, Vanna understood and allowed Elena a little time to recover herself when the black mass had been handled. Once more, Elena gave another piece of Vanna's blockage a shove, setting it into motion before their minds. In this one, Vanna got closer to home. Again, she was a woman dressed in the typical Easterlings manner. This time, her newly married husband, who also had long fingernails indicating that he belonged to the Lord Castas, brought her to his home. However, he had failed to tell her that she was his fifth wife. She was shocked and humiliated to see four other wives as she shuffled into her new home.

An argument ensued and Elena both heard the lies and felt the utter betrayal that the woman felt, along with her total humiliation, none of which the new husband could handle. He slapped her and nearly knocked her over. Still she refused to listen to reason — his words. In utter frustration, the husband came up to her and using his nails, ripped out her eyes. Blackness and pain flooded into the woman's mind and Vanna's. Elena knew that this one was terribly real to Vanna, who was shaking and crying now, though Vanna still held onto her for dear life. While the rest of the image was entirely black, the pain and voices subsided. The black mass dissipated.

Elena guessed that might have been the biggest blockage preventing Vanna's *mentales* from fully activating. As she watched carefully, the remainder of the black mass rapidly vanished, unseen by either woman. Finally, Vanna began laughing. "I'm free of it at last! Total success, Adriana. You were right. It worked. Thank you, Elena, thank you! Whoa, is my *mentales* ever powerful!"

At that instant, Elena saw her make a connection, a very powerful one, she sensed from the sheer amount of mental energies suddenly released. For an instant, the entire room blazed brilliantly white, as if it were filled or flooded with some kind of energy. As the bright light began to fade, a woman appeared among them. To Elena's eyes, she seemed to be composed solely of energy, shifting and shimmering, yet she looked like an Easterlings woman, though she wore only a thin, shimmering gown, pure white. Elena noted that she was not wearing a fetter skirt. Why she thought that important, she couldn't say at the moment, perhaps because she again felt like an outsider.

The woman spoke telepathically. *Well done Vanna Tiofela. After a long sleep, I am awakened to the world once more. I accept you as my High Priestess, Vanna. You may call upon me when you need me. Ariana is already awakened I see and active. Calder is not, nor is Wystan. That is good, but unexpected. Alleric will awaken soon, I will see to it. This time, it is again a man's doing, but not a man of Tierra. Alleric must be awakened, if only for a short time.*

Is this place your choice for my new temple?

Yes, Lysandra, Vanna sent.

Then be it known from this moment forward, that Matera is a Holy Site that no man may enter, a haven for the women of Tierra who are in need, a center for healing and for death. There are men here and an outside woman. They will be sent away.

Elena would have gasped, but her tied lips prevented it. Savina, who had apparently heard none of these words, vanished from the room, as if she had not been there at all.

Not long after that, she heard the horses and carriages fleeing from the oasis as fast as the horses could go.

As before, only women seeking the sanctuary of Matera will be able to see this oasis. I have placed my power and will in this oasis. I must go now to awaken Alleric. He has work to do and so do you and I.

The brilliant energy vanished along with the shimmering energy form that was Lysandra. The other women that Elena had seen quietly joining them shortly after they entered were crying joyful tears. Elena and the other nine kidnaped women looked from one to another without any idea what had happened or how or why. The ten were mystified. Elena glanced back at Vanna; she seemed particularly radiant and composed. Adriana now nudged Elena away from Vanna's embrace and she too was crying. What was going on, Elena wondered, but continued to refrain from using her *mentales* to ask.

Free their lips, Adriana. The time for their silence is ended, Vanna sent to all the women present. Women shuffled up to the ten, but Adriana herself untied Elena's lips.

"I am sorry that we had to do this to all of you, but as you have seen it was necessary and we were extremely desperate," Adriana said apologetically. "I owe you all a full explanation, but come, let us serve you as our most honored guests — the first women to have come to Lysandra's Holy Temple at Matera. Food and drink. I will serve the Lady Elena myself.

Still awed and quite confused about what had just happened, the ten captives-turned-honored guests took their seats, while the other women shuffled off to fetch the refreshments. Martha broke the silence, "What just happened? What did Elena do to Vanna? Who or what did we just see? A goddess?"

Adriana explained, "The ancient goddess Lysandra, Goddess of Life and of Death. She gives and she takes. She is one of the ancient penta-pantheon. She and the other four have been sleeping for centuries and have only now awakened once more. Tierra is in dire trouble, especially we women, for Lysandra has always looked out for we women. None of the other four do, according to the legends handed down to us. Vanna is my mother. It was she who told me all that I know of the penta-pantheon. The recent disaster that has befallen our world has once more awakened Lysandra, who has heard the wails of too many women and was roused by them."

She sighed, "Ours is a long story. Please, let us dine and drink and I will try to tell you what I know to be true. When the *mentales* gifts came, both Vanna and I received them, but hers was blocked from use. Yet, she is the chosen one of Lysandra, but was unable to make contact because of the blocked *mentales*. We spent years trying to find a way to undo it and to bring Lysandra back into our world once more, but we could not break that black barrier. I hit upon the idea of trying to find the right woman who could do this for her. I sought out other women around the Arad who also had the gift. These women who you see here are those that I found. Most have healing abilities, as expected of a priestess of Lysandra. However, none of us could break the barrier surrounding Vanna's gift."

"I heard there were many with the gift in the Midlands, but had not the way to get there myself. And even if I had come among you, our customs are so different. I doubted you would have come if I were to ask you to come with me to Matera to see if you were the one who could break Vanna's block. Besides, I had no idea what such a gift might be that could do what Elena has done. I might have spent my life traveling back and forth with nothing to show for it, meanwhile many, many women in dire need and plight would perish because Lysandra did not have her Holy Temple in operation."

"I thought of a plan that, in the end, did work. I got a clan leader, Serafino Lucca to marry me and take me into his clan as a Lords Castas. Next, I maneuvered him into seeing he needed to have many more *mentales* gifted women in his clan so that he could breed hundreds of such people and gain power. I carefully helped him plan a way to abduct you and bring you here to Matera, where I would see if any of you could help mom break her barrier. I am truly sorry for having done this to you. I hope that one day you can find it in your hearts to forgive my ruthless ways. Yes, if none of you had been able to do this for mother, I am really sorry to say you would have been taken by Fino and bred like cattle. I can only say I had truly hoped that once you were off the *bacal* leaves, you could contact your people and arrange for a rescue somehow. I was prepared to help in that regard. Still, I am sorry for the way I mistreated you."

"Yet, Elena was able to free that awful blockage from mom. Her gift is very rare and very special. Elena, we owe you everything. You may always call upon us to help you in anyway and at any time in the future. You will become a legend we pass on to our children and never forgotten."

"With the blockage removed, mom was able to reach Lysandra and answer her pleadings. Now our oasis here will become a Mecca for women in need, a holy sanctuary for the women of Tierra. Mother's healing powers are enormous but are dwarfed by Lysandra's, though she also brings death as much as she brings life. She is the Goddess of Life and of Death. Whether a woman's fate is life or is death is wholly in Lysandra's hands. We are here to serve Lysandra and the many women who will be making their pilgrimage here seeking only the kind of aid we can provide."

Martha looked over at Vanna and asked, "Why then didn't she cure Vanna's blindness? She still has no pupils."

Vanna grinned. "I no longer need eyes to see. My vision is restored fully, but not via my body's eyes." Martha thought about that one and noticed she was eating and drinking just as the rest were, not the way she imagined a blind person would be handling it by feeling with her hands.

Adriana continued, "I can expand a little on what Lysandra said about Matera. Since this is now her Holy Temple, no man can ever see this oasis or ever enter it. Any such attempt will meet with total failure. This is a woman's haven; it is not for men, not ever. They should beseech the other gods and goddess. Lysandra's energy protects us here always. We cannot be harmed by any from outside our Holy Oasis. You all heard her driving the men and Savina away from here. I am afraid that Fino will be incredibly disappointed when he discovers his plan and work resulted in nothing for him."

"Some of us will stay here to maintain our Holy Temple and to help those who come here seeking sanctuary and healing. Others of us will wander the lands telling those in need that help can be found here, but it will be up to them to get themselves here. I now understand something I did not before I made this long journey to the Midlands. And that is why Lysandra chose this place for her temple. Women of the Easterlings will have a much harder time getting here than women of your lands and those of the Westerlings. I believe you can see why, if only in your fetter skirts."

"Tell us about the others in the ancient penta-pantheon," Elena asked, her interest and curiosity was roused. She'd never heard of them before, and neither had many others here. Nearly everyone had long forgotten the ancient gods and goddesses. That would be changing though.

"Neutral Alleric is at the top of the pentagram, all powerful, but seldom mixing in our affairs. I believe that Lysandra wants him to do something about our awful weather that is destroying us all. Calder is the God of Waters. He used to be worshiped by those who make use of the oceans and rivers, but those are few. Wystan is the God of Battles and Warriors. He is the men's god and he loves to create conflict and strife so that men fight and he can watch and enjoy. Some say that he is perverse. I am glad that he still sleeps. Finally, there is Ariana, the Goddess of Fertility. Lysandra has said that she too has awakened. From so many deaths, I can see why she and her powers are needed now. We followers of Lysandra do not know much about her and her ways, save that she loves to see women and animals fertile and bearing healthy children. I don't know what Lysandra meant when she said that Ariana is now active. She was surprised to see that our plight was not caused by our men as it usually has been in our ancient history, but rather an alien man."

"Wow, so I really was seeing a real goddess! Incredible," Elena exclaimed very much impressed.

Martha then asked, "Well, now that you are freed from this Fino fellow and Gavino, why don't you remove your arm bindings and these awful skirts? You can even hardly walk in them, to say nothing about how impeded we with our elbows chained to our waists." *Surely now they will throw off these wicked bindings.*

Adriana gasped, shocked with Martha's suggestion. "Never in my life have I ever seen a woman over five years old who was wearing anything but a fetter skirt! Wearing such loose fitting dresses as we saw in the Midlands is, well, just unthinkable! We are not men; we are women. To walk like they do, taking such huge steps — why that is scandalous! No woman in her right mind would ever dream of doing such an awful thing. Doing that would be giving up part of what it means to be a woman. Besides, we women use our skirts as a subtle way to control our men. We force them to have to slow way, way down and think about us and help us. We don't have the strength of men; we cannot compete with them, as the women in the Midlands seem to think they can. No, we recognize our bodies have not a man's strength, but we make them put their full attention on us this way. Easterlings women have worn these fetter skirts for many centuries, a long standing tradition."

"As far as the elbow bindings go, we have come to enjoy them as well. Unwittingly, men have again given us a way to control them, another way for us to gain a tremendous influence over all men. Never before have all men paid so much attention to us women and our needs since they started elbow bindings. And we also love the nightly tube bindings as well, because our husbands now pay a whole lot more attention to us at night. They have to. They are responsible for binding our lower arms before we turn in for the night and then to unbind us as their first action in the morning when they wake. Never before have we had men paying so much attention to us and we like it."

"You see, at first, many rebelled against the elbow bindings and the tubes at night, but there was simply nothing that they could do to avoid it. You know men; once they get an idea in their heads, there is no stopping them. Yet, women also saw that in being bound, especially at night, they gained more ways to control their husbands. It is subtle, but very real to us women."

"But surely now that you are free of men," Martha rather protested, "you will want to be free of these bonds. In the Midlands, we women don't need such things to interest our men. They are naturally interested in us."

"While we live here in the Easterlings, we will continue to follow our traditions, Martha," the blind woman spoke up with some authority. "To do otherwise would alienate other women of our lands from us. They would look upon us at best as odd or even sacrilegious or worse, downright scandalous. Men would then have justification to cause us harm, as we would be violating their sense of how women should act and appear. It will be enough that we will be a Mecca for women in need. Both men and women of the Easterlings expect us women to appear as we do, in our fetter skirts with elbows bound to our waists. To appear otherwise would cause irreparable upset and loss of respect. Is this not the case in the Midlands when a woman there appears naked when walking to the marketplace? Or if they cut their hair short like a man's? Or they wear men's clothing?"

"Well, it is too cold to go naked, but I see your point," Martha admitted. "Still, it seems a horrid practice to me."

"I suppose that it does," Vanna admitted, "just as Adriana was appalled at the customs of your land. Yet, these are mere customs. What is vitally more important is the work that we are to do for Lysandra and the women in need. You ten were kidnaped from your homes and countries. I must make that right with you. If ever you have need of our healing, contact me. I will see that each of you knows how to direct a woman in dire need to us." She focused and Elena felt a tingle in her mind. She looked in that direction and had a well-defined map leading from her home here to Matera. Elena thought that this was very interesting indeed. *How did she do that? I'd like to be able to do that trick.*

Vanna continued, "There, that is done. Those of you who wish to return to your homes, I will get you there shortly. However, some of you may now wish to stay with us and serve Lysandra and the needy women of Tierra. If so, then we would welcome you among us here at Matera."

"What about having a sort of branch Holy Site in the

Midlands?" asked Martha. "It is some two thousand miles overland from my home in Pinewood to here, if that new map in my mind is correct. That is a very long way for a woman who is in dire need of your healing to travel. She could well perish long before she arrived here."

"Hum, you do have a point, though it is just as far from our northern lands here too," Vanna pointed out. "What you do not know is once I am contacted by the woman or on her behalf by another woman, then I can reach out to her and bring her here with my gift, just as I will be returning you to your homes shortly. They need not travel overland, not when I have Lysandra's gift. Yet, it would be good to have emissaries in the Midlands, spreading the word among women that there is a place of refuge from the evils of men. Some of you who might not wish to stay here with us could become our ambassadors."

"I'd like that very much," Elena spoke up hastily. "I am very much impressed with meeting a real goddess. It would be good to have others around who can help when bad things happen to us. Mom and the others in our tower are doing all that they can to help folks learn how to control their *mentales* gift a little."

"Yes, Adriana has been telling me about the work that your people are doing in the *Círculo de la Torres*. I am very much impressed with this. We here also are in need of what your people there are calling basic training. While we cannot travel to one of your towers, might it be possible for some of your women to travel here and train our women? There are not too many of us in the Easterlings who have gotten the gift," Vanna both explained and asked.

"Oh, I am sure someone can come, though it is a long way to travel and the risks are great. As I understand the men, there are numerous bandits and hostile kingdoms in the way," Elena replied. *I sure don't know what all I should. I ought to have been paying far more attention to these kinds of things! I am not a little girl anymore.*

Vanna smiled. "Don't worry about overland travel. When we arrange for one or more women to come to us, I will bring them here, as I will take you home, Elena. Then you will know what I am saying. However, it is getting late. It is time that you make your decisions. Do any of you wish to remain with us?"

Nadine, Shannen, and Molly decided to stay and help with their healing skills. The others wanted to return home, but promised to act as their emissaries. "Okay then. Remember always our location must be kept a secret from all men. Only give out your map to the women who are in dire need of us." The five promised to do so.

Vanna then took Elena aside and sent, *Elena, I am also giving you a gift. Our minds have been very close and I saw what troubles you the most. Rest assured that your children will not inherit what you inherited from your mother. Your children will be normal.*

Oh thank you! I know I should not be so concerned over it, but I am. Mom has tried to get me to see that it should not be an important thing, but it is to me and my sister and brother.

Don't worry. For what you have done, this is the least that I can do for you. I will see that your sister will also have normal children. I cannot do anything for your brother though, for he is male. Now then, imagine the place where you would like to be at home and I will take you there right now.

I don't understand. I would like to be in our dining room. How can you get me there?

Like this. Vanna focused her gift and energies flashed. She held onto the image of Elena's dining room. Then next thing Elena knew she was standing there among her family and friends, who suddenly gasped, shocked to see her appearing among them, as if by magic.

Drina shrieked. "Elena! Elena! It is you. My god, what happened to you? Ernesto! Get something to cover her! She's nearly naked!" She rushed to her daughter's side and threw her leg around her, hugging her close and hiding her nakedness from the others. Ernesto hastily wrapped a towel around her chest and hugged her, pelting her with loving kisses, filled with his tears of joy. Then, the others surrounded her.

"Are you really all right? Unharmed?" Drina asked, adding her tears to his.

In a very fast rush of words, Elena said, "Yes mom, I am fine, only I am in desperate need of a bath and get me out of this awful skirt that the women there wear. I have had an adventure, but we have to tell Marisol that there is another *mentales* gift. Somehow Vanna brought me here from where I was at a moment ago in the Easterlings! Mom, I saw a real goddess, a real one! She was an ancient goddess, Lysandra. Way cool! Bad men kidnaped me and nine other women for our *mentales* gifts, but Adriana outsmarted them and had me use my gift to help Vanna unlock hers and then she helped Lysandra appear."

"Okay, okay, let's get her bathed and into her own clothes pronto. Then, slow down and tell us all about it," Holly brought order into the jubilant scene. Later on, Marisol added teleport to her lengthy list of the special gifts.

Most of the later discussions focused on the ancient penta-pantheon. Only Holly had some idea of these ancient legends, though not much. They had been dormant for at least five centuries, maybe more. Few now even knew of them or that they had once been worshiped here on Tierra. Holly sent off messages to all those she knew, asking them if they knew anything about the ancient gods of Tierra. The vast majority knew nothing of them; most didn't even know there were ancient gods.

Some days later, she heard from a former Advanced Witch of Malaca, Abvera, Westerlings, one Arcelia Ascención. *Hi, I have found an ancient journal that speaks of the Penta-pantheon. Its pages are yellowed and quite breakable. Some of the ink is faded and is illegible. I will read what I can, though. There used to be five of them, three males and two females as I understand the writings.*

The head of the Penta-pantheon is Alleric, the All Ruler. He cares little for mankind, but loves our world and cares for its needs. Do not call upon Alleric for he will seldom answer man. Calder rules the waters of Tierra, rivers, lakes, and the sea. Call upon his blessings before setting sail and your voyage may be upon calm waters. It is said do not raise his anger by taking more fish than you need, for his wrath can be terrible.

Wystan is very active in the affairs of men, pushing, encouraging, and aiding them to fight worthy battles. He is a god of wars. Pray to him before entering a battle, but if you do so, do not show unworthiness on the battlefield, for Wystan is known to slay those who display cowardice in battle. It is said that he watches over the wars among men, bestowing riches upon those he deems worthy of his honor. His enemy among the gods is Lysandra, the Goddess of Life and of Death. She is devoted solely to the women of Tierra and has been known to strike down men who have harmed women, even those men who have been highly favored by Wystan. It is said she alone has the power to contain the mighty warrior Wystan and he hates her for that very reason.

Lysandra gives life back to deserving women, though she is equally likely to take it from them. Some say that she is a fickle goddess who cannot make up her mind. It would be wise for a woman to pray to her only when in dire need or when she has been greatly wronged by a man. In the latter case, Lysandra has been known to give death to the men who have so wronged the beseeching woman. She and Wystan are usually highly involved with mankind.

Ariana, the Goddess of Fertility, is more neutral, spreading her gift among animals as well as mankind. Women, who have trouble conceiving, often pray to Ariana for the gift of a child. It is said if they place a newborn lamb or rabbit upon her altar, she will answer their prayers.

María Isabel, the last know High Priestess of Lysandra, has said that with Lysandra's founding of the fifteen kingdoms, she had at last gotten Wystan under her control. With a lasting peace finally arriving on Tierra, the Penta-pantheon quietly retired into slumber. She lived about five hundred years ago, around the time of the founding of Abvera. There, does this help you, Holly?

Holly replied, Thank you! I can tell you that we know for a fact that Lysandra is awake and active once more. She has said that Ariana is also awake and working her magic

234

once more. She alluded to the fact that Alleric must be roused, and she was surprised to see the disaster that has befallen Tierra was not Wystan's doing. He still sleeps, according to Lysandra. One of our women here at our tower met Lysandra.

Incredible! She has met the goddess personally? Incredible, Arcelia repeated herself. *For some time now, I have suspected that Ariana might have been awakened. Here the plants and trees are changing. Around a tree or bush's fruits, a silky pod has developed. It opens in good weather and closes in cold weather, protecting the delicate fruits and nuts. Only Ariana could be having this effect on our world. But Lysandra is awake — now that is news. Do you have any idea if she has chosen a new High Priestess yet?*

Yes, a Vanna Tiofela, an Easterlings woman. If you have any women who need sanctuary of assistance, let me know and I can work out a way for you to get in touch with the High Priestess. It seems that the Church of God is doomed. Both women chuckled at this detail.

Arcelia added hastily, *It would be wise to keep all this information confined to us women. If Wystan is asleep, it would be best to keep him that way. If men know the ancient gods are around, they will surely summon Wystan and wars will inevitably follow. It's bad enough trying to survive now without men fighting more battles.* Both agreed to continue to keep this information from men in general, though Holly would not keep it from the men of the towers. They certainly would not be praying to Wystan or trying to rouse him.

She also knew that sooner or later men would realized the ancient gods were still around and call upon Wystan, but perhaps that would not happen in her lifetime. She found it fascinating that Arcelia was attributing the adaption of the plants to the new, harsh environment to the goddess Ariana. Still, these new cold-protecting pods were providing valuable silk-like thread and cloth, replacing cotton, which no longer grew in the Kingdom of the Angels. She had heard cotton was now thriving far to the south, however. Was Ariana behind some of these changes?

She did discuss this with both Dita and Doctor Zosia, both of whom expressed doubts that gods and goddesses had anything to do with Nature and its process to enable the plant and animal kingdoms to adapt and survive. Neither woman dared contradict Elena and her testimony that she'd seen the goddess Lysandra. They were products of Rigel-3 and Imperium science, which had nothing to do with mystical gods and goddesses, just pure science.

Whether Ariana was real and had taken direct intervention with the plants of Tierra or not, Holly made no decision one way or the other. However, she and everyone else noticed that the extremes of daily weather shifting began to moderate that fall. The four-day pattern of the last few years seemed to mellow out, though the Rigels attributed it to a lessening of the planet's wobble, a natural dampening force. In the back of Holly's mind she could not help wondering if this was Alleric's doing? If so, she hoped he would do more to set things right or at least get them in a better balance.

Part IV Rise of the Towers

Chapter 13 Mechanics of *Mentales*

"Stop writing in that infernal journal! I didn't raise you to be a nearsighted bookworm," the elder man, Amo Hank Roundtree-Wycombe-Brom griped, holding back his rising anger with his twenty year old son. Amo was now the formal title applied to men who had the *mentales* gift, while women were called Ama, a convention from the Westerlings towers now accepted across Tierra. It was the summer solstice, late June 1070. Forty year old Amo Hank was the leader of the Brom *Círculo de la Torres*, often referred to as the Fire Tower by the locals. Here those gifted with the ability to affect or create fires were trained to use their gifts properly. His wife was Ama Linda Waters-Wycombe-Brom, thirty-seven. The custom now was to append the line of inherited *mentales* to one's formal surname.

Felix re-enforced his mental barriers, suppressing his utter annoyance at being so rudely interrupted. *One day dad, you will learn to respect me. Hell, one day the whole world will respect me!* Reluctantly, he put down his quill and rose. His father's eyes scanned his son up and down, adjusting his sash. Every tower had their own colored sash worn over their shoulder and chest identifying their personnel. "You must look your best for your betrothal ceremony, son. No back talk, your mother and I have researched your bride-to-be in depth. It is the very best match that can be made, unless you want to hitch up to an older woman." He watched for his son's reaction to his taunt.

Felix's mouth twitched, the only visible indication of his disgust for this new custom of breeding for *mentales* gifts. He knew darn well it was absolutely necessary. His own gifts came from his genes, carefully bred two generations now. Still, he found the whole process dehumanizing. He and his bride were being mated only for what they could bring for their children. Felix had managed by protests, angry outbursts, and even a temper tantrum to delay the inevitable. Today, he knew from the set, stern face of his father he could postpone it no longer. He sighed and allowed the old man to adjust his sash.

Felix had never met his fifteen year old bride to be. *Well, that's not entirely true,* he thought. *I saw here once at the summer festival when she was six.* He was a gangly boy of eleven then and had hardly noticed her among all the other children of the towers. "Let's get this betrothal ceremony over quickly," he said without any hint of passion in his voice. He followed his father out of his private study on the third floor of the Brom tower. *One day, I will occupy the top level, as soon as dad passes. Well, I must be ready to don the leadership of the tower and I will be. No one is more qualified than I am. I ought to be leading now, not dad.*

They walked down the circular stairs and stopped outside the women's quarters. Ama Linda Waters-Wycombe-Brom was dressed in her nicest pod-silk dress — the blue looked good on her, but she was starting to show her age. His two younger sisters, both giggling, stepped out into the hall behind their mother. Val was eighteen and already betrothed and would be marrying in the autumn to Alberto Bolivar of the Bettingham tower. She wore an emerald green dress. Val gave him a fast thought, *You look handsome tonight. Mind your manners and don't embarrass her.*

Why would I want to do that?

You being you, that's all. Mom and dad will kill you if you upset her. Be warned. She tossed her long black hair back.

His youngest sister, Sally was sixteen and wore a pink dress. This was her golden opportunity to be seen as a young woman by many eligible men. She knew their folks would never consider a marriage for her just yet, but certainly, within two years she expected to be married. In all likelihood, it would be to a man she'd be seeing here tonight. Thus, she intended to make as good an impression on all the young men. *You look handsome, big brother.*

Thanks sis. Make sure you memorize names with faces tonight. You know dad, he'll want to marry you off soon. She blushed. Her eyes met his and he knew that was precisely her plan. The women fell in line behind the two men and they headed on down to the main floor, where the ceremony would be held, along with the dance and celebration. Already most of the tower and their families were present, and they could hear the dance music playing. Amo Hank paused momentarily at the oak door, glancing first at his son's appearance and then the women. Satisfied they were putting their best foot forward, he led them into the large assemblage. Nearly fifty men, women, and children were dancing or standing by the refreshments table chatting.

As they entered, the music stopped and a short fanfare announced their arrival. A bass voice spoke, "Amo Hank Roundtree-Wycombe-Brom, Ama Linda Waters-Wycombe-Brom, Amo Felix Roundtree-Waters-Wycombe-Brom, Ama Val and Ama Sally." A brief round of applause greeted them before the music resumed.

"Dance with me brother, last dance before you are betrothed," Val teased him. Reluctantly, Felix complied, taking her offered hand. For an instant, the two felt the electric tingle as their *mentales* charged bodies met, creating an intimacy unlike those without the gift could ever experience. For a second, Felix wondered if his promised wife would give him this kind of touch, one that opened herself to him as he was opened to her. For all her teasing, Val was close to him, far closer than their father, who always seemed indifferent to his children's emotional needs. "Emotions are for women," he always declared when pressured by his wife. Still, Val and Felix treasured the moments of touch they shared, though infrequently ever since Val had come of age at fourteen. It would be unseemly for them to touch excepting at formal settings, such as this dance. He sensed Val wanted one last touch before he would marry. After that, who could say when they would ever get such an opportunity again?

"At least she isn't a pig," she whispered in his ear, when their steps brought them close. He could smell the lavender of her bath waters on her skin. Felix thought, *She will make him a fine wife*.

"Well, that's something. I take it you saw her when she arrived?" he asked, though he knew very well that she had. Of course, the women greeted their arriving guests, though it was taboo for the men to meet their prospective bride upon her arrival. Rather, she needed to bathe off the road dirt and dress herself to reflect her very best. Such was the custom and Felix had gone along with it, not wanting to be interrupted from his research work.

Once more, the music stopped abruptly and the bass voice announced, "Amo Walter Ewa-Wiola-Wycombe, Ama Drina Ewa-Wycombe, Ama Lilly Ewa-Wiola-Wycombe, Amo Tommy." All eyes turned to the new arrivals as they walked stately up to Amo Hank and Ama Linda. As required, Felix moved hastily to his father's side, prepared for the formal presentation.

He got a good look at his young bride-to-be. Lilly was barely fifteen, too young to marry he thought, but then his father thought differently. She had inherited a light grey skin color from her Rigel-3 ancestors, Dita Ewa and Doctor Zosia Wiola. Her hair was a rich, lustrous black, falling to her thighs, an ornate bluebird clasp held some of it in place in the center of her neck. She looked very thin and tall, again traits these lines inherited from their Rigel-3 ancestors. Originally, her eyes had also been black, but had turned the typical yellow with brown spots when her *mentales* blossomed. She seemed to be frail and thin, but Felix also knew Rigel women were both very tall and extremely thin by Tierra standards, at least, that is what he'd seen when he once visited the Exchange City and saw the aliens first hand. Her face was roundish with thick dark lashes and bushy eyebrows that somehow looked slightly too strong for her features. She was not overly attractive, but then she was not ugly either. If her *mentales* gifts were as promised, then she would add a good deal to their line. That was the proposal agreed to by the two fathers.

As they moved close to the three, Felix could not help sensing her, if only her surface feelings. She was nervous and her eyes were taking him in, just as he was appraising her. Felix could have pushed a little and read her thoughts, but among these telepaths, that was akin to mental rape, something Felix was loathed to do. He contented himself to her surface emotions. *So young,* he thought.

"Amo Felix, I am honored to present my daughter, Ama Lilly Ewa-Wiola-Wycombe, to you. I offer her hand to you in marriage," Amo Walter said quite formally. Felix did detect a hint of pride in his voice, a pride married with a sense that he was getting the better deal in this arranged marriage. *Well that remains to be seen,* Felix thought in answer, though the Amo could not hear it through Felix's mental barriers. Now it was his turn and he sensed his father holding his breath, praying Felix would control his temper and not embarrass everyone here.

"Amo Walter, it is I who am honored and most pleased to accept the hand of the lovely and talented Ama Lilly to be my bride," he bowed politely to the older man and reached out to take Lilly's hand being offered to him by her father. Here would come their first intimate contact! Although it was the lightest, barest touch of their hands, hers upon his, with telepaths, this contact was electrifying and very intimate. Only their mental barriers kept their inner thoughts apart. Their surface feelings would be interchanged immediately upon the touch of flesh.

Felix found himself holding his breath, though he didn't know quite why. He felt the tingle of energies and sensed her extreme nervousness. Felix countered it by focusing on sending out a calm, sure, certain kind of emotional flow, which she picked up on and held to her, steadying her nerves with it. As required and rehearsed with his mother, he gently turned her body around to face her parents and the throng of partygoers.

He said formally, "I give you my future bride. We are to be wedded midsummer." There, he had finally said the irrevocable words his father had been trying to get him to say for the last two years. His word, once given, could not be broken except in unusual circumstances, such as the bride having some unreported fault in her body or gift. He felt Lilly's heart flutter and her pulse raced, but to her credit, she focused her *mentales* and was almost at once calm and collected once more. *All to her credit,* he thought behind his mental barriers. *She at least has control of her body. That is a good sign.* "Ama Lilly, may I have our first dance?" he asked politely, feeling relief sweeping over the young teen and guessed she was unused to such formalities.

"Yes, please!" she replied, a bit too enthusiastically, quickly biting her lower lip slightly and lowering her eyes. Like

Felix, she knew the motions and actions of dancing would not only take the pressure off her, but would also relieve the slowly building tension in her body.

As they began their first graceful steps with all eyes watching them, he said, "I find dancing much more pleasurable than the stiff formalities."

"So do I," Lilly gushed. "I was so nervous. I hope I didn't embarrass you too much."

"Not at all. You dance well, Lilly."

"Thanks, mom had me practicing until I thought my feet would fall off," she readily admitted with a giggle. A bit later, she asked, "You are not too disappointed I have so much Rigel-3 blood in me?" Suddenly, Felix got a flash of intense worry that escaped her mental barriers.

Until she asked, he had not really given that aspect of this marriage much thought at all. As if anticipating his thoughts, she explained, "I have Rigel blood from both my grandmothers, Dita Ewa and Doctor Zosia. I know I am terribly thin and my skin is light grey. My hair is way too thick for a Tierra woman. I hate that I am already taller than you are. It is embarrassing to me."

"Lilly, I am not disappointed over that." He knew his answer was terribly important to the young teen, perhaps setting the tone for their marriage. "Your grandmothers were legends and extremely able women. I have only admiration for the work they did for us all. I can see you are thin, but perhaps in time as you mature you will fill out some. As for your height, it is no matter to me. I've heard Dita was six inches taller than Norwood."

"Oh indeed she was. She had to lean over for their lips to kiss," she giggled again.

"So don't fret, Lilly. You are an attractive, young woman, who is only now beginning to blossom into womanhood," he complimented her as best he could. He felt her body relaxing and knew he had nullified her greatest fears. *Well, this is a good start.* What he really wanted to know was what was the nature and strength of her *mentales* gifts. That was the key issue, but it would be impolite to ask her just now and mental rape to go ahead and just find out for himself, though he could have done both. *Time enough when we are married to ascertain that. Best not make a scene or dad will have my head this time.*

She asked, "Is it true that your grandmother was the famous Marisol Bolivar-Wycombe, the one who created the Master Catalogue that documents all the forms that *mentales* gifts have taken?"

He smiled, "Yes, she was my grandmother, though I only knew her as a young child. She was charming and very brilliant, as I recall." *I do take after her, don't I? I have extended her work enormously. Without her catalog, I would not have all the skills I possess today.*

Lilly offered, "I've inherited a lot from my grandmothers too, on both sides." Oh how this teased him. He would so like to dive in there and see just the nature and depth of her gifts, but again he reminded himself now was not the time. Lilly sensed his unease and quickly backed off, knowing it was very impolite to arouse any male and then not to be in a position to satisfy his needs. It was frustrating to her that she couldn't sense just what his needs were that she'd somehow pricked. Her gifts did not lie along those lines, unlike the offspring of the famous Drina Esteban, who, it was said, always knew what another wanted. That, she thought, would be a tremendous gift, extremely useful. So much so, that her father had been sorely tempted to marry her to one of the Esteban young men. Well, she was satisfied with Felix now that she'd seen him. He wasn't ugly or fat, just five years older than she was, and he was somewhat handsome. She could not expect more, not with her alien bloodlines.

That was always an ever-present barrier, one she could never escape, born home to her every time she looked in the mirror. It was not that she thought of herself as alien as both her grandmothers had been, rather she looked different than everyone else around her. It was not just the greyish hue to her skin that set her apart. She was tall, taller than nearly everyone else at her tower, save her mother and siblings and cousins. If that wasn't enough to bother a young teen just coming into womanhood, she was also extremely thin like her kin. Coupled with the enormous bosoms sported by every woman on Tierra, she considered she was terribly freakish looking. Having thick eyebrows didn't help matters either.

Because of her physical appearance, Lilly spent her energies on perfecting her *mentales* gifts. Her sole idea was her prospective husband would overlook her alien physical appearance if she were powerful and skillful enough with her gifts. When her father told her of the arranged marriage, Lilly had to exercise all her will power to quell the uprising of wild emotions. On the one hand, she despised the fact she had no choice in whom she was to spend the rest of her life with and whose children she must bear. Over and over, she had the notion that love was not important, that if she were lucky, in time she could learn to love her husband, and perhaps, he, she. This was so unlike the love stories she'd heard as a small child from her grandparents on both sides, who had married for love and nothing else. This was especially true for Doctor Zosia and Dita, the two aliens from Rigel-3. The simple fact she had no choice whatsoever in who she was to marry not only frightened her far more than she dared even admit to herself but also made her feel like rebelling and running away to join the Sisterhood. *How dare they do this to me!* That thought took more to suppress than anything else had, but this evening she had managed to bury it deeply in her subconscious, thankfully.

Analytically, she was fully cognizant of just why a specific man was chosen for her. The breeding of the special *mentales* gifts was vitally important for everyone's survival on Tierra. The exceedingly harsh change of climate had taken a vast toll on human life. Crude estimates placed the population loss during the first decade of adjustments at nearly twenty-five percent, a large number of those being women and children. Here in the central Midlands and in eastern Westerlings, that is, areas close to the Plateau Grado where the psi-crystals refinery had been, the losses were a staggering thirty-five percent. Again, the heaviest percentage had been with childbearing mothers, especially those who had some *mentales* gift. These days, the towers kept sharp watch on such mothers and the *Mentales Rules* were strictly followed in such cases, drastically lowering the number of deaths during childbirth.

Still, those with these gifts were saving Tierra from utter chaos. Some were healers and some worked hard on keeping the weather somewhat moderated so crops could flourish. Miraculously, overall conditions had improved around 1006 when the planet ceased its wild wobbling. To this day, no one knew how that had come about. Grandmother Dita had said that even the Rigel-3 scientists were baffled about how that had happened. As she reflected upon the time she heard these tales from her old grandmothers, Lilly began smiling again. Even the alien women's bodies had changed. Dita had said that her boss, who also was a telepath, had her eyes change color to the usual yellow with brown spots and her bosom had become soccer balls, whatever that word meant. Grandmother Zosia had said any Rigel-3 woman who spent more than six months on Tierra found her bosom enlarging, much to their shock and dismay. Again, no one knew just why, though speculations ran wild.

No, if the humans of Tierra were going to survive here, the simple facts of life dictated that the various lines of *mentales* gifts had to be both preserved and strengthened. This had been drilled into her since she was five, giving credence to all the arranged marriages. However analytical the reasons were, it did nothing to prevent the sudden shock Lilly felt when her father announced to her that she would be getting married mid-summer, barely three months away, with her betrothal ceremony less than two and to a man she had never met. Her mother had corrected her on this point; she had met him once when she was perhaps five. In her mind, that didn't count, she couldn't remember him. Besides, he too was a child, though perhaps ten at the time.

For weeks, Lilly had been such an emotional wreck over this marriage that she had not even been able to continue her studies and *mentales* practicing. All day, she spent trying to keep her wild emotions at bay, to keep from broadcasting her emotions to all the telepaths in the tower. It was one thing for her to be so upset and quite another for her to allow her feelings to disturb all the others in her world. That she could, but would never, do.

If all this was not sufficient to keep her continually upset, the week before her betrothal ceremony, another whole arena of fears and worries opened its ugly door in her mind. Sex. She was only fifteen and had heard only wild whisperings and coy teases about this most intimate sharing between a man and a woman. She had no notion of what it was like, what was expected of her. Nothing. She was still almost a child in her mind. A week before this ceremony, her mother had had a long talk with her, a scary one at that. Her mother's words came back to her as she walked into the Brom tower that betrothal afternoon.

"Remember always that you and he are telepaths. Even the slightest touch will bring about a deep intimacy, a deep rapport with each other. Men arouse easily, often at the slightest hint. Thus, you must be extremely careful of your physical actions. Never do or say anything that might arouse your husband, unless you and he are ready to satisfy his needs. Failure to do so results in a telepathic agony that everyone around you two will sense and will have to work on blocking out."

"But what about my needs?" she'd asked, poignantly.

"Yours do not count, dear. After all, your husband is providing for you."

Her mother made it sound like she would be a mere slave to her husband's every desire and need. She'd resented that and retorted, "So I am just as fettered and bound as the Easterlings women, is that it?"

Her mother just laughed. "They are physically bound and there is a huge difference between us." Well, just then Lilly didn't see the difference. At least she thought she could deal with being physically bound. Mentally bound was an entirely different matter, entirely.

She had also explained that when Lilly was pregnant, she should encourage her husband to feel free to take other lovers. Further, if he were to fall in love with another woman, it was acceptable for those two to have their own children, which would be called fosterlings. It would be her responsibility to help raise any of her husband's fosterlings. That she was also allowed to have outside affairs even to the point of having her own fosterlings didn't set well with Lilly.

In short, the whole topic of marital sex was a vast mystery to the fifteen year old, young woman. This tended to frighten her whenever she allowed her mind to look at it. Hence, she did her best to suppress this as well.

For Lilly, the evening was over at last and for that, she was extremely grateful. Pulling up the warm quilts in her guest bedroom, she finally allowed herself to relax. So much had happened so quickly, she thought. The only thing that gave her a cozy comfort was the physical tower here at Brom. Its arrangements and room layouts were identical to that of her own tower in Wyth. Indeed, Drina's husband, the stonemason Ernesto, had designed all four towers in the Kingdom of the Angels. Thus, at least she would have a solid familiarity at this new tower. All she would have to learn is whose rooms were whose. In this, Lilly took a good deal of comfort. She could not imagine what it would be like to also be moving into a wholly unfamiliar tower in which she wouldn't know where anything was located and would be constantly forced to ask for directions — utterly embarrassing and humiliating. She was at least being spared this.

The wedding day came too soon for both. "Felix! Stop your infernal tinkering and get dressed! The ceremony is in an hour," Amo Hank growled angrily at his son, who was busily engaged in yet another experiment of his.

"She'll still be there in an hour," Felix countered, though he knew this would only infuriate his father all the more. Sensing his father about to try to use the Command Voice on him, he knew he'd pushed the man to his limits. "Okay, okay, I'll get ready. Don't blow a vessel!" Hastily, Felix changed into his fanciest suit and then adjusted his tower's sash over his shoulder. He finished up by fastening his short sword around his waist. He glanced in the mirror and wondered for an instant what Lilly saw in him. Quickly, he discarded that line of thought. No way could he know that, not without going into a deep rapport with her and not without her full consent. He brushed his hair a little, pivoted on his heels and headed to the waiting room where his father would be waiting to escort him into the main room on the first floor, the same room where his betrothal dance had been held. This time, the room was decked with fragrant summer flowers and ferns. He liked the ferns, though. This was one of Nature's new wonders. After the climate changes, ferns began growing wildly all over these rocky foothills of the Angels. Felix discovered that he loved these three-foot tall plants.

His father looked him over from head to toe. Felix sensed his father was anticipating something being wrong or out of place, but he knew there wasn't. He was twenty and perfectly capable of dressing himself properly, though he didn't like to. "Acceptable," Amo Hank said as if begrudging him this much. *In a few hours, old man, you will have no more control over me and my life! That's something at least.* His father added, "Don't make a fool of yourself today, and embarrass us all in the process. And treat the bride right. She is only fifteen and almost too young to be married."

"Some marry at fourteen, father," Felix retorted the obvious truth. Still, he knew his father was doing his best to remind him subtly of her virginity and her tender age. *If Lilly thinks she is marrying an experienced man, boy does she have a surprise coming. I'm just as much a virgin as she, though older. I've never had the time for cavorting around, there is too much to learn, far too much. Damn, I hope marriage does not place too great a demand upon my time!*

In a nearby room, Ama Drina Ewa-Wycombe was adjusting the fall of her daughter's wedding dress, lavishly done in white pod-silk. Five petticoats helped hide the young woman's thin frame and added to the illusion that she was not so tall. The top of her large bosom, contrasting in a light grey color, held a large pear cut emerald resting above her cleavage on a gold chain, a gift from her father. She wore her hair as she always did, draped across her back, a portion held in place by her bluebird clasp at the back of her head. Lilly was very nervous in spite of her nearly constant use of her *mentales* skills at calming her body.

I am losing my childhood; my whole life will be gone minutes from now! God am I ever scared! Soon I will belong to this man I don't even really know! Oh god! How did I ever get into such a position? She knew darn well how, she just was having a very difficult time accepting it and all it implied. For a moment, she realized she could faint or even better suddenly have a bout of Verge Sickness. Surely that would postpone the wedding indefinitely. As soon as the notion took shape in her tumultuous mind, it evaporated. Within a tower with so many gifted in the healing arts, she'd be back on her feet, probably within an hour. Worse case, they would pump her full of *bacal* tea, wiping out her *mentales* and get her married anyway, letting Felix deal with her afterwards.

"There, Lilly, you look absolutely beautify. If I say more, I think I will break down and start sobbing! My little girl is so grown up now. Why only yesterday it seems I was helping you to learn to walk. How time does seem to fly."

"Mom, I'm scared," Lilly finally admitted it to her mother.

She smiled, reassuringly. "Dear, I was positively terrified on my wedding day! I don't know any woman who isn't one big case of nerves on her wedding day. It is only natural. You are leaving your childhood behind you and moving into womanhood, starting a new phase of your life. Rejoice in it, my child. All women go through this as well. I'm sure that Felix is nearly as nervous as you are. From all we have gathered, he is a virgin too, and probably as frightened by it as you. See, you already have something in common with your husband."

"That's not a good thing to have in common, mother, nervousness," Lilly replied. Somehow, her mother's words, while meant to be reassuring and comforting, were not.

A solitary gong sounded, causing Lilly to jerk. "It's time. You look very pretty dear. Give me a last hug, my precious baby." Arm in arm, the two stepped out of their room and into the Main Hall, where some fifty had gathered to witness the ceremony, though most were looking forward to the dance and festivities after the brief wedding ceremony. Her mother led her to her waiting father, who took her arm in his. Accompanied by a wedding march, they walked from the back end of the hall up to the front, where Amo Hank and Amo Felix were standing, awaiting them. For a time Lilly focused on simply walking and not tripping over her petticoats, giving her reeling mind something with which to deal.

At the front, the two fathers placed their children's hands together, bowed and backed away. Normally, as the tower leader, Amo Hank would have presided over the ceremony. However, today, Amo Lance Waters, the second in command, officiated. The ceremony went by in a whirl for both bride and groom, who remembered little of what was said. When they shared their first kiss, only then were both brought back into the present, as the electric touch of their lips brought each a brief, but intimate shared reality, a harbinger of what was to come. Mechanically, the couple turned to face the gathering and receive their applause. Then, the dance music began, and Felix turned to Lilly and they shared their first dance as a married couple.

After that, all unmarried women wanted a chance to dance with Felix. Superstition suggested dancing with the groom on his wedding day brought them good luck and a fine marriage as well. Likewise, the young men wanted a chance to dance with the bride. They were more interested in being very close to this new addition to their tower. The afternoon flew by rapidly. At last, Felix was reunited with Lilly, as the dance paused for dinner. Everyone had an hour to freshen up before the banquet.

"My dear, if I may, I'd like to give you my wedding present to you," Lilly said rather shyly. "I know that I know so little about you, but I do hope that you will love what I have to give to you."

"I'm sure I will. I do like presents," Felix admitted. "I've got one for you as well, Lilly. I guess that we are in the same boat, so to speak. I don't know the first thing about you either, but mom did learn a very little about you — I mean beyond your *mentales* gifts, that is," he amended himself.

Lilly flushed a little. *So he is as ignorant of me as I am of him. Is this good or bad?* She offered him her arm, "I'm afraid we will have to go out to the stables for your present, Felix."

Felix chuckled, "Strange, I was just about to say the same thing."

251

Lilly smiled, a little relieved. "About the only thing I know about you, Felix, is you have a real passion for the Hilliard Heights Sisterhood horses. I took the liberty of getting you the finest three year old stallion they had this year. I am a good judge of horses and I picked him out for you. I hope you won't mind."

Felix grinned, "Well, that is something. You heard right. The Sisterhood there raises and trains the very best horses in the land. This is also the only thing that I have heard about you, Lilly, that you love horses too and are a good rider. I got you the best three year old mare they had." Both laughed, releasing tensions between them.

"I am a good rider, though I wear pants when I ride. I simply hate riding like a lady, sidesaddle. I am a fast runner too, when I am not hobbled in these darn petticoats. No one at our tower can catch me. Fleet foot, that's my nickname. Is yours really Fire Man?"

Felix laughed, "Yes, Fire Man, that's me. These two are beauties. Thank you for a most thoughtful and useful gift, Lilly."

"Likewise. I wish we could just go riding right now, skip the darn formal dinner and all that," she sighed a little.

"I do too, Lilly. I hate these formal dinners. Yet, if we did that, my father would skin me alive, yours probably would too." Both laughed and petted their new horses, dappled greys.

As they walked back, Felix warned her, "Don't be surprised if some of my cousins play pranks on us. Some are rather ornery, though why they should do it on a person's wedding night eludes me."

"I think that might be because they are a tad jealous of your happiness," Lilly replied as they entered the tower once more, heading to the dining hall.

The evening passed quickly for the young couple, though Lilly continued to use her gifts to keep her growing fears of the coming bedroom time from her mind and from also being broadcast to everyone present. She, as well as everyone else, knew that the marriage had to be physically consummated in bed before it was a sealed, unbreakable bond. Already some marriages had been dissolved because the young couples failed to be able to perform. Quite why they could not do the deed eluded Lilly, but then so many things eluded her at this point in her life.

Felix dreaded the coming event. He was escorting Lilly to his bedroom and thus, her new bedroom. Legally, both knew they would have to perform shortly, and both were growing more nervous with each step as the room drew closer to them. Ordinarily, serving women would undress Lilly and prepare her for the wedding bed. Similarly, Felix's friends would also prepare him as well. However, both had insisted they were perfectly capable of preparing themselves, much to the chagrin of the young men and women around them. However, as Amo and Ama, they had this right to take care of their own needs.

As they stepped into his room, he noticed that the staff had cleaned it up. "Darn, someone has messed up my papers," he grumbled and headed to his desk, very annoyed. "I'll lose hours of time reorganizing my many papers!"

Meanwhile, Lilly studied her new bedroom and her *mentales* gifts kicked in. "I fear that someone is playing pranks on us, Felix. I think the bed holds some surprises for us."

"Well, someone has cost me plenty of research time by messing up my papers here. Why don't you take care of the bed for us? I won't be but a minute. Darn it, why did they have to tidy up the place?" Lilly laughed.

"Well, do you like sleeping on a bunch of dried peas?" Lilly called out and then giggled a little.

"Idiots, what are they thinking?" Felix commented, coming over to lend her a hand picking them up.

"Careful of the sheet there. Someone had rigged a trip wire to that bucket up there. I don't know what it's got in it, but it cannot be good," Lilly cautioned him.

Standing on a chair, Felix undid the trip wire and brought the bucket down carefully. "Water. We'd have been drenched in our bed. Excellent observations, Lilly. Well done. Any more surprises in store for us?"

Lilly focused her mind and searched. "Nope, that is all. I guess it's safe for us now. Can you help me out of this dress, please? How are we going to sleep? I mean should I wear a night gown or?" her voice trailed off. *Or what? Damned if I know what is expected. He is roused a little. Oh god, what do I do now?*

Felix awkwardly began untying her gown. *What am I supposed to do now? This is so awkward and embarrassing. God, she is shaking too. I wonder if she is as scared as I am? Well, no point in trying to hide it from her. As soon as we kiss, she will know.* "Lilly, I'm nervous myself. I've never undone any woman's dress before nor have I bedded anyone. I don't know what you need, but I promise you if you let me know what you like I will do my best for you."

"You are? Me too, I'm terrified. I, I will, but please tell me what you need too. I am so ignorant of all this," she admitted, knowing full well as soon as they kissed, he'd know it anyway. No hiding from *mentales* gifts while in rapport.

"Well, I think this first time we both should bed naked. That way we will not have to deal with clothing issues. It's going to be hard enough on us both without adding to it. I've made extensive studies of *mentales* energies. I know how it works, but knowing how it works is little comfort to me just now," he admitted sheepishly. He pulled back the sheets and observed his wife's form, embarrassed at his own arousal from merely observing her. She too began to feel strange pangs she'd never felt before and realized she too was being aroused by him and his closeness to her.

He crawled in beside her and they kissed. At that moment, their mental barriers went down and their senses heightened. With the head blind, a passionate kiss was as close as they could come to sharing each other. When one loves someone, they try to be as close together as possible. On the other hand, enemies try to be as far from each other as possible. Yet, when two telepaths kiss and go into rapport with each other, the closeness takes on a whole new dimension. The two spiritual beings move closer together than their bodies, almost blending into the same space. Certainly, their minds nearly merged together, so much so that each felt what the other was feeling. Lilly immediately knew she could sense what he needed and he, her. An hour later, two extremely satisfied people finally fell into a comforting, restful sleep.

Lilly's pent up fears had evaporated as had his. Felix knew this physical aspect of his marriage would work out just fine for both of them. He fell into a deep sleep with her fragrance of lavender in his senses along with the gentle feel of her long, black hair settling on his chest, her huge bosom resting against his side.

The next morning, when they arose and were dressing before breakfast, Lilly asked, "So what is all this research you are doing? Is it permissible for you to share it with me?" *I do hope I have some purpose in this marriage other than being a brood mare.*

"Sure. Are you sure you want to hear all this?" he asked. He added, "I'd rather not have you just be a brood mare either."

"Very much so. I'm sorry. I forgot to put up my mental barriers this morning," Lilly replied, her face quite flushed.

"Well, between us, let's not have barriers. I don't think I could live that way, not unless we have to, Lilly. Come on, let's eat and then I can go over my researches with you."

An hour later, the two reentered the bedroom long enough for him to retrieve his notes and then headed into his study in the next room. "Okay, where to begin? It all has to do with energy, Lilly. What I have found is there is no difference between the energies that are used to run our bodies, our minds, or even bolts of lightning. It is all the same thing, energy. We who have the gift have an increased ability to generate mental energies, thousands of times stronger and in a larger volume than the head blind. This mental energy we generate to power our gifts travels along the same nerve channels in our bodies, particularly reusing the channels that also control our reproductive systems. They do dual duty, routing our sexual drives and routing our *mentales* energies too."

Lilly broke in, "Grandmother Doctor Zosia said we have a larger pituitary gland which is responsible for our *mentales* gifts. Mind you, I've no idea where this thing is or what it does, only its name. How does that fit in with what you are saying?"

"Yes, she is right. This is the gland, which controls the body's production of chemicals that are used to create the energy that drives our *mentales*. For example, Lilly, it is chilly in here. The servants have cleaned out the ashes and set wood for a fire in the fireplace there. Watch." He focused and great flames sprang up, as if the fire were already roaring.

"Now, how did I do that? Well, all matter is composed of tiny particles. With the wood particles, if they reach a critical temperature, they combust. That is, a reaction takes place between the wood and particles in the air, releasing other vapors, including the smoke we see. All the original wood and air particles are still around, still present, though some have joined or bonded together with others, forming new things, such as the smoke. What I did was to raise the temperature of the wood. How? All these particles that compose the wood are vibrating. I have observed that in all things, the tiny particles vibrate proportionately to the ambient temperature. The higher the temperature, the greater the vibrations; the lower the temperature, the smaller the vibrations."

"Is it possible for these particles to not vibrate at all?" Lilly asked. "This is very akin to what I do when I am healing a wound. I move the tiny particles and join them to make larger blocks, eventually becoming large enough to block the blood flowing from the wound."

"Yes, you are right. You can see them too. No, I have never seen these particles in complete rest. Even in the coldest temperatures in the dead of winter, the particles in anything outside are still vibrating, albeit not as much as they would if they were at room temperature."

"Now this is how the monks of Skylar Abby have become masters of their bodies. We've all heard stories of how they can sleep on a stone slab in a room that is way below freezing and yet be perfectly warm, though they sleep naked. They simply focus a little energy on their body's particles thereby warming them up. While this is a simple explanation, I admit I cannot do this myself. I can make the logs burst into flames, but I cannot make my body warm when it is cold outside."

Lilly giggled, "I can't either — warm my body up like the monks can. Still this is similar to what I do when I need to unblock the nerve channels of someone who has Verge Sickness. I get the pile of particles to get back into motion and into flow once more."

"Yes, it is all related, Lilly! I am so glad you too can see this. I have been trying to get others in the tower to see this, but they simply refuse to accept such a simple explanation." Lilly was pleased by his compliment.

"I suppose we should begin by having you share with me all of your *mentales* gifts. I will be logging them in my journal. Then, it is only fair I tell you of mine," Felix suggested. She sensed this was somehow vital for him to know. *Well, it is only fair my husband knows about my skills. He may need to call upon them one day.*

He added, "I know this will sound more like we are a couple of brood mares, but I do need to know about you and you, me." She smiled, *My thoughts precisely. I like this man.*

"I seem to have part of four *mentales* lines, stemming from Aurora, Ally, Dita, and Doctor Zosia, as well as from Norwood. I don't seem to have picked up much from my other grandfathers, though." She rattled off a lengthy list of healing skills she had, far more than any other single person at this tower did. That alone impressed Felix. Not only wounds and injuries, she could deal with poisonings as well. Her ultimate healing skill allowed her to fully heal another, while taking on that person's illness herself and subsequently healing herself, albeit far more slowly. "I also have Norwood's legendary skills as a negotiator and leader, the Command Voice, the Dominate skill, and to Control Other's Minds, but I don't like to use them much. I admit I have not practiced them much at all."

"But I also have a lot of the gifts that Grandmother Dita had. I can sense the history of an object or what recent traumatic events have happened around a location. I never get lost and always know which way is which. I use these a lot, especially when I am out riding. I sometimes have a sense of the future, like Grandmother Aurora, but that one is too scary. I've not done it much. Also, I've got Grandmother Ally's gift that allows me to drive others away. I think that is better than allowing the parties to fight. I guess because I don't like to fight that's why I don't have any of my grandfathers' gifts.

They were fighters, you see. That about sums me up."

"Incredible, Lilly! You have so much to offer. I am very pleased to have you as my wife." She breathed a sigh of relief, knowing he accepted her gifts and that he was even pleased with them meant everything to her. "Now this brood stallion must tell his." Both giggled at his tease. "Well, in a way it does sound like we are nothing but a breeding pair."

"My gifts are a merging of the old Brom and Bolivar lines. I can do basic healing, which comes from Zoe Roundtree-Brom and Linda Waters, Tammy Lane-Waters' daughter. I also inherited Zoe's huge skills with fires. If it involves fires in any way, I can do it. That's why my nickname around here is Fire Man. But in many ways, I am more indebted to my Grandmother Marisol Bolivar-Wycombe. She's also given me total access to all her copious research notes. I can go into Deep Rapport with someone and learn the nature of their gifts, just like she used to do. I also picked up a touch of her skill in making believable Illusions, though I am not too good at it yet. I also have the Wycombe legendary skills as a negotiator and leader, the Command Voice, the Dominate skill, and to Control Other's Minds. They came from Palmer Wycombe, I think. Like you, Lilly, I don't like to use them much. I also inherited their Combat Sense, and I can sense when danger is near too."

"Well, you have impressive gifts yourself," Lilly replied when he finished.

"Oh this, dear Lilly, is only the barest beginnings! I've been going over Marisol's notes and her published catalog of known gifts. I have discovered two key principles. One, the more one uses a gift, the better and more powerful it becomes. Two, we *can* learn to execute gifts we do not have."

"What? That's impossible. I thought we could only do what we were given," Lilly replied, growing confused. Surely, he didn't mean what he was saying.

"It is possible. None of my relatives can see through another's eyes or hear through another's ears. Yet, I have been diligently working on developing these two skills myself. While I am not yet perfect with them, I can do them."

"Perhaps, they were part of your gifts and simply lay

dormant," Lilly offered a reasonable explanation.

"Yes, I thought that too, Lilly. That's why I picked these two at random from Marisol's catalogue. I have stayed away from the more challenging and difficult ones for now, picking the simpler ones, since I have to figure out how to do them on my own. I assure you, neither of those two was in my gift, not even remotely. Yet, now they have become part of my arsenal so to speak."

"But that means we can learn to do anything that is in Marisol's Catalogue of *Mentales* Gifts!" Lilly exclaimed, suddenly in awe of Felix.

"You have that right. Now then, are you sure you want to join me and help me in my research?"

"You bet. I hate sewing and doing menial women's things. I feared I would be put on a shelf now, only making babies for you. I'd give anything actually to help you in real research! That is really what is important, don't you think?"

"Vitally so, Lilly! Vitally so. Welcome to my *mentales* research! I sometimes get so wrapped up in it I forget more mundane things. I hope that won't bother you."

"Not at all, as long as we can go riding when the weather is nice."

"Deal. Now that you are a part of my research, there is a bit more to it. This must be kept between you and me for now, but I am on to something revolutionary." He lowered his voice, "If it pans out, it represents immense power, absolutely mind-boggling power for anyone who has the gift! I am working on a psi-energy booster. Lilly, it does seem actually to work! Imagine this scenario. An army is invading the Angels. With my booster in hand, I start a fire, just like I did in the fireplace a while ago, only this time, the entire forest erupts in flames, wiping out the entire invading army and not a single life is lost on our side! It will make wars totally obsolete! That's a dream of mine, no more wars of any kind!"

If Lilly had any doubts, now they were completely dispelled! No more wars. Oh how any sentient person with *mentales* would dearly love to have that come about! "Where do we start?" she asked eagerly.

"Well, first, we need to get you learning how to do one

of Marisol's skills that is not in your background. What would you like to be able to do, gift-wise, that you cannot do now?" Felix asked, admiring his wife's attitude.

Lilly thought for a minute. "You know, I love horses and love to ride. I have always been envious of those whose gift is to go into rapport with animals. I don't want to control them so much as to understand them and their needs so I can help them or not make them do something they'd rather not do. Horses, specifically. It's the Rusden Tower's gift."

"Excellent. That gift is not in either of our lineages. Perfect choice, Lilly, perfect. If you can learn Animal Rapport, then that is proof we can learn to do other things with our *mentales* gifts. It is my theory right now that given the proper training and ability to generate the needed mental energies, psi-energies to be specific, there is no skill in Marisol's catalogue we cannot do."

He continued, "Of course, the hard part of this is working out how it is done. Those with the gift inherently never even think about how to do it; they just use it. In our cases, we have to work out how it is done, and then train our own minds to be able to execute it and bring it about. That's exhausting work, Lilly, but it does work."

"I'm totally willing to work hard at it, Felix. Really, I am. I know that I am awfully young, but I am willing," Lilly replied.

"It is good I finally have one person in the entire world that I can share my work with!"

"And I am thankful to have a husband that doesn't want just another brood mare," she replied with a coy grin. He gave her a loving kiss and sensed what she desired most at this time.

"Come on, this is a rare sunny day. Let's try out our new horses, shall we?" Felix suggested. The light in her eyes told him he'd guessed right. Time enough for more research later.

When they returned from their long ride, Felix was anxious to work with Lilly. If he could somehow get her to learn this special gift, his theory would be proven, as far as he was concerned. What better time than when they were already hot and sweaty and with their fine pair of horses. "Okay, Lilly, let's get started on learning your new skill. I think the starting point is to get into rapport with me and then see if you can shift it over to your lovely new mare somehow. Sorry, I can't be more specific on how to shift it over to her."

She complied and he felt her slipping easily into rapport with him. He felt her youthful enthusiasm and an eagerness to learn he'd not sensed before. He realized Lilly would never ever accept a role of only being a housewife. Her mind was too expansive to be limited to only the most mundane chores. That's what servants were for, he reminded himself.

After several days of trying, finally Lilly managed to go into rapport with her mare. She was so elated and excited about it she lost her focus and thus the rapport. "I did it! I did it! Felix, I actually did it, if only I hadn't gotten so excited and lost it." She flushed, realizing her loss of concentration had blown it.

"Super well done, Lilly. Okay. Rapport with me. Let's try it again."

A week later, Lilly no longer needed the crutch of going into rapport with Felix first. She could focus on her mare and slip into rapport with her fairly easily. From this initial point of contact, she began to see what she could sense, learn, and feel about her mare. Felix, on the other hand, felt that his theory was entirely vindicated now. Time to move onto the next step — amplification of *mentales* energies a hundred-fold or more. Perhaps, there was no upper limit. Mind boggling.

In many ways, Lilly was also a test subject for Felix and his experiments, though he never used that expression around her. He brought her into the current research he was conducting just prior to their marriage. "Here are some of the psi-crystals the ancient Advanced Witches, such as our great-grandmothers used to use to enhance their mental powers. According to the old journals of Marisol, the prospective witch would go out into the wilds just north of here in search of their very own psi-crystal. Apparently, only one specific psi-crystal would work per witch. I believe that phenomenon has to do with the specific wavelengths of the person's mental energies, with each being slightly different from each other."

"I've seen some of my grandparent's psi-crystals.

Aurora and Ally's huge ones are on display in Wyth Tower," Lilly explained.

"Okay, now I have been going out in the field looking for a psi-crystal that is attuned to me. I've found this one here, which is probably close, though not an exact match. What I want you to do is to watch the fire in the fireplace. First, I will use my gift and start a tiny fire. Use a small amount of mental energy. Then, I will hold onto my psi-crystal and use the same small amount. Watch the difference first, Lilly."

He created a small fire, about two inches tall and then put it out. Felix picked up a small two inch long psi-crystal. While holding it, he repeated the process. Lilly was quite surprised to see a foot tall flame appearing. "Whoa! That's at least six times larger, Felix!" Lilly exclaimed.

Felix smiled; he knew it was. "Yes, now this time, I want you to carefully monitor the psi-crystal when I do it. Pay close attention." She did and he again activated his fire, then hastily put it out.

"The crystal glowed a pale blue-green glow while you were doing it, Felix."

"Thanks, I always wondered what the psi-crystal's response was. I can't use my gifts and watch the psi-crystal's response closely at the same time. Hey, I have an idea. Let's see if another theory of mine is correct or not. I think each of these psi-crystals responds to a slightly different emitting wavelength. Go into rapport with me and hold onto the psi-crystal. Then use one of your gifts. Let's see if it is amplified, shall we?"

She took the psi-crystal in her hand, squeezing it firmly. Then she easily slid into rapport with Felix, something she had grown to love to do now. Once there, she almost forgot about what she was to do. At last, she decided to go into rapport with her mare, stabled a long way from their study high in the tower. Ordinarily, she was way too far from her mare to even attempt her animal rapport. However, suddenly, she was in touch with her mare's mind, a most comforting, warm feeling. Her mare loved her. She broke the rapport and exclaimed, "I reached her! Felix, I reached my mare all the way from up here! It works!" She gave him a tight hug.

"So it is simply a matter of wavelength after all. Lilly, we are on to something most powerful!"

"I need one attuned to me!"

"Lilly, there is more to all this. I came across something even more interesting just before we got married. I was pulled off my research for our wedding. This is important; trust me on that. Our psi-crystals are bluish or greenish. I've tried some of both colors and apparently color makes no difference in the amplification process which appears to be tenfold."

"That is an incredible amount, dear," Lilly replied, awestruck by the magnitude of the amplification.

"Yes, but not nearly what I have in mind. Here, let me show you. Join with my mind and I'll show you the active particles within the psi-crystals." She moved into close rapport with him and saw what he was seeing, the tiny particles embedded within the crystalline rock. Then, she backed out. "I call them silicate particles. They are extremely common on Tierra, found nearly everywhere. Okay, now here is a sample of Midlands' glassware. Again, go into rapport with me and I will show you the particles."

She did so. *They are the same, these silicates?*

Yes. Now watch the particles while I use my gift. She watched fascinated as the tiny particles responded to him. They broke their rapport and Felix explained, "Even when imbedded within common glass, the silicates respond to our psi-energy. I looked long and hard for this particular glass, which happens to be slightly attuned to me. If you noticed, the silicates particles are very far apart. Hence, the overall amplification is nominal, but there nonetheless."

"Quite. But are you saying common drinking glasses can be amplifiers for us?" Lilly was slightly confused, not following where this was leading. Suddenly, she got a glimpse of the future and gushed out, "You have another glass to show me?"

Felix nearly jumped out of his pants! "How did you know that? Yes, that's what is so incredibly important here."

"My gift. It just kicked in and I saw you showing me another glass."

"Amazing woman. Precisely correct. Lilly, it was a sheer

accident I discovered this glass! By a most round about manner, I came across this glass, made in the Easterlings. One of the women, who went there years ago to establish the eleventh tower there at Adelmira, brought a small collection of fine glassware back with her. I was admiring them one day and also using a bit of my gift, when I discovered this particular glass. Okay. Enough prelude. I am going to hold the glass in front of me so that you can see the fireplace through the glass. Watch the glass and the fireplace, dear." He focused and energized the particles in the wood. Flames a few inches tall erupted, which he quickly extinguished by slowing the particles' vibrations way down, killing the reaction known as fire.

"My god, the goblet actually amplified it, Felix!" she exclaimed.

"Precisely. Imagine my excitement when I discovered this! Now, why is this so vital? Again, rapport with me and I will show you these grey-white crystals that are imbedded within the goblet." She did so and saw grey-white crystals instead of the blue or green ones.

As she pulled out of the rapport, she struggled to make sense of this. "The particles are different from the silicates, yet they seem to be there in about the same proportions, which is hardly any present or is it better to say that they are very far apart? So this means that these crystals amplify psi-energies many times more than do the silicates found in the common psi-crystals."

"Lilly, you amaze me. That is precisely correct. Take it one step further, dear," he complimented her enthusiastically and then pushed her slightly.

"Well, if we could find these grey-white crystals in a denser concentration, like in the psi-crystals, then it is reasonable to expect that they would amplify psi-energies many times more than our blue-green ones do," she put two and two together at last. "Where do we find such crystals? Do they exist? Oh! Somewhere in the Easterlings!"

"Brilliant, Lilly, brilliant. Yes, precisely correct. This is what I was researching when dad ordered me to get married. It is why I was so hesitant. This discovery is potentially vastly more important than getting married. Think of what this can mean for us! If we can find these particles, which I'm calling germanium for lack of a better word, in a larger crystal form, the amount of amplification of our psi-energies will be huge! You could reach your mare from miles away. Just think of the possibilities this could offer anyone with the *mentales* gift!"

"So when are we going?" Lilly asked.

"Huh?"

"To the Easterlings in search of these germanium crystals, dear," Lilly replied, as if suddenly traveling several thousand miles across bandit-filled lands, hostile kingdoms, and potentially a war or two meant nothing at all.

He picked her up and twirled her around before giving her a passionate kiss. Then, he calmed down. "We need to go as soon as we possibly can, before we get snowed in totally and have to wait until the spring thaw." They only had to travel some three thousand five hundred miles!

"The hell you two are going to go riding off to Adelmira on you own! Do you think that I am some kind of utter fool?" Amo Hank raged. The two had just told his father of their plans to ride off to the tower at Adelmira, Alba, Easterlings. "That's four thousand miles. You'd get waylaid and killed or captured a dozen times over!"

"Well, dad, this is vitally important," Felix attempted to interject through his father's anger.

"Yes, father-in-law, Felix is right. This is critically important. We will go with or without your permission," Lilly retorted.

"What? You think this is vital too? Oh hell. There is no sense arguing with the both of you! But I'll not risk the lives of either of you two. Your children will be entirely too valuable for Brom Tower to lose before they are born. Give me some time to arrange something. Foolish kids anyway."

"Dad, think of it as being our honeymoon." Felix tried a different approach and saw his father mellow out some.

"Well, you ought to have a honeymoon. Are you pregnant yet, daughter?"

"No, not yet. I am only fifteen, father," Lilly replied, flushing to the roots of her hair. He was talking openly of such things and she barely knew her new father-in-law.

"Of all the infernal places to want to honeymoon! You know that they will probably insist on binding your wife, don't you?" From the expressions on both their faces, he knew that he had scored a point. Neither had.

"Well, if that is what it takes, then I will do it," Lilly replied stoically, though she had no idea what it meant to be a bound Easterlings woman.

A week later, the two found themselves accompanying a small but heavily guarded caravan carrying a dozen women to Adelmira tower and a large supply of items to trade with those in the tower. This was their yearly swap.

Chapter 14 The Amplification of Psi-energies

The caravan left the tower at Brom on the twenty-fifth of July 1070, stopping in Wyth for a couple of days, adding more wagons of supplies and guards. From there, they traveled mostly eastward to Bettingham where more was added. After that, they followed the Wyndl River down to Wye, where the Wal River joined the mighty flow. Here, a day was spent ferrying all the wagons, carriages, and horses across the mile-wide river. Next, they headed slightly north of east to Northend near the headwaters of the Brooke River. Then, it was due southeast into the wild lands of northern Matruk down to the southern edge of the Buku Hills and Adelmira. All told, they covered closer to four thousand miles, arriving on the fifteenth of October, having spent just over a hundred days on the long journey.

However, the many days were not wasted. On the contrary. Felix, now considered his new bride to be extremely valuable, but not in the same way as both of their parents. Besides his wife, she had become a key, valuable research assistant to him. Hence, he felt obligated to help her learn to protect herself, especially while spending so much time exposed as they were. On top of that, he too needed to learn to fight better so she could depend upon him, if the need arose.

This aspect of their training, as he began calling it, took on two very different aspects. First, he knew he needed to be able to handle a sword far better than he could. True, he had been given basic training as a teen, but mostly it was to merely hold his own. He was expected to use his *mentales* skills should an attack come his way. Still, out in the open wilderness, he felt he should be more competent with the blade. Further, Lilly had no exposure to swords or daggers. He wanted her at least to be able to defend herself if needed. Second, those with *mentales* gifts could be attacked by others with the gift. Called telepathic combat, these forms were dangerous for those with the gift.

The leader of their guards was one Captain Sheldon Smith, a forty year old veteran who also had the *mentales* gifts of combat arts. He agreed to train them both with weapons and to work with them on mental attack methods. Ama Alice Rains, a forty-five year old mother, whose children were married, was one of the women who was going to spend a couple of years helping out at Adelmira. Her husband had passed away in a hunting accident. Having spent time in towers herself, she decided to donate two years to the Easterlings, who needed assistance in training their people with the gift. She was a master of mental defense methods. Hence, the two complimented each other.

Although Felix and Lilly both rode their new horses, they did their practice and learning sessions around the campfires at night. When they stopped in Wyth, Felix was able to pick up some of the new extremely high quality blades being crafted from imported, high-grade iron ore by the weapon smiths of Haverhills. "I feel like a Sisterhood fighter," Lilly teased him as she strapped on the short sword for the first time. Both chuckled. Each had a new short sword and dagger. That this was also the favored combination that the Easterlings fighters used was not missed on them. Captain Sheldon worked with them primarily on defensive moves.

Once they were comfortable with that, he switched to the mental forms and Ama Alice stepped in to assist them in learning how to defend themselves as well. As with all *mentales* actions, each required the usage of their finite reservoir of psi-energies, some required more than others did.

Captain Sheldon was a master of all five known forms of mental attacks. "My personal favorite form of attacking others is what I call the Psi-Shock. You send out a huge wall of uncontrolled psi-energies that hits everyone within the expanding cone from me, head blind and *mentales* alike. It is costly to use and I can only get off four of these in one day. If I am successful, the head blind collapse unconscious for a time, while others believe that I've mortally wounded them and often retreat from combat, yielding the field to me. With this form, you just let loose a volley of psi-energy without much thought about it. I like it because I can impact a number of opponents with one shot."

He went on, "Now if I have a single combatant who is very dangerous, I then use the Neuron Crush. It's not as costly to use. I focus my psi-energies onto the opponent's neurons. If successful, my opponent suffers actual wounds, often bleeding from their eyes, nose, and ears. Nasty. Used several times in succession, it can kill."

"Another tactic is called the Ego Assault. Costing about half as much as the crush, it does require me to send out thoughts designed to attack the person's own ideas of self-importance. If I win through and send out the right thoughts, the victim stands around in a daze for a considerable time. Of course, with this form of attack, it is best used when you have some knowledge of your opponent. Otherwise, you don't know what the person might be sensitive to, you see."

"About as costly as the assault is the Subconscious Uprising. With this attack, you attempt to arouse your opponent's subconscious fears and dreads. If you are successful, you drive him temporarily mad. Finally, the cheapest cost is the Mind Stab. With this attack, you send out a single dagger-like bolt of psi-energy. If it is successful, you disable a bit of his *mentales* gifts until they have rested fully. Personally, I seldom use this form because I am more interested in winning the battle. If there are many opponents, I opt usually for a Psi-Shock first. If there are particularly powerful *mentales* opponents around, then I opt for the crush or uprising because if successful, they are out of the combat. Only if I have prior knowledge of my opponent do I take a gamble with the Ego Assault."

Lilly looked a little white. "These sound rather nasty. How do we defend ourselves from them? How do we know which one will be used to attack us?"

Ama Alice took over at this point. "The second question is easy. You don't. You put up what you think will serve you the best against what you guess you might be hit with and hope for the best. The first question is more difficult to answer. There are also five defense forms to protect yourself, Lilly. Some are simple and cost you nothing at all to put up. Of course, the protection isn't so good that way. There are others that are a bit costly to use, but provide better protection. The worst aspect of defending is some forms of defense are good against certain types of attack but really poor against other forms of attack. Choose the wrong defense and you could be aiding your attacker. Choose the right one and you are hindering his attack as well as defending against it."

"Now the cheapest one that costs you nothing at all to use is called the Blank Mind. It costs nothing because all you do is put all thoughts out of your mind, hence its name. It is particularly effective against only the Subconscious Uprising attack since you are holding all thoughts out of your mind. With other attacks, it helps the attacker somewhat, as there are no other thoughts for those attacks to have to penetrate first. With the Mind Cloud you throw up a host of random thoughts which makes your mind seem totally confused to your attacker. It is a good defense except against the Uprising and the Neuron Crush. You could probably put up dozens and dozens of these each day. Very cheap."

"The Thought Chant is a more expensive defensive mode and requires you to chant the same thought over and over, rather like a monk. It is effective against everything except the Uprising. Then, there is the Mental Fortress, which costs even more to put up, but is effective against all forms. The ultimate defense is the Steel Will and is the most costly of the defenses to raise. My guess is you could throw up five of these each day. It gives you the absolute best protection against all these attacks. It is my favorite, mind you. I don't want a man messing with my subconscious."

Alice flashed them quick smile before continuing, "Now, first, I will be teaching you how to use these defenses. The problem is, from all that we know, these cannot be taught to anyone who does not inherently have this gift initially. Same is true for the attack forms. Either one has it initially or he doesn't. What Captain Sheldon and I are saying is that do not be surprised if you only have one or two of these. We will find out which ones, if any, that you have, and then get you up to speed in their use."

Felix spoke up. "Do me and Lilly a favor. Assume we do have each of these and work with us to get the details down pat. We will let you know if we simply cannot master one of these." Sheldon and Alice shrugged their shoulders, but agreed to do so.

By the time they arrived at Adelmira, both Felix and Lilly had mastered all the attack forms and all the defense forms, shocking both Captain Sheldon and Ama Alice. Both subsequently assumed that miraculously both had these ten as part of their original *mentales* gifts. Little did they know that neither had any. Felix had once again proven his theory that one could learn to execute other *mentales* actions for which their original endowment had not provided.

The trip itself had been mostly uneventful, due primarily to their large numbers and *mentales* personnel. Some armed encampments were encountered in the long stretch between Wye and Northend. Captain Sheldon suspected one or more minor wars were about to break out. They encountered what they guessed were five groups of bandits on the long haul down from Northend. However, because of their size, they were not attacked and that they were bandits remained mere speculation.

The oasis known as Adelmira was located at the extreme southern edge of the Buku Hills, the land of mesas and some five hundred miles north and slightly west of the large coastal city of Turda, Alba. Officially, they were in the Kingdom of Lucca, whose major oasis was at Lucca, some two hundred miles further north. Adelmira had a population of close to one thousand, having doubled in size in the last twenty years, as the tower's influence continued to grow. Surrounded by mostly inexpensive and easily constructed adobe homes, the imposing grey stone, five story tower dominated the entire town and surrounding desert lands.

Adelmira was a crossroads town. One track led due north paralleling the eastern edge of the Buku Hills, leading to Lucca and beyond. The south track led eventually to Turda. The eastern track led out into the vast sand dunes of the desert land of Arad. Of course, the western track led into the interior of Matruk and the breadbasket of the Easterlings. Eventually the track veered to the southwest and arrived in Southbend. Trade goods much needed in the desert kingdoms flowed through Adelmira. Known only to select few women, the northern track led also to the hidden village of Matera, the safe haven and sanctuary for women, run by the High Priestess of Lysandra. Only a woman in need could actually see the village when she approached it. All others merely saw more uninhabited desert wilderness. Ama Alice knew of Matera though, but said nothing about it to the other women and certainly not to the men in her party.

As the caravan rolled into the main mud packed streets of Adelmira, Lilly held her hand across her mouth as she gasped, "Oh my god! Felix, look at their women!"

There were many open air markets lining the street. Women wearing their fetter skirts shuffled along, taking slow and tiny steps. They wore no clothing of any kind above their waists. Well, it was very hot here and the women and men of the caravan were drenched with sweat on a daily basis. However, it was not so much the exposed giant breasts that so shocked them both. Rather, each woman had copper chains binding her upper arms just above her elbows to a band around her waist. All wore their long brown hair in two long braids lying down their backs. Even from this distance, Lilly could also see that many of the women had awfully long finger nails as well.

Felix whispered, "My god, Lilly! What have I gotten us into? Maybe I ought to send you back with the caravan."

"Why? Why would any woman endure this?" Lilly whispered back, totally aghast at what she was seeing.

"I can't imagine why, Lilly. We've heard the Easterlings bind their women, but I never dreamed it would be this bad."

Lilly swallowed hard. *If these women can somehow endure it, then I can too. I will not be left behind. Felix needs me and I won't let him down, not ever. He has treated me as an equal and I refuse to disappoint him.* "I'll stay, Felix. I'm sure somehow I can manage this. Look, if all the Easterlings women can, then it must not be that awful, though I expect it takes an enormous amount of getting used to, don't you think?"

"Dear, I cannot imagine how anyone can get used to this. Are you certain you want to stay? It is going to be terrible for you."

"Yes, we are on the verge of the most significant discovery since the arrival of our gifts. I won't let you down. I refuse to do that, Felix." She said very determinedly, hoping somehow, someway she could manage this.

As they approached the tall tower, they passed a small adobe home which had a large sign painted in crude letters on a warped piece of board. It read simply, Sisterhood House. "What do you make of that? The Sisterhood has a presence even here?" Felix asked, though he didn't expect Lilly to answer the latter one.

"Amazing. I wonder how they manage?" Almost as if in answer to their questions, a woman stepped out of the doorway and stared at the incoming caravan. She was short, but she looked as bound as all the other women of Adelmira and Lilly's brief hope vanished even before she could vocalize the thought. The woman's eyes were yellow and she followed the caravan and riders as they pulled up near the main double doors of the tower. Only then did Lilly notice the woman had ducked back into the home. So much for the Sisterhood, she thought.

A bound woman opened the doors allowing another woman to slowly shuffle out to meet her expected guests and trade caravan. "Welcome to Adelmira. I am Ama Floriana Via, the leader of the tower. My esteemed guests, if you will follow me inside, the caravan can pull into the stables behind the tower. There, the goods can be unloaded and our return goods loaded. Dinner will be provided for your men."

Captain Sheldon nodded and took charge of the caravan, while the two wagons with the ten volunteer women, including Ama Alice pulled up closer to the doors. Felix and Lilly dismounted and followed Ama Floriana, failing utterly to walk slowly enough behind her. The older woman chuckled, noticing their sudden spurts of motion. "I can see that you two have never been to the Easterlings."

Lilly joked, "Surely, it doesn't show!" Both women laughed.

Shortly, they entered the Great Hall, quite similar to that in Brom. At once, all dozen felt more at ease in surroundings that were familiar, though not exactly. Layouts of the eleven towers were quite similar, though there were some differences. They took seats indicated by Ama Floriana, watching her move slowly to her seat at the head. Several other women shuffled in carrying pitchers, clay mugs, and a tray of dates and wheat biscuits.

After Ama Alice introduced her ten volunteer women, Ama Floriana asked, "And you two, Amo Felix and Ama Lilly, am I to understand that you wish to spend some time traveling about our lands?"

"Yes, Ama Floriana, we do. We wish to travel around the mesa lands. This is possible, is it not?"

"Yes, but. It is the law of the Kingdom of Lucca that all visiting women must follow our traditional dress codes. The only exceptions are the filthy Sisterhood renegades, but I am sure that you are not one of them, Ama Lilly." She had a tone of absolute and utter scorn when mentioning the Sisterhood and the two decided not to press that issue.

Lilly spoke up, "Yes, Ama, I am prepared to make the attempt, but I am afraid that we are totally ignorant of your customs here."

Before she could continue, Ama Floriana raised her lower right hand, indicating that she wanted a word. "That is most understandable. Our ten new volunteers will also need to learn our ways. The first order of business will be to get you women all bathed and into our outfits. Then, we will help you learn how to deal with them and answer your many questions. Always outsiders have many questions about our Easterlings customs. Plus, I will have our stable man teach Amo Felix his proper duties for you, Lilly. It is not proper for a woman to teach a man, you see. Now Felix, someone will show you to your guest room, a bath has been prepared for you. Your lovely wife will join you later on. Rafe will be told to come to you and give you your instructions after dinner. At the moment, he is overseeing the unloading of the caravan."

A woman shuffled in and beckoned to Felix. He followed her, with a backwards glance over his shoulder catching the other eleven women following Ama Floriana. After showing him his new quarters, she suggested he unload their things and bring them into their quarters before taking a bath. "Our heat will make you Midlands folk sweat. Already your shirt is soaking wet. You have a lot to learn about life in the desert, Amo." She teased him slightly. Well he knew that was true and did as asked.

Ama Floriana explained to the eleven women who were being helped into their local dress, "You see, the women of the Easterlings have worn fetter skirts for many, many centuries now. About the worst thing a woman can do to embarrass herself is to be seen outside of her bedroom not wearing her fetter skirt. At night in your bedroom, your husbands or fellow women will assist you in removing your skirts. We do not sleep in them, of course. The desert heat is such that women almost never wear any kind of top, save in the winter time and then only the thinnest of silk blouses."

She continued, "All women also are bound, as you are now being bound. For any woman, this is considered to be a high honor; men must therefore always consider our needs. They cannot ever overlook women of the Easterlings, not ever. While we put fetter skirts on our girls when they reach their fifth birthday and they soon get accustomed to them, you eleven may expect to take quite some time getting used to walking in them and in the special ways we women do our things with our upper arms so bound. We will be teaching these to you beginning now."

"Further, at night, our men further bind our arms in leather tubes such as this one. They tie our arms behind our backs as we go to bed. It is the duty of a man to do this great honor for his wife, but here, we women do it for each other, honoring ourselves. Of course, it is the man's first duty when he rises in the morning to undo the tubes, release our arms, and help us into our fetter skirts. Thus, here in the Easterlings, our men give women a *great* amount of attention and special care. We must strive always to be worthy of such a great gift. Lilly, your husband will be instructed on how to care for you. You need not worry about that detail. Now, I see that they have you all properly dressed. It is time that we help you learn to walk and do the normal things we women do. We will show you how. All you need is a brief period of adjustment. The main thing is we must always work together, you see."

Lilly didn't see, for she was miserable. The fetter skirt was so very tight and she could only move her feet two inches. She kept fighting against the chains that held her upper arms at her sides. That she was naked from the waist up had become a completely minor consideration. At least she was no longer sweating to death, as she had been the last couple of weeks while doing nothing but riding while wearing her thicker blouses. *Minor adjustment period, bah! This is more like disguised torture!*

But is it any different than your brand of torture in the Midlands? A voice appeared in her mind. Whose? Lilly looked around, but all the women seemed preoccupied helping the eleven as they began to wobble, trying to figure out the shuffling walk without falling down. The voice definitely was feminine in nature, but whose? Lilly lost her balance and tried uselessly to catch herself, but of course, reflexively, she used her arms, which didn't move as expected. Only the quick reach of her helper's hand kept her from taking a spill. She looked aside and gave the Ama a brief, but pained smile.

A bit later, they were sitting down to take tea, thus showing the eleven how to deal with dining. Lilly was very glad to be sitting at last. Although she followed the explanations and emulated their movements, her attention was still somewhat on the mystery voice. *What did she mean by my brand of torture anyway? Who sent me that. This is sadism against women, pure and simple.*

Isn't it also sadism in the Midlands, only of a different variety? There was that voice again.

What do you mean? Who are you? Where are you? She thought that this was the better question, as she again glanced around the table. All the women seemed preoccupied with their own struggles to dine.

I'm Fel. We'll meet later. Best not to let the Amas know that I'm chatting with you. Just think about your own Midlands' fetters. We'll talk later. Promise. Oops, Ama Flo is starting to catch on. Bye. The contact was broken abruptly and Lilly focused on learning to dine by herself.

That done, the eleven were again set walking; this time

moving around the tower's first floor. *How can they possibly go up even one step in these skirts? I can't lift my foot more than an inch!*

Ama Floriana explained, almost as if in answer to her thoughts, "Now Lilly here will not need to go up the stairs as guests are allowed only on this first floor. So we'll leave Lilly to practice getting around here, while I show you how to manage the stairs." Even though she was being left behind, she was still curious and made her impossibly slow way after the large group. Well, they were going just as slowly as she, so her pitiful speed fit right in. Lilly took a strange comfort in that but wondered why she did.

The leader was still explaining to the new volunteers, "Normally, our men will carry us up stairs, but throughout the Easterlings, there are very few stairs. They lift us up and into carriages and wagons when we need to travel. However, here in the tower, there are only a few men. To get ourselves up, sit on your butts and use your hands. Like this, ladies. I'll take you to your new rooms. Your bags have already been brought up to your rooms. Ama Gina has used her Move Object gift for you already. Handy *mentales*."

Well that would be handy for a woman to have! So that's how they do it, crude, but it works. They are going up, Lilly thought. As the women moved awkwardly upwards, she decided to continue her practice walking. Might as well explore the rest of the first floor.

Sometime later, Lilly found their guest bedroom. A man was just leaving as she slowly shuffled her way into her new room. "Lilly! Wow, are you sure that you are able to manage this? You look, well, enticing," Felix said.

He's getting aroused! Hell, now what do I do?

I see you without your blouses only at bedtime, dear. I'm sorry about responding to your form. Felix was too embarrassed to come right out and say her naked bosom and struggled to control his aroused emotions. Hastily, he changed the topic, "I have been briefed on how an Easterlings man is to behave. I am supposed to move as slowly as you do and to care for your needs. I am supposed to be anticipating what you are unable to do and to be there for you, as you need it. I don't know I am that aware of such things yet. Please, Lilly, let me know if you need something and I don't quite see it fast enough."

"Will do. I can't believe how tedious and slow walking actually is. I'm told we are to anticipate things and make our actual trips as efficiently as possible, getting as much done on one walk as possible," Lilly explained a little.

"I'm afraid it only gets worse at night. While I am to undo your laces and free you from your fetter skirt, I am supposed to bind your arms behind your back with these leather tubes before we go to bed and then to undo them and get you back into your skirt first thing in the morning before we head off to breakfast. Lilly, are you sure you want to continue with this? There is still time for you to head back with the caravan. I would never ask you to endure this awful torture."

Lilly sighed. Part of her wanted to do just that, to flee from the Easterlings with all possible speed. Yet, she had a goal. "No, I want to help find these crystals. The importance of them vastly exceeds my minor discomfort. Honestly, I am not being physically harmed, just inconvenienced and slowed down to a snail's pace."

"Okay then, I promise you I will do my best to assist you. Oh, I am supposed to brush out your hair each evening and then braid it first thing in the morning. Apparently, this duty falls to me because we do not have any women servants with us. We had not thought of bringing along any servants."

"You know I don't like having others doing things for us that we could do ourselves. We are not helpless just because we have the *mentales* gifts. So are you going to have to braid your hair too?"

Felix flushed, "Yes, but damned if I have a clue how it's done."

Lilly smiled, "Got it. I really don't like mine braided, but it is not that hard."

"Thanks, love. I supposed I should practice walking with you. He said I would need to gauge my steps when I am with Easterlings women and I would need a lot of practice with that, if I am to be seen as comfortable around women here."

"I'm supposed to be practicing walking, so let's have at it. The sooner we get used to all these strange customs, the better. Any idea how soon we can get on with our search?" Lilly asked.

"Not yet. No chance to ask anyone. I suspect we can get more information at dinner."

The two practiced walking together and Felix's heart went out to Lilly who really was struggling with the restraints but continued to persevere. Suppertime did not come too soon for him. After the nice meal featuring may new delicacies that neither had had before, including dates, figs, and relatively hot spices, both were ready for tea and chat. While the many tower dwellers headed off to their rooms, Ama Floriana finally had the chance to chat at length with her guests.

"Okay, I know that you've come for a visit. No one comes to Adelmira for a honeymoon. So what exactly did you have in mind? Will you be staying here in the tower? It may not be ideal for you to stay in our only inn. I'm told it is not up to your Midlands standards," she both asked and advised.

Felix took a breath and explained, "Actually, Ama, we wish to roam around the Buku Hills. We are looking to sample some of the crystals found here and take them back with us. Lilly and I are doing some experiments on crystals."

"Well, this *is* a strange visit. It would not be wise of you to wander on your own. The hills and desert are dangerous to those who have not grown up here. One must always know where the oases are located. Without water each day, your horses will not survive and you may be able to get by a day or two at most without it. On top of that, there are patrols of the king. Sometimes they are not too friendly to foreigners. Though by following our customs, they might not object too badly."

"We suspected this would be the case, Ama. We have a half-dozen soldiers who will act as our bodyguards, but you are right. We were hoping to hire some local guides here in Adelmira. Can you recommend any? We need them for a month or two. The time is variable, depending on what we find. They should know the hills and nearby desert regions and able to guide us properly."

"Ah, that is the key factor, variable time," Ama Floriana replied, but with a frown. "Usually our guides ask for specific times. They arrange their schedules well in advance and will not take kindly to your more meandering approach. I mean, you are not planning to go to a specific location and back again. Am I guessing right?"

"Yes, exactly. It is more like a search and we will not know precisely where we need to go until we are there and find what we are looking for," Felix replied, not wanting to divulge more than he had to about his mission here in the Buku Hills.

Ama Floriana frowned, "Then my guess was correct. I've not done such things myself but I have made arrangements for others before. I will make inquiries for you, but I am not too hopeful. The men usually insist on very *precise* travel schedules."

"Ama, what about the Sisterhood?" another woman spoke up. "Isn't this just the sort of thing they would undertake?" From the grimace on Ama Floriana's face, Felix suspected this was a sore point with her.

"Well," she stared at Felix, "would you even consider women guides?" From her tone, Felix sensed a deep-seated dislike or perhaps even hatred of the Sisterhood.

Although he didn't want to offend the tower's leader, he needed guides. "In the Midlands, some of the Sisterhood women make excellent guides. I suppose that is true here too. So, yes, we would consider them. I understand why the men would need a precise destination. We are not their only clients."

"Yes, precisely. If you are *sure* you could accept those women as guides, then I will send someone to ask them for you," Ama Floriana begrudgingly volunteered.

"Thank you, you are most generous," Felix replied diplomatically. The woman who had mentioned the Sisterhood volunteered to run the errand and soon began her long shuffle out of the room and tower. Meanwhile, Ama Floriana was only too happy to change the topic. She was eager to hear the latest news from the Kingdom of the Angels. They learned she had done her basic training there many years ago, but she had not enjoyed the Midlands customs, though she had followed them.

Somehow, Felix could not imagine her not wearing her fetter skirt and arm bindings. Later she excused herself and asked them to wait on her messenger.

A half hour later, the woman shuffled her way into the Great Hall. "They have agreed in principle to be your guides. However, they wish to meet with you and hear what it is that is needed before they give their agreement to serve you. The woman you need to see is Andreina Giola. She said if you are in a hurry, you could drop by their house yet tonight. Otherwise, come by in the morning at your leisure."

"Thank you, Ama. I believe the morning will be just fine. These women are good, right?" Felix answered and decided to probe a bit. Was he making an enemy of the tower's leader?

"Oh yes, I personally think they are the best guides, but they get so few contracts you see. Men, well you know how prejudiced they can be. I sensed you both are more open-minded about these things. That is why I suggested it. Honestly, you'd never get any of the male guides to agree to your needs."

"Thanks, yes, I suppose we are. I take it Ama Floriana doesn't like the Sisterhood women," he led the conversation a little and was rewarded.

"Oh my yes, she hates anyone who dares defy our Easterlings traditions. You know she spent two years in the Midlands, Angels kingdom, training to lead our tower. She was forced to disregard our traditions and follow yours. I don't think she has ever forgotten that. The Sisterhood is rebelling against all we hold honorable and sacred according to Ama Flo. Not all of us do, though. She means well, don't get me wrong."

"Thanks, no, we can see she has only the best of intentions. We will visit them in the morning then," Felix ended the conversation. His suspicions were validated and that meant he should judge the Sisterhood women on their own merits. He didn't need to color them ahead of meeting the women.

She looked pleased and bid them good night. Felix rose and put his arm around Lilly's waist as she got up from the table. "I think it best if I stabilize you, my love."

"Please do! You have no idea how much better it is with your arm around me to support me. This is so hard, Felix, but I am making it go right for us. I hope you don't mind. I never thought to ask you if you minded me putting you in this position!" With his stabilizing arm, she felt more confident and less afraid of falling. However, she suddenly realized if she came along on the search, she would be drastically slowing him down! She'd be a hindrance and not a help. Her body tensed up noticeably to Felix.

"Oh, I don't mind at all, Lilly. I am more concerned for you. If I am going to be in the Easterlings for a couple of months, I am certainly going to encounter women and have to deal with this anyway. I'd much rather it be you than some woman I've never met. Besides, this is supposed to sort of be our honeymoon too, you haven't forgotten that, have you?" His tease unlocked the sudden tension that had built up in her.

"Of course not, silly! I am *always* looking forward to our bed times," she answered with a coy grin, a tease of her own. She sensed his arousal beginning and smiled again. Six hundred tiny shuffling steps later, they had covered nearly a hundred feet to their bedroom. Once inside and the door shut, she turned and gave him a hug and passionate kiss to thank him for being so patient with her.

After a bit, Felix sighed, "Now comes the hard part, my dear. I am supposed to help you out of your fetter skirt. It is so hot that I suggest we don't put anything else on." She agreed. "But I am to undo your braids and brush out your hair. I haven't a clue how to proceed. You'll have to," he began, but she interrupted him.

Lilly sensed the embarrassment that emanated from Felix and kept him from having to say more. "I'll give you step by step instructions; just get me out of this skirt first. Ah, what a relief!"

Later on, Felix asked, "I am supposed to use this leather tube to bind your arms behind your back now. Are you sure we should do this? I mean no one will be the wiser if we don't."

Lilly considered this. As much as she wanted to ignore this detail, she decided against it. "Someone might make a nightly check on our well-being for security reasons. Ama Floriana might well have the gift to look in on us to see how we are faring. She did seem to go out of her way to help us all with their customs. I can see no reason to upset her. When in the Easterlings, do as the Easterlings do. Obviously, their women all endure this at night, so it cannot be harmful, just annoying. We should do as their customs dictate, dear. I'm supposed to put my lower arms across by back like this."

"Okay, then here goes. Let me know if it is too tight. He looped the leather over her lower arms and laced the ends together, effectively binding them behind her back. Her fingers did protrude slightly from her sides. He helped her into bed, blew out their lantern, and crawled in beside her. After a passionate kiss, they dropped into a deep rapport with each other and their passions exploded once more.

Later, both were sweating but deeply satisfied. Lilly whispered, "Now that *was* kinky!" He chuckled but agreed. The morning came before either realized it, having had a sound, restful sleep. It took him a considerable period of time to get Lilly's morning needs handled. She found a way to braid his hair for him. Her reach was severely limited, but if he sat on the floor and she on a chair, she could manage. At least his hair was barely shoulder length. Together, they retraced the hundred feet to the Great Hall for breakfast, only to find that indeed they had been extremely slow with the morning necessities.

Ama Floriana gave them both a royal smile as they slowly entered the nearly empty room. "I am so glad you chose to follow our customs. For this, you have my respect, Amo, Ama. Not many from the outer lands do so. I am honored you two have." She chatted with them as they dined, but Felix knew they had scored highly with the tower leader. He didn't know if that was really needed or not, but it certainly didn't hurt. Little did he know that his impression on her would be vitally needed later on.

Fed, the two headed off to meet with the Sisterhood woman as instructed. Although the Sisterhood house was just over a block away, the two got a very good look at life in the small oasis. They moved along very slowly and could see others going about their morning business. Felix saw several men accompanying their wives, moving just as slowly as he was. Various sounds drew their attention: men calling out their wares in the open air market a street away, the caravan men barking loading orders, and the chatter of distant voices. Odors were even more prevalent. Lilly smelled fresh baking bread mingled with a strange dry air and the various date and palm trees that lined the edge of the cool waters. Peace, calm, routine. If asked, those would have been how she would describe the village life this morning. The air was quite warm and she was glad that she wasn't wearing the heavier clothing of the Midlands, because she knew by now she would have been drenched in sweat and it was just early morning.

The Sisterhood adobe home was typical of the many houses in Adelmira, square some forty feet on a side. The flat roofs were thatched with palm leaves laid between thicker logs. Wood was at a premium and only a rough threaded, tapestry-like rug served as their door. A few wealthier homes actually had wooden doors, though the wood was extremely rough, weatherbeaten, and quite crudely planed compared to the fine woodworking of the Midlands. Smoke curled up from their chimney as the two approached the entrance. Felix tapped lightly on the adobe beside the rug door. "Hello?"

Shortly, a woman's hand appeared, pulling the rug back, revealing a young woman's weathered but kindly face. Her alto voice was soft, "Ah, you must be the Midlands couple wishing to hire guides. Welcome to the Sisterhood home in Adelmira. I am Andreina Giola e Zurra. Please come in and take tea. Let us discuss your needs." She was the eldest of the four Sisterhood women at twenty-seven. She was tall with well-toned muscles. Shocking both Felix and Lilly, she wore traditional male white pants that were tied loosely at her ankles, though she too wore no top. Her skin tone was a uniform tan. Although Felix felt ill at ease around half-naked women, Lilly felt a kinship with her, though she stared at the wholly unfettered woman.

The small home was divided into quarters and they entered the room that served as business office, dining room, and living room all rolled into one. Later they learned two other rooms were bedrooms and the forth was their combination kitchen and pantry. A window to the street was opened allowing a hint of the hot outside air inside, but the quarters was remarkably cool, unlike their tower room. Their table was a crude wooden construction, but serviceable. Instead of chairs, two long benches paralleled two sides of the table and Andreina motioned them to have a seat.

As they made their slow way there, another woman entered, bound identically to Lilly, carrying a copper teapot, with six copper cups balanced on a copper tray. She was a year younger than their host. After serving the tea, she took a seat beside Andreina, just as two more bound women made their way into the room from their bedroom. Both of these women were twenty-five. Once everyone was seated, Andreina introduced her group. "I am our leader, Andreina Giola e Zurra. This is my free-mate, Bernardetta Zurra e Giola. We don't use the Ama titles around here."

"Just call me Betta, please," she said with a smile. Andreina's face was round with bushy brown eyebrows. She had high cheekbones and a rounded nose. Betta was slightly shorter with a squarish looking face, thick lips, and thin brows. Her complexion was nearly as tanned as her free-mate.

Seeing the questioning looks, Andreina explained, "Women cannot marry other women, just as a man cannot marry another man. Yet, we can live together as a married couple if we take the free-mate pledge, which is much the same as a marriage ceremony. The e in our surnames tells you that we are free-mates. We append an e and then the surname of our mate. We've been free-mates for five years now."

"This is Gabriella Fulvia e Fina and her free-mate Felisa Fina e Fulvia. Both were twenty-five and tanned as well. Gabriella was not as tall as Andreina, but just as well built and strong. Her eyes were a tad sunken. Combined with her protruding nose and thin lips, she reminded Lilly of a bird. Felisa had an oval face, rather angelic looking. She was soft-spoken, preferring to be called Fel. Yet she was also a very chatty young woman, as they would soon discover.

Felix introduced himself and his young wife. Then, Andreina got down to business, "I'm told that you are looking to hire knowledgeable guides for this area. Can you be more specific in what you need?"

"Yes, we wish to wander around the Buku Hills and adjoining desert lands looking for some unique crystals. We wish to gather a large number of samples. However, we do not know where they may be found or how long or how far we need to travel. I anticipate spending up to perhaps two months in our search. My guess is we probably do not have to stray more than a couple hundred miles from here, but I just don't know. It is all so wildly variable, dependent upon what we find and how fast we find it and so on. Can you help?"

"Yes, this is the kind of assignment we prefer. Ten silvers per day for mere guidance. Fifteen silvers per day if you also wish us to provide transportation, wagons, provisions, and such so we do not have to be constrained to moving from oasis to oasis. Seventeen silvers if you wish us to also prepare three meals each day. Thirty silvers if you wish us to fight raiders and such, but if you do not have that in mind and we do run into trouble, we would ask for an additional ten silvers per battle."

"I have no intention of fighting battles, though we know nothing about raiders. Captain Sheldon and six men will accompany us as our bodyguards. If we are attacked, it would likely be very helpful if we could depend upon your help with that. I think it wise if we take your seventeen silvers per day package, since we are not familiar with your desert. Let us advance you your pay for say a month. If we are out longer, we can settle up on our return here," Felix proposed.

Andreina grinned, "You have dealt with the Sisterhood before, I take it?"

"Is it that obvious? Yes, we live just south of your Hilliard Heights ranch and we get our horses from them," Felix answered. "So yes, I know generally that one should offer half payment up front."

Andreina grinned, "That works for us. Indeed, we really do appreciate your business; we are nearly broke. So many Easterlings refuse to hire us, though we are most competent. I hope in time to prove that to the men. Anyway, we will use this day to make the arrangements and gather the supplies for say a month on the trail. Mind you, the grub will be trail food, not the fine dining of inns."

"Works for us. We will be ready."

"Good. Now then, about apparel. As you and everyone else can see, we four are wearing the double horse earrings, which identify us as Sisterhood members. However, where and how you are proposing to go, you must accept our orders on your clothing. If not, we cannot guarantee that you will not die of heat strokes."

"What do you recommend?" Felix asked.

"First, it is extremely wise of you both to have Lilly here dress as an Easterlings woman. If she wasn't a bound woman, then anyone who we meet would know at a glance that she is a foreigner and would likely pick a fight with you. However, Lilly, out in the desert heat, you should be wearing a light silk blouse or you will burn rather easily. We will provide them for you and a head wrap as well. As for you, Felix, you need to dress as a male Easterlings man. If you like, we will provide appropriate dress for you as well. For heaven's sake, hide that sash of yours! That will cost you an additional five silvers and we will send one complete set of clothes by the tower later this afternoon so you can be ready in the morning. We leave after an early breakfast."

Felix handed over the coins and asked, "Might I ask why you dress as I, yet these other three dress as Lilly?"

All four laughed, as if this was some hilarious joke. Finally controlling her levity, Andreina explained, "Look as guides, you can hardly expect us to be bound women. No, I am in charge. Gabi is my second and she too will dress as a man when we ride out. Fel is an excellent cook and both she and Betta will dress as Easterlings women. However, if trouble comes, they will change into men's dress so that they too can defend themselves and fight. When we are around Adelmira, if we dress as Easterlings women, we create far less of a disturbance among the villagers, who only barely tolerate our presence. Fel can tell you more about this as we ride. Now then, this means that one wagon will carry the passengers while the second will carry our water and food supplies. I assume that you, Felix, will want to ride, as well as your seven men. They too will need to dress as Easterlings men and we will arrange clothing for them as well. It is wisest if the party gives no easily recognized appearance of being foreigners. Much safer. Lilly can ride with Fel, while Betta drives our supply wagon. Gabi and I will ride and lead the way. Acceptable?"

"Of course. This is working out perfectly," Felix complimented her. She flashed him a smile.

So have you seen that our binding is not any different from your brand of torture in the Midlands? That same woman's voice appeared in Lilly's mind once again, startling her. She glanced quickly across the table at the four women. Fel gave her a faint smile and slight nod of her head. Now Lilly knew who had sent her that original message while she was entering the oasis. It had been Fel whom she'd seen watching them from her doorway. Lilly realized that she must have good telepathic skills to have sent that through her mental barriers. All four women had the telltale yellow eyes with brown spots, which Lilly found comforting and reassuring.

Andreina rose and her fellow Sisterhood women followed her lead. Felix helped Lilly up and accepted Andreina's handshake, sealing their deal. He noted her shake was both strong and firm. He also was aware she had her barriers up solidly and only the faintest psi-energies were felt from her touch. "Expect one of us later today. We have much to arrange before morning," she added as the two made their slow way to the front door.

Lilly wore a thin white silk blouse and a light, white, hat-like affair on her head to protect her from the direct sunlight of the open desert. Felix felt ill at ease as he stood beside her wearing a loose fitting white silk shirt, a heavier but white loose fitting pants whose legs were tied above his ankles. He looked at his sandals with their highly recurved toes, they looked so strange on his feet, whereas Lilly's sandals looked wholly acceptable. His head was wrapped in a turban, again white. Captain Sheldon, standing beside him, wore identical clothing, as did the other six guards. Each of the men wore their swords around their waists, a dead giveaway that they were not Easterlings, who always used curved scimitars and daggers. While Felix knew they would not withstand close scrutiny, from a distance they would appear Easterlings and that was the effect that Andreina desired.

Already she and Gabi had come by to inspect their horses. "Look, if we are to be your guides, we must satisfy ourselves of the soundness of your horses. In the middle of the desert, you will not be able to obtain a new one, should yours falter," the alto voice said forcefully. After inspecting their two, she smiled, "Hilliard Heights stock, right?" Felix smiled and replied that they were. Captain Sheldon and his six guards also had their mounts pass her inspection, much to Felix's relief. More and more, he realized that he was entrusting his safety and that of Lilly's to these four women. It had not helped his nerves when Ama Floriana had bid them farewell and said that she would not be held responsible for their safety in the hands of the Sisterhood. Well, she was definitely prejudiced against them, he justified.

Their two saddlebags lay close to his feet as they waited for the four women to meet them just outside the tower an hour after dawn. Soon, they saw two wagons rolling their way. Each had two horses pulling them with another horse tied behind it. Andreina and Gabi walked in front of them, while Fel and Betta drove the wagons. Each wagon had a thin silk roof-like affair over their tops some four feet above the sides of the wagon, providing shade for the drivers and anything in their beds. It was held up by four poles. All the sides were open to the air. The rear wagon was heavily laden with water, salt, and their food supplies. Bedding and spare clothing were in the front wagon. Lilly noticed that both Fel and Betta were dressed and bound just as she was, while the other two wore men's style clothing and carried both a scimitar and a dagger around their waists.

Andreina barked, "Men, mount up, time is a'waisten. Amo Felix, toss your gear into the wagon and watch how I lift Lilly into the wagon." Felix flushed; he had no idea how Lilly would be able to manage getting into the wagon by herself. As he realized this, he also knew it was his responsibility as a man to lift her in and thus had no idea how best to do it. Hence, his flash of embarrassment. He watched as Andreina put her hands beneath Lilly's arm pits, lifted her up, carried her to the wagon, and then lifted her gently up, sitting her rear on the bench beside Fel. She kept her arms out, steadying Lilly while she pivoted into place beside Fel. "Next time, you do it. Mount up. Guards at the rear. You and your captain ride up front with us." Hastily, they obeyed and the small caravan rolled on down the hard sand-packed street.

Within minutes, they left the small oasis of Adelmira behind them. Lilly turned to look back at the tall palm and date trees that marked this desert watering hole. A slight pang of desolation struck her; they were leaving the relative safety of food, water, and shelter, heading out into the bleak, hot desert lands.

Once clear of the oasis and prying ears, Andreina pulled close to Felix. "Okay, Amo. Where to? What are we looking for? We can't properly guide you if we do not know what and where."

"Thank you for your discretion. Of course. This is rather hard to explain. Back home, I acquired some glassware goblets made here in the Easterlings."

"Naturally, we have lots of sand and many glass blowers make quality pieces. So?"

"Embedded within one of the goblets are some grey-white crystals which I have named germanium, for lack of a better name. They are in the silicates family though. My assumption is that somewhere out here, we may be able to find pure specimens of these crystals, much like the psi-crystals that the ancient Advanced Witches used to use. We don't want to mine for them, rather we were hoping to wander about and pick up a fair number of them from the ground."

"You mean that this is nothing more than a stone-gathering mission? You want to wander the desert picking up pretty rocks?" Andreina exclaimed sarcastically, in complete disbelief of what she was hearing. Her three companions moaned and then laughed.

Felix suddenly realized that all along she must have been thinking he was only providing her with some vague cover story for some important mission. "Oh, I assure you, Andreina, this is a vitally important, critical mission that we are on."

"Rocks?" she said in complete disbelief.

Felix raised his arm and the party halted. "Captain, have our guards fall back out of earshot. I will explain." He barked his orders and looked at him curiously. All four Sisterhood women leaned forward to hear, none more so than Betta who was the farthest back. He positioned his horse a bit closer to her so she could hear as well.

"Okay, mind you, this must be our secret. No one else on Tierra knows about this and we need to keep it that way for a time." He noticed that all four women were suddenly paying very close attention to what he was saying, and perhaps a bit impressed they were privy to some deep mysterious undertaking. "Let me begin by reminding you of the ancient Advanced Witches. If you recall, they were supposed to have used special psi-crystals that greatly magnified their *mentales*-like powers. For any given witch, only one specific crystal out of all the thousands that lay on the ground would work for them. It was said that they were somehow 'attuned' to their personal crystal."

"Yes, but what has this to do with us? We are not witches," Andreina countered.

"Absolutely everything Amas, everything. I've discovered that each of us with the *mentales* gifts generates psi-energies, but at slightly different frequencies. Each of the psi-crystals that are found all over the foothills of the Goza Mountains resonates at its own precise frequency. Lilly and I have shown repeatedly that if we find a psi-crystal that resonates at our personal frequencies, then that psi-crystal will amplify our energies, often five to ten fold."

"Hum, now that is most interesting, tenfold? But how does it work? How do you find the right one for yourself? Hunt until you find it?" she asked.

"That's how they used to do it or so I've been told, secondhand, mind you. The right psi-crystal begins to glow when you touch it with your own psi-energies. If its own frequency is not the same as yours, no glow occurs. However, Andreina, just as I was marrying Lilly here, I discovered that the grey-white crystals, which are embedded within that

Easterlings goblet I came across, have the same resonating frequency as I emit with my psi-energies."

"So?"

"So that tiny, nearly invisible grey-white crystal amplifies my psi-energies at least a hundredfold. Lilly's too when she is in rapport with me and radiating at my frequency. A hundredfold. Can you imagine what that would do for each of your own *mentales* gifts — having their effects magnified a hundredfold?"

"Good god! A hundredfold?" Andreina was stunned. So were her three companions and Captain Sheldon.

"Please, keep our secret a while longer. We are in search of these crystals. We want to find a bunch of them and with luck find some that resonate with our frequencies. Once found, we need to see if they really do magnify our psi-energies that much. If so, then we will inform everyone with the gifts and start finding the right crystals for each."

"Good god, man!" exclaimed Captain Sheldon. "Do you realize the kind of power that we would have? A few of us could wipe out an entire army of head blind soldiers!"

"Precisely, but not that we want to do that. No, my aim is to give those of us with the *mentales* gifts that kind of power so when the rest of Tierra sees it, they will never again fight their petty wars. My aim is forever to eliminate wars from Tierra! If just a few of us can wipe out an entire invading army, then no one in their right mind would ever again foment wars. Permanent peace can come to all Tierra." Felix waxed philosophical.

"Incredible!" whispered an awed Andreina.

"Just what do they look like?" asked Fel, startling Lilly, who was sitting beside her with her full attention focused on Felix and Andreina.

"I've only seen the tiny crystals embedded with the glass. Thus, I really don't know if they can be found in large sizes or even what they would look like as large stones," he admitted. "That's part of our problem, you see."

Fel replied, "Well, I have a grey-white crystal. It is my good luck charm. Here, take a look at it." She leaned over and asked Lilly to use her hands to undo her blouse and then untie the leather string that held a small pouch nestled between her massive breasts. Bound as she was, she could not manage this herself. Lilly fumbled at it, but soon retrieve the pouch and handed it to Fel. "Here, have a look at it. It is my good luck charm. I was in Dead Man's Canyon and nearly dying of heat, lost, and disoriented. I spotted this sparking thing and made my way to it. Right beside it was a yucca plant and I was able to get enough fluids from it to survive until Andreina found me. I've kept it on me ever since. My good luck charm."

Felix moved his horse over to the wagon and took the pouch from her hand. Carefully opening it, he found a grey-white crystalline stone or rock about an inch in size. He closed his eyes and focused his mind onto the structure of the stone. After a minute, he opened his eyes wide. From the huge grin on his face, all six knew this must be what he was looking for. "Brilliant, Fel! This is a pure geranium crystal. While it is not attuned to my frequency, it is precisely what we are looking for! Can you take us to this place?"

"Aye, Dead Man's Canyon is about a hundred fifty miles north of here," Andreina answered. "No water for miles and it's a very remote, desolate area, near the base of a mesa."

"Why is it called Dead Man's Canyon?" Lilly asked out of curiosity.

"Oh because someone once found the bleached bones of a dead man there," Fel replied. "The floor is littered with these stones. Surely you can find hundreds of them there."

"Now we have a destination! Okay, let's get going," Andreina took charge once more and they got underway, continuing on the same northern track they were on before the chat. Lilly carefully retied Fel's good luck charm back around her neck and buttoned up her blouse for her.

"Well, who would have thought that my good luck charm would be so important? It has indeed brought us good luck once again, see Gabi?" Her mate turned in her saddle to cast a loving smile back at her. Fel grinned.

Fel continued to chat. "So Lilly, have you now seen that you Midlands folk are just as bound as the Easterlings women are?"

"Huh? I still don't understand you Fel. Being bound like

this is awful! You can hardly even walk and can't go up even the tiniest step. With our arms tied like this, we can barely function at all, to say nothing of how we are while sleeping. It's horrid," Lilly replied, but she noticed the other three women were listening to the two of them chatting as was Felix.

"Yes, there is no doubt the Easterlings women are physically bound and your Midlands women are not physically bound. Yet, Easterlings women are not otherwise bound as your Midlands women are," Fel went on merrily.

"What do you mean?" asked Lilly somewhat exasperated. She still had no idea what Fel meant by her cryptic comments.

"Look, are you free to marry whoever you desire? Can a Midlands woman determine her own fate? Can she do whatever she desires? Wear whatever clothing she chooses?"

"Well, no. Our parents arranged our marriage. I was told about three months before my marriage that I would be marrying Felix here. Same with him, he was ordered to marry me. Well, I've always really known I would not be allowed to marry whomever I chose. No, I could never fully do what I desired. No, women almost never wear men's clothing. It is not proper."

"See, you are just as bound as the Easterlings women, Lilly. Only your bonds are more invisible than ours are, which are plainly visible to all eyes. In some ways, it is better to have the bindings clearly visible than to have to deal with hidden, invisible bindings," Fel pointed out. "All women on Tierra are bound in some way. Here in the east, we wear our bindings for all to see and do not hide them and pretend that they are not there as you westerners do. That is the biggest difference that I can see. We are totally open and quite clear with our limitations, while your people tend to hide them and pretend otherwise."

"Even your men are bound, but they seldom even recognize that they are. Felix had no choice in his wife. I bet he has had little other choices either. Here, our women are free to marry men of their choices. Well, that's changing now. *Mentales* gifted are being bred now just as they are in the Midlands. Other than those, even though there are the Castas, we can marry whomever we desire, excepting of course no same sex marriages are allowed — another barrier you see. Still, we bound women are free of many other invisible barriers that you Midlands women have. How many of your husbands care for your needs each evening and morning? Ours give us their full and undivided attention at least an hour each time. We are cared for in the mornings before they do anything else."

"Out on the streets, if we need any help, dozens of strangers will rush to our aid without our even asking. That's how close attention our Easterlings men pay to women here. Further, if some evil man should harm a bound Easterlings women and his crime becomes known, entire villages have been known to go after him obtaining a swift and effective justice for the woman. Can that be said of Midlands folk? I think not."

"Easterlings women accept their bonds but receive a great freedom in return. Midlands women do not even see many of their bonds and have drastically less freedoms as a result."

"I see what you mean now, Fel. I have not thought of it that way, but yes, we are bound but with invisible bindings. We do not endure physical restraints, unless wearing five petticoats counts, yet we are tied up just the same. Perhaps there is something to be said about being able to see your bonds. Certainly, there is less mental and emotional stress over them," Lilly admitted.

"True, do you realize your men are equally bound? Poor Felix, he probably hated being forced to marry. I suspect he wanted only to continue his researches. He's that kind of man, you know."

"I know, but so am I — that way too. We sort of mesh together really well."

"That is highly fortunate for both of you. He is not the kind of man who will ever settle down and be domesticated." Fel and Lilly giggled a little.

"But can I ask you about this, Fel?" She nodded. "You four have joined the Sisterhood to gain your freedom. How is it that you still wear your bonds? I don't understand it. You could be riding your horse and have complete freedom of motion like Andreina and Gabriella have."

"Betta and I do not need to be unbound to drive the wagons, but that's not the main reason. You see, here in the Easterlings, an unbound woman is looked upon with utter and complete disdain and contempt by both men and women. They are seen as destroyers of our whole culture. Since we four live here and were born as Easterlings, we do not want to destroy our own culture, perhaps change it, yes, but not destroy it, accepting in return the hidden bonds of the Midlands. Already as Sisterhood women, we are looked upon in contempt and disgust by all. We agree there is no need to add to others' hatred of the Sisterhood. Thus, we willingly and knowingly wear our bonds when we choose to do so. That is a huge difference. We are in control of it, choosing when and where to be bound. We do not see any need or any benefit to be gained by flaunting our choice of physical freedoms before our people. It only increases and magnifies their hatred and prejudices against us — those of us who would be free. It is enough that we know we have a choice and can exercise our choice. In that, we four are free."

"Gabi and Andreina are the better leaders and guides and thus they go unbounded far more than we do. Their work requires it, ours does not, unless we are called upon to fight. When we are bound, our free-mates treat us as men would, you see. We reciprocate at those times when they choose to be bound. Always, we try to minimize the disruption we create upon others by our choices of freedom."

Fel chatted on, "But don't think just because we four have become Sisterhood members that we four are free of all bindings. On the contrary. We have merely swapped physical restraints for additional hidden ones. As Sisterhood members, we have to follow all their rules too. As I see it, anyone living life has to accept some form of barriers, whether they are physical or mental ones, but barriers to freedom they all are, in one way, shape or form. Everyone has barriers, just as everyone has certain freedoms. We four have exercised our personal choices of barriers and in doing that we have a tremendous feeling of satisfaction and peace. Our barriers are of our own choosing, though to a more limited extent, so are our freedoms. I think every woman ought to be free to choose her own barriers, not have them enforced upon her unwillingly and often unknowingly as is the case with you Midlands."

"You see, Lilly, all life has some barriers to overcome. All life has some freedoms to use in overcoming them. There is no life when all is barriers with no freedoms at all, and, equally, there is no life with all freedoms and no barriers to overcome. Each is equally death, though an all-barrier death is probably horrible."

"I can see your point. I have had no choice of the barriers in my life or even freedoms for that matter. I think that I have been exceedingly lucky to have been married off to Felix. At least I am able to help him with his research, something that intrigues me and in which I am keenly interested," Lilly admitted. She asked, "Do all women in the Sisterhood marry other women?"

Fel laughed and so did Andreina. "No, Lilly, but that is a common misconception nearly everyone has of the Sisterhood. No, we are free women and have chosen to marry out of a deep love for our mates. It just happens with we four that we are all women and that we have had the convictions to follow through on our love despite the social ostracization that comes with it."

"But don't you want to one day have children and raise a family?" Lilly asked.

"Of course we do. What a silly question. Once we have earned enough money to support children, we plan to have them. We've already picked out men to bed to get us pregnant. In fact, we hope this trip will put us over the top of our financial goals so that at least two of us can have a baby. Later on, the other two will have theirs. Again, with us, particularly so because we four have the *mentales* gifts, it is our choice of when to have a child and who the fathers may be. You, I am afraid to say, have no choice. You will be expected to bear many children. How long do you think your father and his father will tolerate you not bearing them their precious children with their expected *mentales* gifts? A year, two at most?"

"Point taken, I did feel like I was supposed to be

nothing more than a brood mare when I was married off to Felix. I am utterly thankful he doesn't share his father and my father's ideas about that!" Lilly admitted frankly. She found it was so easy to speak of these intimate things with Fel. Perhaps it was because she was so open about them.

"Speaking of *mentales* gifts, it is pretty amazing that all four of you have such similar gifts," Lilly pointed out.

Fel gave a laugh. "That's what everyone says, but it isn't true at all. Heck, before I met Gabi, I had not the slightest direction sense. I could get lost in Adelmira! Okay probably not that small a place, but you get the idea. No, we all didn't originally have similar gifts. My big thing was cooking, I've a knack for it. My biggest gift used to be starting cooking fires and such things. That and an empathy for others. After I met Gabi, well, things changed. She actually taught me to sense directions and all manner of *mentales* gifts for trail survival. Betta taught us all several healing skills. Andreina taught us all Combat Sense and how to defend and what to Anticipate in terms of the opponent's strategies and tactics. Over the last five years, they have served us well. Andreina couldn't heal anything when she first met Betta, but Betta was able to teach her how to heal fairly well. We four have learned a whole lot of *mentales* skills from each other."

She lowered her voice a little as if letting Lilly in on some secret, "I suppose I shouldn't be telling you this. The tower leaders will pooh-pooh it, but you can learn new gifts you weren't born with."

Lilly laughed this time. "Felix has already learned this himself and taught it to me. I've learned to do some things I never knew I could do! We even did a random test using Marisol's catalogue of gifts. We chose one at random and then I learned how to do it. Pretty amazing, plus we believe the more that you exercise your skills, the more that you can learn and the better you get at them. Probably it is just like learning anything new, practice makes perfect."

Now the countryside began to change. Initially, to their left the Buku Hills were nothing more than sharply descending slopes, rocky with tufts of hardy grasses fighting for life in scattered patches. Now, they entered the true mesa country.

The hills rose far higher and the steep slopes changed into sheer cliffs of unclimbable rocks, loose and slippery as well. Talus piles formed small mounds at their bases, before giving way to the great sands of the Arad desert off to their right. Fel pointed out by the time they reached their destination, these eastern sides of the great sloping mesas would rise over a thousand feet above the desert floor over which they were passing.

Andreina explained they would need eight days to reach Dead Man's Canyon, primarily because they needed to take a more zig-zag course so as to always reach a water source within two days travel. However, after the sixth day, they would be leaving all sources of water behind them until they retraced their route. There was no water to be found within two days ride of the canyon. Hence, Andreina had allowed for this, adding several more water barrels at the first oasis they passed through late the first day of their journey.

Both Lilly and Felix watched quite interested, as Andreina led them to their first oasis watering stop. She handed the village leader a silver and led the horses in pairs to the watering trough. Each oasis made a little profit on providing water to the traveling caravans. However, she explained if they were not classified as a caravan, the water would be given to them freely.

On the third day, a band of twenty riders intercepted them. Although a little worried about the approaching riders, Andreina pointed out, "Look, the women are totally safe, no matter what. Harming a bound woman is a worse crime than murdering someone. Believe me, no man will harm them, the penalty is too steep. Now if we are all killed, they may well ask them to join their band or clan, purely out of survival needs, but they won't be harmed."

When the well-armed riders drew close, their leader looked them over, especially the three women in the wagons. "Well, I see you have another party, Andreina. You may pass. Word to the wise, two bands of raiders have been seen here in the west. Stay alert." She thanked him and they headed off to the south. Andreina hastily explained these men were Lucca soldiers out on patrol.

The next day, they did encounter one of those bands. Another well-armed group overtook them. However, their leader, noticing all the yellow eyes wisely decided to move on. "Now that is one smart raider," Andreina pointed out. "Had they attacked us, I doubt it very much if one of them would have survived." Felix didn't ask why she had that notion however. She added, "Don't worry, when we get to our destination, there won't be any raiders there. There is no water. Water is life here in the Arad."

On the eighth day of their journey, as the sun sank behind the now tall mesa edges, the party halted. Ahead of them lay two sheer mesa walls with a steep sided canyon lying between them. "Here we are. That's Dead Man's Canyon there. The ground is littered with these crystals," Andreina pointed out. We will set up camp there at the entrance of the canyon. It is not safe to camp closer to the cliffs. Rocks often fall crashing into the talus slopes there at the base of the cliffs. Tomorrow we can start this search."

Chapter 15 Discoveries

After arriving at a suitable spot to camp, Andreina and Gabi dismounted, temporarily tying their horses to the wagons, while lifting their spouses down. Felix hastened to emulate their action, carefully setting Lilly onto the ground. Then, they went about setting up the camp as always. The four women were extremely efficient, having done this many times before. As she had for the last six days, Lilly contented herself with helping Fel set up her portable stove and prepare their supper. She and Fel had become very close friends.

After breakfast the next morning, they took one wagon on up into the canyon to begin their explorations. Everyone, except the guards who remained at the camp with the second supply wagon, rode in this one. "Fantastic, they are everywhere," Felix exclaimed as his eyes began spotting the grey-white crystals. Most were from a quarter inch across to perhaps an inch in size. At last, Andreina stopped the wagon and the group dismounted.

"Keep an eye out for scorpions and winder vipers," she cautioned, as Felix handed out sacks in which to put the gathered crystals. While Lilly found it very awkward to gather the stones, she, Fel, and Betta persevered and gathered what they could as well. At noon, they returned to the base camp so Lilly and Felix could examine their find.

After a light lunch, Felix had Lilly join him in laying all the stones out on the wagon bed and then playing their own psi-energies over the lot. They were, of course, looking for any crystal, which resonated at the frequency of their particular energies. "By golly, here's one that matches me," Felix announced, holding up a small crystal.

"Okay, Lilly, let's see if our theory actually does work of if we are on a wild goose chase," he teased.

"He's a Fire Starter," Lilly whispered to Fel, as they all stood back watching Felix.

He held the crystal in his hand and gave it a slight squeeze as he focused and then stopped. "Lilly, we should do this experiment properly. Fel, get me two small, identical sizes pieces of your horse dung charcoal, please. Lilly, I want you to monitor me and make sure I am releasing the same level of psi-energies as I Create Fire on these two. First, I will do it normally with my gift and then I will attempt to do the same using the crystal here, making sure I am emitting the same level of psi-energies."

It took Fel several minutes to do that much walking and for an instant, he had the notion that he should have asked Andreina or Gabi to fetch the charcoal. However, he realized that had he done so, he would have affronted Fel and the other women, since the charcoal was entirely the responsibility of Fel. He thanked her as she finally shuffled up with the two small pieces. He walked out onto the stony ground twenty feet away from the camp, placed the first one there, and jogged back to the others.

Fel said, "You know we four can also monitor you too, don't you? Wouldn't it be smarter to have five of us monitoring your power levels to make very sure it's the same?"

"You can?" he said somewhat surprised. "Well, why not. Let's do it. More validation this way." He felt the five minds touching his, and when they were ready, he focused and Created Fire within the charcoal. It erupted into flames as expected. He was the Fire Man, after all.

"Cool! You do it as well as I do," Fel praised him.

He took the second one and headed out to place it before changing his mind. "You know, if this crystal performs as we suspect it might, then a thousand times more powerful might create troubles for us if it is that close. I'm going to play it safe and move it out a hundred feet."

Once he returned, again the five slipped into rapport with him and monitored his psi-energy output. He squeezed his hand onto the crystal and Created Fire once more. Nothing could have prepared them for the effect. The entire charcoal brick was totally consumed by fire within less than a second, creating an enormous ball of fire fifty feet across, rising an equal distance into the sky. "Holy cow!" Felix exclaimed.

"Hell fire!" Andreina exclaimed.

"Shit!" Fel added.

"My god!" Captain Sheldon uttered shocked beyond

belief. He'd never seen such an explosion before.

"Yahoo, it works," Lilly added. "It was about the same, Felix. The crystal does indeed amplify our psi-energies enormously! What a find! Glad that you put it way out there, dear. That was a bit too close for comfort."

"Now how do we go about finding crystals that are attuned to us?" asked Andreina. "You were right, Felix. This *is* the find of the century!"

For the next hour, the group of *mentales* gifted poured over each of the crystals they'd gathered up, looking for ones attuned to their own unique frequencies. Though the four Sisterhood women and Captain Sheldon had no idea of frequencies or even what that meant, they looked for crystals that seemed to glow in their presence. By evening, all were disappointed. None had yet been found, save the one that had matched Felix.

The next day, they again went crystal gathering, spending the entire day collecting bags full. During the gathering, Felix realized they were coming from the crumbling sheer cliffs of the mesa edges. At least he knew their source. The following day, they again began searching the new and quite large pile of crystals for ones attuned to them. Fel was the next to find one that matched herself. Everyone gathered around to see if it would work for her. Since she was used to starting fires, she opted for the same test that Felix had done and used a bit of charcoal too. Gabi carried the small brick way out from their camp, nearly two hundred feet this time.

"Ordinarily, I'd never be able to get it lighted this far away, but I'll try," Fel admitted. "Squeeze it while I do it?" she asked of Felix, who nodded. She did so and focused. To her astonishment and the others too, the small brick literally exploded in a bomb of flames equally as large as Felix's had been!

"My god, Fel! You are deadly with that thing!" Gabi exclaimed, quite astonished. Now they all threw themselves into finding more that matched themselves.

Another day passed without anyone discovering another matching crystal. "I sure wish that there was a more efficient way to go about this," Lilly said quite disgusted. "If only we could attune the crystals to us instead of the other way around! Well, why not?" she looked up at Felix. He shrugged. It didn't seem to work that way was his only answer.

Lilly stared at yet another disappointing crystal and focused her psi-energy into its crystalline form. Fel, standing beside her looking for another for herself, shouted, "Lilly! It's glowing! Have you found one?"

"Er, I don't know. It seems to be attuned to me now anyway. I wonder if it works right?" Lilly replied. "I guess I ought to test it." She did, but not in the spectacular ways of Felix and Fel. Rather, she attempted to exercise her rapport skills. To her amazement as well as the others, she suddenly shifted into all four women and even Sheldon before she realized it! "Whoopee, it works. Felix, you try it! I focused my energies on the crystal and somehow attuned it to me. It works the other way around!"

Felix came over and glanced at her crystal, which was now glowing. "See if you can change it to match you now," Lilly suggested.

He complied, focusing his energy onto her crystal. Energies flashed. The crystal shattered. Lilly shrieked and collapsed! "What happened?" Fel cried out as she knelt down beside her new friend. "What did you do to her?" she accused Felix.

Felix dropped down to his knees, focused and began examining Lilly's body for signs of damage. His voice sounding quite distance said, "She is unharmed, but has a massive headache." Slowly, he soothed her frazzled neuron endings and got her energies flowing once more and Lilly came around.

"What happened? I got a blinding head pain," she said softly.

"Felix darn near killed you, that's what happened," Fel answered her quite angry with Felix.

"No, something with that crystal, Fel. Help me up, dear. We have to figure this thing out before someone does get seriously hurt," Lilly suggested.

Felix focused his energies on another crystal. "Okay, Fel. Look, I have this one attuned to me. It is glowing. Now try to change it to become attuned to you."

"Well, if it kills you, I won't be blamed," she insisted.

"No, I am, this is my theory that we are testing."

I hope it gives him a bad headache. It will serve him right for harming poor Lilly. "Okay, then. Here goes." Fel focused on the crystal, attuning it to her unique frequency. The glow dimmed out as its frequency began to change. It flared up, shattered, and Felix crumpled to the ground, dazed. This time, Lilly knelt down and used her healing skills to get his damaged neurons soothed and the energy buildup flowing again.

"Thanks love. We now know that once a crystal has been attuned to someone, trying to change it to another both destroys the crystal and harms the owner to which it is attuned," Felix concluded. "I don't think we need to study that effect any further. What a headache!"

He then suggested, "Okay, how about each of us picking a crystal that we like and attuning it to ourselves. Let's keep them on our person and see how long the crystal's effects last." This suited them all and before long, the five women and two men each had a glowing crystal and began testing the crystals impact on their *mentales* gifts. All were most impressed with the drastic increase in the effects of their gifts both in range of coverage and its magnitude.

Lilly then asked another question. "The crystals come in various sizes. I wonder if the amount of amplification is proportional to the size of the crystals?"

Several days were spent working out this detail. By and large, they could discover no significant difference between the smaller ones and the larger ones that they had found. However, there wasn't that huge a difference in their sample sizes. Hence, they headed back out, searching for much larger crystals, which they quickly discovered were far rarer. After an entire day's search, each one had found only a single crystal that was approximately two inches wide.

The next day's testing proved valuable. Size mattered! With these larger samples, Felix estimated that the amplification effect had doubled, bringing another round of cheers from the group. As they sat around the wagons eating their trail dinner, Andreina said, "Well, Felix, you were not wrong in saying that yours was a vitally important, highly valuable mission. This is an enormous find! World shaking."

The question now was how best to proceed with their discovery. "We should scour for even larger ones," Captain Sheldon suggested. None disagreed with that.

However, Andreina pointed out, "We are running low on water. If we want to stay more days, some of us will have to make a water run today. It's two days to water and two back again and there are four days of water left, three if we are all here. I can take two of your guards with Betta and me to fetch more." This was agreeable to all. Felix certainly was not ready to give up the quest. He had far more questions to get answered. Were there even larger crystals to be found? Were there other locations that had them? Were they common at the talus slopes of all these mesas? Could anyone with the *mentales* gift be attuned to a crystal? If so, how could the person be instructed to do it? The seven of them were obviously highly practiced individuals. Would those with lesser gifts be able to attune a crystal to themselves or would a powerful one need to help and if so, how? As if sensing the hesitancy of Felix to leave, she added, "We'll bring back more food and twice as much water as we had. It should give us another ten days out here before we'll need to make another water run."

She added, "We should keep this a secret between us all for now. Perhaps even later, we should keep the location of these crystals also a secret, known only to a few chosen leaders. Some of the head blind really despise us, and if they knew about these crystals, they might come here and somehow destroy them."

After Andreina and her smaller group left, the others discussed what to do next. "Since size matters," Felix said, "the next question to ask is there any quality difference between these crystals? Are some of a purer form than others? If so, does that make any difference?"

"Well, one cannot go around with one of these that is a foot in diameter, no matter how powerful it makes the person. There is obviously a limit to the physical size, one that is optimal," Lilly pointed out. "Besides, another question that we ought to be asking is will there be adverse consequences if one attunes himself or herself to one that is too large and too powerful for them to properly control? Can children be entrusted with one, for example?"

"Well, you two have already given us a gift of enormous magnitude, the crystals. Let us help find some answers," Fel offered. "At least looking for the crystals is something that goes at the pace of us women." Lilly giggled. Indeed, everyone had to walk ever so slowly with their eyes on the ground, looking for the larger ones. For once, the women's speed of movement was not a hindrance. While the others were off obtaining more water, the smaller group visited first the talus slope to the south of the canyon and then the one to the north. Substantially larger crystals were found closer to the talus. Evidently, they came out of the rock strata as portions weathered away and came sliding down. The action also tended to break up the larger crystals. However, the constant danger of another rock fall made them all leery of getting too close. Still, they found fifty good sized samples that were around two inches across.

Felix and Lilly spent the next two days analyzing the crystalline purity of all the larger samples and taught Fel and Gabi how to do this as well. "Focus on the tiny particles," Felix said, after bringing Fel into rapport with him and showing her what he was seeing at the particle level of a crystal. By the time that Andreina and the others returned heavily laden with water and more dried trail food, the two Sisterhood women were getting quite good at analyzing the purity of the samples. The vast majority were roughly equivalent in content, only a handful were "duds" — Fel's term for those that had major impurities.

Felix then tested the impure ones and found that the results obtained when using them were wildly variable and sometimes unpredictable. In normal use, then, the impure crystals would be a severe liability. Thus, Felix established the rule that only pure crystals be considered for use.

One of their guards, John, had very limited *mentales* abilities, just barely enough to Sense When Danger Is Near. Felix, while monitored carefully by the five women and

Captain Sheldon, then attempted to have John attune a crystal to himself. Quickly, it became apparent to all seven that those with lesser gifts would need to have help attuning a crystal to themselves. Felix made several failed attempts with John before Fel made a promising suggestion. "Why don't you go into rapport with him and attune it for him that way?"

"Good idea," Felix replied. He focused on John and slowly adjusted his frequency to match the guard's. *I wonder how many of us can easily go into rapport with strangers? Ah well, first see if this works. In theory, it might. After all, I am now resonating at John's frequency. If the crystal only responds to a given frequency, then after I attune it to his, after that, it should respond to John himself.* He went ahead and attuned one of the smaller crystals. When it was glowing brightly, he terminated the rapport. The acid test came next. John was asked to use his gift while holding the crystal.

"I can do it more easily," John replied.

Felix was not convinced. "Try staring into the glow of the crystal, focus on it and then try it again."

John complied and a huge grin appeared on his face. "Wow! Now this *is* something! It is many times better! Incredible. I feel so powerful this way!"

"Conclusion, gang. Focusing on the crystal's glow greatly aids the amplification process. That's got to be part of the rules of crystal operation," Felix pronounced.

"Well, we need to make a User's Guide to Crystal Operation," Lilly suggested.

"Great idea," Fel praised her, "but there is only one problem with that." Lilly gave her a questioning look and she added, "Most cannot read."

"Oh. Had not thought of that. Well, we still should have the guide written up and have the person who is handling the attuning process go over the rules with the new owner of the crystal," Lilly amended her proposal.

Next, Felix attuned John to one of the larger crystals. Now came some exhaustive tests. In the end, after a day's work, they concluded that indeed the size and thus power amplification had to be matched to the user. John simply could not handle the larger magnification of his weak gift. The slightest error on his part was magnified enormously by the two inch crystal. He had to be content with a one inch crystal. This very significant finding caused both Felix and Lilly to reconsider everything in light of this. They could not just unleash this on the world, sending out nice crystals to everyone with the gift. If the wielder was not matched with a power amplification that he or she could manage, disasters would surely follow.

By now, the five other guards had become keenly interested in the work. All had no *mentales* gifts whatsoever. They were head blind, to use the derogatory term. Felix, ever curious, decided to see if he could attune one of these to one of the very small half-inch crystals. After going into rapport with the man and attuning it to the man's ordinary brain energy waves, he then began a series of tests.

"Hey, I can now do tricks with this. Watch this," he said happily. He bent a copper fork in half. "I can bend forks just by thinking about it. This is cool! You know, I don't feel so left out this way. Can I keep this one?"

Felix smiled, "Sure it is all yours. Your stone will only work in your hands." He was very pleased, but of course, the other four guards also wanted one. Felix didn't want Lilly to go into rapport with the men and he spent a half-day getting the others attuned to their own small stones.

"So even the small crystals will have some use. These could easily be marketed and sold by the towers. Of course, someone in the tower will have to do the attuning process for them," Felix declared happily.

"Okay, on to the next question," Andreina moved them forward. She liked to be in control when possible, Lilly noted. "Betta and I found a problem with them while we were off getting more water. When we have them strung around our necks, the continuous glow that they give off attracts undue attention to them. Also, when Betta touches mine, man do I ever get an electric shock. She does too. Likewise, if I should touch hers, she gets a bad jolt and I get the backlash. Something has to be done about that. Can they be turned off somehow or are they permanently turned on, once they've been attuned to someone?"

"Turning a stone off nearly wipes out the person and it destroys the crystal," Felix stated. "So no, once activated, they can't be turned off. So we need a cover for them, like a lantern slide. Open when you want light, and shut when you don't. How about a leather bag?"

Betta got out her patching kit and sewed up a small one for hers. She and Andreina tested it. "Ouch, it's better but not good enough. That stings. Ideas?" She tried a bit of wool and even a small strip of cotton; all dampened the effect some and did hide the glow completely, but still Betta received a light shock when her mate touched her little bag. At last, she tried a bit of silk, which was much more costly than the others. This seemed to work very well and the group added another rule to their ever-growing list.

Andreina then asked, "Is this the only place where they are found or not? Shall we pack up here and head on up the line and see if the next mesa also has them?" She was anxious to get moving once more, hating to be stuck for long periods in one place. The next day, they began to head on north to the next mesa some ten miles distant.

Again, their searching yielded more of the crystals. Having collected some fifty really fine ones, they stopped gathering them and put their attention on discovering more locations where they could be found. During the next four days, each mesa edge had the crystals, however, the steep edges continued to rise higher and higher. The number of crystals lying close to the beginning of the desert sands diminished. Apparently, they came from a specific layer and as the cliffs rose higher, that layer also rose higher. This meant that the exposed crystals had a greater distance to fall and more and more frequently, the larger fragments were broken into many smaller pieces when they finally hit the talus slopes at the base of the mesa.

At last satisfied of their location, Felix decided it was time to return to Adelmira. They reversed their direction and picked up their pace. As they rode along, Felix reached a decision. "Andreina, when we get back, I will make a formal presentation to the towers. Obviously, as those with our gift learn of the amplifying crystals, they will want crystals of their

310

own. If it is acceptable to you, I will place the acquisition of these crystals into you four's hands and thus the Sisterhood. I will have the towers contact you and place their orders for the raw crystals through you. The Sisterhood can then arrange for their shipment to the various towers, who can then dole them out. Probably the Sisterhood ought to charge a nominal fee to cover your expenses and give you some profit from this venture. Just don't make your price too high or I expect others will try to figure out where these are coming from and come here on their own."

"Felix! Thank you, that is uncommonly generous! It will give the Sisterhood far more respect and will enable us to finally be able to afford to start our own families," Andreina replied, her mellow voice full of unexpected emotion. Never before had anyone truly shown her such trust and respect.

"You four have earned all that we can give back to you. But I do have one question. If it's too personal, you don't have to answer. Just how will you be able to have your families? I don't quite understand, you are free-mates," Felix asked.

Andreina chuckled. "Yes we are, but that does not mean we can't bed a man for the sole purpose of becoming pregnant, silly. Betta wants to bear our first child, while Fel does for her and Gabi. After they have theirs, then Gabi and I will have ours."

Felix grinned, "Of course, I understand that, but do you have the men lined up who will bed with you? Won't they want to become the baby's fathers?"

"We hope to find men who are willing to have fosterling children. If not, I suppose we can get one drunk and do it. He'd never know," Andreina laughed. "Unless you are volunteering, Felix," she gave him a coy grin and he flushed red.

"I, ah, I'd have to get Lilly's permission," he muttered, rather wishing he'd kept his curiosity in check.

Lilly, who'd overheard them, spoke up, "Felix, it is fine with me. I am almost sixteen now, but I really am not ready to face being pregnant and then a mother. Not so soon, unless you insist, Felix."

"No, I certainly am not insisting, Lilly. We both ought to

agree on it before we have a baby," he answered, as she knew he would. *At least I have some choice on when I have to bear a child*, she thought.

Lilly then said, "Dear, if you want to be the father of Fel's child, er, Fel's and Gabi's that is, it is fine with me. Or Betta too. We owe these four so much. Without them, we may never have found the crystals and I really like them. *Especially Fel. She's become my best friend. How I am going to hate to part with you, Fel!*

We can always chat this way, Fel replied. "You'd consent, Felix?" she asked rather pleased. She could not have ever asked for a better breeding line for her child, hers and Gabi's.

"Well, yes I would Fel, as long as I could perhaps visit him or her whenever I am in this part of the world," Felix replied.

Fel said sternly, "You consent to the fact that any child will be raised as Gabi and my child and in the Sisterhood?"

"Of course, I live about four thousand miles from here. It cannot be otherwise. Yet, if something happens to you and you have no way to continue to raise the child, please send him or her to Lilly and me to be raised as our fosterling. Okay?"

"Yes, that is as it should be," Fel agreed. Starting that night and on alternating nights, Felix slept with Fel and the other nights with Bernardetta. By the time they reached Adelmira, both women could sense their pregnancies had begun.

Meanwhile, Gabi and Andreina alternated sleeping with Lilly and taught her many things she did not know, not the least about how women could deeply satisfy themselves. While Lilly didn't consider herself a lover of women, she gained a very deep appreciation of these four women and their bonds to each other. After those evenings, she often wished that her own mother had taught her such things, and she promised herself that if she ever had a daughter, she would pass these things along to her. Her daughter would not go into a marriage so ignorant of such things as she had.

Chapter 16 Tipping Point

Andreina looked their campsite over before turning in for the night. "Last night out on the trail," she sighed. "I will miss it. No question of that."

Betta tossed her head back slightly and laughed. "That's an understatement! I've known that ever since we first met. Sometimes I think your home is the open desert sands. You are as predictable as the bees around the fig blossoms, dear."

"Well, I do love it out here. So peaceful. No men to mess up everything," she replied.

"Now that's true enough. Guards posted?" Betta asked, though she need not have. Andreina always saw to that.

Andreina replied, "Yes, two on duty every three hours. We should be in our adobe house tomorrow night," she answered. *Something's out there. I can feel it, but I can't get a handle on it. I've not seen any real signs of trouble. Besides, we are within forty miles of Adelmira so there should not be any bandits this close. I best not get the others worried over what's probably nothing at all. I will stay alert tonight though. Something just doesn't feel right.*

An hour after the shift change, the bright white Echador rose. Nearing last quarter, the moon cast faint shadows of their wagons and tethered horses onto the dark sands of the southern Arad desert. Nothing had happened and Andreina finally dozed off herself. A dozen armed men, wearing black to conceal their bodies as much as possible, slowly crawled towards the campsite. Four headed directly towards the two guards who were milling around the remains of the charcoal campfire. One was sipping hot black tea. For over a month now, they had stood guard duty during the night hours and nothing whatsoever had appeared. They were quite bored, but their pay was good, exceptionally so for this long a trip.

One dark man tossed a small pebble towards the horses, one of which made a slight noise, attracting the attention of the two guards. As they turned to look, the four men leaped to their feet and attacked them from behind. Neither man stood the slightest chance and died nearly instantly, their throats cut and their hearts stabbed from the double attack of scimitar and dagger. The slight noise roused Andreina and Gabi as well, who were laying with Lilly in one of the two wagons. Andreina rose and sat up. Instantly, she saw that they were being attacked and drew her scimitar and rose to jump out of the wagon to attack them. Gabi was sleepy-eyed and a bit slower reacting.

A dozen men now rushed silently over the sands and before Andreina could even get out of the wagon or begin to counter the attack or even warn the others, a scimitar sliced across her chest. Reeling from the sudden, sharp pain, she felt a heavy blow on the back of her head and darkness flooded over her. Gabi went down almost as rapidly, but was not cut. The noise and motion roused Lilly who tried to sit up, but was constrained by her nighttime bindings. She didn't make it to a sitting position as a man knocked her out as well.

"I told you, Donato, this would be child's play. Now let's get them to the tent and handled before one of them rouses," Ezio whispered.

Donato Lucca smiled. Yes, this had been too easy, but then they had spent over a month planning this ambush, taking every precaution they could think of to ensure the capture of the two foreign *mentales* gifted were taken alive and unharmed. Well, unharmed as yet, he thought.

An hour later, Donato Lucca, the first-born son and heir of the Lucca clan, led his wife, Adelina, to the tent. "Everything has been prepared, just as we planned, my love. I leave them in your care. We will drag our footprints into the sand so that even if they can manage to find some way to see, they will only see empty desert. Signal me if you have any trouble or when you have their pledges in hand. Tomorrow around supper begin to apply persuading pressure."

Adelina smiled, and gave her thirty-six year old husband a loving kiss. "I will not fail you, my lord. They will be broken and become valuable *mentales* to our clan." She was tall and thin, but her abdomen bore the marks of childbirth, thrice now, though she was barely thirty, but had also already lost four other children in miscarriages. Adelina looked forward to the day when Donato would take over as *Jefe* for her clan, making her the most powerful woman in the Lucca clan and territory, something for which she'd schemed for the past sixteen years. She'd used her beauty and wiles to charm Donato, and he'd married her, elevating her from the lowest Castas into the Lords Castas. Now she was about to prove her mettle; she would not fail in her task. She would break these two foreigners and add two more *mentales* gifted to her clan.

Standing at the tent's entrance, she looked around. She had a charcoal stove, well supplied with horse dung charcoal. Inside the tent, she had two huge water kegs and a number of food sacks, along with copper cooking pots and pans. She also had a goodly supply of *bacal* leaves. Donato had already poured sufficient *bacal* into the unconscious forms and had handled their eyes, according to her specifications. Now, she turned her attention to the six unconscious forms, lying on blankets on the tent floor. The other three guards had been killed outright. The guard leader had been spared, for he too had yellow eyes, and Donato changed his plans when he discovered this. Perhaps he too could be broken into their service as well, but Donato knew he had little leverage over the guard. Still, they would try. However, the repugnant Sisterhood women would be kept under *bacal* influence until they were no longer needed. Donato suggested perhaps they could be used as leverage with the two foreigners and maybe even this soldier guard.

She shuffled her slow way over to the forms and examined their eyes. *Perfect, my idea is working extremely well. No need to mess around with unwieldy blindfolds I cannot easily manage and remain bound myself. I certainly won't disgrace Donato by making him unbind me. No, this is far better. Hot wax poured into their closed eyes, now dry and hard, have sealed their eyes shut. No way can the wax be easily removed. It's embedded in their eyebrows and lashes. They do have a weird appearance; it's like they don't even have eyes or eye sockets any longer, just a smooth yellow wax where their eyes should be. I'm glad that Donato took my ideas for the men too. What a joke. Now they are bound as Easterlings women. Ha!*

She took her seat inside the tent near the door and

leaned back to doze until they roused. She would then have her hands full caring for them, all the while breaking them. *Patience, Adelina, patience and you will be rewarded. The damnable tower is taking away all the mentales gifted we need. Well, looks like we will get two or maybe three out of this. I wonder if I can possibly break the four Sisterhood women? Hell, they are married. Repugnant, but still, if I could break them too, we could have seven added to our clan. Now wouldn't that be something?*

Andreina roused, her head throbbing. *Attacked!* She tried to rise from her position of lying on her back. She couldn't and she gasped, attracting the attention of the dozing Adelina. She could not move her arms, which were fastened securely within a leather tube across the small of her back. Andreina recognized her situation immediately. Occasionally, Betta would play the dominate and bind her at night. She knew that her arms were bound and that she could not free herself. Worse, her legs were bound tightly in a fetter skirt, though her feet were bare as was the rest of her from her waist on up. "Why can't I open my eyes? Help, we have been attacked," she called out, trying desperately to rouse the others. Were they even alive? Then she remembered that she'd taken a bad wound across her chest and tried to sense how badly she was bleeding.

"Calm down Andreina is it? I healed your chest wound. I'll explain it all later when the others wake. Yes, your three Sisterhood women are just fine as are the three foreigners, though the five guards have been killed and buried in the desert sands," Adelina calmly reported to the panicking fighter. "Yes, none of you can see, and we have all of you, including the two men nicely bound. Kind of cool, don't you think, to bind these two foreign men?"

"Why? Why can't I see? What have you done to us?" Andreina pleaded, more frightened than she had ever been in her life. She felt utterly helpless and a complete failure. Felix and Lilly had depended upon her for their safety and she'd led them into a trap!

"Your eyes are buried under a half inch of wax, so don't even try to open them. You can't, not until we soften the wax.

It will be quite a chore to remove the wax, that's for sure. Anyway, this is lots better than a blindfold. I really can't handle those at all well. Now lie there and rest 'til the others wake," she ordered. Andreina did so, trying to use her psi-powers only to discover that she was now head blind. From the foul aftertaste in her mouth, she knew *bacal* had been forced into her, deadening her *mentales* gifts wholly. Damn, she cursed silently.

A while later, Adelina roused them all and repeated her warning about their eyes. "You women are wearing your fetter skirts and are bound for nighttime sleeping. You two men, well, you get to experience what we Easterlings women endure for our men. I have you bound just as we bind our women each night, plus I have you both wearing fetter skirts as well. If you haven't noticed, I've been giving you *bacal* so no *mentales* tricks on me. Those are out. Now then, explanations will come over breakfast, but first, I will walk each of you in turn outside the tent and help you go to the bathroom. I have breakfast waiting. Oh, you will notice you are bare from your waists up and have no sandals on. That's to prevent you from trying to wander off in the desert. The sun will fry your head and torso and the sand will burn and cook your feet. So don't get any such ideas in your heads. I'll help the women first. My name is Adelina Lucca, by the way."

As she approached each woman in turn, she asked them their name and helped them get to their feet. Each noticed that their hair was un-braided now, adding to their discomfort, since it was uniformly quite long. She held each woman's arm securely, as she led them the sort distance out of the tent. Such was necessary since they were blind and had no use of their arms, which made walking in their fetter skirts quite challenging, just as Adelina intended.

Felix and Captain Sheldon had a terrible time adjusting to their restraints. Adelina even fell down herself trying to support them as they kept falling themselves. However, Felix did get the sense that her fingernails were quite long as she assisted him. *Lords Castas,* he correctly surmised. *She must be some kind of important leader, perhaps a clan leader. But what is this all about?*

Almost an hour later, Adelina was exhausted. Handling them in their situation was harder than she had anticipated. Still she sat down and began feeding them in turn. "We are out in the middle of the desert, miles and miles from anywhere. It is just you and me here. Even if you get free, there is nowhere for you to go before the desert and the sun pickle you. I've a goodly supply of food and water, enough for as long as it takes. Okay, here's the deal. We've killed your five head blind guards."

Sheldon groaned, *Those were good men, damn her!*

She continued, "Our objective is simple. We want Felix and Lilly here to willingly join our clan and use their *mentales* gifts as we dictate. Sheldon, it would be nice if you were to join us too. As far as the Sisterhood guides go, we don't want anything to do with them! However, they will be kept here for a time before they are released. If you four don't do anything to antagonize or harm me, then no harm will befall you. After all, it is a high crime to harm a bound Easterlings woman. You are just along for the ride at the moment."

"You want Lilly and me to join your group and use our gifts as your leaders order?" Felix summarized what he thought that she was indicating.

"Precisely. Are you prepared to do so now? I caution you, my gift is to know when a person is lying or withholding some of the truth," she replied.

"Hell, no! Never. Lilly and I will never ever become your puppets! So you might as well just kill us now and be done with it. We will never give you that, not ever," Felix burst out, venting his pent up anger and frustration.

"He's right, never. So kill us and be done with it," Lilly added bravely. *So my life ends here in the desert just as we come up with the greatest find of the century. I won't even have the chance to bear his child even.* She had a sick feeling in her stomach. Until this moment when it seemed she would not get the chance, she'd not been ready to have a child. Now she suddenly found herself passionately wanting to bear his child.

Adelina smiled, though no one could see it. "Yes, you are telling me your truth at this moment. However, everyone has their price. For some it is higher than others. It is my job in the days ahead to help discover the price you will pay to swear allegiance to our clan and use your gifts for us. I assure you, at some point, the price will have become high enough that you will willingly agree. It will not be your deaths. That helps no one, certainly not us. We need your *mentales* gifts, and we are prepared to find the price you will pay. Just as I once had mine, so will you. I will leave you with something to think about, Felix, Lilly. While I dare not harm the Sisterhood women, Lilly here is a foreigner and I can hurt her all that I desire, bound or unbound. You both will join us; it is just a matter of how much I have to dole out for you to reach the price beyond which you will not go."

"If you hurt Lilly, I swear that I will kill you!" Felix burst out vehemently. "I'll hunt you down like a cur and kill you."

Oh god! She's going to hurt me until Felix gives in! Oh god, what have I done to Felix? Lilly's mind alternated between imagined tortures of herself and Felix caving in to her demands because of her pain and suffering. Seeing no other avenue, she tried to will herself to die, but it did nothing, of course.

"We will begin after breakfast, while the light is good. I am a qualified, competent healer, that's part of my gifts. So don't worry, I will not allow her to die, though she may well wish she could before we reach the price that you need, Felix," she said dryly.

"What kind of a hellish beast are you, Adelina?" Felix asked snidely, his whole body straining against the unyielding restraints. If he could just get free, he'd strangle her now! *I can't even enter her mind to console her and help her. God, Lilly, I've failed you utterly! What kind of man am I to allow this to happen to you?* "Have pity on her, she's only sixteen." He tried a different approach. Could this unseen woman harm a child?

"If you will truly agree right now, then I won't have to harm her," Adelina countered and he glared at what he thought was her face. Fear swelled into Lilly as she strained to hear what the unseen woman was doing. Was she still feeding the others? Her stomach knotted and she began to think she might vomit at any moment.

After what seemed an eternity, Lilly felt something metal being forced into her mouth. Her jaws were forced wide open. She tried to fight back but was helpless and could only wiggle her head a little as she lay on her back. Then something was pricking her gums and soon she felt them go a little numb. Adelina's body sank down upon hers and she felt something on her front teeth now. Then came the immense pulling pressures and bursts of excruciating pains. She screamed unintelligibly and tried to move her head, but Adelina held it solidly with her legs and continued her work.

"What are you doing to her?" Felix screamed struggling somehow to get to his feet. With a great effort he did. As he tried to move towards the sounds of Lilly's screams, Adelina launched out with a swift kick, and he went sprawling onto the ground, knocking over some unknown things.

"There, she has lost her front teeth. I've left her big molars for now. Give me a few minutes to heal her up and stop the blood loss," Adelina commented with a sense of satisfaction. A half hour later, she left Lilly lying and moaning softly to herself. "Now think about it and we'll see if you've changed your mind at suppertime." She rose and they heard her leave the tent, though from the sounds, she had to be nearby.

"Lilly! Lilly, what has she done to you?" Felix wailed, crying though his tears did not seep out from the wax seals over his eyes.

"My front teeth are gone," she said, but her voice sounded awfully strange now, scaring her even more. She broke down and began crying too.

Others whispered ideas during the day, but no one had any real way to make this torturing woman cease. The four Sisterhood women felt terribly guilty. They had failed as guides, their charges were being tortured, and they were helpless to prevent it. Recriminations flew thick inside the hot tent that day.

After supper, Adelina removed the remainder of Lilly's teeth, amid a storm of curses, protests, and death threats. Poor

Lilly only cried herself to sleep; she was now a toothless woman, whose speech was almost impossible to understand. How could she ever eat again, she wailed, wishing she could just die in her sleep.

The next day after breakfast and latrine usage, Adelina proceeded to announce, "So that was insufficient payment. Today, we will remove her fingers on her left hand, one at a time. Just say when you have reached your limit and are ready to unconditionally and willingly submit to my will."

Searing, excruciating pains throbbed through her left bound arm as one by one, beginning with her pinky, she felt them being severed. Once the heavy jolt of pain flashed, she could no longer feel that finger. After each, Adelina kept checking to see if she'd reached the proper payment for Felix. "Well, no matter. Tonight, I'll remove the arm at her elbow. It's useless now anyway." Oh how she was giving them all something to think about during the day. As before, she left them alone to rant, curse, rave, feel guilty, sympathize with Lilly, and anything else they cared to say — all part of the process of finding the proper payment they would accept to give up and join her clan. She'd found hers thirteen years ago.

Later that afternoon, she did as promised. Lilly screeched from the hideous pain just above her left elbow and quickly lost all feeling in her left lower arm. She fell unconscious from the pain, thankfully. After enduring the expected outbursts and curses, she sat back and chatted.

"You see, I was in the same position as you are now, only some sixteen years ago. We used to live in a small village of Waterhead, some fifty miles east of Northend. That fateful day, raiders from this Lucca clan came to our small farmstead, just outside the village. They killed my husband; he didn't have the gift, you see. They kidnaped me and my three year old daughter, Sally, and brought us here to the Easterlings land. We both have the gift. That's what they want, to add more of us who have the *mentales* gifts to their clan. *Mentales* equals power to them. Once here, they tried to get me to join them, but like you, I foolishly refused."

Felix wished that he could somehow see Adelina. He was sensing some deep seated grief or thought that he was.

321

Lacking anything else to go on, he decided to act on it. "So what happened to you? Did they cut off your arm too?"

"Oh no! That would not be the way of it. If I were cutting off your arms, that you could endure. It would not be the price that you'd be willing to pay. Heck, I bet you'd let me cut off all your appendages and still not yield to me. No, I won't harm you, Felix, only your pretty wife here. Just as they got to me, so will I get to you."

"Oh dear god! Not your three year old daughter," Felix had a sinking feeling in his guts. She was right; she could carve him up and he'd maintain his own integrity, but Lilly? Now that is entirely different! He was not certain how much longer he could take it. Poor Lilly was being made to suffer on his behalf, crippled for life just because he would not yield to her.

Adelina sighed. He imagined what awful past memories and emotions were going through her mind. "Yes, my little Sally. They cut off her left arm at the elbow, but not before one by one cutting off her fingers and then her hand — all the while forcing me to watch them do it. Every time I passed out, they roused me and then continued until at last, I yielded. I found my price, but it was too late. Sally died. A year later, I bore him a daughter, Felisa and then another, Nicolina. They have the gift too. I then miscarried four more and I am now no longer fertile." He sensed a deep disappointment or resentment in her. Perhaps, it was a heavy guilt. Lacking any visual clues, he was only guessing.

"Enough of my life story. They found my price, just as I will soon find yours. Tomorrow, we will start in on her right hand and fingers. If that doesn't work, then perhaps I will start in on the Sisterhood women. Perhaps you will feel more compassion for them than you do for your own wife. However, I will leave Lilly's upper arms intact. Otherwise, she cannot be bound when she becomes a true Easterlings woman. You don't need arms and hands for your *mentales* gifts. Name your price," she chortled. "Time for sleep. Tomorrow will be here soon enough."

"Maybe I can just die, Felix. Please don't give in to her because of me. I can't live if you do that," Lilly sobbed.

"I won't my precious Lilly. I won't give her the

satisfaction of breaking us. We'll both probably die before she gives up," Felix whispered back to her before breaking down completely and sobbing like a child. *Her voice sounds so funny without her teeth. Even if we could somehow break free, what kind of a life could she have now? Oh god, why did I ever bring her along with me? This is all my doing! I can never, ever make this up to her. How could I? What she is sacrificing for me is beyond words! If I surrender to Adelina, all Lilly has and will continue to suffer every day of her life will have been for nothing! Yet, can I allow her to mutilate the Sisterhood women? They are totally blameless, innocent of everything. God, what do I do now?*

Fel listened to the brief whispers between Felix and Lilly and among the four of them. Poor Captain Sheldon had already sunk into a deep apathy, saying little. His last words were to the effect that he had failed utterly to protect his liege and that his life was now less than worthless. She knew she could not count on him. She knew the situation was getting desperate. Lilly would lose her other arm tomorrow. Of that, she had no doubts, for neither would give in to Adelina's demands. They had too much integrity for that. No, tomorrow the bitch would start in on herself and her three Sisterhood mate and companions. Reaching the depths of despair, her mind drifted to the rumors of the ancient goddess Lysandra.

What the hell, it can't hurt. Goddess Lysandra, hear my prayer. We women are in dire peril. I've never prayed before, so I don't know how to do it. I can only say that I love Lilly and Felix and my free-mate and my two dearest friends. We are all utterly doomed unless you can help us somehow. I don't know what I need to do to beseech you to help us, but if you will let me know, I will do anything. Please, save us from this horrible nightmare. They will not give in to Adelina's demands, and tomorrow she will cut off Lilly's remaining arm, making her a helpless invalid for the rest of her life, and then she will do that to the four of us. We will all surely die and I don't want us to die. I want us to live. Betta and I are carrying Felix's children and perhaps that will account for something. We have always tried to help women of the Easterlings, but now we are failing. If Adelina gets her way, we will no longer be able to even help ourselves. I don't know what else I can say except please help us somehow, please. Oh yes, I am Felisa Fina e Fulvia, goddess.

There, I did it. I can't think of anything else that I can do except keep from breaking myself. I won't. I'll die first. God, I hope she doesn't mutilate my Gabi!

Suddenly, Fel saw a ghostly, shimmering image in her mind along with the thought, *How much are you willing to sacrifice for these two men and four women?*

Everything I have. That's not much, Goddess Lysandra. I'm sorry I don't have much to sacrifice for them.

That is enough, dear child. Your sacrifice is accepted.

Thank you, Goddess Lysandra. The image faded. *God, I wish I could tell the others, but maybe I dare not say anything. Yet, it might give them some hope. Hope. They need some now.* "Gang," she whispered, hoping that Adelina would not overhear her, "I just prayed to the Goddess Lysandra, and she answered me. She said that she would help us!"

"Fel! You didn't?" exclaimed a very worried Gabi.

"I did. She said that my sacrifice was accepted."

"Oh god, Fel! What did you sacrifice?" Gabi's heart sank. She had heard many wild tales of the sacrifices that the Goddess of Life and Death demanded of those who beseeched her.

"I don't really know, but I did it to save you and everyone else," Fel whispered back. "We'd best be quiet." Gabi's real concern started Fel worrying about just what Lysandra was going to take as her sacrifice. *Well, whatever it is, I will pay it to save everyone. That's the very least that I can do. When we Sisters give our pledge, we must honor it. We have little else except our word of honor.*

At dawn, they heard Adelina stirring. All of a sudden, Adelina shrieked, "Winding vipers! Winding vipers! Don't anyone move!" her voice filled with terror. Felix and Lilly couldn't really move anyway but held still not knowing exactly what a winding viper was other than perhaps a snake of some kind.

Not so with the four Sisterhood women. Fel whispered, "Winding vipers are deadly poisonous. One bite and you are dead within minutes! Oh gods and we can't even see it! Do as she says, even if you feel something slithering over you!"

They strained their ears listening for Adelina and trying to guess what she was doing. Adelina had awakened and was just stretching her cramped legs when she saw the six foot long, thick viper slithering into the tent. It stopped before her legs. After she gave her warning, she knew that she had to do something or the viper would likely kill them all. She reached for her small dagger, but because her upper arms were bound, she had to slide it out of its sheath in a number of small lifting motions.

Unfortunately for her, that attracted the viper's attentions and it struck her, biting her in her upper left arm. "Hell! It bit me. I'm dead. Take that." She slashed out wildly, though the viper bit her twice more before she killed it. Already she felt her body growing numb and collapsed onto the ground.

Her voice barely a whisper, she said pitifully, "I'm dying. Bit three times. Please, rescue my two daughters, Felisa and Nicolina from the Easterlings. Our camp is a mile north of here. Please, take them back to . . ." Her voice died off to the faintest whisper and none could hear her last request properly.

After a period of silence, Fel whispered, "Is she dead? Can anyone hear anything? I bet Lysandra did that for us. Gabi, roll over closer to me."

"I don't hear her breathing," Felix whispered nervously. "I wonder if there are more of those snakes around here?" He heard Gabi trying hard to move her bound body closer to Fel. *Well, now we are in a fine mess. We have lost our only caretaker. What do we do now? I can't break these bonds, but I must.* He strained and failed for the hundredth time. *Now I've gone and gotten us all killed, a slow and painful death!*

Although she was lying on her own hair, Fel managed to wiggle and push her head onto the back of Gabi. For an hour she used her teeth to work on undoing the ropes that threaded through the leather arm binding, lifting her head up and pulling the ropes out of one hole after the next. Her neck began aching but Fel persevered. Convinced that Lysandra had sent the viper, she was determined to get Gabi's arms free somehow! "They are coming loose, Fel! I can feel it. Keep on doing whatever you are doing!" Gabi exclaimed, with a newfound burst of hope. Then her lower arms came free. "Fel! You miracle worker, you did it. My lower arms are now free. Hang on everyone. I am going to try to free Fel's lower arms and then we can get the rest of you too. As soon as she can get hers free, together, we can get ourselves out of the waist chains and the fetter skirts. Patience everyone, we are going to get free somehow!"

After what seemed an eternity to Felix, Fel's voice called out, "Gabi's got mine free. Now we are going to undo the waist chains and then get out of the skirts. This is working!"

Felix was never so happy to have his physical freedom as he was when Gabi finally got his arms totally free and his fetter skirt off. That he was totally naked didn't register with any of them. They couldn't see anything at all. Hastily, he felt his way over to Lilly, who took the brunt of the torture, maimed for life. "Lilly, I can feel your left lower arm! It's still there! Your fingers — she didn't cut them off!"

"I can't feel them, Felix. It is as if they aren't there. Are you touching them?" Lilly asked. How could they be there and yet she couldn't move or feel them? She was flooded with hope and dismay at the same time as she felt Andreina's hands finally freeing her right arm. As soon as she could, she felt for her left hand and fingers herself. "God! They are there; I can feel them with my right hand, but I don't sense or feel them with my left. I can only feel my own touch just above the elbow, as she said. Still, it feels like she didn't cut them off. What's going on? Oh, thanks, I am really glad to be out of that skirt, Andreina."

While the four Sisterhood women worked together to free Captain Sheldon, who continued to sit quietly in a deep apathy, Felix tried to remove the wax from his eyes. "Well, I can't pry the wax out of my eyes. Damn. I think that if we can lay in the sun for a time, that will soften it. Didn't she say something about having to heat it up so it can be removed?"

The seven soon crawled on their hands and feet out of the tent, following the heat of the sun, fumbling around the body of Adelina. They felt the hot sand and lay on their backs, their faces towards the very hot sun of the Arad desert. "I bet we are going to get a bad burn," Fel whispered, though she didn't know why she ought to be whispering. They still heard no one else around them.

Sometime later, Lilly complained, "I feel like I am positively baking. Sweat is pouring off my face and body. I feel icky."

"Okay, everyone, try to see if you can get the wax out of your eyes, but be careful. It's probably going to be very stuck to our lashes and brows," Felix suggested. "Ah, it is working a little, I can see light." A half hour later, everyone had gotten most of the wax out of their eye sockets and could see for the first time since they were captured.

Looking around, Felix saw nothing but scorching desert sands. Already the seven were extremely sunburned on their front sides. The solitary tent sat near the base of a dune along with a small portable stove for cooking. They all crawled back inside to escape the baking sun, though it was even hotter inside. There lay the dead snake and the lifeless corpse of their torturer. Off to the far right were a number of water barrels and a stack of food. All headed for the water!

While the women busied themselves with making a meal, the two men, using their hands, dug a shallow grave for Adelina and buried her and the remains of the viper. When they rejoined the women, everyone looked at each other and burst out laughing. Everyone was stark naked and very dirty, but they were alive. While the women had already examined Lilly, Felix now took the time to examine very carefully her injuries. He was amazed that although she had her left arm, hand, and fingers intact, she could neither move nor feel anything with them. "You are right; it's like they are somehow dead. Let's see your mouth. God, she really did pull them all."

"I know. How am I to eat now? I talk so darn funny. I don't want to be this way. But go look at Fel. She's in a bad way, Felix."

Until now, he'd thought that everyone was in good shape, excepting Lilly of course. He turned to Fel, who was sitting quietly off to one side not helping with the meal preparations. "Fel?" he said as he sat in front of her, looking her body over for signs of injury. Then she looked up in his direction. "Oh my god! Fel! Your eyes!"

"I know. Gabi says that I don't have any pupils any more, just yellow-brown eyeballs. I can't see anything at all, but that must be the price Lysandra said I must pay for her help. She sent that snake so we could be saved. I will be all right, I think, Felix. After all, we promised to keep you safe, and we have mostly failed. I had to do something to save us. It worked. Lysandra is real, though she looked sort of ghostly to me in my mind," Fel explained, trying hard not to break down. *Focus on what you did for them, that they are now alive and safe. Focus. Don't start bawling, Fel!* She was able to stifle her swelling fears and emotions, for now anyway.

When the food was ready, Felix personally helped Fel with her meal. "Thanks, but I think that I am going to have to learn how to do it myself, even if I poke my face with the spoon," Fel attempted to make light of her situation. *After all, what else can I do about it? I willingly made the sacrifice and we are now safe, well mostly.*

Once Fel was managing to eat by her own means, he mashed up a bowl for Lilly. "I am doomed to only eat mushy food from now on. Well, I wish I didn't sound so funny. I can manage with my dead arm somehow, but this is so weird. Gumming my food! Oh I am like an aged old crony now!" She became quiet as she began gumming her food.

With a full stomach, Andreina stated flatly, "Well, Felix, we will return all your silver to you when we get back. We have failed miserably to protect you and Lilly especially. I feel so badly for her and it is all our fault."

"Andreina, enough of that silly talk. It is as much my own fault for even allowing her to come on this journey in the first place. The blame is all on me; I will have to live with it forever," Felix lamented.

In her toothless voice, Lilly added, "No, I am to blame and now I have to live with my own failures for the rest of my life, as long as that may be."

"You are all wrong, you know," the apathetic voice of Captain Sheridan broke in. "The fault is all upon me and my late guards. We failed to protect you as we were pledged to do.

My life is now worth less than nothing."

Fel, listening to her friends, suddenly began laughing. "Oh hell. There is more than enough blame to go around. Please, let's forget the blame and guilt trips. I got us this far, but I can't get us any further now. What the hell are we going to do now? Wait here until someone else comes to see what happened to Adelina and then recapture us? Or wait until the water runs out? Stop the guilt trip and figure out what we do now."

"She's right, of course. Okay, what do we do? I yield to you sisters. You know the desert and what we have to do to survive," Felix asked. *She's right. We are not out of this yet.*

Andreina took charge. "Look around for clothing that we can wear and sandals. We aren't going anywhere without them, turbans too." They rummaged but found nothing but their fetter skirts. "Well, they obviously wanted to trap us here. We can't possibly go far during the day; we'd not get a mile before our feet burned to a crisp. Even if we wrapped them in bits of our skirts, we'd die of heat stroke; our heads would boil."

"We could travel at night," Gabi suggested. "Look, she did say that their main camp was maybe a mile north of here. Let's mark the sun and leave a line in the sand pointing the way. Surely, we can walk a mile barefoot, say after the desert cools down a bit. But we only have the one dagger to fight off the entire clan."

"And we are very vulnerable, naked as a beetle-bird," Andreina added disgustedly.

"We can't manage the desert wearing our fetter skirts," Betta added, "so we go naked a little longer. Maybe we can sneak into their camp and steal some clothes and weapons."

"Hey, my *mentales* is returning," Fel broke in, eager to share her news. All were very relieved as they too soon began sensing theirs returning, albeit slowly as the *bacal* drug wore off.

As they milled around waiting for sunset, Betta chatted with Fel. "You know, I bet your eyes are meant to be proof positive to Lysandra's intervention on our behalf, Fel. Felix listened in, curious to know why she thought this.

"You see, if you were just fine like the rest of us, we would all rather not believe your story. I mean there are winding vipers here in the desert, though they usually do not bother humans unless we provoke them. One could speculate it entered the tent looking for some shade and attacked Adelina because she tried to prevent it from doing so. However, your eyes tell us something else happened entirely, Fel. None of us can possibly explain what happened to your eyes. I've never heard of such a thing happening, except maybe very rarely a baby is born that way. So your blindness is Lysandra's way of making believers of us all," Betta finished up what she thought was perfect logic. Fel smiled and accepted her views. It made sense to her.

Later after supper and full dark, they tested the sands. Finding them still too hot for comfort, they waited even longer. Lilly continually worked with her left lower arm and fingers, hoping to rub some sensation back into them. "Still dead?" Felix whispered, seeing her trying yet again rubbing them.

"Yes, they just dangle there like some lifeless dead weight. I wonder what she really did to me?" Lilly replied in her strange sounding toothless voice. "I keep hoping that sooner or later some feeling will come back in them. I have to keep hoping, Felix, the alternative is too horrible to think about." She fought back a flood of tears once more and he held her close.

"Damn, I can't even kiss properly now," she whispered as her passionate kiss merely pushed her lips into her mouth, frustrating her all the more. Felix gently touched her cheeks with the tips of his fingers, rousing her into a rapport with himself. At last, he could share her grief and fears; their gifts had fully returned. He knew how deeply she was wounded, but could do nothing about it at the moment.

"That sounds like a major sword battle going on up ahead of us," Andreina whispered. She, Gabi, Felix, and Sheldon were approaching the Lucca encampment, having insisted the others remain behind. Felix allowed Andreina to carry the dagger; he planned to use his fire gifts if they had to fight the men. Slowly, they made their way up the sand dune before lying down to survey the scene below them, some five hundred feet distant.

The camp was large. Dozens of tents arranged in a giant circle enclosed a small herd of horses and their own two wagons! However, in the dim moon light, they could see men running in many directions fighting wherever they could. Many fallen bodies could just barely be made out in the dim light. *We will wait this one out,* Andreina sent them. *Thank god, we have our gifts back!* The fighting slowly subsided as more and more combatants fell. From the position of the moons, Andreina estimated it was around two in the morning when they no longer saw anyone fighting or even moving around down below. She wisely held them back another hour before they cautiously began moving silently down the side of the dune.

Approaching the edge of the camp, one by one the companions began mechanically picking up scimitars to use to defend themselves. However, no one challenged them. *This is really spooky!* Andreina sent. *I've never seen so many dead men before. What the devil happened here? We should start checking the tents to see if anyone else is even alive here. Use extreme caution.*

They entered tent after tent only to find supplies and bedding in them, no occupants. Then, Andreina opened one flap and heard a faint intake of breath. *Someone is in here. Careful.* "Who's there? Come out where I can see you. Mind you, we mean you no harm, but we are armed if you try anything," she barked both sternly and forcefully. A young woman raised her head up and stepped out from the shadows. She had been in bed, Andreina concluded. Her hair was down and un-braided. Her arms were bound behind her back in the traditional way and she wore only the thinnest of a silk nightgown. Then, another slightly shorter girl stepped out of the shadows hiding behind her older sister.

"Is, is it over? You are not of our clan. You must be Nerezza's. Have we lost?" the older teen asked very nervously, glancing from person to person. Her eyes fixed upon Felix and his bare form. She needed no reply. A small exhale told all. *We've lost, Nico. We now belong to these Nerezza men. They have come for us. See, the men are ready to take us now. Be brave. We must do our duty to the victors. We must not show them that we are weak and unworthy.*

I'm afraid, Felisa. I'm scared.

Just do like mother always told us. Remember what she explained to us. I think if they are mentales, it won't be so bad. If not, well, Nico, we must show them that we are strong and worthy of them.

But I'm shaking so badly I can hardly walk! Where is mother? Why can't we see her?

I don't know, Nico, I can't reach her anymore. I, I think that she is dead too. It is up to us to honor the victors now. Just do what I do, Nico. It will be all right if we do the ceremony right. They will have to accept us.

Felisa bent over and shook her long hair forward partially covering her bosom. She meekly stepped forward and knelt before Felix. Her sister followed her motions and quickly knelt before Captain Sheldon. In a shaking voice, Felisa said, "We honor the victors of this battle in the centuries old tradition of *sesso disposto* as proclaimed by Wystan the Bold. We beg you to then accept us as tradition dictates."

Felix looked down at the young woman, scarcely older than Lilly. He could barely see her in the bit of moon light that shone through the tent flaps. *What is she doing? What does she mean? Oh my god.* "No, wait a minute, please." He backed up a little, cursing the fact that he was completely naked before this young woman.

Andreina grasped what the teen was both saying and now trying to do. She smiled and then explained, "Felix, Sheldon, one of the customs or traditions, if you choose to call it that, is after the battle, the victorious leaders are honored by the reigning Lords Castas — that is, the leader of the losing clan's wives or representatives. Ex post facto, that's you two men. It is a matter of great honor for these two women to perform this ceremony for you. It seems that these two young women are insisting on it. If you do not allow them to do this, you will greatly dishonor them both. For them, it would be tantamount to a total and utter rejection of themselves, which usually means that they would then commit suicide rather than live as wholly dishonored women. Of course, if you consent to the ceremony, then they will expect to become part of your harem."

"Harem? What?" exclaimed Felix, growing more frustrated with each explanation. "But I am happily married."

"The custom of the Easterlings is much different than those of your Midlands. Here, a Lords Castas man is expected to have many wives and children," Andreina added, enjoying immensely the discomfort of Felix and Sheldon. *Men!* she thought.

I'm damned either way. If I don't let them do this, they will kill themselves as dishonored women. If I do it, then they will expect to become my wives. Lord, help me!

Gabi sent both men, *You should allow them the ceremony. Later, we can sort it all out. Here, a woman needs the physical support of a man in order to live. Except for us in the Sisterhood, women here with their binding customs cannot live alone — at least not easily. It would be a life of complete humiliation; something a woman cannot easily bear here in the Easterlings.*

But this is a sexual thing, Felix protested.

So? Gabi replied. She added, *Are you so high and mighty that you cannot allow these teens to retain what little remains of their dignity and honor?*

Her words stabbed him like a knife. "Please, continue with your ceremony. I mean you no dishonor."

Felisa pressed her body against his; he could smell her scent of exotic eastern spices. Intoxicating, he thought. Gently, she pushed him back deeper into the tent to her bed. He lay down and she gently swept her long hair over his body before mounting him. From a corner of his eye, he saw Sheldon being similarly treated. Then, Felix became wholly absorbed in the rapport that only two *mentales* gifted can share. He sensed that for her, this was her first time and was as gentle as possible with her, yet she insisted upon riding him. Such was the custom; she had to prove to him that she was worthy of him. That much he gained from their closeness. He also now knew that she was the daughter of Adelina. Her dying words came back into his mind.

The two Sisterhood fighters quietly backed out of the

tent. Sometime later, Andreina whispered, "Felix, Sheldon, we've found our clothes. We've got to pack up what we can and get out of here before sunrise. The jackals and scavenger birds will soon be here. Hurry up, will you."

"You have done very well, Felisa. Now it is time that we pack and leave here," Felix whispered gently to the young woman. "May I unbind your arms so that you may pack your things?"

"Thank you, Felix. I am pledged to you now. Yes, my sister and I will pack. Will we be taking a wagon?" she asked. The relief in her voice put him at ease, finally. She was untrained and because of their close rapport, he picked up her message to her younger sister.

Nico, now we can continue to live! They will have to look after us. I know, sis, we will never get the chance to be First Wives, but we have shown them that we are honorable and by custom, they will have to look after us now. We can live. Mother would want that for us.

Is she really dead, Felisa? Sheldon and Felix both felt the overwhelming grief that she bravely fought down.

Felix took a gamble. "Yes, if your mother was Adelina, then she is dead. Sheldon and I buried her outside the tent. She died a brave death; she gave her life to protect us all from a deadly winding viper. While she killed it, the snake bit her several times. With her last breath, she begged us to come find her two daughters and rescue them. You can be very proud of your mother, Felisa, Nicolina. Now, we must hurry. I hear the jackals already." He and Sheldon had gotten the leather bindings off their arms, freeing their lower arms.

"Thank you. We will dress and pack now," Felisa replied. Felix and Sheldon both sensed the two teens desperately wanted to be alone to morn for their mother and they quickly stepped outside. At once, Gabi handed them some of their spare clothes and the men dressed as quickly as they could. Meanwhile, Andreina had begun to hitch up their horses. Gabi dashed off to assist her companion, hitching up the third wagon that belonged to the Lucca clan.

Dressed, the two men joined them. Andreina barked, "Finish this up. Gabi and I need to scavenge what we can that is of value. None of us wants to return here in the daylight. The scene will be too gruesome. Trust us." They did as she asked.

An hour later, they arrived back at the solitary tent and Betta, assisted somewhat by Lilly and Fel, had a morning breakfast waiting them. Over breakfast, Felix outlined what had happened to them, vis a vi the role that Adelina had in it, answering the teen's questions about Lilly's condition and Fel's blindness. They did not mention Lysandra's intervention, allowing the teens to focus on their mother's bravery in saving her captives from the viper.

Both teens had fiery red hair, long and thick with a slight waviness, perhaps due to constant braiding. Felisa had a round face but high cheekbones, attractive but with a pixie look about her. She and Lilly were perhaps the same age, Felix guessed, but her bosom was substantially larger than his wife's was, quite similar to her deceased mother. On the other hand, Nicolina was much younger and taller than her sister was. In many ways, he thought that she must take after her Easterlings father. Felisa definitely did not have the Easterlings look about her, though she dressed and acted the role. Remove the braids and bindings and she'd be seen as a Midlands woman. In contrast, Nicolina's face was oval with very marked features. Her flaming red hair was similar to her sister's hair and that of her mother and the only hint that she was not of pure Easterlings breeding. Only recently filling out, she looked a bit on the thin side, especially so because of her height, nearly six-two, a good five inches taller than Felisa. Nevertheless, she was significantly prettier than her older sister was. Both women wore their nails precisely five inches long, carefully manicured as befitting the Lords Castas.

After eating, Felix, a supporting arm around the two bound women in their fetter skirts, walked over to the crude grave. He left them there to privately morn their mother.

Lilly, Betta, and Fel now wore their skirts as well and had donned their waistbands and chains as well. "It is still the custom, dear," Lilly gave her whispered explanation to Felix. "Besides, the two teens are more comfortable with us dressed as they are. Have you seen the awful looks that they shoot at Andreina and Gabi? If looks could kill," she added with a coy grin.

"I know where we are now, Felix," Andreina broke in on them. "My gifts have completely returned. We are about five miles deeper into the desert than we should be. We will still be home by nightfall, if we start soon."

The two men helped the two Sisterhood women load up what was valuable here, including the tent, stowing the gear in the third wagon. Felix then led the two teens back to their wagon, lifting each up and helping them get seated in the bed. He arranged their sun cover sheet over their heads while Sheldon climbed up to drive them. Felix then assisted Lilly, while Gabi and Andreina lifted their free-mates into the sun-shielded wagon. At last, days behind schedule, they continued on their homeward journey.

Nicolina began chatting with Captain Sheldon. "Which of these women are your wives? Lilly belongs to Felix, that much we know."

He laughed. "I am not married, Nicolina. Those four are Sisterhood free-mates."

"Oh! I did not know. That means that I am now your First Wife, Sheldon. I am really proud and honored! I know that I am only fourteen, well almost fourteen, but I will do my best to please you, always. I have the gift like my sister and mother and father."

Sheldon was about to protest, when he had a flash of insight. *My god, this is all that she has left now! She's lost both parents, the planned future they had for her, her clan, friends, home, absolutely everything except the clothes on her back. She's holding on tightly to the only thing that remains to her — the traditions of her people and her honor to them. If I deny her this, it will completely destroy her!* He forced himself to reply, "You are already doing very well, Nicolina. I am most pleased with you." *Well, I am not lying, I am pleased, more so than I might care to admit.*

The two teens chatted a bit and then fell silent as the heat of the day increased. At noon, they halted to rest the lathered horses and water and salt them as well as themselves. "Felix! Andreina, come quick. The teens. Something is wrong with them," Captain Sheldon called out.

Felix and Andreina rushed to the rear wagon that their newly acquired string of forty horses were attached. "My god, they are burning up!" Andreina exclaimed, pulling her hands from their foreheads. She looked up at the sun shield, but it looked normal. Meanwhile, Sheldon got a water keg and rags. Carefully, he began wiping their heads with them, while Felix examined the girls. "I'll fetch Fel — no, damn it, she can't see now. Okay, Betta, she's second best at healing." She raced to her wagon and lifted the woman down, but carried her swiftly to the back wagon, lifting her into the wagon, unwilling to waste precious time while Betta took her hobbled steps.

Betta grinned, "In a hurry are we," she teased and then set to work on the sisters. While both men wanted an immediate report, Betta would not be hurried. At last she said, "Well, my bets are on Verge Sickness."

"What?" exclaimed a very worried Felix. They were out in the middle of nowhere and had no way to treat the young women.

"Well, it is to be expected. That was their first time; their bodies have now gotten their *mentales* energies confused and mixed up with their sexual drives. Compounding it is the shocking loss of their mother, the nasty attack on their camp in which their father and all their acquaintances were killed and everything else. It is a wonder that they haven't had a complete mental breakdown before now. I'll ride here with them and keep water on them. Its evaporation will help keep their fevers down. For heaven's sake, get us to our home by nightfall where we can treat them properly."

"Yes ma'am!" Sheldon replied. As soon as his horses were watered, the group continued along the track towards Adelmira. Just after dark, they finally pulled in to their small adobe home. By mutual consent, they decided not to take the two women to the tower but to try healing them first. "Look, they have already had their whole world shaken. If they sort of waken inside a tower, they could freak out even more with total strangers around them," Sheldon explained his viewpoint.

As soon as the women were lifted down and began making their slow way inside, Betta ordered, "Bring them into the front room. We will get *bacal* tea going at once and then Fel and I will see what we can do."

A tense hour later, Felix, Lilly, Sheldon, Betta, and Fel finally compared notes. While Felix and Sheldon's healing skills were minimal, they had a vested interest in the welfare of teens. Fel spoke first, "Yes, they both have come down with a really bad case of Verge Sickness, compounded by the fact that they are now both pregnant. Men, honestly didn't you think?"

Sheldon's face crimsoned, "But if we hadn't, that too would have destroyed them. We were damned either way, Fel. Honestly, we had no choice at the time. What can we do for them?"

"When they get it this bad, they usually die," Fel said sorrowfully.

"Damn, damn! Isn't there something that we can do for them?" asked Felix. Guilt swamped his mind too. Like Sheldon, he saw no other route available than the one they had followed. Culture and tradition meant everything in the Easterlings.

Fel thought for a time. Already *bacal* had been given and had begun to dampen out the teens' *mentales* energy production, which was blocked from flowing by their reproductive systems that had been activated. "Well, with our new crystals amplifying our powers, maybe we can get the huge blockage undone. Let's give it a try in the morning. Right now, we all need a good night's sleep."

After breakfast, Andreina and Gabi headed off to handle the horses and gear they'd brought back. The others gathered beside the very sick teens. All uncovered their new crystals and Fel began to examine Felisa first. She didn't need her eyes, rather she used her healing gift as the young woman's nervous system became visible to her in her mind. She smiled, sensing the growing life within her womb. Probably the teen did not yet know that she was pregnant, though it was primarily behind the energy blockage. Fel did her best to dislodge the dammed up psi-energies, but failed. "I've never seen anyone so blocked before. Betta, have a try."

Betta failed as well. "Even with the amplification, I just can't get enough psi-energy to bust it loose. If it doesn't go into flow soon, we will for sure lose the both of them. Ideas?"

Felix groaned, but this pronouncement was what he had anticipated. He and Sheldon had slipped into rapport with her as she went about her work and had pretty much witnessed her failure to dislodge the wall of psi-energies. No one said anything for a minute.

At last, Lilly said, "Look, what if we all could get into a close rapport with either Betta or Fel and then we all flow our own psi-energies to her. Maybe with our combined forces she can bust it loose?"

"Lilly, that's brilliant. I don't think anything like that has ever been tried before," Felix replied, hope kindled in him. They set to work on this novel idea. Felix could easily slip into a total rapport with Lilly alone or with Fel or Betta simply by matching their unique wavelengths of their psi-energy fields. However, each person's frequency was different, and some were closer than others were. Sheldon's was vastly different from Felix's, for example, and the two simply could not get into an intimate rapport with each other. There was also some male vs male resistance to such closeness within both men.

A half day later, they were about to give up Lilly's idea when she had another suggestion. "Say, let's try it this way. Betta, you slip into rapport with Fel. Then I'll slip into rapport with you. When I am all set, Felix, you slip into rapport with me. Once he's in, Sheldon, you see if you can join us."

Betta slipped in with Fel, her vision became black, which was just what Fel was seeing; she had no vision. Betta forced her feelings of guilt and sorrow over what Fel was enduring and saw Fel as she was, a beacon of strength and faith. A bit later, though she now had no way to measure the passage of time, minutes or hours, she didn't know how long, Betta felt the loving touch of Lilly's youthful mind joining with hers and Fel's. Both women keenly felt Lilly's monumental sense of loss and frustration over her mutilations that were permanent. In a close rapport, nothing can be hidden from the others; it would not be a rapport if it was so hidden. No, one has to accept wholly what the other is, or rapport does not occur. Again, Fel and Betta let go of their own sorrow and sympathetic feelings towards Lilly's awful physical situation.

As soon as they did so, Lilly slid into an intimate rapport with them. The closeness instantly reminded both Sisterhood women of their own free-mates and the similar intimacy that they always shared each evening. Even Lilly now felt it quite strongly and it was even sexual in nature. Unknown to her, her mouth grinned a little with envy of the two women. Then, she also picked up the two tiny sparks of new life growing within each of the two Sisterhood women. They in turn picked up her own desires now to have a child.

After a time, Felix began to match his frequency to that of the trio. He knew that he was not actually strong enough to break up their rapport with his bungling efforts to join them. Theirs was far too strong. Sweat poured from his forehead as he labored to alter his natural psi resonances. Just when he thought he just couldn't match them, he felt himself slipping into that intimate rapport. In a flash, he was one with the three women. Their thoughts, emotions, and feelings were his just as his were theirs. All four fluctuated slightly as they began to face that which defined and was the being called Felix. They felt his guilt for having helped precipitate Felisa's Verge Sickness, his guilt for not having been able to prevent Lilly's mutilations, and more. *Tonight, Lilly. I promise we will make it so,* he sent her as he duplicated her now strong desire to bear him a child. She smiled; a little embarrassed all heard him as well. Nothing could be private when in this kind of close rapport. It passed swiftly.

Now it was Sheldon's turn to attempt to match the resonating frequency of the group of four of them. Each time that he approached the proper frequency, a blast of repulsion psi-energies cast him out from the groups. After several attempts, Lilly realized what was happening. She sent to them, *Stop Sheldon. It is never going to work with both you and Felix in it. You two cannot go into a deep rapport with each other because each sees the other as an enemy to your own sense of maleness.*

Well, I am not a lover of men, and it does spook me, Sheldon sent back.

Same here, Felix added.

I will act as your regulator instead. We ought to have

one of us watching over our physical bodies, Sheldon sent.
*Your body is getting quite cold, Lilly. There, I've adjusted
your blood flow. Okay, I'm monitoring everyone. Go ahead.
I'm keeping my fingers crossed.*

Betta, reinforced by three other's psi-energies, began to
push and shove Felisa's massive blockage of her own energies.
Suddenly an electrical spark gapped between Betta and Felisa,
very nearly breaking their rapport. Physically, Sheldon got a
workout getting all five bodies smoothed out. *Well, that's
started to alleviate it,* Betta noted. Joined as they were, so did
the other three. She did as much as she dared and then turned
her attention onto Nicolina, who was in perhaps even worse
shape, being almost too young to bear children. *Obviously not
or she would not have been having her monthly cycles.*

Again, an electrical spark gapped from Nicolina and the
group, raising havoc with their physical bodies. Sheldon again
worked rapidly to calm heartbeats, get breathing regular, and
release tension in muscles. Sweat poured from his face as well.
It was challenging and hard work monitoring so closely five
bodies at the same time. At last, Betta could do no more, she
dare not. *We must allow their bodies to adjust before we
continue.* One by one, they dropped out of their close rapport
only to find that their bodies were ravenously hungry. That
they all smelled food didn't help.

"Food's ready," called out Gabi. Andreina and I went
ahead and whipped up something.

"Thanks love. I am famished. Who would guess this
kind of work burns up so much energy?" Fel gushed.
"Someone lead me to the food." Several chuckled, but Felix
noticed that it was nighttime. They'd started around noon.
Time had flown by and he'd not even sensed it.

Over dinner, Felix said, "Well, we five have just done
something that's never been done before. We've joined in a
kind of psi-circle, merging our energies into one huge one.
Together, we are immensely more powerful than we are alone.
It was most impressive and incredible. Thanks to our healers
too, the teens are doing better."

"Yes, they are, but they are not out of the sands just
yet," Betta cautioned him.

"Let's call it a *Círculo de mentes* because that's what we were when we were joined. Betta had the combined energy power of four of us," Lilly said. She always liked having proper names for actions and this one seemed most appropriate to her. The others accepted her term.

"When you do it, you best have a regulator on duty. I am worn out from keeping all your bodies going at peak efficiency," Sheldon added.

"He's right. Without him monitoring our bodies, we'd have all run into major problems," Felix noted. "Always have a regulator present when a *Círculo de mentes* goes into action. Add that to your collection of rules, Lilly." She grinned and did just that.

Sheldon added, "We really need to study this whole *Círculo de mentes* thing. My mind is whirling with the possibilities of being able to control that much psi-energy."

"He has a vital point," Felix pointed out. "While the crystals alone are incredible, our *Círculo de mentes* will open up an entire new world of possibilities! We have to study them before we dare release our findings of the crystals on the world."

"So we are not returning to the Midlands anytime soon?" Lilly asked.

"We can't right now; winter has come to most of the Midlands. We'd have to wait until the spring thaw anyway," Felix replied.

"Well, I don't want to stay in that stuffy *Círculo*, dear."

"You can stay with us," Fel offered. "We can add a back room or two onto our house or maybe even get us a new home that's bigger."

Andreina spoke up, "We can afford it now. Gabi and I sold off all the stuff that we brought back. We've got us a small fortune. Here's your cut, Felix. I gave you half."

"Nah, we don't need it, Andreina. Get a bigger house and consider it payment for our keep," Felix replied, bringing broad grins to the four Sisterhood women's faces. This idea greatly appealed to them.

Chapter 17 A Time for Healing

The next morning, Lilly's heightened senses detected what she now wanted. Her beaming face told Fel and Betta mountains. *Congratulations Lilly*, Fel sent her and Lilly's toothless grin broadened. By breakfast, everyone knew that she was also pregnant. As they ate, Captain Sheldon teased Felix, "Well, in a few months you will be a father four times over. Think of all those diapers you will get to change." Felix growled and then smiled. Somehow, he'd gone from not even thinking about some distant time of fatherhood to being one four times in probably the same month!

After eating, Fel and Betta went to check on the two patients. Their fevers were down, but not gone. Once more, the five formed up their *Círculo de mentes*, with Sheldon acting as their regulator. This time, Betta and Fel were able to unblock another batch of the teen's psi-energies far more swiftly, completing it by late morning.

Meanwhile, Gabi and Andreina went off looking for a larger home or for a way to enlarge theirs. "We ought to move farther from the tower, Gabi. I am sick of the insults that they toss at us every time they see us or our free-mates," Andreina suggested as they walked like men along the streets of their village, passing the many women who shuffled along with their tiny two inch steps. Neither minded the insults and taunts from other women of the village. That was to be expected, since they had thrown off their fetters and had followed their hearts in love, breaking two taboos at once. This they could understand, coming from the women of the village, but not from the intelligent and gifted women of the tower.

"Say, what about the old Patrizio Inn on the north edge?" Gabi had a sudden bright idea. "It's been empty for over a year since they built their new inn on the southern edge. We would have plenty of rooms and a stable for horses too." Andreina liked the idea too and they changed direction and headed to check it out. While it was in somewhat disrepair, the old inn could sleep a dozen, with a large dining hall and big kitchen and pantry. Both women liked the stables and large corral, though hauling water from the oasis ten blocks away would be a pain. Gabi spotted an old water wagon in one stall. "If it could be fixed up, it would make fetching water lots simpler."

Around noon, the two returned home having purchased the old inn for a hundred silvers, one tenth of their currently available funds. Of course, they used telepathy to make sure it was acceptable to their free-mates first. "We have a lot of fixing up to do," Gabi declared as she ate and watched as Felix mashed up Lilly's food for her. *God, that has to be horrid for her!*

"We can lend you a hand," Captain Sheldon offered and the conversation changed to what the two women thought would have to be done. Felix volunteered to sit with the two teens while the others went off to inspect their new home. He watched as the three fetter-skirted and bound women shuffled slowly out of the front entrance. Andreina and Gabi had their arms around their free-mates, while Sheldon held Lilly securely. He imagined their twelve block walk to the new home and again wondered why the women of the Easterlings would ever put up with such. Still, the love shown by the two couples suggested the why. He had a sudden burst of pride in his Lilly and wished he'd gone instead.

At last, he focused his attention on the two still unconscious teens. They were pretty and so young to be so close to death. Verge Sickness was often far worse for young women than young men. He mused about the reasons behind it but could only surmise that it was because their bodies were more complicated than males. He rubbed a cold wet cloth across Felisa's forehead. Her fever was way down and Fel had been cautiously optimistic about their recovery. As he did so, Felisa stirred and moaned a little.

"There, there, you will be fine, Felisa," he said softly to her. Her eyes opened for the first time in days.

"What's happening to me? Felix, I'm not feeling so well," she whispered.

He sensed her rising panic. "Easy, easy. Relax. You and your sister are fighting a really bad bout of Verge Sickness. Fel, Betta, Lilly, I, and Sheldon have been tending you both. Your fever has broken and that's a good thing. Drink?"

She tried to rise up, but being bound at her elbows coupled with her overall weakness, she couldn't. Felix gently lifted her unbraided hair off her shoulders and then lifted her into a sitting position. She took the clay mug and drank the water greedily. "Easy. We need to get fluids in you but they have to stay down. Here, let me get the kinks out of your stomach." His light rapport with her allowed him to feel what she was feeling, a sharp tensing of her stomach as the water hit it. He focused and adjusted the neurons around that area.

"That's better. Thank you. I am so weak. I ought to have my arms bound behind my back when I am in bed like this, my husband," she whispered.

"Yes, I know, but we didn't want to bother with that while you were so ill. You have been unconscious for nearly three days now."

"Oh. Oh, okay then." *Oh god! I have shamed him already! Sick for three whole days and nights! What he must think of me now!*

Again, her mind was open; she was untrained in even the basic skills of blocking her thoughts from being broadcast to all telepaths around her. "There is no shame in being ill, Felisa. You have not shamed me. Rather it is I who have shamed you. I should have delayed your *sesso disposto* until you and your sister had recovered from your heavy losses and shocks. Our loving indirectly brought on your Verge Sickness and Nicolina's too. Please don't think less of me because of that." He'd cleverly turned it around on her.

Her eyes were wide open and her look of total sympathy shook him. "Oh no! You must not think that of yourself, my husband. You could not know nor could I. We both did what simply had to be done and you were gentle with me. For that, my sister and I will be forever grateful." Her fleeting shame and guilt feelings had vanished completely.

"I have another surprise for you, Felisa. You are going to have our child. You are also pregnant. So is your sister."

Felisa's face lit up. "I am? We are so blessed so soon! Oh my husband, this is the best news ever! I will be a good mother and teach our child our many traditions. He or she ought to have our joined *mentales* gifts too. I have some of mother's ability to tell when someone is lying to me. I will use it for you whenever you need it. Just let me know, my husband."

"Now that is a very useful gift, Felisa. Now lay back and rest. You have been very sick. I need to tend to Nicolina now."

"Okay. I am so weak. Nico, she prefers just Nico."

As he wiped her brow, Nico's eyes fluttered and she woke too. "What? Where? Oh, you are not my new husband," she whispered faintly.

He helped her up and got some water in her too. "No, he is off with the others to see our new home. This one is too small for all of us now so we needed to get a bigger place. He will be back soon. He's been at your side these past three days." He went on to tell her about the same things that he'd told Felisa, including the fact that she too was pregnant. As expected, that brought a smile and a brightness to her face. He overheard Felisa's telepathic message to Nico. *Now they know that we both are fertile women, Nico, and they will want to keep us as wives for sure! We don't have to worry any more.* Nico flashed a grin at her sister before lying back down.

The men assisted Andreina and Gabi in making the needed repairs to the new Sisterhood home, while Lilly, Fel, and Betta looked after the recovering teens. Rapidly, they regained their strength but both new just how close they had come to dying. While the men and the Sisterhood women were off at their new home working, and while out of earshot of the two teens, Felix and Sheldon discussed what they should do about them.

"Look, they somehow think we are now their husbands," Sheldon complained. "We haven't been married, not by any rules I know about."

"You are comparing these circumstances to your Midlands culture," Andreina replied.

"What? Are you saying because we had *sesso disposto* that she and I are wedded?" Sheldon asked both protesting and confused.

"In a way. You see, both of them are Lords Castas; their parents must have been either clan leaders, equivalent to your kings I think though I am not entirely sure, or their father was his direct heir. When two rival clans or kingdoms in your terms, Sheldon, go to war, and the victor kills the rival king, what is to become of his harem, his wives? You see, in the Easterlings culture, women are bound and thus highly dependent upon their husbands for their survival. Husbands dote on them and pay far more attention to their physical well-being than I saw when I was in your Midlands getting Sisterhood training."

"The harem wives of the dead king have two choices. One, they can request to be sent back to their own parents in utter disgrace, there to live out a pitiful existence or they can execute the *sesso disposto* ceremony in which they demonstrate that they would be viable wives for the conqueror, especially if they can also quickly show they are fertile. In the case now of *mentales*, this aspect has grown enormously — being fertile translates to bringing forth more children who have this rare gift here in the eastern lands. Custom dictates if the conqueror finds the women willing and able and especially if they are proven to be fertile with them as well, then the conqueror is obligated to add them to his harem as his wives. If they are unable to please him, unable to bear children within a few years, they are then returned in total disgrace to their parents or other relatives."

"So you see, these teens are deeply rooted in the Easterlings customs, even though their mother was born in the Midlands. In spite of Nico's age, both managed to execute the *sesso disposto* custom. They were on top, were they not?" Both men flushed at the hint of such an intimate thing. "So they felt they had been successful and you then must accept them into your harem and provide for them as you would your wife or wives. That they are now both pregnant is rather like an official seal of approval."

Sheldon then said, "So what you are saying is we should not have allowed them to do their *sesso disposto* ceremony?"

Andreina sighed, *Men!* "How can I say this? If you had denied them the right to perform their *sesso disposto*, that would have caused them even more troubles, and they may well have not recovered from their Verge Sickness. They would have lost their will to live. No matter what choices you might have made, one thing is certain. They would have gotten the Verge Sickness anyway. Their lives were up-heaved so badly and so suddenly and at the worst possible time for them as they came into womanhood, they would have gotten sick from that alone. If you toss in total rejection, they would not have desired to live. My bet is they'd have died in spite of our mammoth effort to save them."

"I see. So we must accept the fact they believe they are our wives now," Sheldon concluded.

"Yes, make the best of it. Nico is pretty and a fine young woman as far as I can tell. Very much on the useless side as far as I am concerned, but then you know me," Andreina teased him.

"You mean because she insists on being bound?"

"Yes, and her very long nails. While they are sexy, they are not very practical. I do not believe either teen knows much about managing a house, much less anything else that Gabi and I do."

"So I'm stuck with nothing more than a pretty wall flower who gives good sex?" Sheldon asked bluntly.

Gabi broke into a hearty laugh. Both men flushed. Andreina answered, "Well, that is one way of looking at it, Sheldon. However, you should talk with them and find out what they are able to do. I'm sure their parents taught them something. Most likely they are knowledgeable about people and motives, able to assist their husbands in ruling their clan, that sort of thing. But I like your image: wall flowers. Cool. That's one thing that we cherish in Betta and Fel, they can be wall flowers when they wish and can be fighters when they need to be, and they have a knack for keeping a home in good order, unlike Gabi and me, who hate household chores, though we can be wall flowers when we choose to be."

Felix took all this in and then asked, "Sheldon, the real question is how far can we trust these teens? How far will their loyalty go to us? We are both virtually strangers to them. We have conflicting customs. Do we bring them onboard with our crystal discoveries and get them attuned to one so that their gifts are amplified too? Do we trust them enough to bring them into our experiments?"

"Good question, Felix, and one you'd better be asking," Gabi pointed out. "My thoughts are if you treat them with kindness and respect and help them maintain their self-respect with their traditions, then they will have no reason not to be loyal to you. It is possible when other clan leaders meet them and see their situation; they might attempt to bribe them and even to steal them away from you, but only with the women's consent, mind you. If they felt they were not being respected or were mistreated, they would have reason to consent to treasonous acts. Lacking that, they have very little choice but to be loyal to you both; they are utterly dependent upon you now. Bound women have a difficult time supporting themselves by working for a living. Only the lowest Castas women even make such an attempt to survive on their own in the world. It is just too challenging to do that while being bound. We chose the Sisterhood to escape that eternal mess. None of us has ever regretted it."

They got back to the mundane chores at hand. Felix, who had never done a hard day's labor with his hands before, felt a rush of satisfaction at the end of each day. His blisters felt good somehow. By moving day, the teens had fully recovered and wanted to help with the move. However, Felisa and Nico took their new husbands and Lilly aside. Felisa asked, "Please, my husband. Why are we still with these Sisterhood women? They are looked upon with disgust or worse by our people. Yet, we are going to move into their new home and share life with them. Nico and I do not understand this. Lilly has said that you are heir to a great *Círculo de la Torres* in some far away land. Why is it that we do not go to our *Círculo de la Torres* here in Adelmira?"

"We chose to live with people who we trust, respect, and admire, Felisa, Nico. While those in your tower here are fine women, we do not count them as our close friends. These four Sisterhood women have been our trail guides, protected us, taught us many of your customs, saved our lives, and two are bearing my children. Out of all the people in Adelmira, these four women, outcasts in your society they may be, I trust with my life and that of my wives. I respect them and admire them.

They are our friends and have shared in my *mentales* experiments. In fact, both of you owe your lives to their immense healing skills. By living with them under their roof, I know my wives and Sheldon's wife will be totally safe from harm. Those four women will give their lives to keep you three safe from harm. Does that help you understand?"

"Yes, thank you for explaining this, my husband," Felisa replied, thinking this through. At last, she accepted his explanation. The packing and moving got underway.

When they were finally ready and the wagons loaded, Andreina sent to Felix and Sheldon, *You should walk with them to our new home. I know it will be very slow walking and take quite some time, but they will feel honored to walk at your side to their new home. Gabi and I will take the wagons on ahead along with our free-mates.*

Felix spoke up, "Lilly, Felisa, will you accompany me as we walk to our new home?" Sheldon said something similar to Nico. The sudden smiles on both teen's faces spoke volumes of Andreina's wisdom.

With one arm around Lilly's waist and his other around Felisa's, steadying them both, they began their twelve block walk. Sheldon and Nico walked just behind them. Felisa held her head high, walking proudly through the streets of Adelmira, albeit with two inch steps. By now, both men were somewhat accustomed to moving slowly. He knew that he had scored a small victory with Felisa and Nico. Even Lilly seemed to be enjoying the long walk herself. Walking along so slowly, Felix suddenly realized that at this leisurely pace, he was able to get a very good look at the world around him, quite different from what he was accustomed to seeing from his normal walking speed or from horseback. The world seemed to slow down somehow, and he spent much more time with his wives as a result. Was there something else behind these strange Easterlings customs? He leaned over and kissed each on their cheeks in turn, bringing smiles to their faces.

Later, he led them into their new suite — well, two adjacent rooms connected with a doorway in their middle wall. He'd removed the door. This will be our study and workroom and this will be our bedroom. I see that they've already piled our things in here, so why don't you ladies start unpacking and I'll fetch us something to drink?"

With their few things stored in their new drawers and their bed made, Felix gathered Lilly and Felisa together with Sheldon and Nico. "Nico, Felisa, it is time that we bring you formally into our lives, that you may share even more with us." He carefully explained what they had discovered about the special crystals, though he carefully avoided giving away where they had actually found them. Finally, he presented each teen with her own large crystal. He and Sheldon helped them attune their stones to themselves and then test them out. Both teens were shocked to discover that their gifts were incredibly amplified by these stones.

"I swear Felix that I will always be faithful to you and I will always use my gifts to help you. Just let me know what is needed and when. Lilly, I will be faithful to you as well, assisting you always in any way I can, since you are Number One. I will protect you with my life as is proper for Number Two. I so swear, Lilly," Felisa stated very formally and properly. Nico told Sheldon something quite similar. "I know I will always be second to you, Lilly. That is only right and proper that I am, since you are his first. Felix, you must always kiss her before you kiss me. Always help and satisfy Lilly before me. It would be a terrible offense for you to do me before her. It would be an awful slap in her face, her honor."

"Got it, Felisa. If I make other goofs, I trust you will tell me about them right away. I certainly do not wish to dishonor Lilly or you." She smiled.

That evening as the three prepared for bed, Felix wondered how in the world this could possibly work out with all three sleeping in one bed. Already, Felisa had unbraided Lilly's hair, but Lilly was having a very hard time doing hers, because her left arm was totally useless. "Will you allow me to brush out your hair, Felisa?"

"Yes, that will be proper. Lilly, I am so sorry your arm is dead and useless. I feel just awful having you try to do it one handed. You won't be upset if he does mine?"

Lilly laughed, "Not at all. So many things are so damnably hard for me to do now and my voice sounds so funny without my teeth." Felix then brushed out her hair, with Lilly giving him pointers. Then, he helped each out of their skirts and into a thin nightgown. He pulled their covers down, but Felisa stepped up to him holding their two leather arm bindings. Lilly saw her and said to him, "Dear, you should do me first, right Felisa?"

She nodded and corrected him a little. "Pull the strings tighter. Our lower arms should be quite snug but not overly tight. Let me check. Yes, now you have it right." She positioned her arms behind her back waiting her turn. "A little tighter. There, you have it just right. We ought not be able to move them at all. Now Lilly, toss your hair over your front like this." She then showed her how to slip easily into bed such that her hair would lie between herself and Felix. She got back up and made sure that Lilly did it right. "No, now you slip in, Felix. I will be last on this side of you. Remember to kiss her before me. Do her, then me. Never the other way around. I must always be second."

The next morning over breakfast, Felix announced, "Okay everyone. I have decided that it is time we do more research with our new *Círculo de mentes*. We will introduce Felisa and Nico to it. What I want to do is to see if there is anything our combined powers, amplified by both the joined circle and our crystals, can do to somehow heal Lilly. Question one: is there any way that we can somehow grow a new set of teeth in her mouth? Question two: what has been done to the fingers on her left hand, her hand, and just below her elbow? We know that Lilly experienced intense pain as if they were actually being cut off. Yet, they were not. So what has been done? Question three: can we find a way to reverse it and restore Lilly's fingers and hand?"

Gabi added, "Question four is what can we do to help Fel be able to see again?"

"But I can't have my eyes back. I promised Lysandra," Fel protested.

"No, dear that you can't, but surely something can be done," Gabi suggested. "But thanks to Felix, we know that we all can learn to do other gifts."

Nico volunteered, "Maybe if she could have one of the

little things I can do, that would help. It is mostly a little trick, I think. I can see from someone else's eyes."

"Say, would you allow me to join with you and see what it is that you see? Perhaps this is the answer for Fel," Felix asked politely. He didn't know if Nico would allow such an intimate contact with another man other than Sheldon. If so, he'd go with Sheldon's opinion.

"Well, I suppose I should," Nico said hesitantly, looking at Felisa for confirmation. Felisa nodded and shortly Felix joined with Nico. *Amazing, Nico. Yes, this will help Fel immensely. Good idea.*

Can we really learn how to do new gifts, ones we were not born with?

Sure. It is hard, but we all have done just that. You will see. Will you help Fel learn how to see like you do?"

Yes, that would be the right thing to do, I think.

When they formed up their *Círculo de mentes*, Felix found that the teens were very adept at merging into the total rapport with Betta and Fel and they accepted him almost as easily. Sheldon took up his usual position as their regulator, while Gabi and Andreina provided physical protection of them all, swords at the ready, though no one expected any real trouble to come their way. However, with the others lost to the real world around them, someone had to take responsibility for their safety. Later on, Lilly added that detail to her growing rules book.

After a day's study, Felix came up with a plan. Over dinner, he explained his idea. "We are going to build her a new set of teeth, one tooth at a time. I can see the tiny particles that ought to be in one's tooth. I will filter them from her blood and deposit them one particle at a time in their proper place. Given enough time, we ought to be able to make her a whole new set of teeth."

That worked, though it took them six months of tedious work. Lilly had to drink a considerable amount of goat's milk to keep the needed particles readily available for Felix to move into position. When they finished, Lilly's new teeth looked completely like her original ones. She could not tell the difference because every tiny difference that she detected was quickly remedied by Felix.

During these early weeks, Nico and Fel worked together and within a week Fel was able to see through another's eyes. The other person was only vaguely aware that Fel was actually seeing what they were seeing. After this point, Fel always kept some of her daily psi-energies back to power her new sight. By the time Lilly's teeth were remade, it was second nature for Fel to see from other's viewpoints.

Felix also discovered the major basic gifts that Felisa and Nico possessed. Both had an uncanny ability to tell when another was either lying or not revealing the whole truth. Secondarily, they both were able to heal others in various ways. Felisa also could absorb another's illness by bringing it into her own body and, once there, curing it. Nico, on the other hand, had an uncanny ability to empathize with another. Of everyone in the small group, Nico could go into rapport with anyone else with the greatest of ease.

Now that Lilly could eat properly, they all took turns trying to discover what had been done to her arm and fingers. This time, Felisa found the answer. Neurons had been severed around each finger, her wrist, and then just below her elbow. Almost three months later, the *Círculo de mentes* had rebuilt those destroyed neurons, particle by particle. At long last, Lilly was whole once more, just in time for the many births.

With five births expected within a few weeks of each other and with all acutely aware of <u>Marisol's Mentales Rule Book</u> and particularly Rule 3A that dealt with childbirth in which mother, father, and baby were known to have the gift. Felix decided not to gamble and sent for the tower's midwife. Nilda was fifty and very pudgy, nothing to look at, but she was a veteran, having delivered nearly three dozen children.

"Expect everything to go wrong and prepare for the worst," Nilda explained to the whole group when she first met with them. "That way, we can be thankful when none of that is actually needed. Now then, with five of you so close, it is best that I stay here with you. I don't like having to be roused out of bed at three in the morning and go shuffling across half of the city only to arrive too late to be of any use."

"Of course, Nilda. We have a room prepared for you,"

Lilly replied. "We will also see to your nightly needs, of course."

"Well, that is as it should be," she said sternly, glancing at both Andreina and Gabi, who wore men's clothing as far as she was concerned.

July of 1071 became known as baby-month. Fel was the first to give birth. Nilda insisted that Felix go into rapport with Fel and share in the pain and joy of the birthing. His job was to keep both mother and child calm and relaxed as much as possible, monitoring their nerve channels and helping eliminate the attendant channel blockages that resulted in pain for the mother and child. He received an education before his four children were finally born. Under Nilda's guidance, all minor problems were handled before they could threaten either mother or child.

Felix allowed Fel, Betta, and Felisa to name their baby daughters as they desired, while he and Lilly decided on their son's name. Fel named their daughter Tecla, glory of God, after Lysandra. Betta gave birth two days later to their daughter Vitalia. Barely a week after that, Felisa gave birth to their daughter Savina, meaning follower of a different religion, since Felix was from the Midlands. Savina was destined to have flaming red hair, like her mother. Three days later, Sheldon and Nico had a daughter whom they named Pierina. Two days later, Lilly gave birth to their son, Tom.

In July of 1073, the next round of babies was born. Felix was the father of Andreina's son, Basilio, Gabi's son, Dario, Felisa's daughter Michela, and Lilly's daughter, Rosina. Sheldon and Nico had a son whom they named Dante. After that point in time, Felix intended to return to the Midlands and they wisely agreed to put off having more children until they had made the arduous journey back to the Kingdom of the Angels.

Chapter 18 The Genesis of the Brom Compact

By August, the mothers and babies were doing fine and Felix decided that it was time to share their discoveries with the Adelmira *Círculo de la Torres*. Because this particular tower had no males present in positions of power, he decided to have Lilly and Felisa accompany him, though they had to bring along their infants. Midmorning, a baby in each arm and a large bag over his back, Felix stepped out into the sunbaked street and waited for Lilly and Felisa to join him. Both women look positively beautiful and radiant in his eyes as they slowly shuffled to his side.

The long walk was enjoyed by all. "See, this is another reason for having bound women," Lilly teased him. "You get to carry our babies for us."

He laughed, "But I'd do it anyway. Both are as beautiful as their mothers."

"Ha, once maybe," she teased back. Both Felisa and Lilly thoroughly enjoyed the rather large amount of attention Felix gave to them. From her own experiences growing up, Lilly knew Felix was giving her and Felisa at least ten times as much attention as her father had given her mother, brother, and herself as they grew up. She saw this as yet another benefit of the binding tradition of the Easterlings. Men had to pay far more attention to their wives than was ever done in the Midlands. She suspected the bond between husband and wife here was much closer and stronger than in her homeland, and she attributed it now to their tradition of bindings. Even the overall pace of life seemed much slower here, time to observe and notice the world around you, something she'd rarely done while growing up back home. *If only men could learn to be this loving without women having to be tortured with these bindings, the world would be a better place.*

Midmorning, they sat on one side of the long table in the tower's Guest Dining Hall, watching as the women shuffled in and took their seats. Eight women had been chosen to meet and learn from Felix. Then, if they found what he had to teach warranted it, all the others in the tower would join them. All were Amas, of course. Leading the women was the tower leader, Ama Floriana Via, the stern, highly opinionated woman they had met when they first arrived here over a year ago. Benigna, Clara, and Domenica followed her. They recognized them from their previous short stay here. Two of the volunteers from the Midlands followed behind them. They recognized Alice and Lana at once. The two had accompanied them on their long journey from the Midlands to Adelmira last year. Both gave Felix and Lilly a broad smile and nodded at their baby, who Lilly was now cradling since she was seated. Two other women who neither had seen before brought up the rear, Alessia and Ambra.

"Thank you all for coming. Lilly and I wish to share with your tower some absolutely stunning discoveries we have made. Your tower is the first to receive our gifts, and, when you learn the magnitude of them, you will better appreciate the enormity of what we are doing for you. Now then, let me begin at the beginning," Felix began, once the introductions and small talk was finished. Several women were somewhat pleased Felix had a small harem going now, as was the custom here in the Easterlings.

"You have noticed these crystals we three have hanging around our necks, covered in a special form of silk found in the Midlands. I call them Germanium Crystals, for want of any name known to me. When found in nature, they are inert. Yet, they have a unique property. They can be attuned to any person's unique psi-frequency. Even the head blind can be attuned to one of these. What do they do? Simply put, they amplify our psi-gifts almost a hundredfold, depending upon the size of the crystals. The one an inch or less amplify perhaps tenfold. The ones that we are wearing expand our energies a hundredfold. Once attuned to a person, they glow continuously and when used, the glow can become blinding for a brief time. Once attuned, they cannot be attuned to another person or 'turned off.' In either case, the crystal shatters and is destroyed."

"This is only the beginning of our discoveries and

researches. Without further discussion, I will hand each of you an inert crystal. We three will then help each of you become attuned to your crystal. We encourage you to see for yourself what the crystals can do. To activate them, merely hold them in your hand and squeeze them."

Two hours later, the eight women were more than "convinced" of their amazing discovery. All resistance to the new ideas had vanished completely. "Do you realize the tremendous importance and impact of these stones, Amo Felix?" Ama Floriana said, highly enthusiastically. Gone were all traces of her stern, stoic countenance.

"These are amazing, beyond description even," Ama Alessia added. The others added more explicative words to the mix. Their new crystals worked perfectly, amplifying their *mentales* gifts a hundredfold or so. "I am able to see across all the Easterlings lands now and with the greatest of ease! Unbelievable!"

"You said this is only the beginnings of what you and Lilly have discovered," Ama Alice added. "I cannot imagine what else there could be!"

Lilly grinned, "Oh, I assure you, there is a whole lot more!"

"We must have these for all our women here," Ama Floriana stated. "How are we to obtain more of these crystals? What is the price that we must pay for them?"

"With them comes immense power," Felix answered. "It is my request that all those who desire a personal Germanium Crystal obtain theirs from their local *Círculo de la Torres* along with help in attuning it to their own psi-frequency and training in its proper use. You here will be the dispensers of these crystals to all those in the Easterlings. With the power we hold, coupled with the rest of what I will be sharing with your tower first, it is time we put an end to these constant wars among the clans and kings. I'm sick of all the senseless wars and attendant carnage."

"Felisa here is one such victim. Her parents were killed in a clan battle that left only her and her sister alive. Alone in the desert, they would have perished had we not found them. My friend and I have taken them on as our wives to prevent them from dying or from having to live the rest of their lives in complete disgrace. These petty wars and disputes simply have to end. With the powers we with the *mentales* gifts can now possess, it is my wish and belief that we can put an end to all this senseless bloodshed. That is my sole goal: to end all wars on Tierra, beginning here in the Easterlings."

"How will such an admirable thing be possible?" asked Ama Alessia. "You do know that Wystan has been awakened and is fomenting wars across the world."

"When you have received all my gifts and have been fully trained in their use, you will see that there is nothing that we, as a unified tower group, as a *Círculo de mentes*, cannot do. That is the name we are calling our special group. We have discovered that it is possible for a whole group of us to join in a close rapport, combining our individual, greatly amplified psi-energies into one huge pool, controlled and directed by one of our group." He paused to let the idea be absorbed.

"We put this into practice. At the time that we rescued Felisa and Nico, we were being held prisoner and Lilly was being tortured. All her teeth had been removed and her left fingers, hand, and lower arm had been made dead, wholly unusable, unfeeling, and useless. Using our *Círculo de mentes* and its combined power, I was able in six months' time to remake all her teeth. See for yourselves. Her teeth are back, as good as before they were pulled. We found what damage had been done to her neurons and made new, replacement neurons and now she has regained the full use of her left arm. A miracle, as far as I am concerned."

Once more, the meeting broke up into a lengthy chat, with the women examining Lilly's teeth and left arm. At last, Ama Alessia spoke up, "He is speaking the whole truth. All is as he has claimed. Truly, a new day has come to Tierra. Perhaps Wystan can be defeated after all!"

Felix then continued his presentation. "Now, Ama Floriana asked about the crystals. Because of the vital role that the Sisterhood here in Adelmira played in the acquisition of them, I owe them a very great debt. Henceforth, as I have promised them, all needed inert crystals will be acquired from the Sisterhood. Only they and I know where they may be found. By our agreement, they will only charge a nominal fee to cover their expenses in acquiring them, plus enough profit for them to survive."

"The Sisterhood?" Ama Floriana grumbled, clearly disapproving of his choice.

"Absolutely. I cannot trust men with this task." That comment brought affirmative head shakes from all eight women. "I trust these women with my life and have done so. They and they alone can guarantee the safety and integrity of these precious crystals for us. Ama Floriana, you can send word to the Sisterhood here in Adelmira, requesting as many of the crystals and their sizes that you desire, and they will bring them to you in exchange for their small fee. I leave the disbursement and training of the recipients up to you and your tower here. When I return to the Midlands, I will be doing the same thing with each tower there as well."

"Well, we can live with this arrangement," she acknowledged. Ama Floriana realized just how powerful this would be making her tower here in Adelmira, the lone tower in the entire Easterlings lands.

"I thought that you would. After we get everyone here attuned to their crystals, we will begin training you on how to form and operate a *Círculo de mentes*. In addition, there is one more discovery that Lilly and I have made. While we are all born with some initial *mentales* gifts so excellently catalogued by Marisol, what we have discovered is we all can learn to use other gifts that we were not born with!"

As expected, this shook them all up considerably. Until he announced this, it was common knowledge one only had and could do those gifts he or she was born with, bred for in many cases these days. That one could learn to do other ones was not only startling but also opened vast new doors, if it was so.

Thus began a year-long training session. There were twenty women housed in the tower but a dozen men also received their crystals and some training. Additionally, Ama Alessia and Ama Ambria brought another fifteen women into the tower to be fully trained as well. Felix began working with them in small circles of four at a time and worked with two such circles each day. By fall, the initial supply of crystals had been exhausted, and Ama Floriana put aside her bias and met with Andreina to work out delivery of another hundred such crystals. Those were destined to go to the known men and women who had the gift and were part of the many clans scattered over the Easterlings. Just how they would be handed out and trained had yet to be worked out.

In December, Ama Alessia asked to meet privately with Felix and he agreed only if Felisa and Lilly were also present. He'd grown to trust Felisa and her truth gift. Per Alessia's request, they met just after noon on the north side of the small oasis, out in the open, where they could be spied upon, but not overheard. Felisa pointed this out to them as the three slowly reached the designated location. He helped the women sit upon the hard packed sand, and they took the opportunity to cool their feet in the clear, blue, life-giving waters. Soon, they saw Alessia making her slow shuffle towards them. Felix rose and assisted Ama Alessia to sit beside them.

"Thank you for meeting me this way. As you know, I have the gift of far seeing. Right at this moment in time, there are ten battles or wars as you call them that are ongoing across the Easterlings. I believe another six are close to being executed as well. I bring this to your attention because as you also know, Ama Floriana is about to receive the next batch of the crystals and will be starting the long, slow process of handing them out to the many men and women throughout the Easterlings who have the *mentales* gifts."

"Yes, I am aware of her plans to do that. I didn't know there were so many wars in progress, though. Damn them anyway. Don't they realize how devastating they are to everyone?" Felix's ire rose again.

"Much is Wystan's doing, I suspect. I too have a problem with what Ama Floriana is planning to do. If she gives these crystals to the others outside the tower, then they will most certainly be asked by their leaders to use their enhanced powers to help them win their petty wars. This bothers me enormously, as I hope it does you," she said calmly, but not without conviction.

"I agree. It is time that we put an end to these petty

wars," Felix replied.

"But how?"

"I have given the tower powers that greatly exceed any single person who has a crystal. I think the answer lies in making the *Círculo de la Torres* of Adelmira the sole ruler of the entire Easterlings lands. The clans can have their leaders and kings or whatever, but all answer to the higher ruler, the *Círculo de la Torres*. With their combined circles, they wield enormous powers now. It is time we of the *mentales* gifts assume full responsibility for ruling and governing our world. Only we have the power to stop these infernal and wasteful wars and petty battles. We must do so. I have given us such enormous powers so that none can defy us, if only we exercise our will and responsibilities, assuming the mantle of rulers."

"So you would put Ama Floriana and her tower women in charge of all the Easterlings lands?" she asked.

"Yes, I do not believe she would start a war or a battle. I know she is biased against the Sisterhood, but she has proven to at least be fair with everyone."

"Okay, then I accept your suggestion. How will you be able to get this implemented across the Easterlings? A century ago, we had four huge kingdoms, but now we have hundreds of smaller clans spanning nearly three thousand miles north-south and two thousand east-west. The tower here is but a tiny dot in all that vastness," she pointed out.

"We use our gifts. I know it will take some convincing, but it can be done. It is high time that we take responsibility for leading our world into a century of peace and growth and prosperity," he said with conviction, though not truly answering her question.

She is hiding something. I've sensed it for many days now. There is something that Alessia is just not telling you. She has not outright lied to you, but she is withholding something of importance, I think, Felisa sent him.

"I take it that you have strong doubts about all this, Ama Alessia. Is there something you are not telling me that I ought to know?" he decided to act upon his wife's intuition.

He sensed a brief elevation in her body's temperature and a twitch in her right hand. He knew he'd hit the mark somehow. *Damn, he knows something. How much, I wonder? Are my barriers that weak? Calm. There. He has built this whole relationship on trust. Yet, am I somehow making him think I am breaking that trust? If so, this may well lead a man to very wrong actions. Trust must go both ways.*

"Few know this. Can you three be sworn to absolute secrecy? Can you promise me never to relay what I am to tell you to others?" Ama Alessia asked formally. All three swore and she accepted their pledges.

"I am the High Priestess of Lysandra, leader of the secret Matera Sanctuary for Women. Only Ama Floriana knows of my identity. The others accept me as an Ama from a nearby village. We provide sanctuary and protection for women who are in dire need and peril. More, I dare not say."

"Thank you. By chance did you have anything to do with Fel Fina-Fulvia's prayer?" he asked.

"I heard her prayer and relayed it to Lysandra, Goddess of Life and Death. Our goddess did as she thought appropriate. No more can I say of that, for I know no more."

"Okay. Are you then satisfied with what I am proposing, that the tower here become the sole ruler of the entire Easterlings lands?" he asked what he thought was far more important.

"If you can somehow bring peace to our lands, then I am satisfied. Though I cannot help wondering if in doing so you will be upsetting Wystan?" she replied.

"I deal with men, not with gods, Ama Alessia. I will do my best to end wars. I have pledged my life to that end. It is the reason I have done all the research and experiments to date. Wars must end soon."

"Few women will argue against that, though many men will. Good luck with it. I must go now. Thank you for seeing me."

"Thank you for trusting us," he replied. She smiled and he helped her get to her feet and begin her slow shuffle away from the waters.

"Say, Lilly, your nails are now as long as mine. At last, I can let mine grow again," Felisa pointed out.

"Yes, I can now scratch my nose without bending over,"

Lilly added. "Dear," she explained to Felix, "the long nails extend the reach of our hands." He chuckled and helped them rise.

As the new year came, 1073, Ama Floriana and Felix began the massive project, beginning with the clan leader here in Adelmira, Adamo Adelmira. First, he was given a demonstration of just what the crystals could do. Then he was presented with what became known as the Brom Compact to sign. As experience was gained, Felix altered the wording slightly, but it remained intact in its essence.

Brom Compact

I, _____, swear my allegiance to the _____ tower and proclaim that they are the sole rulers of the lands called _____.

I swear to never start or participate in any battle or war that is not sanctioned by my tower beforehand.

I swear to carry out the laws and orders of my tower.

Twice a year, I will send a representative to my tower to receive the latest news and orders, if any.

In return, I will provide my tower _____ annually so that they may be free to spent their entire time ruling our lands without distractions.

In return, my tower will provide security for my clan and prevent any wars or battles from entering lands under my control.

I retain the right to rule my lands as I choose, but I will obey any laws that my tower dictates, as these supersede mine.

Any matters that I cannot settle peacefully, I can bring to my tower for their adjudication, and I will abide with their decisions.

I and any of my people who have the *mentales* gift shall receive a Germanium Crystal from my tower.

Said crystals will be attuned to the person and they will receive the necessary training to use it from my tower, all at no cost to me or said persons.

This crystal agreement applies to all present and future residents of my lands who have the gift.

This contract applies now and into the future, independent

of time.

Should I or my heirs break the compact, it is understood that the tower will take appropriate actions to bring us back into compliance by any and all means of their choosing.

Signed _____

Date _____

Witness _____

The representative of the Kingdom of Adelmira signed without any persuasion needed. The crystal demonstrations convinced him. However, most were not so easily persuaded.

For example, the Adriano and Fonso clans were engaged in a war over land rights. Ama Floriana had no choice but to intervene. Using the power of her combined *Círculo de mentes*, she put an end to the battle. One by one, the men's weapons were ripped from their hands and discarded a long way away. Those who were engaged in close hand to hand combat were picked up bodily and tossed some distance apart. She used any means possible to halt the battle, short of harming the men, just as Felix had anticipated. Apparent supernatural powers can be a mighty convincer. Once the two leaders were convinced that she would not permit them to continue their battle, both men began to listen to reason. Of course, she then had to send copies of the compact to where they were located to have them sign. In return, they sent back many of their *mentales* gifted to be given their crystals and trained.

Most of the haggling was over what tribute had to be sent to the tower yearly. In this, Ama Floriana was very clever. She took what that land had in plenty, usually food, livestock, or horses. In time, the tower would have an abundance of food at all times and could begin to be an effective ruler over the vast lands of the Easterlings.

All this traveling took far more time than Felix had anticipated. When his second round of fatherhood came in 1073, they'd only begun to get the hundreds of clans to sign. While he wanted it to happen overnight, he soon realized with the limited resources of the tower, it would be years in the doing. Ama Floriana began adding staff, especially men, to handle the long distance traveling to get the compacts signed, while her people monitored those who had promised to sign and were awaiting the arrival of the compact. More than once, she had to intervene a second or third time, before the leaders physically signed.

To help Andreina and Gabi, four more Sisterhood members arrived in late 1073. Already the fees that the Sisterhood was making had accumulated to a substantial sum, bringing notice to their top leaders back in Hilliard Heights. They promised to send another eight volunteers in the summer of 1074.

While Felix and Sheldon helped with the next round of their wives' childbirths, Felix commented, "This is taking far longer than I anticipated, but it is going to work. We should start making plans to return to our homeland." With this in mind, they all agreed to forgo having more children until they finished the long journey home. Unfortunately, this did not happen until early 1080. So many details had to be worked out, problems solved, small modifications made, that Felix felt he could not depart until he was certain that the Easterlings would be fully handled.

In January 1080, he received word that his father had passed away in his sleep. That meant, as heir to the Brom tower, he had no choice but to return there as soon as possible. Besides that, all the other towers were demanding that he return and bring these incredible stones with him and train their circles as well. Word spread during those eight years. He had little choice now. Fortunately, the Sisterhood also anticipated this move and sent along three dozen of their fighters to escort him and his precious crystals back to Brom tower.

Chapter 19 Adjustments and Implementation

"Family meeting, family meeting," Felix called out, then added, "big family meeting!" His nine year old son, Tom, laughed.

"That's more like it pop," he teased his dad as the many women came shuffling into the large dining room of the Sisterhood home. "Come on, Dante, Basilio, Dario — sit by me." He waved his hands to the three seven year old boys, who were only too eager to get away from all the women and girls.

The four Sisterhood free-mates, Andreina, Betta, Gabi, and Fel, took seats at one end of the long table and their two daughters, Vitalia and Tecla, sat quietly beside their mothers. They knew their father was going to be leaving soon and that they would be remaining with their mothers and their free-mates, along with their two boys, Basilio and Dario.

At the other end, Felisa and Lilly sat on either side of Felix. Felisa's two daughters sat beside her, Savina and Michela. Lilly's daughter Rosina sat beside her mother. The four boys sat along one side, in between them. Opposite them, Captain Sheldon and Nico sat with their daughter Pierina who was next to her mother. This evening, all the women were bound as was the custom here in the Easterlings. Andreina and Gabi knew the significance of this meeting and dressed accordingly. For them, this would be a parting of ways, and they wanted Felix to remember them as Easterlings first, Sisterhood women second, and that they had free choice.

"Okay, I see that everyone is here. Good. I have received the news that my father has died in his sleep. What does this mean for us? Simple. I have no choice now but to return to Brom tower in the Kingdom of the Angels, Midlands. As his only heir, I am now the leader of that tower and I cannot do otherwise than to don that mantle. I must continue with my life's mission of ending wars everywhere on Tierra. To do that, I must get the Brom Compact in force both in the Midlands and in the Westerlings lands. Hence, within a few days' time, I must finally return to my homeland, far, far to the west."

"Lilly and I have spent nearly a decade here among the Easterlings and I dare say she and I have learned a lot about you, some good, some not so good. We've made lifelong friends here and we will sorely miss you. I don't know if I will ever have the opportunity to return for a visit, but I will try. No promises though."

"I've called this family meeting, big family meeting, to allow some of you a choice. Lilly, Tom, and Rosina will be returning with me. Per our agreement with these fine Sisterhood dear friends, our children will remain here with you, their mothers, unless you women chose otherwise. Vitalia, Tecla, Basilio, Dario, I am not abandoning you. If you ever wish to come to the Midlands, just let me know. You will always have a home there with me, if ever you want it. That goes for your mothers too."

"The hard decisions must be made by Felisa and Nicolina here. The customs and traditions in the Midlands are vastly different from here in the Easterlings. Binding of women not only doesn't exist, but would be highly frowned upon. If you were to appear bound as you are now, you would be looked upon as some kind of freaks, just as we must have first appeared to you when we arrived. Women's dress is quite different. Fetter skirts simply do not exist in the Midlands and even so, they would be wholly impractical. You see, our climate is vastly different than here."

"Summer days in the foothills of the Goza Mountains are unlike even your wintertime days here. On a good day, the temperature in the afternoon might reach into the eighties, but it also rains heavily by afternoon, turning to sleet and sometimes snow by evening. In winter, the snow depths can reach over ten feet before the spring melt comes, sometimes thirty feet in big drifts. Here the land is rather smooth and sandy. Where we come from, the land is very hilly and rocky. In fetter skirts, you would not even be able to walk through the streets of our town, too many ups and downs for you to navigate. Women often wear pants out of necessity."

"What I am trying to say, Felisa and Nico, is that if you were to accompany us back to our home in the Midlands, you would have to change not only your dress, but discard your bindings and learn totally foreign customs. For example, in the Midlands, no man has more than one wife; we don't have harems. In short, this is an enormous bunch of changes for you, and I have no right at all to force you into this nor do I have any right to ask you to do this for me."

"So Felisa and Nico, Sheldon and I want to give you a choice. You can come with us but you will have to make many drastic and possibly uncomfortable changes and adaptions to our culture or you can stay here in Adelmira. If you wish to stay, I will guarantee your keep. You will not want for funds or a place to live. You can say that your husbands are off on a long business trip to the Midlands, for that is the truth of the matter. We will try to return for visits, but I cannot say if that will be possible or how frequently. If you prefer, you can be free to take other husbands. Still, Sheldon and I will provide for the raising of our children. In no case will we forsake our loving, darling children. They, like you two, are precious to us."

Felisa, fighting back tears, asked, "You do not love us? I would not then be your Number Two wife?"

"Oh no, Felisa. I do love you. I have grown very fond of you. I would like nothing more than to have you at my side opposite Lilly. You would be called my Royal Consort if you came back with me. But if you and Nico come with us, you will have so much you will have to change, from discarding your bindings and skirts, to learning to dress as Midlands women, to learning a whole new set of values and even our language. You will have to give up so much and make so many changes that I must let you decide for yourselves if you want to do this. Sheldon and I both know these changes will be terribly hard for you to make. We love you too much to force this upon you."

Nico spoke up, her voice deeply troubled. "You, you are giving us free choice? But we are bound to you and Sheldon. We must always do what you ask of us. That is our way."

In that instant, Felix finally understood Felisa and Nico and all the other women in the room, including Lilly. All women on Tierra were bound; none was truly free to make any and all choices in their lives! The bound women of the

Easterlings dramatized this with their physical bindings, while the Midlands women, like Lilly, were bound by cultural and mental bindings, just as strong and powerful as the fetter skirts and copper chains of the Easterlings. She had no choice but to marry him and bear his children, a brood mare disguised as a woman. Only the Sisterhood women could approach the freedom that the men of Tierra had, but even they had their own bindings, different from the others, but constrained nearly as effectively. Only the women in the towers had more freedom of choice than the other women of Tierra, but they were just as bound, bound to the towers.

I told you so, Andreina sent him. She couldn't help gloating, having argued this point on many occasions with him.

Dear, you will have to make the decision, Lilly sent him.

No matter how much he wanted to change this, to give women the same freedom of choice that he had, he knew in that instant he could not suddenly with one sweep of his hand change centuries of traditions and customs, no matter how badly he wanted to do so. Even worse, he saw he too was not entirely free, but was bound as well. He had no choice but to return and take his father's place; he had to marry Lilly and bear more children with their supposedly merged *mentales* gifts. *We are all stuck in barriers of different types. What then remains? Is there no hope at all?* He sighed; he could see none, save making the world a safer place to live by eliminating wars and battles.

"Okay, then I will make the decision. I love Felisa and our children. I will ask you come back with me to my home in the Midlands. I will do all I can to help you adapt and adjust to what will likely be a very difficult time for you. Our customs are very different from those here, Felisa." Sheldon told Nico much the same thing. Both men saw vast relief and huge smiles appear on the two sister's faces.

We will not be abandoned, Nico! Felisa sent to her sister. "We will do our best to change and make you proud of us, my husband."

He grinned lovingly at her. *She has no idea how hard it*

is going to be for her and her sister. "Thank you, I cannot ask for more. Andreina, Gabi, what about your sons? I know that Fel and Betta will be raising our daughters here."

Andreina sighed, "You know us only too well, Felix. Yes, our boys are almost too old now to be staying with us in the Sisterhood house. Rules, you know, but then we all knew this day would come. As much as Gabi, our free-mates, and I love our two boys, we want them to have the best chance to make something of themselves in life. We will accept your generous offer to take them with you."

"Oh boy! Basilio, Dario, you get to come with us!" Tom exclaimed very excitedly. Both younger boys grinned broadly; they had so hoped that they'd be allowed to go with Felix. Already, they had suffered a lot of teasing from the other local boys in Adelmira for being Sisterhood bastard boys.

"I swear to you that I will raise them no different than Tom and give them every chance possible," Felix promised, knowing how difficult this was for the four to give up their two boys. If only they had had two girls, they could have kept them. Still, he also knew that Vitalia and Tecla would also be given a choice later on; they would not have to become members of the Sisterhood if they didn't want to do so.

"Thank you, Felix. We know you will do just that," Andreina replied. "All I ask is you and Lilly continue to eliminate wars and strife on Tierra. That alone will allow all of us a better life."

"You can count on that, Andreina!" Felix answered.

"Cindy Rogan, Trailmaster," the tall, fit Sisterhood woman shook Felix's hand solidly. Her short shirt sleeves revealed well-toned arms. She had very short, black hair and a face with strong features. There was a bit of a husk in her voice. "Thirty-six fighters, sufficient food, and clothing for all your party, Amo Felix. My two seconds and Navigators, Cassie Fields e Watson and Bree Watson e Fields." Two shorter women stepped forward and shook his hand. While Cindy was as tall as he was, the other two were four inches shorter, but equally well-muscled. Good fighters, he presumed, judging by the way the two carried themselves. Cassie had sort black hair,

371

while her free-mate Bree had equally short brown hair. All three women's hair was at least a foot shorter than his. He'd allowed his to grow, as was the custom here in the Easterlings.

All rode the fine mounts from Hilliard Heights. They had three supply wagons and three carriages with them as well. He guessed that Cindy was perhaps forty while her two seconds were in their mid-thirties. "Thank you. Are you being well paid to escort us back? If not, I will see to it when we arrive."

Cindy gave a hearty laugh. "Aye, that we have been. You must be a very important man. You realize these are the very best Sisterhood fighters in all the Midlands? You must rate," she declared.

Felix noticed all three had the distinctive yellow-brown eyes. "Yes, we are perhaps the most important group on Tierra at the moment. Once we get going, Lilly and I will give you three and any others among you who have the *mentales* gifts a very big thank you present."

"Not necessary, Amo, we are already quite well paid. We ought to get underway as soon as possible. I don't know how any of you can stand this infernal heat here. We are all melting. I think I've lost ten pounds of sweat so far," she jested.

"You need the proper clothing to survive the heat," Lilly pointed out. That the many other women were staring at her fetter skirt and waist chains that bound her arms, she ignored. "We are all packed and ready, dear."

Cindy gave Lilly a look of dismay but said kindly, "That's good. The sooner we get underway, the better. I've horses for the boys, if they want to ride, but perhaps it would be best to have them ride in a carriage until we are well underway. Ama, will you wish to change clothing before we start?"

She asked politely, Lilly thought. "Not until we clear the Easterlings. This is going to be hard on the others. Let's give them some time to get used to the trail difficulties first." She knew that the girls and the two sisters would be mortified to be seen unbound while still within Easterlings lands.

Ever practical, dear. Good idea, Felix sent her.

"Can we have a private word with you, Amo Felix?" asked a serious looking Cassie. He nodded and she, Bree, and he moved off to the side of the Sisterhood inn where they could not be overheard. At first, he thought that they would launch a protest against the women traveling bound. Cassie unrolled a crude map of the Midlands and the Easterlings. "Here's the situation. Our commission is to get you all safely to Brom tower. Safely is the key word. Right now, we have known wars or battles taking place at these known locations marked with red dots."

"Good god! They are all over the place," Felix exclaimed. "I had no idea things have gotten this bad."

"Well, it looks perhaps worse than it is. It is winter and they have toned down somewhat. Some are small scale, you know. However, we had a devil of a time getting through them on our way here. We avoided the major ones, but still we don't want to take any risks with your safety. The safest route lies along the northern route, up here north of Walsham and Chester, coming down through the safe zone of Hilliard Heights. The problem, Amo, is we are two thousand miles south of the northern passage and it is the dead of winter up there. Can they possibly survive the harsh, bitterly cold travel?"

"I see your point. I doubt it. They've never been far from here; it's always hot around these lands. When we came here, we followed the Wyndl to Wye and went eastward to Northend before turning south. Is that out?" he asked.

"Yes, there are five different conflicts in that region that we know about. Plus, there is the usual heavy winter snow to hamper us. While we have our best fighters with us, we don't want to fight if we can avoid it. So our thoughts are to go south from here down to the sea coast, follow it over to Madya at the mouth of the Wyndl. From there, we parallel the Brockton River to Hayden's Crossing, then up to Oakham, Haverhills, Exchange City and on into Bedworth and home. Of course, we would be skirting five areas of known conflict along the way. We've heard that somehow you have gotten all these conflicts settled here in the Easterlings. If so, then it would be safe to head south through Alba and Matruk. We came here from the north, coming south from Northend."

"Yes, you've heard right. Most all have signed my Compact though there are still a few in the far north who have not."

"Well, while it sounds safer to go south then, what are the temperatures like and the weather and water situation?" Cassie asked the key questions she needed to know.

"Extremely hot and dry up here. Matruk, however, has become the Easterlings' breadbasket, though technically the land really lies within the Midlands. If we go straight south through Alba, the climate moderates significantly, since the rains can get through. No hills to stop them," he replied.

"Okay then our southern route seems the best considering the time of year and the women. The trip will be a little longer than the northern route and possibly a bit more dangerous, but it is the wisest," Cassie concluded. "We'll let Cindy know." They headed back to the group. Already Sheldon had lifted the women and girls up into one of the carriages. The boys commandeered the other carriage for themselves.

"We are ready to shove off," he told Felix. "I'll drive the boys, unless. . ."

"Perfect, Sheldon. I'll take the women. Okay, Cindy, lead on. We're ready." After he climbed into the driver's seat, he and everyone else began waving farewells. Then, they were off. Once clear of the oasis village, Cindy, Cassie, and Bree took point. Their supply wagons pulled in behind the boy's carriage, and the dozens of riders fanned out along their flanks with several bringing up the rear.

"Mom! Do you see all these man-women riding along with us?" Savina gushed. "They are all wearing pants! None of them are bound. Are they nuts or something? What's the matter with them? Are they like Aunt Gabi?"

"Yes, they are Sisterhood women. They are from the Midlands and have different customs," Felisa answered, also somewhat disturbed by them. She was used to Andreina and Gabi, but they were only two. Here were three dozen of them, quite unnerving to say the least.

"Well I don't like their customs! Did you see how they were all staring at us? I checked myself, but my skirt was fine, my blouse buttoned, my braids are straight and not messed up," Savina retorted defensively.

Lilly answered for Felisa, "They have probably never seen many Easterlings women before, Savina. In their eyes, we look weird, perhaps more so than they do to us. Women in the Midlands and Westerlings are never bound, not ever. Nor do they wear fetter skirts."

"Oh how hideously awful!" Savina exclaimed, which was what Felisa and Nico were thinking as well, though they politely didn't vocalize their opinions yet.

Lilly replied, "Well, as awful as it seems to us, our skirts and binding are simply not practical in the Midlands. Look, could you easily get yourself into and out of our carriage?"

"No, of course *not*. It is a man's *duty* to help us," Savina spouted what she had learned from her mother and others.

"Quite right. However, in the Midlands, the ground is very hilly and rocky. So much so that dressed as we are, we could not walk even five feet without a man carrying us. We simply cannot have men carrying us wherever we need to go, now can we?"

"Well, not *everywhere*, I suppose," Savina gave in a little.

"Also the weather is very cold and chilly, even in the summertime. Here, it is always hot. So we will need to wear much warmer clothing, particularly warmer tops. Plus, we need to put on heavy, warm coats and cloaks too. We simply could not do that while our arms are bound. In the Midlands, it is wholly impractical for us to go around dressed and bound as we are now."

"But, but we'll be dishonored, disgraced! We'll be naked without them!" Savina protested. "Mom, can't you talk dad into letting us be bound while we are inside the house?" she pleaded.

"I will, dear. I'm sure that he will allow us that much freedom and respect." Felisa certainly hoped so. To go to bed beside him unbound was a horrible sacrilege, a total disgrace, a complete dishonor both to her and to him. Of this, she was absolutely certain. Countering this was the equally strong admonition to never, ever disgrace her husband in public. She began to feel torn between the two.

When they finally made camp that night, the girls held their heads up proudly as Sheldon and Felix lifted them down from the carriage. The Sisterhood women wisely kept their distance from the two families, though they posted guards around them. Savina continued to keep her head up that evening, though she covertly spied on the women who were still staring at her and the others. It was a standoff.

Later when the men laid out the blankets for bed, each girl took her usual pose, placing her lower arms behind her back, waiting for Felix or Sheldon to come and bind them for the night. As they quietly proceeded to do so, Cindy sent him, *Amo! It is not wise to tie them up so, especially at night. How can they sleep? If we are attacked, they will be helpless!*

You know it and I know it, but they do not. They expect to be bound at night. I think for now it will be easier on them if we do it. I am hoping in the next few days that I can nudge them out of their traditional ways, he replied. *Already, they have sacrificed not having their hair unbraided at night. One small step at a time, please.*

The next day, they began heading due south through the relatively dry, rolling hills, though the Buku Hills could still be seen on the horizon some distance behind them. Before long, the tough desert grasses began to give way to lush green. Deer trails sprang up, leading seemingly nowhere. Around noon, the dark rain clouds swept over them, but only sprinkles came down. Felix explained that the clouds had already deposited their rain on the Midlands and had almost none left for the desert lands of the Easterlings. Felisa and Nico began to grasp why their homeland was so dry. They were still in the Easterlings, northern Alba to be precise, but the lands here were nowhere near as desolate as at Adelmira. The third day they passed by a rural farmstead and a small forest patch.

After that, the landscape changed once more. Now rolling hills covered with tall grasses and occasional splotches of forest rose before them. The rains came in measurable amounts, though still not in any real quantity, just enough to get the riders wet and make life more miserable. It was still hot and now muggy. Savina asked him where all the people were and he explained they were taking a path to avoid population centers because there were so many open conflicts in progress. This she accepted.

Felix spent hours each evening looking over the maps of Cassie and Bree. Their route would be taking them past three of the six towers that were not in the Kingdom of Bettingham, which had four of them, and one was his Brom tower. One of the remaining three was just on the other side of the Goza Mountains from Oakham tower. Many of the conflicts in progress lay in these areas. Slowly an idea began forming. If he stopped at these towers, doled out enough germanium crystals, and taught them how to attune a person to them, they could get started on getting the various *Jefe* and petty kings to sign onto the Brom Compact. While he wanted to give these to his own four towers first and use them to help convince the others to go along with his grand plan, it seemed foolish to waste this opportunity, especially since he would be passing at least three of the towers.

A week into their journey, he'd made up his mind to stop at each of the three towers on their return path. However, dividing up the lands each tower would control and protect was extremely difficult. In the Easterlings, the problem was simple. There was only one tower; hence, that tower was responsible for the entire third of the continent. True, much of it was desert lands, save Matruk and part of Alba. With the other ten towers and with four residing in the Kingdom of the Angels and nearly all up against the Goza Mountains, there were no natural boundaries he could definitively use to divvy up the Westerlings and Midlands easily. Further, some zones contained the Midlands and Westerlings breadbasket areas, where crops now thrived. In the back of his mind, he had a gnawing suspicion that no matter how he divided up the lands for the towers, tower conflicts could well result. Still, it had to be done if his dream of ending wars and conflicts between the hundreds of small kingdoms was to come to fruition as it was happening in the Easterlings now. He shut that gnawing suspicion out of his conscious mind and focused on how to divide up the lands among the towers.

At last he just drew some lines on the map, the best he

could devise. That night, he activated his crystal and joined with Lilly and Felisa, drawing upon their psi-energies to maintain his enormous telepathic conference. He pulled in all the ten tower leaders and two of their subordinates as well, along with Ama Floriana of Adelmira.

Yes, the hints that you have been picking up from the Easterlings are true. Lilly and I have made some powerful discoveries. He outlined the effects of the germanium crystals and Ama Adelmira backed him up on the hundredfold amplification process. *Without them, I could not hold thirty-four of you in this massive telepathic link. I am bringing a beginning supply along with me, enough at least to provide one to each of your tower members, perhaps a few extras.* He outlined how they could get as many as desired through the Sisterhood and many did just that the very next day, though he didn't know about that just yet.

The power that one crystal gives us mentales is almost beyond description. Yet, it goes farther. Lilly and I have devised a way for the tower-trained to join together in what I call a Círculo de mentes. Each member flows their psi-energies to the leader, who then uses it to do what is needed. It is beyond imagination the total power that the leader then wields. I will let Ama Floriana tell you about it.

She did so enthusiastically for a half hour, describing how she was able to monitor the entire Easterlings lands, stop wars and battles by tossing their weapons away or lifting the combatants up and depositing them elsewhere.

I am returning to my tower at Brom now. On the way, I will be stopping at Rusden, Oakham, Haverhills, Bedworth, Wyth, and Brom. At each, we will deliver the first of the crystals, show you how to attune them to yourselves, and get you started on how to form your own Círculo de mentes. He then went on to describe his Brom Compact in detail. *I have drawn up a rough plan of the lands that each tower will control and be responsible for. I tried to do it as fairly as I could, but some tweaking will be inevitable. I'll deal with that when I finally get to Brom tower.*

He then outlined the lands to be controlled by each tower, suggesting that those in Duero tower make a journey over to Oakham tower so that they could get theirs at that time. Valen, Portillo, and Bettingham towers would get theirs later on when he and they could arrange to meet in the spring, once the mountain snows melted enough to allow passage.

Brom tower would control Hilliard Heights and all northern lands above Chester. Bettingham would control a northeastern slice covering Stockton, Chester, Walsham, and on up to the northern seacoast. Bedworth would control the lands some fifty miles south of the Southfork River all across the Midlands, including Wye and Northend, all the way to the Buku Hills, a long narrow track. Haverhills, just to the south of Bettingham, would control a similar west-east track that included Wycombe all the way to the Brooks River, the natural border with Matruk. Oakham, lying just south of Haverhills, would control a similar west-east track including Leedsburough on over to the Brooks River. Rusden would be responsible for all lands to the south of it, including all old Bashir over to the Wyndl River, where Matruk began. In the Westerlings, Duero tower would control old Almendia, while Valen would control old Trujillo, leaving Portillo to control old Abvera and Zamora, the latter of which was now largely uninhabitable due to the extreme cold.

Historical note: On behalf of Felix Brom, it must be said the tower leaders did not like the proposed lands they were to control. However, because of the sheer magnitude of what Felix Brom was giving them, none voiced any disagreements, choosing instead to bide their time and see how this all played out. Also, that Felix totally ignored the aliens at Plateau Grado and Exchange City also would play an important role in the future, though he had no such ideas at this time.

After the long conference ended totally satisfactorily from his point of view, with Sheldon's help, Felix handed out four of the large crystals to the four *mentales* gifted women among the three dozen Sisterhood women. Cindy, Cassie, Bree, and Linn Beckworth became the first Midlands folks to receive the amplifying crystals. Linn was their band's truth teller. All four were staggered to discover how greatly their powers were being amplified by the crystals. "My god! No wonder they chose us for this mission!" Cindy exclaimed.

"Maybe they should have sent an army to bring you safely back!"

"I would feel far safer among you women," Felix replied. "Besides, we've lived nearly a decade with your Sisterhood women in Adelmira.

"Yes, understandable and I must say that you did them a tremendous honor by giving them the children they so greatly desired," Cassie replied with a knowing smile. "Bree and I checked on that, you see." She gave him a flirting wink and Felix nodded, smiling at these two free-mates while wondering if one day they too would desire to bear a child for themselves. After this point, the four women held Felix in a far higher regard and that attitude was also reflected in the many other Sisterhood women protecting them.

Felix then made a decision based on both the traveling conditions and his women and girls, modified by his own sense of wanting to get on with his huge plans as rapidly as possible. "Can we change our route to head towards Southbend and then head straight west, shaving perhaps a thousand miles off our journey?" he asked Cassie, Bree, and Cindy. "This way, we could spend more nights at local inns. I know that increases the dangers, but it will shorten the journey considerably."

"Southbend? That's a den of assassins and thieves," Cindy protested, but she mellowed a little. "Yes, the women are having a most difficult time camping out at night. I can see your point. Honestly, when are you going to set them free of their bindings?"

"When we clear the Easterlings, Cindy. It is going to be traumatic for the older ones, but I figure when they are among normal women, they will be less reluctant to the drastic change. God, I hope so."

Bree spoke up, "Well, I've been through Southbend once. Despicable city, but there are good roads and plenty of inns now that Matruk has become a breadbasket land. We could send a message to Rusden and Woodhill's Sisterhoods and ask for more fighters to meet us in Southbend. Perhaps we could get a few more from Leedsburough too. Are you sure that you ought to have brought the Easterlings women back with you?"

"No real choice, though I gave them the opportunity to stay," Felix justified. *I wonder if they really will be able to adapt and adjust.* For the first time, Felix began to worry about Felisa and Nico. The children, he assumed, would adapt more easily.

Cindy and Bree used their telepathic gifts that night and the next evening they reported that another dozen Sisterhood fighters would meet up with them somewhere around Southbend. They continued to make around forty miles each day. With the countryside becoming more hospitable and stopping at the occasional village inn, the women began to relax more, enjoying the trip through the Easterlings breadbasket lands. While the winter fields were brown and bare, often they encountered a little snow as well. The children loved to stop and play in the snow. Felix continued to caution them that in Brom, the snow depth would be many feet at this time of year. He didn't realize they had no conception of such a thing, let alone what that implied.

On the second of February, they rolled into Southbend, the largest city in Matruk with some thirty thousand inhabitants. Except for the Sisterhood women, this was the biggest city any of them had seen, including Felix, who was used to the smaller cities of the north. Here was a city in which you could get absolutely anything that you desired, for a price, of course. The great granaries rose like giant candles on the north side of the city, New Town, as the locals called it. During the last hundred years as Matruk became a breadbasket country, many farmers had immigrated here. The city's population nearly doubled and expanded to the north forming the New Town. Here the wealthy moved and naturally, this was the safest area in Southbend. Old Town became poorer and here thievery, assassins, and the black market thrived amid a myriad of shops.

The Sisterhood house was located on the western edge, officially within Old Town, but adjoining New Town, pushed as far away from the normal inhabitants as possible. A contingent of fifteen more Sisterhood fighters met them as they approached the huge city, alerted telepathically by Cindy.

She wanted an escort through the city, especially since they would have to pass through the heart of the Old City to get to the Sisterhood complex, where they decided the group would be the safest.

As they moved slowly through the packed streets, that Southbend had become a sort of melting pot became evident. Some men wore the traditional white Easterlings turbans, shirts, and pants and bound women shuffled along their slow paths, so also were brown skinned men and women displaced from Bashir far to the south. Their women wore long robes and were definitely unbound. Further, they caught sight of some Midlands folk as well. It was a strange mixture of bound and unbound women and a colorful display of men's dress patterns that greeted their eyes. Small boys darted through the crowded streets, carrying large copper vessels, hawking drinking water.

Felix noted the shops as he drove past them. Swords, scimitars, linens, soap, candle, herbs, saddles and tack, rope, rugs — a myriad of shops, large and small, crammed into every available space in some crazed jumble. He wondered how anyone found anything here at all. It was a confused maze. Worse, the streets were not laid out in any order he could see, twisting this way and that, as if the city planner was doing a drunken walk as he drew out the street plans. More than once, he spotted thieves in action with little difference whether the victim was bound or not.

With all the mounted Sisterhood fighters surrounding their carriages and wagons, the locals gave them a wide birth, but all stared at this strange sight. Seldom had there been such a large group of Sisterhood fighters in one party, which most assuredly called everyone's attention to them. Only their reputation as wicked fighters kept the inquisitive at a distance. At last, Felix realized the danger he had put them all in by insisting on going through Southbend.

As they maneuvered down a particularly crowded street, Felix saw a revolting sight. A grubby bearded man led a string of seven bound Easterlings women chained together with copper chains affixed to their waist chains, forming a long line with another equally grubby looking man bringing up the rear. Slavers, he thought disgustedly. Worse, as they drew closer shuffling along with their tiny steps, he saw that their arms were bound behind their backs, as if it were nighttime. The women were between their late teens to early twenties or that was his best guess.

As the line drew close to his carriage, the lead woman appeared to stumble and she fell on the ground. Lacking the use of her arms and constrained by her skirt, she had an extremely hard and awkward time regaining her feet. Meanwhile the lead man growled at her, but his eyes fixed solidly on Felix, who had to hold up the carriage or run over the woman. Instantly, several Sisterhood fighters moved closer, placing themselves as close as they could to him, but they were unable to get their bodies and horses between the man and fallen woman and his carriage. The slaver said nothing nor did he do anything but stare hard at Felix and the women inside. He sensed no telepathic thoughts, but the slaver did have the yellow-brown eyes and was presumably blocking his thoughts. Eventually, the woman managed to get to her feet and the slaver finally broke eye contact and gave the line of women a tug. The slow shuffle of the bound women began once more and soon Felix was able to get his team of horses walking again.

Bree pulled up beside him. "What was that all about? Did he threaten you?"

"No, he just stared at me, nothing else. Strange, but I'd sure like to go back and free those women," Felix replied.

"Can't. He's a slaver and he's got a right to his property. Those women are of the lowest Castas and his property," Bree said, spitting on the dirt street where the slaver had just walked.

Inside the carriage, Felisa and Nico were rather upset by it. "My god, they had their arms bound in the sleeping position and yet were forced to wear their day skirts! That is not done, not ever! Why were they chained together?" Felisa asked.

Felix called down to her, "Slavers, dear."

"Oh, well that still doesn't give him a right to so mistreat and humiliate them!"

"I would like to stop and free them from those men. Slavery is totally outlawed in the Midlands," Lilly said somewhat antagonistically, though she realized she really could not have done any such thing herself, being bound still.

Felisa gave a startled gasp, "Oh no, Lilly! Those women have nothing at all and would perish if those men would not have taken ownership of them. They probably had no other choice but to sell themselves so a man would take care of them and provide them with food and a place to live. Still," she softened her voice, "they should not be humiliating the women. The seven were of the lowest Castas. Did you notice that their fingernails were all very short?" Felix tuned out their conversation and focused on the street ahead.

She went on, "If you are in the lowest Castas and if you are of age and have no suitors, no husband and your parents cannot afford to keep you, then you have very few choices left to you, unless you have the *mentales* gifts and could then hire out to some clan leader. Those women didn't have yellow eyes and likely had no other choice but to sell themselves to those men, who are then obligated to feed, house, and care for them. That is our way, Lilly. Men must care for women someway. It is a good system in that all women can have a way to survive somehow." Lilly couldn't believe what Felisa was saying, but then, she'd seen much of it already. Grim, she thought, glad that she was finally going home.

The Sisterhood home consisted of a large stone building, two stories tall with a large stable and courtyard surrounded by a low two foot wall of field stones. A plump woman came out to greet them, the House Mother, Celia. "Welcome Amo Felix Brom to our humble home. I have reserved some rooms on the first floor for your use." She seemed friendly enough and soon they were settled inside. The accommodations were rather Spartan and Felix got the distinct notion that many women had temporarily vacated their rooms to give his party the three rooms they needed. He did notice their four *mentales* gifted guides were also given a room, but the dozens of other women merely made their sleeping rolls around the large courtyard out in the open.

"My god, Celia! Real wheat bread!" exclaimed Lilly,

tearing into the hot, steaming loaf fresh from their ovens. "I haven't had real wheat bread in over a decade! It is a super luxury in the Kingdom of the Angels. Usually our bread is made from nut flower and oats, far coarser than this. Mind if I eat the whole loaf?" She was teasing, of course, but Celia seemed very pleased. Even in Adelmira, the bread had rice flour and other grains diluting the small wheat content.

"Wheat, we have in quantity here in Southbend. I'll make sure to send along some extra loaves with you tomorrow," Celia offered, much to Lilly's great pleasure.

Over their meal of roasted foul and gravy, Felix announced, "Tomorrow, ladies, I want you to begin wearing your new Midlands dresses. Already you can see that half of the women here are unbound. We will be heading due west from now on and soon you will see no bound women at all. Besides, we will be heading into areas where they are known conflicts. We may have to fight a battle or two. I want you to be able to at least move easily on your own."

The next morning, Rosina complained, "Dad, I am utterly naked!" She was no longer bound, but dressed in a normal Midlands dress with tall socks and sturdy boots.

"Me too," Savina added.

"I am humiliated to be seen like this, my husband," Felisa whispered to him. "Is this really the way your women dress?"

"Yes, though we will don much warmer clothing when we get further north," Lilly explained. "A Midlands woman would feel utterly disgraced if she had to have her husband carry her about as Felix and Sheldon have been doing for us. We must carry our own loads, but we simply could not do so if we were wearing your traditional dress."

"Next, he'll be having us wear pants!" wailed Savina, who broke into a fit of tears.

He did notice the women kept their upper arms at their sides, as if they were still bound, refusing to move them. Also, they continued to take tiny steps, though there was no reason for it. He figured that it was their silent protest and let it go at that. They pulled out right after breakfast and Felix left a large tip with Celia, certain now she'd made huge adjustments on their behalf.

That night as they made camp, Felix got an earful from the women and girls complaining they could not possibly sleep without being bound. They even resorted to sobbing when their begging went for naught. *Give them time to adjust, dear,* Lilly sent him.

"Girls, we must somehow find the strength within us to do this and not disgrace your fathers," Felisa whispered to the girls and her sister as they prepared for bed, unbound for the first time in their lives, that is, since they were five years old. By morning, all had red eyes and little sleep. However, they continued to put on a brave face, Felisa continued to insist on that.

Felix then discovered that both Felisa and Nico were not faking. Their upper arms had been bound to their sides since they were five years old, close to twenty years. Not only did their upper arms have almost no muscle tone and were quite thin, but also they really could not move them around much at all. Certainly, they could not raise their arms; they had extremely limited movement around their shoulders. He went into Regulator mode with Felisa and discovered huge deposits in her shoulder sockets that prevented her upper arms from much movement at all. He felt that the *Círculo de mentes* could remove the deposits, given time. However, the children and Lilly were still able to move their upper arms, though they all complained that it hurt them to do so. Lilly continually worked hers, determined to get back her full range of motion.

Around noon, a little excitement broke the monotonous journey. A band of a dozen hunters came upon them. However, seeing the large band of Sisterhood fighters, they wisely chose to watch the caravan pass them by. After that, they stuck to the well-traveled routes and passed by many tiny hamlets, rural farmsteads, or bands of hunters, the latter when they were near patches of forests. Once, a patrol of soldiers encountered them, but again gave the Sisterhood women a wide berth. Felisa noticed they too seemed to hold the Sisterhood women in great disdain. *Well, at least we have that in common,* she thought.

As they approached the Wyndl River around the third week of February, the weather turned noticeably chillier and cloaks were handed out. Occasional snow filled the air, accumulating a little each night, but melting by day. Once ferried across, they were plowing their way through ever increasing depths of snow. The cold and snow were entirely new to the desert dwellers. At first, the children loved it, making snowballs and tossing them. Around the campfires, they rolled small snowmen. However, soon the snow was too cold to pack. The newness wore off and the constant cold began to take its toll on them. Now Felix was very glad for the warmth of the various village inns along the way, however overcrowded they were.

The second week of March, they neared the Kingdom of Woodhill and came upon a recent battlefield, where the snow was trampled and red-hued, but they had missed the actual battle. Five times they were stopped by soldiers on patrol, but the presence of such a strong Sisterhood group and some "Fire Man persuasion" from Felix defused the situations. Everyone breathed a sigh of relief as they entered the Kingdom of Rusden in mid-April.

Here, they laid over for a week, while Felix and his party doled out a dozen crystals, taught the tower men and women how to attune them, and going over the basics of how to create a *Círculo de mentes*. He also gave them a copy of the Brom Compact to copy and get all the many kings or *Jefes* to sign.

Mid-May, with flowers sprouting up everywhere and farmers out working their fields, they reached Oakham. The three representatives from Duero tower were also there waiting on them. Once more, they spent a week getting these two towers educated and more crystals delivered.

Of course, the children and the two Easterlings women were utterly amazed at the impressive sight of the tall, snow covered Goza Mountains, and the amount of snow that was still present, though melting rapidly with each day. Since Oakham was cradled in the foothills, right up against the mountains proper, the terrain was rocky and quite rough. At last, Felisa and Nico began to see that they would be unable to walk anywhere outside a home in their fetter skirts, but that did not give them much comfort. Both still felt constantly humiliated while wearing the Midlands dresses.

Mid-June, another week was spent at Haverhills, and then they pushed on to Bedworth. As they went through Exchange City, they got their first look at the alien spaceport and watched as the huge silver ships, belching fires, came slowly to the ground or rose up into the sky only to become a tiny speck before vanishing entirely. This gave the women and girls something to talk about for quite some time. After stopping at Wyth tower, they finally reached home, Brom tower, where folks from the Bettingham tower were also waiting to get their crystals and training. It was July and midsummer when they arrived home at long last. Brom, with its tall tower dominating the view, the rugged foothills, and the snow-capped peaks of the Goza Mountains, captivated the newcomers.

Chapter 20 The Brom Compact Takes Effect

It was now early June 1082. Felix finally began to relax. His grand plan to end all wars on Tierra was coming to fruition made possible by his invention of the unlimited weapon, a combination of the germanium crystals and the tower's *Círculo de mentes*. During the past year, more and more *Jefes* and kings had been forced to sign the Brom Compact. He grimaced as he recalled the "by force" methods so many of the other tower leaders had been using.

Many of the towers outside the Kingdom of the Angels had male leaders. These used very persuasive means to force them to sign. One *Jefe*'s mountain fortress had a huge chunk of its outer stone wall disintegrated, a massive breech. Another two, who were massing armies to do battle, had half of their men destroyed by fires. Those who steadfastly refused to sign suffered greatly at the hands of these male tower leaders, until they at last had no choice but to concede and sign the compact. The towers with women leaders used far less destructive means to bring their rulers to sign. Two groups preparing to battle for a stronghold found their weapons flying off a half mile from their hands. Others found their soldiers lifted up and deposited a thousand feet away.

No matter which tower was involved, they gained the signatures by a clear demonstration of an almost unlimited power, the unlimited weapon against which no single king or *Jefe* could possibly stand, even with their own *mentales* gifted and their new crystals. The *Círculo de mentes* were just too overpowering.

Felix had spent the past year training the various tower members, sharing all that he and Lilly had learned. It had been quite a challenge, squeezing in enough hours each day to accomplish all that he wanted, but now he could finally relax a little. Fully half of the local *Jefes* and kings had signed onboard with the compact. These were the more important ones, located close to the various towers. True, the distant rulers, such as those in Walsham and Northend, had yet to be contacted, but he was sure it was just a matter of time before the various towers expanded outward to encompass them as well. Now, he could sit back and watch the ultimate weapon bring peace to all Tierra at last.

In celebration of his success, he, Lilly, and Felisa decided to have more children. Both women were now two month's pregnant, due sometime in late December. Because of their heightened senses, Lilly knew hers would be a boy, and Felisa knew hers would be another girl. The excited women already picked out names, John and Annetta. Felisa compromised and "Easterlings-ized" the name Anna, which Felix wanted.

Still, Felisa and Nico were not adapting at all well to the Midlands and its vastly different culture. They simply did not adjust to the physically unbound state of women in this land. At night, though Felix refused to allow them to be bound, they still slept with their arms behind their backs as if they were still bound properly at night.

After a year of being freed, both women's shoulders still had not adjusted and they still continued to have very little range of motion at their shoulders. So even though they wore no chains, their upper arms still remained at their sides and they used their lower arms they always had done. Although he had promised to see if the *Círculo de mentes* could undo the deposits that blocked their shoulders from moving much, the pressures of his great work left him no time actually to pursue this cure.

Worse for Felisa and Nico was the simple fact that for the last year, Felix and Sheldon had been so absorbed in their vital work they had spent very little time with them, only at night when they slept. Even then, the men were so tired and spent they fell asleep rapidly. For the two women, this was almost intolerable.

They were raised as bound women and that meant their men spent a great deal of attention on them and their needs. In terms of time alone, at least a quarter of each day, the Easterlings men's attention was on their wives and their needs. Now the two women, unbound, had at most an hour each day in rapport with their husbands. This shocking loss of attention nearly drove both women mad.

Yet, neither was unintelligent. Rather, they made an attempt to understand the new culture in which they were immersed, if only for the honor-sake of their husbands. They found the women of the Midlands were bound in an entirely different way, mentally bound. While they expected the marriages of *mentales* gifted women to be arranged, they were shocked to learn that most women's marriages were arranged in one way or another. An innkeeper, for example, needed to marry a woman would was gifted at helping run his inn. So it went. They were appalled at all the restraints that Midlands women faced and with no apparent return benefits from their husbands, wholly unlike that of the Easterlings. By June of 1082, both Felisa and Nico pitied Lilly and the way that her life was laid out for her. They didn't see her active role in the experimentations of Felix made up for it in any real way. Thus, the two women grew more and more miserable with each passing week, ignoring wholly their intense dislike for the cold and snow that seemed to last almost year round — an exaggeration on their part.

Felix sensed their growing unrest and he incorrectly thought the best thing for them would be to have another baby. They readily agreed and it had happened, but to his dismay, pregnancy did little to help the two women out of their doldrums and discontent.

Beppe Faustino Lucca was nineteen when Felix and his party were captured by Donato and Adelina, and held prisoners and tortured in the tent in the desert. The youngest brother of Donato Lucca, thirty-five, his birth was both unexpected and lucky. Unexpected, because so many of their *mentales* bred children died in childhood of Verge Sickness. Lucky, for an entirely different reason: his unique gift. He first discovered it when he was nine. Beppe had been out riding in the desert and had foolishly ridden his horse into a heat stroke. With no other choices, he began walking across the desert back to their oasis. However, at the top of one dune, he spotted his home several dunes distant and bemoaned the fact that he had to walk nearly two more miles in the heat of the day. He imagined walking into his village where the cool, blue waters beckoned and the next instant found himself doing just that. Having no name for what he'd done, he began to call it "jumping" for that is what it seemed to the nine year old boy. Later, he learned that it was called teleporting and was an exceedingly rare gift.

So much so, that his older brother, Donato, desperately wanted to have that gift bred into his own clan-leader line. Thus, he promised Beppe that he could marry his own daughter, Felisa, when she was eighteen, two years from the time of the abduction. As Beppe grew up, he coveted Felisa, who knew nothing about this proposed marriage. She rather disliked the cowardly boy. Beppe was with Donato in the camp when the kidnaping occurred and was watching Felisa covertly as she prepared for bed. Then came the surprise attack and Beppe, as usual, took to hiding rather than fighting. When he saw Donato slain and the battle lost, he used his gift to abandon the camp, arriving safely some two miles away. He could only use his gift once per day because one jump used up most of his available psi-energies. After a good night's sleep, like all *mentales* gifted, his energies were restored. Thus, when he finally jumped back to the camp to see what had happened and perhaps to steal away with his betrothed Felisa, he found only the desert scavengers hard at work.

Someone had confiscated the horses and much of their gear. He tore through his brother's tent looking for traces of Felisa. At last his panic subsided. She had not been killed. Rather, it appeared that she had been taken away by an unknown group who had been barefoot when they came into the camp. Strange. He spent the day piecing together survival gear, a scimitar and dagger, water skins, dried food, and a bedroll. With no other viable options, he set off on foot tracking his betrothed Felisa, swearing that one day she would be his, one way or another.

Months later, he finally tracked her down in Adelmira. To his dismay, she was now married to a foreign man and living with the infernal Sisterhood women. She was again beyond his reach. A man possessed, he had to do something to survive, and he began to use his jumping skills to his advantage, becoming first a thief and then an assassin. He learned that these foreigners came from the far northwestern Midlands and that they were not planning to return there anytime soon. He reasoned that they would in all likelihood travel through Southbend on their return journey, whenever that happened. Hence, he made his main base of operations in that large city, where he could use his unique gift to full advantage. When the germanium crystals began to be distributed, he donned a disguise and received his crystal. He discovered that by using it, he could teleport over many miles now and use his gift three times each day! One of his "Southbend industries" was dealing in female slaves. By the time that Felix was to return to the Midlands, he had an extensive spy network established throughout northern Matruk and Alba. Thus, he was alerted to the travel plans of Felix, although the arrival of so many Sisterhood fighters from the north also would have alerted him to those plans.

He dare not directly confront the Sisterhood fighters, but he contented himself to monitoring the location and thus daily progress of his beloved Felisa. Later each night, he used his gifts to sense her general location, her unique frequency or wavelength. He was pleased that she was at last coming towards Southbend. He was dying at least to catch a glimpse of her. Her fiery red hair, was it still so long and beautiful? He had to see her, if only for a moment. He worked out the timing and the route. Leading a small band of his captive slave women, he moved them slowly along the narrow street and ordered the lead slave to take a stumble and fall at precisely the right moment. When she did so causing his line to stop and forcing Felix's carriage to halt while she pathetically tried to get back up, he saw his betrothed once more. Longing swelled in him once more, he just had to have her! Then, they were moving again.

Carefully, he made his plans to follow them, but always a very discrete distance behind them, usually several days' travel time. He wanted nothing to do with the powerful Sisterhood escort. No, he had waited a decade to claim his promised bride, he could wait a little longer, but the foreign man who was stealing her away, destroying her honor and self-pride, forcing her to become unbound — he would have to pay, pay with his despicable life!

Slowly but surely and always a couple of days behind them, he followed Felix and party all the way to the small village of Brom with its tall tower. Again, she was just out of his reach and he took a lowly position as a helper for the local coppersmith. He used his position to watch and learn the secrets of the tower layout. While he occasionally saw Felisa walking around the town, his hatred of Felix and what he had done to her overrode his desires for her. He could sense her deep sorrow and misery. Honor demanded that he slay Felix and then take his beloved back to the Easterlings lands. So while many times he could have reached out, touched her, and then, using his gift, teleport them both far away. But first, he had to obtain justice. Thus, he took to listening and asking innocent questions of the staff women who worked in the tower as cooks, maids, and cleaners when they dropped by the coppersmith's shop. In time, he learned the layout of the tower, and where Felix and his harem slept. Slowly, his plans came to fruition.

As Captain Sheldon was preparing for bed, he happened to notice a wagon parked just beyond the rocky bend in the path that led from the small village up to the tower. Strange place for a wagon to be parked this time of night, he thought. "Excuse me a minute, dear," he whispered to Nico and left their bedroom. He went down three flights of stairs to the two guards who were on duty near the entrance door. "There's a strange wagon by the bend. Probably nothing, but go check it out will you?" The two grabbed their swords and obeyed. Sheldon turned to go back upstairs, but changed his mind and waited for the guards' report.

A half hour later, they reported. "Boss, it's loaded with supplies for a trip, two horses, but no one is around. Probably they just forgot something," one said rather bored.

"Okay, keep an eye on it," he asked and headed back up the stairs. He told Nicolina about the wagon, answering her questions about it. She, too, noticed it while he was downstairs. Satisfied, he finished binding her in the traditional manner, which he secretly continued to do for her, and they turned in. She slept so much better this way, he had discovered. Before long, Nico was sound asleep. Sheldon tossed and turned.

Something isn't quite right about that wagon. His thoughts kept going back to the wagon. *It should not be there.* Although the hour was late, he stole out of bed and put his clothes back on. *If someone had troubles, they ought to have just walked the thousand feet to us and asked for help. If the wagon and team are okay, why would someone who forgot something leave the team there instead of turning them around and going back to the village? We are not expecting any guests either. Something's not right about that wagon. I'm going to see for myself.*

He headed down the stairs, but not before checking the next room. He heard Felix, Lilly, and Felisa's quiet breathing. All three were asleep. "Going to check on the wagon myself," he told the two guards, who were fighting the boredom by playing cards. He stepped outside and felt the chill of the summer's evening breeze. *No rain tonight for a change,* he thought. He looked around the area. All seemed quiet, though the two moons did cast a pale glow over the landscape, fleeting in and out of the thick clouds. As he walked slowly to the wagon, his eyes took a survey of the land and found nothing out of the ordinary, as far as the faint illuminations showed. At the wagon, he inspected it closely, his curiosity growing by the minute.

Hiding in the dense pines on the rocky slopes behind the tower, Beppe Faustino Lucca waited patiently. He saw the lanterns going out in their bedroom. *Let him get to sleep, patience will be rewarded. Vengeance shall be mine soon now!*

Finally, he acted. Holding his crystal that hung from a thong around his neck, he focused his mind, forming an image of their bedroom, constructed from a tapestry of hints provided by the tower maids. He held on to that and got the idea that he was now standing beside their bed. Psi energies activated, his crystal amplified them, glowing bright blue for an instant. He was there in their bedroom, tripping over a chair and stumbling over their boots set beside their bed ready for the morning. All three roused from their sleep by his clumsy noise. He acted as fast as he could in the very dim moonlight that came in from the windows. He brought his dagger down hard, thrusting it into the chest of Felix, just as he was rising. Lilly tried to deflect the blade with her hand, but she was too slow in her sleep-disturbed reactions. Blood gushed out from his wound and his body slumped back onto the bed. Lilly screamed.

Beppe grabbed Felisa's shoulder and focused once again, getting the idea solidly in his mind that he was now standing beside his waiting wagon with Felisa at his side. Time enough later to properly dress and bind her. He cast that errant thought aside and refocused his thoughts. Again, his crystal flashed its telltale blue light. Beppe and a shocked Felisa were standing beside his wagon. She screamed.

When Beppe touched her, her mind was wide open and she instantly picked up his thoughts and intentions, particularly that he thought he was betrothed to her and that he was fanatically in love with her. She saw instantly he was planning to take her back to the Easterlings with him and that he'd just assassinated Felix. She recognized his face as that same man who was so brutally mistreating the line of women in the street, the Slaver. She also saw he'd assassinated twenty other men as well, so open was his mind to her in that instant. Hence, she involuntarily shrank from his grasp as they arrived beside his wagon. Her mind fought to grasp what had just happened to her. She was in bed, just sitting up and now she was standing in her nightgown beside a wagon some distance from the tower. She also saw Captain Sheldon behind Beppe.

Sheldon had heard Lilly's scream and was just about to race back into the tower when suddenly a strange man appeared in front of him, holding onto a shocked Felisa, who was struggling to break free from his solid grasp of her right shoulder. He acted without hesitation. His sword stabbed the man through his ribs. Its wide blade, parallel to the ground and his ribs, slid in easily, and as the man twisted to face his attacker, the motion aided the blade to slice through his heart and arteries. Gasping, he dropped to the ground, staring pitifully up at Felisa before his eyes closed forever.

"Felix! Stabbed," Felisa finally managed to say something coherent. Leaving her to walk back inside the tower by herself, Sheldon raced as fast as he could. His dear friend stabbed? How could he have been so careless? Self-deprecating curses flew through his mind as he took the stairs three steps at a time. He dashed into the bedroom, his eyes taking in the horrific scene before him. His long years of soldier training kicked in. Light. He quickly moved from lantern to lantern, until he had all five lanterns going at once. Now he could better analyze what needed to be done.

When the assassin disappeared taking Felisa with him, Lilly was still sitting up in bed, leaning over her bleeding husband. Felix wasn't dead yet and that drove her necessity level into overdrive. She focused and her crystal shone in a brilliant blue light as she slipped fully into her monitoring mode, ready to work her healing magic. The blade had severed part of an artery before cutting into his spinal cord. If she pulled the blade out, he'd bleed out long before she could heal the huge slice in the artery. Hence, she took a different approach. She pulled it out a tiny bit and then rapidly began pulling in particles to fill the cut. *If only the whole team were here,* she lamented in a tiny corner of her mind. With the energies of all her circle members, this would be far faster and easier.

This is what Captain Sheldon saw as he got the five lanterns going. Lilly was in deep rapport with her healing work and oblivious to the heightened illumination. Instinctively, he reached out to Nico, drawing her into rapport with himself. Then, he joined with Lilly, who suddenly felt the burst of psi-energies being sent to her, precisely what she needed most now. A bit later, a breathless Felisa came into the room and Sheldon joined her into the circle. Now others of the tower joined them, one performing the Regulator duties that Sheldon usually handled for his circle. Before long, Lilly was drawing upon the psi-energies of a dozen!

Still, Lilly realized she was losing the battle. Each time she pulled the dagger out a fraction and then healed that portion of the artery, Felix lost more and more blood. In desperation, she attempted a new strategy. She focused on the particles of the blade that were still within the artery and separated them, one by one, allowing them to seep towards the surface of his chest, while adding more particles to the side of the artery just revealed. Tedious beyond measure was the task, but at last she had the artery healed, stemming the large loss of blood. Now she could pull the blade out fully.

Working from the inside outwards, she continued pulling in and placing tiny particle after particle, until at last, she sealed his outer skin. Lilly was exhausted beyond measure and starving, as if she'd not eaten for days. Fortunately, the woman monitoring her blood-soaked body was fully aware of her needs and literally picked her up from her bed and carried her out of the room bodily. "I can walk," Lilly heard her faint voice speaking as if from some far distant place. The woman put her down, but had to support her all the way.

Felisa and Sheldon lifted Felix up while the others removed the blood-soaked bedding, while another gently washed off his body as the two held him up. A half hour later, Felix was lying in his bed with clean sheets. He was unconscious, but alive, barely. Sheldon returned to his room and unbound Nico and they headed down to the dining room of the first floor. Lilly had been washed and put into a clean nightgown, which was somewhat too large for her. Already food was being stuffed into her mouth, and the two sat down along with the others to quench their hunger as well.

"He was an assassin from the Easterlings; he was the cowardly brother of my father who left Nico and me to the enemy when we were attacked," Felisa at last began to speak, her stomach finally satisfied. "Somehow he thought I belonged to him and that Felix, my husband, had greatly dishonored me." She went on to describe what she had picked up from his mind when he'd touched her shoulder. "He was that slaver man we saw in Southbend, Nico. Ugly man." They discussed this for a time but soon exhaustion kicked in and they all headed for bed, but not before Sheldon tripled the guards on duty.

I was so wrong to bring you back here, Felisa. I should never have forced you to leave the Easterlings. Felix was too weak to talk. Morning had come and though alive, he knew he was close to death's door.

Hush my husband. It is my duty to go with you. You are alive and that's what matters. She tried her best to suppress both her fears for his health and the many months of isolation and humiliation she had endured for his sake.

No, I have dishonored you, my dear Felisa. I have been so blind to you these past many months. Forgive me, my dearest. It is not safe for you and Nico to be here. I am going to ask Sheldon to take you both back to Adelmira and set up an Easterlings office there for me. When I recover, I will join you, my love. He felt her sudden rejoicing of the mere possibility of returning to her warm homeland, away from the eternal cold and rains of the foothills. Felix knew he had to make this happen for her, if he did nothing else before his body died on him.

But it is my place to be here at your side and help you recover, my husband. Felisa protested in the proper manner she had been taught by her mother. She was unable to squelch entirely the huge longing to return to her homeland that had swelled up in her mind and heart. Somehow, Felix had unlocked it all in that instant.

I know dear, but Lilly will look after me. I want our daughter to be raised in the proper Easterlings traditions, Felisa. You and I know that she cannot around here. Please, if only for our new daughter's sake, go with Sheldon and Nico and prepare us a proper home in Adelmira. Lilly and I will join you when my health returns. Please, do this for me, my dearest.

If this is your wish, then I must do as you ask, my husband. Felisa relaxed. She'd said her piece as a good wife was obligated to do, but he'd insisted — no ordered her to return. Felisa suppressed the utter elation swelling within her; she would be going home at last.

"How are you feeling this morning?" Sheldon asked after breakfast. He'd come up to check on his mentor. He tried to conceal his shame at having failed to protect him yet again.

I can't move my legs yet. Too weak to speak. I have one last favor to ask of you, my old friend. I need you to take

Felisa and Nico back to Adelmira and set us up an eastern office so to speak. If anything happens to me, if I don't make it, I entrust Felisa and our unborn daughter into your hands. Keep them safe, Sheldon.

But I have failed you twice now.

No, you have not. You killed the assassin before he could steal away Felisa and our unborn daughter. That means more to me than my life, Sheldon. Keep them safe. Do this last thing for me, please.

Yes, my lord. I will guard them with my life. Surely you will recover and join us?

It is my hope, my friend, but. . . He never finished his thought. Both men knew how it would end and neither wished to vocalize it, not even mentally. After a long pause, he sent, *Give Savina and Michela a choice to go or to stay. Same with your two.*

Thank you. How soon?

As soon as you can arrange it. Use the Sisterhood again.

You don't want Felisa to. . .

Right. If she knew, she'd not go and I can't have that on my conscience too. I've caused her so much grief and humiliation, I just can't add more to it.

I understand, but really, what choices did we actually have? We have been just as trapped as the women, only in different ways. I'll suggest that there may be more attempts on her life too.

Good. I am counting on you. If things go badly here, at least some of my line will survive this. Thank you. I'll make sure you have more than enough funds. Best get it started. I will miss you, Sheldon.

And I you. He leaned over and planted a gentle kiss on Felix's forehead, but Felix was unable to respond physically. Without further words, Sheldon turned and headed off to make the arrangements. This was his last memory of the Great Bringer of Peace, Amo Felix Brom.

A quick trip into the small village of Brom yielded results. Linn Beckworth who had accompanied them on their trip from the Easterlings was at the Sisterhood house on another matter. "Is it true? Did an assassin kill Amo Felix Brom last night? Rumors are rampant," she asked. Her concern was genuine, he noted.

"I killed the assassin, but Felix is still living. He's badly wounded and his recovery is not so good. Lilly's working on him again. Close call. That's why I am here. I need to get Felisa and some others out of here and back to Adelmira pronto."

"Ah, so you think that there might be more attempts? Makes sense not to have all your hens in one henhouse when the foxes are about. Well, you want the Sisterhood services again?"

"Yes, Felix requested that I ask for your services once again, Ama Linn. Price is no object, but speed is. We need to leave as soon as possible," he replied.

"Well, you are in luck. I've just finished my business here. Do we need to have as large a force as before or would a more clandestine group be desirable?" she asked.

"We could start with a small group and perhaps add some additional Sisterhood fighters as we go. I would guess it would take some time to muster a larger force. Felix wants us on the road soon, just in case there are more attempts."

"Okay, can you be ready by the morning? I will send out word and arrange everything. We'll come by around eight tomorrow. Let's not take any chances of your group being ambushed on the short way into Brom from the tower," Linn replied. She named a price and he paid it and then some, to which she gave him a flirting grin.

The really tough choice fell to Savina and Michela. Both girls had adapted well to their newfound physical freedom. "Mom, I don't want to go back just yet," Savina answered, pulling on her long braids. "I like it here, but I don't want to leave you either. Can I stay with dad a while longer? I am sure that he can arrange for someone to bring me to you later on."

Felisa sighed, but accepted her daughter's wishes. "I will speak with him. If he agrees, then you can stay. How about you, Michela?"

"I want to go with you, mom. I like it here, but Pierina and Dante are going and they are my best friends, so I want to go too. Please, Savina, you come too," she pleaded with her older sister.

"Let's see what dad has to say first," Felisa suggested. She led them into her bedroom where Lilly was once more tending to his wound. "My husband, Savina wants to stay here with you but if she later on changes her mind, can she be escorted to Adelmira? Michela wants to go with me."

Savina, you don't have to stay with me. I love you too much to have you see me laid up like this.

But I want to dad. Please? I don't want to be bound again.

Yes, you can stay. You and Rosina can share her room. Thank you, Savina. I understand.

"Okay, then we best get packing. Sheldon says the Sisterhood will be here for us by eight tomorrow morning," Felisa whispered, though she didn't really know why she did. Perhaps it was because Felix was not speaking.

Felisa, Michela, come give me a goodbye kiss before you leave, he sent. They did so and left, leaving Lilly to wipe away some tears that trickled down his cheeks. He still had little physical control of his arms, none in his legs.

Lilly, we need very quickly to work out drastically better security arrangements for all the towers. If he could get to me that easily, none of us in any tower are truly safe. Make the contact with all the other tower leaders for me. Then join me with them. We have much work to do before this body fails me entirely!

Early the next morning, Felisa and Michela came to say farewell to Felix. After an emotional kiss, they hastily left and Lilly again had to wipe away his tears. He simply could not bear to say farewell to Sheldon upon whom he had depended for so many years. Sheldon didn't dare see him either, for he knew the fate that faced Felix and knew that if he saw him again, he might not be able to bring himself to leave Brom tower. Instead, he focused on the last request from Felix: to get his wife and daughter to the safety and security of the Easterlings. Late October, he succeeded and in January 1082 Annetta was born.

By July, Felix insisted Lilly stop wasting her time trying to complete his healing. He'd recovered the use of his arms but could feel or control nothing below his waist. "Look, we have to spend our time researching ways to protect the towers. Already several *Jefe* are making plans to try to take over a tower to get around the Brom Compact. I am witness to our vulnerability."

"Yes, true, but those who can jump or teleport are extremely rare, Felix," Lilly protested. She wanted more than anything to restore him to full health, but simply did not have the skill needed at this point. None in Brom tower did, though with the great advances that the tower circles were now making, thanks to their new germanium crystals, it was only a matter of time before someone would develop such skills. Would it be too late for him? This was her greatest fear.

In August, Felix had a breakthrough. "Look at this, dear!" Lilly nearly dropped his breakfast tray she was bringing him. There was Felix on his bed, which he never left, floating three feet off the floor, bed and all. A circular ring of the crystals was glowing bright blue around the floor where his bed had sat. Seeing her surprised look and not wanting her to drop the tray he hastily explained, "The crystals. We can charge the crystals with a specific psi-energy. It took a dozen to lift the bed and me. Watch as I release them one by one." She sat the tray down on the desk and watched in disbelief. One by one, the blue glow of a crystal vanished and as they dimmed out, the bed slowly lowered until it sat firmly on the floor with six crystals still glowing. He extinguished these as well.

"So we can attune a crystal to a specific gift?" she asked, finally grasping what Felix had figured out.

"Precisely, dear. You catch on faster than anyone else does. We can embed attuned crystals around the insides of the tower and activate them. Their effects will be permanent until one of us dims them down."

"We should have an anti-scrying shield and one to prevent teleporting into a tower," Lilly began extrapolating from what she'd just heard.

"Good idea. If outsiders cannot spy on us and they cannot jump inside the tower from the outside, the tower folk should be well protected," he agreed with her.

"Okay, here's your breakfast. I'll get going on the anti-scrying shield now. I've no ideas on how to prevent jumping. I leave that one up to you," she teased him. After fixing his tray for him and giving him a kiss, she left to get to work. How many crystals would be needed per floor? This she could empirically work out.

By late October, all the towers now had these two new protections installed, compliments of Felix and Lilly. At the fall harvest celebration, Felix, still confined to his bedroom, chatted with Lilly. "We have the towers protected now. With the unlimited powers of the towers and our new *Círculo de mentes* in each one, they can at last put a stop to all wars and conflicts across all Tierra! None can stand up to us now. Those of us with the *mentales* gifts, armed with a small crystal and trained in its use, can now step up and share the responsibility for making the world a safe place to live and bring up our families. Think of what we've done here, Lilly!"

"We've accomplished the impossible, dear, a life's work well done. Our boys can grow up in a sane world now," she replied, patting her bulging belly. John wasn't due for a couple months yet, but her pregnancy was more than visible. Felix smiled and pulled her close to him for a private time.

Felix passed away in his sleep that December. John was born a week after his funeral and he never knew his father, only the enormous legend that he left behind. It was not until the turn of the century, 1100, that the last of the far western *Jefe* finally signed the Brom Compact, effectively yielding control of their kingdoms to their tower. While they retained a sort of autonomy over their dominions, ultimately they had to respond and follow the orders from their towers. For a time, it seemed that peace had finally come to Tierra.

Far below the surface of the planet, intertwined in the red-hot silicon-germanium magma, the being known as Wystan radiated a newfound smugness. *They have found the crystals that I sent forth and are using them as I have planned. Soon we'll see **real** battles!*

Nearby and absorbing the warmth that only the magma could give her, the being known as Lysandra replied, *Yes dear.*

Now I will be able to give Life and Death a whole new order of magnitude.

Damn you two! Don't you ever think of me? With all that death, you are going to make me have to work ten times harder than you!

Poor Ariana, Wystan smirked. She flicked a blob of magma his way. He noticed that Calder still slept. *Just as well sleep. You've nothing to do anyway.*

He glanced over at the largest of the five beings, who was just going into a new slumber and picked up a parting thought from Alleric. *The planet is stabilized again and life is adjusting. All is well once more. I am tired. Time to sleep once more.*

The End.

Other Books by Vic Broquard

Without Warning (fantasy)

The Trident Series: (fantasy)
      Volume 1 The Trident and the Book
      Volume 3 The Trident and the Scepter
      Volume3 The Trident and the Resurrection

The Adventures of Elizabeth Stanton Series: (science fiction)
      Volume 1 The Evolution of the Path
      Volume 2 The Great Messiah
      Volume 3 Of Kings and Queens and Troubadours
      Volume 4 Chaos in the Aftermath
      Volume 5 Power Plays
      Volume 6 Age of Exploration
      Volume 7 Abducted
      Volume 8 The Emperor and Empress
      Volume 9 A Job Worth Doing
      Volume 10 Degradation
      Volume 11 The Second Crusade
      Volume 12 When Worlds Collide
      Volume 13 Dark Ages

The Lindsey Barron Series: (fantasy)
      Volume 1 The Rod of the Apocalypse
      Volume 2 The Board of Governors
      Volume 3 The Crown of Moses
      Volume 4 Dominus for President
      Volume 5 The National Health Care Program
      Volume 6 States Justice
      Volume 7 Cross and Double-cross

Zoran Chronicles Series: (fantasy)
      Volume 1 A Dragon in Our Town
      Volume 2 Dragons, Power, Courts, and War

www.ingramcontent.com/pod-product-compliance
Lightning Source LLC
Chambersburg PA
CBHW070834260626
47170CB00007B/2374

Planet of the Orange-red Sun Series: (science fiction)
  Volume 1 When Kingdoms Fall
  Volume 2 Dark Ages
  Volume 3 Age of the Towers
  Volume 4 Difficillis Exitus
  Volume 5 Age of the Lords
  Volume 6 The Renegade Tower
  Volume 7 Rebellions
  Volume 8 The Aliens Return
  Volume 9 Power Struggles
  Volume 10 Guilds, Genetics, and Gods
  Volume 11 Magi, Witches, Swords, and Superstitions
  Volume 12 The Voyage of the Eagle's Seed
  Volume 13 Justifications
  Volume 14 Responsibilities

The Return of the Wizards: Twelve Companions – The Making of Wizards (fantasy)